Italian Renaissance Tales

Selected and Translated, with an Introduction

Cap: Csgangarato   Cap: Cocodrilo

by Janet Levarie Smarr
Professor of Comparative Literature
The University of Illinois at Urbana

Italian Renaissance Tales

*Selected and Translated, with an Introduction
by Janet Levarie Smarr*

WITHDRAWN

 Solaris Press, Inc., Rochester, Michigan

©1983 by Solaris Press, Rochester, Michigan 48063
ALL RIGHTS RESERVED
Printed on permanent/durable acid-free paper
and bound in the United States of America

We wish to thank the University of Illinois Library, the Henry E.
Huntington Library and Art Gallery, and the New York Public
Library for permission to reproduce the illustrations which appear on
the cover and in the Masuccio, Straparola and Basile sections.

Library of Congress Cataloging in Publication Data

Italian Renaissance tales.

Bibliography: p. 281
1. Tales, Italian. 2. Italian fiction—To 1400.
3. Italian fiction—15th century. 4. Italian fiction—
16th century. 5. Italian literature—Translations
into English. 6. English literature—Translations from
Italian. I. Smarr, Janet Levarie, 1949-
PQ4253.A4E5   1983   853'.01'08   82-19575
ISBN 0-933760-03-5

To my parents, who introduced me to the pleasures of Italy.

Contents

Contents

List of Illustrations

Woodcut illustrations from a Renaissance Edition of Masuccio's
Novellino, reproduced in the Classici del Ridere Edition
(Modena: G. Ferraguti, 1929), New York Public Library,
pp.70, 72, 80, 88, 94.

Woodcut illustrations from Giovanni Straparola, *Le Tredici
Piacevoli Notti* (1599). Henry E. Huntington Library and
Art Gallery,
pp.181, 185, 191, 212.

Engravings of the Dance of Sfessania by Jacques Callot
(1592–1635), in Karl Kloss ed., *Jacques Callot, Balli di Sfessania*
(Vienna: Artur Wolf, 1919), University of Illinois Library,
pp.235 (#5), 234 (#6), cover (#11), 233 (#19).

Translator's Introduction

Although Boccaccio's *Decameron* has been translated frequently and even made into a film, the storybooks of other Renaissance Italians are generally unknown to the English-speaking public.[1] Bartolomeo Gamba's bibliography of Italian novellas lists more than 250 *novellieri* or short-story writers; yet many of these authors have never been translated into English, while others are available in archaic English and, even then, can only be found in libraries with large collections.[2] With rare exceptions, none of these tales are to be found in bookshops where they might be acquired to be read and enjoyed by the general public. It seemed to me, and to a number of my colleagues, that this state of affairs represented a serious gap in American letters. Both students of literary history and readers who simply relish good stories were being deprived of some of the most delightful tales ever written. But even more serious was the fact that the roots of the modern novel, as well as the sources for much drama, lie in this largely inaccessible body of Italian narrative materials. Thus, motivated by both scholarly and popular concerns, I undertook to translate some of those tales by authors which are difficult to find in English and, in most cases, impossible to purchase.

What is especially unique to this anthology is the inclusion of framing materials, or stories into which other tales are fitted like drawers in a dresser. My desire to present material not otherwise available was modified slightly by the inclusion of several tales interesting for their relation to other literature. Thus I have included the original stories of *Romeo and Juliet, The Merchant of Venice,* and *The Duchess of Malfi.* There is also a tale which comes close to the story of *King Lear* (Sercambi, 57), and another which was the basis for an opera, *The Love of Three Oranges* (Basile, V, 9). Similarly, I have chosen from the earliest novella book, *The Hundred Old Tales* (ca. 1300), tales which reappear in the writings of Dante, Boccaccio, Chaucer, and Cervantes. I have wanted not only to offer stories pertinent to other literatures, but also to represent as truly as possible the very different qualities of the selected writers; therefore I have preferred to include several tales from each author, rather than a greater number of authors each represented by one tale. I have also tried to represent the wide variety of kinds of novella. Although the majority of writers in this collection are properly from the period accepted as the Renaissance, I have deliberately chosen tales which bracket the period at either end as examples of transitional phases of the novella. Finally, I have selected stories which, to my taste, are among the best and most interesting of their genre, and which remained sharply in my mind long after their hundreds of companions had been read and half forgotten.[3]

I. FORTUNE AND FAMILY: A GLIMPSE AT REAL LIFE

Even a brief consideration of what life was like in Renaissance Italy makes one appreciate two concepts that play a major role in the novella: fortune and family. Fortune, personified as a dominating agent in the world, represents everything that changes and is beyond one's control, from the weather to the possession of kingdoms. As Dame Fortune's wheel spins, the people on it are continually being moved up and down, regardless of their social class. Thus one is constantly at risk, from the moment of birth onwards.

The very continuity of life seemed to be in the hands of fortune. A newborn baby in the Renaissance had a fifty percent chance of surviving past its first year. In order to ensure an adult heir, a woman might therefore have many children; but childbirth endangered her own survival. Males were killed in the constant wars among the Italian city-states. Even when those wars were fought by mercenaries, the destruction of harvests and the interruption of commerce brought hard times, accompanied by heavy taxes. After the official war was over, the mercenaries remained in Italy. These *condottieri*, as they were called, traveled in bands of as many as a thousand armed men, terrorizing and extorting large sums of money from the populace. Plagues, exacerbated by malnutrition, and causing further malnutrition by their disruption of farming and marketing, recurred nearly every ten years. The worst and most famous of these was the Black Death, which in 1348 wiped out somewhere between a third and a half of the population of Europe. A number of small towns were entirely eliminated from the map.

A brief chronology of wars and plagues involving Florence may illustrate the instability of life: during 1369–70 Florence was at war in alliance with the papacy against Milan. In 1374 there was a plague, followed by a famine, and the start of a war in alliance with Milan against the papacy in 1375. Thirteen seventy-eight saw an end of war with the papacy, but also a workers' revolt resulting in a change of government to increase representation. In 1380 there was economic depression and in 1382 a change of government to a more restrictive representation. Thirteen eighty-three ushered in another plague. During the 1390s a long struggle with Milan was finally relieved by the sudden death of the Milanese Visconti in 1402. There was again a time of plague in 1398–1400; 1408–11 saw the war with the king of Naples and an outbreak of plague between 1410 and 1412. Fourteen twenty-four was another plague year, and a new war with Milan continued intermittently until 1447. On top of this, from 1378–1417, the great schism between two conflicting popes threw all levels of religious authority into tremendous confusion. No wonder people felt themselves to be under the power of fickle Dame Fortune!

The realm of commercial enterprise was, of course, also perceived as being under fortune's sway. Italians pursued trade far and wide across the world, from England and Scandinavia to Russia, and south to India and North Africa. Yet travel and the transportation of goods were always high-risk ventures, imperiled by storms and pirates at sea, by bad roads, and bandits on land. In the fifteenth and sixteenth centuries, trade routes were increasingly blocked by the Turks whose expansion westward was a serious threat to Europe. Political uncertainties also endangered the merchant in foreign lands. A businessman would be away from home for months or years at a time, even if nothing went wrong. With worse luck, he might be captured by pirates and sold into slavery, or imprisoned in a foreign jail while his family was left without news of his condition. With high risk came high reward, and a very successful merchant around 1500 might make 50,000 florins in a year! This was twenty times the income of a well-known law professor, sixty times that of a master shipwright, two hundred times that of a soldier or bank clerk, and a thousand times that of a poor day laborer or parish chaplain.[4]

The differences between rich and poor were clearly visible. Palaces and shacks existed side by side, as did homespun tunics and elaborately ornamented clothing of fancy silks. Nonetheless, social mobility — both up and down — was considerable, at least between the middle and upper classes. Alberti, writing in the 1400s, claimed that no family had maintained its wealth and status for more than three generations. A list of principal families in Florence in 1380 shares very few names with that of fifty years later.[5] The wheel of fortune had spun them around.

As economic and political power went hand in hand, the loss of either had wide repercussions for the whole extended family. If things went badly, the family could have a hard time arranging marriages. Its members might suffer harassing taxations and adverse judgments in the law courts, and possibly be subject to exile and the confiscation of their property. On the other hand, with the profits of successful business, a family might marry its children into older houses of established power, thus enhancing its political status and improving the prospects of further gain. These were tricky games to play, however. Machiavelli, who studied assiduously the means of gaining and losing power, asserted that fortune governs fifty percent of even the best-planned manoeuvers.

If personal success or failure, honor or dishonor, affected the whole family, family was also the chief bulwark against the effects of personal misfortune. Members of the family, or "house," might be expected to help each other out of economic difficulties and to defend the honor of their name. A man in political office had more or less authority and could afford to be more or less severe, depending on the power of his family. The judge from a lesser house would hesitate to decide against or to penalize harshly someone with more powerful connections for fear of reprisals. Because public justice was partial, private justice was often a surer resort. Many people went out armed, or, if wealthy enough, surrounded by armed servants. Some families kept their own *bravi* or "ruffians" as a kind of private police force ready to execute their boss's will.

Marriage was the chief means of allying one's family with a family offering political or economic advantage. Therefore, marriage was not an individual matter based on love, but rather a family decision made for the welfare of the whole group. Women were considered marriageable at fifteen; men usually waited until they were around thirty. Time and again the novella shows us a young wife with an older husband, with whom she has little personal rapport, and a younger, unmarried male, eager for a sexual affair.[6]

The parents of a girl had to provide a dowry, and the bigger the dowry, the better was the chance of an advantageous marriage. A wealthy merchant, seeking to marry his daughter to a powerful, established family, or a family with political enemies, striving to overcome this disadvantage, might pay a huge dowry; and conversely, a young man from a good family could shop around for the best financial deal. One member of the Strozzi family, for example, was offered marriages involving dowries of 1000, 1500, and 4500 florins at a time when the total assets of a well-to-do family might equal only 2000 florins or a bit more.[7] Such dowries were an investment on the part of the bride's relatives. Obviously a modest shopkeeper, with assets of a few hundred florins, was not in the same category, but even a wealthy family could be ruined by having several daughters to marry honorably. It was cheaper to send some of the girls into a nunnery, though convents, too, required some payment.

The dowry was often used by the husband to establish himself in business. Widows were the only women who controlled their own property. As widowhood also meant avoiding the dangers of childbirth and controlling the upbringing of one's children, and as the Church supported the ideal of chaste widowhood as superior to remarriage, many women opted to remain single after the death of their husbands. In 1427, over fifty percent of adult women in Florence were widows.[8] The widow is a frequent figure in Renaissance literature, for her sexual experience and loneliness made her susceptible to love affairs, thus threatening the honor of her family.

Family loyalties took precedence over any kind of loyalty to the state, and state interests were identified with the interests of the families in power. But if the individual was first a member of his family or house, he was second a member of his community or city. Other towns were the object of scorn and derision. For example, Boccaccio illustrates the stupidity of the Sienese and the easy virtue of the women of Bologna, while depicting the cleverness of his native Florentines. Of course, there was no Italian nation in the Renaissance; the various independent city-states had different dialects, currencies, and forms of government: the duchy of Milan, the kingdom of Naples, the oligarchy of Venice, and the republic of Florence are a few examples.

Later in the Renaissance, social mobility seems to have become harder to attain. Established families turned into a fixed aristocracy whose control of the nomination lists made access to political power difficult for anyone outside the ruling group. The republic of Florence became a dukedom run by the Medici family with the support of the emperor. Other areas of Italy to the north and south were invaded and reinvaded by the French and Spanish in their conflict for possession of Italian territories. Many well-to-do families dropped out of both politics and commerce and invested their money in large estates which provided a more secure life. In sum, society returned to a kind of feudalism, the aim of which was to minimize both the risk and the enterprise of the Renaissance.

II. The Origins and History of the Novella

In the beginning, the word *novella* meant "short story," but with the lengthening of narratives over the centuries, the term eventually took on its specialized modern meaning of "short novel," which is very far from the original sense of the word. Unlike modern short stories which are usually published one at a time or in slim anthologies containing tales of relatively uniform length, mood, and subject matter, these Renaissance narratives tended to appear in groups of as many as fifty or even several hundred tales by the same author. Such collections were marked intentionally by a tremendous variety in content and mode. Some of the tales are tragic, others comic or satiric, while still others are whimsical, romantic, or erotic. The diversity which marks these collections is symptomatic of the vagueness of the term *novella* which was used interchangeably with more specific generic designations such as *exemplum* or *favola*. No doubt because the word *novella* had a flexibility which alternative generic expressions lacked, it was to prevail as the official name of the genre.

Textbooks of rhetoric, ever since Cicero, had distinguished between three kinds of narrative on the basis of their truth value: *fabula* was totally fictive and fantastic, *historia* was true, and *argumentum* was a verisimilar hypothesis which was not true but could be.[9] Thus Giovan Francesco Straparola (1480–1558?), refers to his narratives as *favole*, while his contemporary, Matteo Bandello (1485–1561) insists that his own stories are not fables but *vere istorie* or true histories. Because the term *novella* meant several quite different things besides "a tale," its meanings were able to include both true and untrue narratives. On one hand, it meant "news," and as such could be used to describe the many stories drawn from recent events by the Florentine Franco Sacchetti (1335–1400), the Lucchese Giovanni Sercambi (1348–1424), and the Milanese Matteo Bandello. On the other hand, it meant "new" or "strange," "things never before heard," and in this regard could be applied to the fantastic fables spun by ser Giovanni the Florentine (second half of the fourteenth century), Giovan Francesco Straparola, and the Neopolitan Giambattista Basile (1575–1632).[10]

Francesco Bonciani, one of the very few Renaissance theorists to discuss the novella, offers a third meaning for the word: "foolish" or "ridiculous" and therefore "an object of laughing reprehension." Thus he defines the novella as "that speech which recounts the follies of others so that we may mock them."[11] According to this definition, novellas must imitate the ridiculous and foolish actions of persons who are neither too noble nor too wicked. Bonciani's narrow definition of the term, however, is immediately qualified by his recognition that Boccaccio had elevated the genre to include the imitation of persons much better and nobler than we, thus raising it in parts from the comic towards the tragic.[12] The qualification was needed, because Boccaccio and many other *novellieri* were expressly interested in presenting a wide variety of tale types and characters of every social and moral level, from the abominable to the saintly. This state of affairs led the critic, Angelo Lipari, to suggest that the *Decameron* was written as an illustrative handbook of the many narrative genres.[13]

Through the centuries, tales which had originated as demonstrations of oriental philosophies were adapted by Arabs, Jews and Christians alike to suit their particular didactic and moral needs. Somehow these brief narratives seemed to contain a wisdom from which all cultures could learn. It is not surprising, then, to find a number of these oriental tales being combined with western story materials even in the earliest European collections of tales.[14]

Among the oriental sources of the novella was a life of Buddha. Written in Sanskrit in the sixth century, this work was soon translated via Arabic into Greek (630 A.D.) becoming in the process the life of Saint Josafat. The *Vita di Barlaam et Josafat* appeared in Latin about the tenth century and spread throughout Europe in French, Italian, and Spanish versions, pieces of it making their way into the famous thirteenth-century *Legenda aurea* or "The Golden Legend," a book of saints' lives.

Another oriental novella source book was the ancient Indian *Panchatantra*. This set of animal fables journeyed through Persian into Syriac and Arabic under the title of *Kalileh ve Dimnah*, thence into Greek and Hebrew, and from there into Latin in the late thirteenth century. From the Latin version, published later as *Directorium humanae vitae* or "The Guide of Human Life," sprang vernacular translations into many languages.

A third collection of stories widely copied in Europe made a similar journey from the east. The parables of the Brahman sage Sindibad, like the *Panchatantra*, came from Sanskrit via Persian and Syrian into Greek by the eleventh century, into Hebrew, and finally into thirteenth-century Latin as *Historia septem sapientum* or *The History of the Seven Sages*. A second thirteenth-century avatar of the *Sindibad*, sometimes called the *Dolopathos*, transformed the King of India — the hero of the original version — into a Sicilian prince in the time of Augustus while the hero's Brahman teacher became the Roman poet Vergil.

Finally, the very popular *Disciplina clericalis* or "Student's Training" was compiled by Petrus Alphonsus, a Spanish Jew converted to Christianity in the beginning of the twelfth century. The stories in his tale collection are translated from the Arabic. Some of them come recognizably from the *Kalileh ve Dimnah* and others from other sources mentioned above.

There were, of course, early western sources of short narrative as well, most notably Ovid's *Metamorphoses* and Apuleius' *Golden Ass*. Valerius Maximus' *Factorum et dictorum memorabilia*, "Remarkable Sayings and Deeds," recounted examples from Greek and Roman history under thematic categories such as Justice, Ingratitude, Friendship, and Patience. Other narratives, although medieval in origin, were thought to be classical. A collection of fables called *Romulus Imperator*, "The Emperor Romulus," circulated as the Roman emperor's translation of Aesop for his son, but was in fact a set of fables from about the eleventh century. The late thirteenth-century *Gesta Romanorum*, "The Acts of the Romans," too had little to do with Romans despite its title; in addition to a few anecdotes from Valerius Maximus, its author appropriated about a third of the *Disciplina clericalis*, other tales from the *Vita di Barlaam et Josafat*, and still others from medieval legends.

The special interest in these tale collections, evident in Europe during the thirteenth century, probably came from the newly founded orders of Franciscans and Dominicans, with their emphasis on popular preaching.[15] For their purposes, anthologies were compiled during the thirteenth and fourteenth centuries which drew upon a variety of earlier sources, often grouping the tales under moral headings or themes. Saint Gregory the Great had not only encouraged the use of stories in preaching, but had compiled his own collection of moral and religious exempla, the *Dialogues*, which now found a new popularity and many imitators. The *Alphabetum narrationum*, "The Alphabet of Tales," containing 800 exempla, was written in the thirteenth century by a Dominican; the same century produced *Il Fiore di Virtù*, "The Flower of Virtues," a collection of examples grouped under the virtues and vices, and the famous popular sermons, *Sermones Vulgares*, of Jacques de Vitry, which included over three hundred tales of all kinds.

In the fourteenth century the French Franciscan, Nicolas Bozon, wrote his *Contes Moralisés*, "Moralized Tales," and the great English Dominican preacher, John Bromyard, produced the *Summa praedicantium*, "The Preacher's Compendium." The Florentine preacher Jacopo Passavanti's *Specchio di vera penitenza,* "Mirror of True Repentance," from the same period, was also strewn with narrative examples. The English *Confessio amantis*, "Lover's Confession," written by Geoffrey Chaucer's friend, John Gower, and Prudenzani's *Liber solatii*, "The Book of Consolation," were in the same tradition, and, like *Il Fiore di Virtù*, arranged their tales under the categories of virtues and vices.

Such was the popularity of these tales with preachers that Dante has Beatrice protest in *Paradiso* 29:103–117:

> Florence has not as many Lapos and Bindos as tales like these that are proclaimed in the pulpit on all hands through the year, so that the poor sheep that know nothing are returned from pasture fed on wind; and not to see their loss does not excuse them. Christ did not say to His first fellowship: "Go and preach idle tales to the world," but gave them a true foundation; and that alone sounded on their lips, so that in fighting to kindle the faith they made of the Gospel shield and spear. Now they go to preach with jests and gibes, and if only there is a good laugh, the cowl inflates and they ask no more.[16]

Boccaccio, echoing Dante's words, refers to the jests of the preachers in his conclusion to the *Decameron* to justify his own collection of tales: " . . . considering that the sermons made by friars to reprove the sins of men are these days for the most part full of jests and nonsense and foolishness, I judged that the same would not sit ill in my novellas. . . ." (My translation.)

History and chronicles provided another narrative source for tellers of moral tales. Of course, history and moralizing were not always separable categories. Valerius Maximus and the lives of the saints, for example, straddle both. The first collection of tales represented in my translations, *Le Cento Novelle Antiche* or "Hundred Old Tales," drew directly or indirectly upon Valerius Maximus, Vincent de Beauvais' *Speculum historialis*, "Mirror of History," and the *Historia Karoli Magni*, "The History of Charles the Great." Similarly, Villani's chronicles of Florence became a source of stories for ser Giovanni, and anecdotes from Sercambi's chronicles of Lucca reappeared in his own novellas. Later on, Bandello had a wider set of histories upon which to draw, including Xenophon, Strabo Josephus Flavius, Machiavelli's *Florentine History*, Vasari's *Lives of the Painters* and a *Description of Africa* by Leo Africanus, the last two having been published in 1550, very close in time to Bandello's writing.[17] Finally, current events were a bounteous source for storytellers. Nearly all the writers in this book, with the exception of Basile, made use of, or at least claimed to be transcribing, recent true occurrences. Sacchetti concentrated almost solely on recent events, commenting on the worthy or foolish doings of his day. Bandello, with an eye to future audiences, took on the role of historian, recording for future memory events worthy of note.

One more set of sources must be included in the formation of the novella: the literature of medieval France. Episodes from chivalric romances, which told the stories of the Trojan War, the conquests of Alexander the Great, and the adventures of medieval knights, were detached and turned into brief tales, to be sung on the street by entertainers and inserted into story collections. Later the process was reversed as Ariosto, Spenser, Cervantes and others folded well-established tales into their long romances. Also from France came the *fabliaux*, some of which are parodies of romance's theme of adulterous love, dealing with lower-class characters rather than knights and ladies. Both high and low treatments were welcomed by the early storytellers who eliminated the differences of style and merely sketched the outline of events. Trickery too was a *fabliau* theme which became dominant in the novella.

The more story collections spread, the more they borrowed from one another, the harder it becomes to trace an author's sources. *The Hundred Old Tales,* the earliest anthology of short stories to be composed in Italian, includes tales from nearly every source mentioned so far. A few notes on just those stories included in the present collection are perhaps sufficient to give an idea of the multiple and crisscrossing streams of narrative which flowed through one book.[18] As a first example, a version of tale no. 21 can be found as "The Story of Sheik Schehabbedin" in the Turkish *Forty Viziers*, in *Meshal-ha-Quadmoni*, "Wise Sayings of the Ancients" by Isaac, son of Salomon Ibn Sahula (thirteenth century), and later in the Spanish *El Conde Lucanor*, "Count Lucanor." Tale no. 31 appears in the *Disciplina clericalis* and later in *Don Quixote* (I, 20). No. 44 seems to be a contemporary anecdote which Petrarch in his *Rerum memorandarum libri*, "Noteworthy Matters" (II, 83) later retells about Dante. No. 69 appears in the *Legenda aurea*, and the first half of it occurs in the *Dolopathos*; but the immediate source may have been Vincent de Beauvais' *Speculum historiale* XI, 46. It shows up later in Dante's *Purgatorio* X and in Francesco da Barberino's *Documenti d'Amore*, "Teachings on Love." No. 73 appears in the *Gesta Romanorum*. No. 83, here about Christ, was told about Buddha in the *Avadanas* and about a Persian sage in the ninth-century *Book of Merzban*.

III. SOME IMPORTANT FEATURES OF THE GENRE

The Hundred Old Tales is the only collection in this anthology which predates Boccaccio's *Decameron*. With Boccaccio the genre was transformed from brief and sketchy outlines or anecdotes to a high level of art, with full attention paid to style of narration and a wonderful richness of psychological insight. The *Decameron* (ca. 1350) was immediately recognized as a masterpiece, becoming the chief model for subsequent writers of tales. As a result, several of its elements became associated with the novella genre.

The first of these elements is the declared use of the low style, that is, of the common daily language which classical theorists had considered appropriate for comedy. Indeed, Bonciani, no doubt basing his remarks upon the *Decameron*, cites the low style as the proper level for the subject matter of the novella.[19] Nevertheless, Boccaccio's description of his style as the "most humble and low" (IV, Introduction) is somewhat misleading; for despite the lively and realistic dialogue within the tales, his language strikes us as formal and measured, and indeed was based on Latin rhetorical models with its long sentences full of dependent clauses and broken into rhythmic phrases. By contrast, the early Tuscans Sacchetti, ser Giovanni, and Sercambi, more truthfully disclaim any rhetorical polish. Sacchetti describes himself as "uneducated and coarse," ser Giovanni as an ignorant "sheep" who knows nothing about writing books, and Sercambi as a man "without learning." Their writing is certainly plain and sometimes even awkward; for whereas Boccaccio had made an ardent study of rhetoric, his early imitators were truly simple shopkeepers and businessmen who tried their hand at writing stories. Therefore it is hard to tell whether the plainness of the early Tuscan style is mere artlessness or an intentional style deemed rhetorically appropriate. Boccaccio had learned his love for rhetorical elegance during his years at the royal court of Naples, and did shift to a notably plainer writing after his return to the mercantile republic of Florence. The two Neapolitans in this collection, Masuccio and Basile, both frequenters of the court, use the most opaque and elaborate styles. Yet even Masuccio offers his stories very humbly, describing them falsely as rough and unpolished; and Basile, with deceitful modesty, subtitled his book an entertainment for children.

The modest apologies of these writers may partly reflect the difficulty of the genre in establishing itself as serious literature. Despite Boccaccio's defense of his work as being closer to the Muses than it seems, humanists of the following generation cited with praise his scholarly Latin works while brushing aside the *Decameron* as unworthy of serious note.[20] Although a few attempts were made by humanists to translate tales from the *Decameron* into Latin or to compose stories in Latin directly, the material seemed by and large unsuitable to solemnization in this way. These stories were not meant to be restricted to an educated audience. Meanwhile Renaissance poetics, with rare exceptions, focused on the genres of antiquity, ignoring the novella despite its wide popularity.[21]

Another aspect of the genre possibly related to its humble manner is the frequency of its address to women. Boccaccio claimed to aim his stories at women in love. Dante, in his treatise *On Vernacular Eloquence,* had remarked that works written in Italian, rather than Latin, were usually intended for a female audience, lacking a Latin education. Boccaccio's address to women might partly, then, signify his aim of writing for a popular rather than a scholarly audience.[22] On the other hand, in the more feudal French court women had been the patronesses of literary men and therefore received the dedication of works of many kinds, treatises as well as poems and romances, and works in Latin as well as in French. As the French were ruling Naples while Boccaccio lived there, he may well have been influenced by both French and Italian traditions. Furthermore, he may have used the idea of a female audience symbolically to reinforce the notion of writing for persons in love. For passion was considered the female aspect of the soul; reason, the male aspect. The implication would be that Boccaccio, as he professed in other works, was writing the *Decameron* to be morally useful to an audience more inclined to hear amusing stories than to ponder moral philosophy. Whatever Boccaccio's reasons may have been, the address to women became a frequent, if not constant, feature of the genre. Masuccio dedicated not only single tales but, more important, his whole collection to Ippolita of Aragon, hoping it would find a place in her library. Luigi da Porto dedicated his love tragedy to a female relative. Bandello, like Masuccio, besides the dedication of specific tales, offered his whole collection to the late Ippolita Sforza at whose suggestion he claimed the volumes were composed. Straparola's frame makes Lucrezia Sforza the suggester and chief member of the audience for his tales, and his second volume begins with a preface "to the gracious and loving women" readers in defense against his critics. Dedications to women could be construed as the authors' acknowledgment that the genre is a humble one and not high literature. In this light, Basile's subtitle offering his book to children can be seen simply as an exaggerated version of the address to women. On the other hand, the ladies addressed by Bandello and Masuccio were of the highest nobility. Masuccio hopes his dedication to so noble and powerful a lady will raise the level of his humble work in the estimation of its wider audience. And Bandello, arguing in his dedication to IV, 18, that women can be just as good as men at scholarly and literary pursuits, points as an example to Ippolita Sforza, "who is daily seen to discuss learnedly difficult passages of Latin." Thus he cannot have dedicated his book to her as a sign of its being in the vernacular, nor as a sign that works in the low style suit women readers because of their lack of education or sophistication. There may, in sum, be no single explanation for this aspect of the genre other than the influence of Boccaccio following in the footsteps of the French court poets.

Since its beginning in Italy, the novella was a secular genre; and yet it remained always close to the exemplary tradition from which it had sprung; close, that is, to the use of stories as educative examples of moral and immoral behavior. As a result, it is peculiar to the novella to discuss within the fiction itself whether or not it ought to have an ethical function. After all, how edifying are stories which frequently deal with illicit love affairs, practical jokes, and clerical misbehavior?

Perhaps as a result of the ethical ambiguity of the genre, those who wrote or enjoyed such literature hastened to ascribe practical value to it. For example, Bonciani spoke in 1574 on the novella in this way: "As we usually have many more pains and sufferings than we need, it becomes necessary for us to procure some mirth."[23] Thus the simple aim of amusement does not suffice unless it can be shown to serve some useful purpose. Fortunately the medical establishment of the day was strongly in favor of play. As a fourteenth-century medical text declared, "a moderate cheerfulness belongs to the regimen of health because it is one of the means of strengthening bodily energy." Recreation was recommended especially for the anxious and troubled as a way of restoring a healthful balance and preventing disease.[24] Thus another fourteenth-century doctor advised that "during this time of pestilence" people avoid melancholy thoughts and attend to cheerful ones for the preservation of their health; he suggested spending time in gardens with delightful company, singing songs and telling amusing stories without tiring oneself out.[25] Boccaccio's Dioneo asserts that the members of his group have devoted themselves to amusement for the sake of their health and lives.

The German scholar, Walter Pabst, attributed a revolutionary role to the *Decameron*, asserting that it intentionally subverted the traditional function of tales as moral exempla.[26] By contrast one of the *novellieri*, Masuccio, linked Boccaccio's name with Juvenal's, thereby implying that he read Boccaccio as a satirist on the mores of his day.[27] The fact of the matter is that a debate exists within the *Decameron* itself as to its own moral seriousness. In the preface, Boccaccio claims that the work is meant to teach its readers what behavior to shun and what to imitate; and the ten tales of the final day announce their topic of magnanimous behavior precisely as providing examples for imitation. Most of the ten narrators, at one time or another, pronounce the usefulness of their tales, although certainly the professed moral may be at variance with the tale's real concerns. It is Dioneo, whose name means "Venerian" and whose self-conscious role is that of bawdy foil to the other "most honest" narrators, who stresses that storytelling is purely for entertainment. In short, the characters themselves argue about the social role of literature.

In any case, one has to modify the view that early novellas were revolutionary because the functions of moral example and entertainment did not follow each other in time but existed simultaneously all along. Many of the old didactic stories were told for enjoyment on the streets or at fairs. Such was the popularity of this kind of entertainment that Bologna in 1288 had to issue a law to prohibit French minstrels and storytellers from blocking traffic on the streets by their performances.[28] *Il Paradiso degli Alberti* by Giovanni da Prato in the fourteenth century describes a storyteller's performance on the street in Florence while the crowd gathers around and even a nun leans out of a window to listen. The same crowds would gather to hear a famous preacher. Was that for education or entertainment? For examples of morality or of fine eloquence?

The question of whether, or what, these stories teach requires a consideration of the tales in context, a task much too ambitious to be undertaken in depth here. Briefly, however, the context is of many possible kinds. First, each tale exists in relation to surrounding tales, to which it is often linked by topic or theme or by a remark from the author. This linking allows ideas to be developed beyond the individual story. Thus frequently the lessons of the book lie in the collection as a whole with its variety of perspectives on a theme. Second, each tale exists in the context of some defined narrator and audience, either inside or outside the fiction. Masuccio and Bandello, who seem to have circulated tales individually before collecting them, accompanied them with letters, prefaces, or postscripts, in which the authors comment on the story and on how they hope it will be read. Boccaccio and many other writers enclosed the tales within a narrative frame, which describes a narrator or group of narrators and the social situation of their storytelling, sometimes including responses from the audience. The frame is such a major feature of these collections that it requires consideration at some length.

The use of a framing tale did not start with Boccaccio but goes back to many of the earlier sources such as Apuleius' *Golden Ass*, the *Disciplina clericalis*, the *Panchatantra*, and *The Seven Sages*. Often in these early collections some wise hermit, sage, or father tells stories in order to instruct a prince or son in the ways of the world and the good life of virtue. In Boccaccio's *Decameron*, ten Florentines escape from town into the hills during the Black Death and pass the heat of day telling each other stories on various assigned topics. At the end of two weeks they return to their homes. Boccaccio's frame became the dominant model for all subsequent Italian *novellieri*. The division of the book into days was imitated by ser Giovanni, Straparola, and Basile. Masuccio emulated the grouping of tales under topics and took over Boccaccio's final topic as his own. The plague setting was reused by Sercambi. Indeed the influence of Boccaccio's framing narrative was so strong that Bandello felt the need to be explicit and almost apologetic about putting together an anthology with no set order or frame. Basile, writing with baroque extravagance for the Spanish royal court of Naples at the end of the novella tradition, set up an introductory narrative only to break down in the end the distinction between frame and content; for the final tale merges container and contained, while its close resemblance to the preceding tale aggravates the confusion. Furthermore, Basile's ten ugly and decrepit old women are a grotesque parody of the usual idyllic group of narrators.

Medieval collections of examples had been chiefly intended for a varied oral presentation, and the later literary use of narrators to tell the stories was a way of continuing at least a pretense of the oral nature of the tales. It is remarkable, moreover, to note how often tales include their own telling by characters within the story. Thus, to pick out only a few examples, Federico makes the bewildered count retell his story several times to the entertainment of the court (*Hundred Old Tales* no. 21); an innkeeper in ser Giovanni's IV, 1 tells Gianetto's wife, who is disguised as a judge, what has happened up to that point; later Gianetto tells the rest of the tale to his barons. The story of Fatso is told repeatedly, in whole or in part, by various characters within the tale, and the text ends with the author's tracing a history of its narration. Indeed, tales often begin or end with an account of how the story spread until it reached its present author, especially in the case of those writers who claim that their stories are true, e.g., Masuccio and Bandello. Most of the authors are explicitly interested in the oral act of storytelling as well as in the tales themselves. They seem to be aware of freezing onto paper the previously variable flow of narration and to be trying to capture in this translation from one medium to another some of the original feeling of fluidity.

Unlike the framing fable of Basile's *Tale of Tales*, most frames are not themselves a story with a plot. Ser Giovanni's enamored monk and nun never get anywhere, for better or for worse. Sercambi's travelers, either because he did not finish the work or because part of it has been lost, are left in the middle of their travels; but even were they to end up back home, not much in the way of plot would have occurred. Straparola's group is also left in midstream, with their lives continuing as usual; the polit-ical flight of Lucrezia's father is left unresolved; there is no neat return.

Collections do tend, however, to achieve a sense of closure by ending on a higher tone. Boccaccio's last day is devoted to examples of magnifi-cent behavior, and his final tale is the moralizing story of Griselda. Masuccio's last topic, in obvious imitation of Boccaccio, is examples of magnificence, justice, and the tempering of passions. Straparola's nights of entertainment end with the beginning of Lent and a turn towards religious activities. These endings often appear as a corrective to the preceding tales.

The contrasts between frame and content are also often corrective in nature. Thus, for example, Masuccio dedicates his third topic, ten tales illustrative of women's lustful and vicious nature, to women of complete honesty and chastity, Ippolita Maria de Visconti and her sisters-in-law, Eleanora and Beatrice of Aragon. Bandello similarly offers his tale about a gluttonous priest to a distinguished member of the clergy, the bishop of Brunate. Such dedications present an obvious alternative to the behavior portrayed in the tale. They are in line with Boccaccio's statement that his book would demonstrate both what to imitate and what to shun. Boccaccio's narrators are consistently described as very honest and mature, and they express their desire to flee from the moral corruption of Florence quite as much as from the plague. Sercambi expresses the idea more heavy-handedly and makes his group not only moral but also much more formally religious, with its clerical members and daily Masses. Their trip becomes an open call to penitence and godly living, provoked by the demonstration of God's wrath in the plague. Sercambi's tales, harp-ing repeatedly on man's avarice, lust, deceit, and vanity, are given moraliz-ing Latin titles: "On avarice" or "On falsehood and betrayal." Their bleak view of man suits the frame's exhortation to penance and a return to God.

Many tale collections are set into a notably gloomy social context of plague, war, political turmoil, or individual melancholy.[29] The merriness of the tales is then purposefully contrasted to the quality of reality as a means of comfort. Boccaccio and Sercambi use the plague; Straparola, the political flight of Ottaviano Sforza. Cinthio's *Hecatommithi*, begun in 1528, makes similar use of the recent sack of Rome. Even Sacchetti, who uses no framing narrative, refers in his preface to the multitude of sufferings in his day from which people are in need of relief. Ser Giovanni Fiorentino refers to his own condition as one "blasted by fortune"; and Sercambi, introducing his own name as narrator for the traveling group, describes himself as "one who has causelessly suffered many injuries done to him with no fault of his."

Straparola uses his frame in a different way to affect the reading of his tales. His group is worldly, and the tales are presented as an entertainment during the carnival season, the period of license which precedes a call to penance. An analogy to Straparola's use of carnival is Giovanni Sabadino degli Arienti's setting of *The Porrettane* (1483) at the baths of Porreta, for baths are a place of notorious license. Boccaccio again is the source for both, having noted in his *Decameron* that the plague was a time of unusual license and the failure of social laws. The variety of Straparola's tales makes it difficult to infer any one aim for the collection. It seems that whereas Sercambi's are moral exempla of human sin, Straparola's are perhaps a purgative outlet or exploration of human emotions of all kinds meant to allow the reassertion of a moral order afterwards. His work ends with church bells ringing to mark the beginning of Lent, whereupon Lucrezia reminds her guests that the bells "invite us to holy prayers and to do penance for our committed faults. Therefore it seems to me honest and right that in these holy days we set aside delightful conversations and loving dances and sweet music, angelic songs and ridiculous fables, and attend to the salvation of our souls." Straparola's careful containment of the tales in time, the clearly respectable nature of the assembled group, and the final reminder of the importance of our spiritual welfare all serve as hedges against a possible misapplication of the fables. His use of fairy-tale material and the word *favole* or "fables" are a further means of separating them from real life.

The concept of carnival, that is, of a time of special liberty from normal rules and social hierarchies, may be very useful for understanding the novella.[30] William Bascom, in his analysis of folklore, has remarked on the frequency of shocking, antisocial, and taboo behavior in folktales of all kinds.[31] Renaissance novellas are not only full of illicit love affairs and clerical scandals, they show an immense interest in scatological humor and pranksterism. The prominence of the trickster in the society of the novella fulfilled the need of both author and reader to participate vicariously in the assertion of human sovereignty during a period which, as we have seen, was fraught with peril. Carl Jung noted that the trickster is recreated every time people feel that their will is being thwarted by accidents which seem somehow intentionally malicious. The trickster does horrible things without any conscience or thought; yet he is amoral rather than evil.[32] He is not quite human; and yet he is a projection of human willfulness onto misfortune. The frequency of pranksterism in the novella may be a restorative emphasis on human will and planning and an attempt to identify the power of malicious accidents with human agency, that is, with human power. Thus it might gird the reader to cope with a life of disasters. Bascom explains the phenomenon as a fantasized escape from real-life restrictions, which allows the culture to continue with all its necessary frustrations. Any system requires rules which at once imply the possibility of their infraction.[33] In part, then, the Renaissance novella may be playfully breaking all the rules, but within a strictly controlled situation. Straparola's use of carnival, ser Giovanni's monastic retreat, or Boccaccio's villa outside the city each create a containing wall between literature and life which allows the narrators greater freedom in their stories than in their lives. Ultimately, carnivalesque themes do more to maintain than to undermine real social order. Not until after the writers of the Reformation had turned the centuries-old comic theme of sinful friars into a serious attack against the holy orders, did the Church try to put an end to such stories.

Related to the carnival is the idea of play, where a special time and space are established in which rules apply that are different from the rules of normal life. Huizinga discusses numerous and contradictory theories proposed by others about the function of play: that play satisfies a need for relaxation, or the urge to exercise certain faculties; that it is an exercise in restraint, or an expression of the desire to dominate and an outlet for harmful impulses; that it is a training for serious work, or an escape into wish fulfillment. All of these, he concludes, may be partly true.[34] He associates play with two other things which, combined, describe many novellas: through its freedom and spontaneity, play is connected to comedy, folly, jest and laughter; on the other hand, through "the impulse to create orderly form" it is linked with art.[35] It is precisely the combination of human impulses towards freedom and towards order with which the novellas are concerned. Marcus's comment on the *Decameron* may be valid for a number of these works: "For the dialectic between the cornice and the tales is an attempt to define a space, bounded by reason, within which man may exercise his passions and appetites *onestamente*."[36]

IV. LATER DEVELOPMENTS

The sixteenth century saw considerable changes in the novella genre. The writer who, after Boccaccio, was most influential and did most to enhance the status of the genre was Bandello. He developed a longer, more elaborate narrative, often following the development of a character or relationship through many years and demonstrating in some cases a realism of observation and a depth of psychological interest unparalleled since Boccaccio. Bandello presents his specific case histories as keys to general truths about human behavior. Some of his historical characters are unforgettable, for through all their particularity they become outstanding representatives of basic qualities of the human psyche. The Englishman William Painter, taking half his English collection of tales from Bandello, was clearly interested in the tales as psychological and moral portraits of a variety of characters. Bandello's longer stories, especially the tragic ones, were immediately translated, imitated, and much further lengthened and elaborated by French, Spanish, and English writers. The interest of these imitators was focused on passion and sentiment, enhanced by the insertion of long inner monologues, speeches, letters, and comments by the author. From Bandello, then, rather than from Boccaccio, one can trace the beginnings of the novel. Luigi da Porto's *Giulietta* was another example of this type of longer romance, which because of its length could—as a rare exception—be published alone, apart from any collection.[37]

The Council of Trent, which met at intervals between 1545 and 1563 to solidify the conservative Catholic position against the increasing influence of Protestant ideas,[38] had a considerable impact on the development of the novella and encouraged it to follow the new directions offered by Bandello. One of the Council's acts was to institute an index of forbidden books in 1559 which included the *Decameron*. By condemning lascivious stories and scandal tales about friars, nuns, and clergymen, the Council suppressed two of the novella's major themes, leaving romance and history as the main viable subjects.[39] As Maier has observed, a result of the Counter-Reformation was thus the shift from comedy to tragedy as the prevailing mode of narrative.[40] Given the principles of decorum, which specified that tragedy be written about noble characters in an elevated style, while comedy treat lower-class characters in a more naturalistic language, this also meant a shift in style from low to high. We can see this change in the subject matter and style of the novella taking place in the works of Straparola, who borrowed passages from the elegant pastoral romances of Sannazaro and Montemayor with which to embellish his narratives.[41]

The lengthening of narrative produced a new kind of frame in which the life of a single character formed the connecting thread for a series of incidents and adventures. This device was developed especially by satiric writers such as the Englishmen George Gascoigne (1573) and Thomas

Nashe (1594), or the Spanish author of *Lazarillo de Tormes* (ca. 1554). In these longer satires the high style was either avoided or used in jest, being put in the mouth not of a noble or middle-class gathering, but of a lower-class scoundrel or outcast. In sum, the development of the satiric or picaresque novel came about as the mirror image of the development of the sentimental novel, much the way that chivalric romance and *fabliau* had mirrored each other in medieval narrative.

Another development which transformed the genre and avoided the Church's criticism was the introduction of folklore and fairy tale. Although medieval collections such as the *Gesta Romanorum* included fantastic as well as real subjects, the early *novellieri*, such as Boccaccio, Sacchetti, and Sercambi, concentrated almost exclusively on the realistic. Ser Giovanni introduced a small number of more romantic stories, but it was Straparola who first turned to folktales and fairy tales as a major source. With Basile the folktale finally took over completely. It was thus Basile rather than the other *novellieri* who aroused the excitement of the French in the eighteenth century, and the Germans in the nineteenth, when folklore became a fashionable subject of study. Basile's treatment of folk materials, however, is highly artful. Unlike the romantics who were enchanted with his work for sentimental reasons, Basile probably thought of his use of folklore not as a return to the roots of storytelling but rather as a playfully baroque combination of farfetched and homely materials with extravagantly artificial style.

A further novelty was the use of various local dialects instead of the established literary Italian based on the Florentine of Dante and Boccaccio. Certainly, Basile's use of the Neapolitan dialect was playful and artful, rather than true to local speech; for he went out of his way to find or even invent Neapolitan words that could be substituted for much more common Italian ones.[42] Another factor at work here, besides a baroque taste for the exotic, was a shift away from Florence as the cultural and literary center. The early *novellieri* had usually been Tuscan: the author of *The Hundred Old Tales*, Boccaccio, Sacchetti, ser Giovanni, Sercambi. But in the fifteenth century other areas of Italy began to rival Florentine hegemony. Masuccio is Neapolitan. Straparola, later on, is from Bergamo, and includes two tales in the Bergamasc and Paduan dialects. Bandello explains that he is writing in his own Lombard idiom, not in Tuscan. Basile pushed this localism to such an extreme that his work has had to be translated into Italian.

Renaissance tales all along offer a wonderful combination of local realism with eternal fable. On one hand, they give us glimpses into life in

Renaissance Italy in a very personal way: how individuals felt about their life and their society, and what they wanted or valued. On the other hand, specific cultural detail merges with ancient myth, as tales which originally came from India or Arabia or classical Rome are given a contemporary Italian setting. Thus, for example, the legends of Hero and Leander or Pyramus and Thisbe lurk behind Straparola's tale of Malgherita (VII, 2) or Luigi da Porto's story of two lovers in Verona, adding a mythical resonance to the narrative. Basile is a master at gliding smoothly from the busy streets of Naples to the most magical of landscapes, from a familiar argument between father and son to encounters with orcs and fairies, or from the problem of nosy neighbors to a goose that excretes gold coins and takes hold of a prince's posterior.

Many aspects of the novella can be summed up by the concept of variety, an aim often expressed by the writers themselves.[43] It is for the sake of variety that the collections of stories mix tragedy and comedy, *fabliau* and romance, briefer and longer narrative, examples of sin with examples of virtue, themes of love with themes of fortune, wit, or anti-clerical satire. Sometimes we can find nearly the same tale retold with the ending reversed from tragic to comic, or with the roles reversed from husband to wife or from upper-class to lower-class characters. One function of variety was simply to hold the interest of the reader, or to ensure popularity by offering something for every taste. Another purpose, however, was to use variety to approach the fullness of possibilities, both of form and of character or example, in order to create a world in small. The hope of thus arriving at a sense of completeness is symbolized by the authors' frequent choice of large round numbers of tales: one hundred for *The Hundred Old Tales* and Boccaccio; fifty for the less ambitious ser Giovanni, Masuccio, and Basile; three hundred for the enthusiastic Sacchetti. Bandello exclaimed about the variety of the world as a perfect object for literary imitation, that it is full of "marvelous and different things . . . worthy of astonishment, compassion, and blame!" (Prefaces to I, 8 and III, 62). Painter, collecting and translating tales from Boccaccio, Straparola, Bandello, and others, comments on his title, *Palace of Pleasure*, by announcing that his palace will include both the glorious deeds of princes and gentlemen and also the doings of inferior persons, "eche one vouchsafing to tell what hee was, in the transitorie trade of present life." He calls his book "a Theatre of the world."[44]

In the preceding pages I have attempted to give readers a necessarily brief history and description of the novella in order to enable them to enter into the context of writers who, despite their being culturally different from us, have established the roots of our own literary heritage.

While aiming to achieve readable English in the tales that follow, I have also tried to convey a sense of stylistic changes by following the author's patterns of language as closely as English allows. Basile's alliterations, puns, and rhymes I have reproduced where I could without changing the meanings of his words; untranslatable wordplay is indicated in the notes at the end of the book. Again at the end of the book is a bibliography listing other novella anthologies where the reader may find more tales to read. The bibliography also includes a number of secondary works in Italian and English to enhance the reader's appreciation of the narratives.

The *novellieri* were of course widely read in Italy in their own time. They were also extremely popular outside Italy, a fact which is attested to by Ascham's complaint in his *Scholemaster* (1572) about the ill effect of Italian books upon the behavior of Englishmen: "These be the inchantementes of Circes, brought out of Italie, to marre mens manners in England; much by example of ill life, but more by preceptes of fonde bookes, of late translated out of Italian into English, sold in every shop in London. . . ."[45] It was perhaps my own love of "fonde bookes" which first prompted me to bring these stories to the attention of American readers. Although a stern contemporary may have judged them *fonde*, or "foolish," I find these tales to be among the brightest narrative jewels of the Italian novella collection.

The Hundred Old Tales

This anonymous collection of tales, named in retrospect by its first editor after Boccaccio's hundred stories, was written by a Florentine between 1280 and the early fourteenth century. It went untitled in most manuscripts, except for MS. Panciatichiano-Palatino 138, now 32, which called it "the book of tales and fine gentle speech." The stories are drawn from classical mythology, the Bible, oriental collections, medieval chivalric legends and chronicles, miracle stories, the lives of saints, and historical anecdotes from all periods. Thus we find Narcissus, Lancelot and the Lady of Shalott, Alexander the Great, the Emperor Federigo II, Saladin, Nebuchadnesor, Hercules, Cato, and St. Gregory jumbled together with contemporary men of court, lawyers, cabbage vendors, pageboys, storytellers, and animals. The preface suggests that people who cannot invent their own amusing conversation may want to retell these anecdotes, presumably in their own words; this may explain the outline quality of most tales. Perhaps, however, the tales were written with an intentional brevity of style; the author, odd as it may seem to us, apologizes for his wordiness and hopes we will not find it tedious!

The first printed edition was published in 1525 at the urging of Cardinal Pietro Bembo, who owned a manuscript of it and remarked on the pleasure of comparing some of Boccaccio's stories with those of this forerunner (e.g., no. 73). Boccaccio was not the only one to borrow ideas from here, however, for tales from this very popular collection appear in the writings of Dante (no. 69) and Chaucer (no. 83) too, and in the later stories of Straparola (no. 97) and others. I have selected tales to show the variety of characters and situations which distinguish this collection. Nos. 31 and 89 are about the art of storytelling and offer some insight into the aims of the anonymous narrator.

My translation is based on *Il Novellino*, a critical edition with introduction and notes by Guido Favati (Genova: Fratelli Bozzi, 1970). It is considerably different from the previous editions by C. Alvaro (Milan: Garzanti, 1945) and L. di Francia, Classici Italiani 45 (Turin, 1930, reprinted as volume 48 in 1945 and 1948). These other editions also include notes and some bibliography. The book has been translated as

The Hundred Old Tales by Edward Storer (New York: E. P. Dutton, 1925). Alessandro D'Ancona, "Del Novellino e delle sue fonti," in his *Studi di critica e storia letteraria* vol.2 (Bologna, 1912), pp.2–163, includes tale-by-tale notes on sources and analogs.

Preface

When our Lord Jesus Christ spoke with us in human form, among his sayings was this one: that from the heart's overflow the tongue speaks.[1] You who have gentle and noble hearts, fit your minds and words to the pleasure of God, speaking, honoring, fearing, and praising our Lord, who loved us before he made us and before we loved ourselves. And if it is ever possible, without displeasing Him, to speak for our recreation, let it be done as honestly and courteously as possible.

And as nobles and gentlemen are like a mirror for lesser folk in speech and in action, noble speech being more pleasing since it proceeds from a refined instrument, let us here recall some flowers of speech, of handsome courtesies, witty replies, fine worthy deeds, handsome gifts, and noble loves enacted in times past. And he who has a noble heart and keen mind will be able to imitate these examples in times to come, and to discuss and narrate them whenever it is appropriate, for the profit and pleasure of those who are ignorant and want to learn.

And if the flowers which we will set forth are mixed with many lesser words, be not displeased; for black is the enhancer of gold, and on behalf of one noble and delicate fruit we are sometimes pleased with a whole orchard, and for the sake of a few pretty flowers we like the whole garden. May it not be wearisome to the reader; for many persons have lived a long time and in their whole lives have had scarcely one noteworthy saying or deed to their credit.

21

HOW THREE MASTERS OF NECROMANCY CAME TO THE COURT OF THE EMPEROR FEDERIGO.[2]

The Emperor Federigo was a most noble lord, and people with talent used to flock to him from all over because he gave generously and showed favor to anyone with special skill. To him came musicians, troubadours and tellers of fine tales, artisans, jousters, fencers, and people of all kinds.

One day as the Emperor Federigo was standing while water was being brought around for handwashing, and the tables were set and everybody was ready to sit down to eat, there came to him three masters of necromancy in long slavic robes.[3] They greeted the Emperor suddenly, and he asked,

"Which is the leader of you three?"

One stepped forward and said,

"My lord, I am." And the Emperor requested him to play some magic trick. Obligingly they cast their spells and performed their arts.

The weather began to grow stormy: lo there was a sudden downpour, with hailstones as big as steel balls, thunder, lightning, and flashes, such that the world seemed to be dissolving. The knights fled through the rooms, some one way and some another.

The weather cleared. The masters requested permission to leave and asked for a reward. The Emperor said,

"Ask what you will."

They looked to the count of San Bonifazio, who was nearest to the Emperor and said,

"My lord, command that man to come to our aid against our enemies."

The Emperor commanded him tenderly to do as they wished. The count set out with them; they led him to a lovely city, showed him knights of great prowess, equipped him with a handsome steed and beautiful arms, and said to the count,

"These men are to obey you."

Then they showed him their enemies, who came to do battle; the count defeated them and freed the town. Next he fought three pitched battles in the field. He conquered the land. They gave him a wife. He had children. Afterwards he ruled for a long while.

The magicians left him for a very long time; then they returned. The count's son was already forty years old; the count himself was an old man. The masters said,

"Do you recognize us? Do you wish to go back to see the Emperor and his court?"

And the count replied, "The empire will by now have changed hands several times; the people now will all be new; to what shall I return?"

But the masters said, "We wish to take you there again anyway."

They set off; they traveled a long while; they reached the court; they found the Emperor and his barons still washing their hands with the same water as when the count had gone away with the magicians.

The Emperor had him tell the story; he told it: "Moreover I have a wife, and a son who is forty years old; also I fought three pitched battles. The world has all turned backwards. How can this be?"

The Emperor with the greatest delight made him tell it all again, and so did the barons and knights.

31
THIS STORY IS ABOUT LORD AZZOLINO'S STORYTELLER.

Lord Azzolino of Romano[4] had a storyteller, whom he bid tell tales in the evening during the long nights of winter. One night it happened that the storyteller had a great desire to sleep when Azzolino asked him to tell a tale. And so the storyteller began a yarn about a peasant who, having a hundred *bisanti*,[5] went to the market to buy sheep and got two for each *bisante*. Returning with his sheep, he found that a river which he had crossed before was meanwhile very swollen by a heavy rain. Standing upon the bank, he solved his problem in this manner: he found a poor fisherman with a little boat, so extremely tiny that it would hold no more than the peasant and one sheep at a time; then the peasant began to cross. The river was wide. He got into the little boat with one sheep and began to float across. He floats and crosses.

At this point the storyteller paused and said nothing more. Sir Azzolino said, "Go on."

To which the storyteller replied,

"Sir, let the sheep get across and then I'll tell you what happened."

It would have taken at least a year to get the sheep across, so that meanwhile the storyteller could sleep very comfortably.

44
ON A QUESTION THAT WAS PUT TO A COURTIER.

Marco Lombardo[6] was a very wise and noble courtier. One Christmas he was in a city where a great deal of clothing was being given away, but he received none. He found another man at court, a minstrel, who was an ignorant person compared to himself and yet had received many clothes. From this there arose a fine saying, for that minstrel asked Marco,

"Why is it, Marco, that I have been given seven robes and you none? And yet you are much better and wiser than I! What is the reason?"

And Marco replied,

"None other than this: that you found more people of your kind than I found of mine."

49
THIS STORY IS ABOUT A DOCTOR OF TOULOUSE, WHO MARRIED A NIECE OF THE ARCHBISHOP OF TOULOUSE.

A doctor of Toulouse married a well-born lady of Toulouse, a niece of the archbishop. He brought her home. In two months she gave birth to a girl. The doctor displayed no anger; rather he comforted the woman and showed her reasons, according to Medicine, why it could well be his own child; and with those words and with a sweet mien, he prevented the lady from aborting. He honored the lady much during the birth; after the birth he took her aside and he said to her,

"My lady, I have honored you as much as I could; I pray you, for your love of me, that you return now to your father's house. I will keep your daughter with me, with great honor."

Things went along well until the archbishop heard that the doctor had dismissed his niece. He sent for him, and as he was a great man, he spoke down to him with many haughty words, mixed with pride and with threats. And when he had said plenty, the doctor made the following reply:

"My lord, I married your niece thinking that I was wealthy enough to be able to furnish and feed my family; it was my intention to have one child a year and not more. But the lady began to have children in two months; wherefore I am not so well off that, if things go on like this, I could provide for them all; and it would not be an honor to you were your lineage to become impoverished. Therefore I beg you as a favor, and so that you may avoid dishonor, that you give your daughter to a richer man than I, one who can provide for her children."

69
THIS STORY IS ABOUT THE EMPEROR TRAJAN'S GREAT JUSTICE.

The Emperor Trajan was a very just ruler. One day as he was going with his large cavalry to fight his enemies, a widow presented herself before him and took hold of him by the stirrup, saying, "My lord, do me justice against those who have wrongly killed my son!" The emperor replied,
"I will satisfy you when I return."
She said,

"What if you never return?"

He answered,

"My successor will satisfy you."

She said,

"And if your successor fails me, you will be my debtor. And even suppose he does satisfy me, the justice done by someone else will not free you of your guilt. Your successor will do well enough just to free himself from his own guilt."

Then the emperor dismounted from his horse and did justice to those who had killed her son; afterwards he rode off and defeated his enemies.

Not long after the emperor's death, the blessed pope St. Gregory came by,[7] and learning of Trajan's justice, went to his statue and honored him with tears and great praise and had his body exhumed. It was found that the entire body had turned to dust except for the bones and the tongue; and this showed how Trajan had been a very just man and had spoken justly. St. Gregory prayed for him to God, and it is said to be a clear miracle that, through the prayers of this holy pope, the soul of this emperor was freed from the pains of hell and went to eternal life. And yet he had been a pagan.

74

How Saladin,[8] Needing Money, Tried to Find a Pretext against a Jew.

Saladin, needing money, was advised to find some pretext against a rich Jew who lived in his land, whereby he might confiscate his immeasurable wealth. Saladin sent for this Jew to ask him which was the best religion, thinking:

"If he says the Jewish religion, I will tell him that he sins against mine; and if he says the Saracin, I will say, 'Why then do you adhere to the Jewish?' "

The Jew, hearing the ruler's question, answered thus:

"My lord, there was a father who had three sons, and he had a ring with a precious stone, the best in the world. Each of these sons begged the father to leave him his ring at his death; and the father, seeing that each one wanted it, sent for a fine goldsmith and said,

"Master, make me two rings just like this one, and put in each a stone that looks just like this one."

The master made the rings so exactly that no one could tell the valuable one except the father. He sent for the sons one by one, giving his ring to each one in secret. Each son thought he had the valuable ring, and no one knew the truth except their father. And so it is concerning the religions, sir; there are three religions; the Father above knows which is best, and the sons, that is we, each think we have the good one."

Then Saladin, hearing this man save himself in this way, could find no pretext to hold against him, and so he let him go.

83

HOW CHRIST, WALKING ONE DAY WITH HIS DISCIPLES THROUGH A WILDERNESS, SAW A GREAT TREASURE.

One day as Christ was walking with his disciples through a wilderness, the disciples, who were following behind him, saw some coins of fine gold shining to one side. Surprised that Christ had not stopped for the gold, they called to Him, saying:

"Lord, let's take this gold, which will provide for many of our needs."

And Christ turned and reprimanded them, saying,

"You desire those things which take from our kingdom the majority of souls that are lost; you will see the proof of this when we return."

And they passed onward.

Shortly thereafter, two dear comrades found the gold, whereupon they were very merry. They agreed that one of them should go to the nearest village to bring back a mule, while the other should remain as guard. But hear the wicked deeds that followed from this on account of the wicked thoughts which the enemy[9] put in their minds. One of the two men returned with the mule and said to his comrade,

"I ate at the village, but you must be hungry. Eat these two breads that look so good, and then we will load the mule."

The other replied,

"I don't feel like eating now; therefore let us load first."

Then they began to load. When they had almost finished loading, and the one who had gone for the mule bent over to tie on the load, the other ran up behind him treacherously with a sharp knife and killed him. Afterwards he took one of the breads and gave it to the mule and ate the other himself. The bread was poisoned; as a result both he and the mule fell dead before they could move from that spot, and the gold remained unclaimed as before.

And our Lord passed by there with his disciples on that same day and showed them the proof of which he had spoken.

89

THIS STORY IS ABOUT THE COURTIER WHO BEGAN A STORY THAT NEVER CAME TO AN END.

A group of knights was dining one evening in a great house in Florence; and a courtier was there who was a great storyteller. When they had dined, he began a story which never came to an end.

One young page of the household, who was serving and perhaps had not had much to eat, called him by name, saying:

"Whoever taught you that story did not teach you the whole thing."

And the other replied,

"How so?"

And he said,

"Because he neglected to teach you the ending."

Whereupon the other became ashamed and stopped.

97

THIS STORY IS ABOUT A MERCHANT WHO CARRIED WINE ACROSS THE SEA IN BARRELS WITH TWO DIVIDERS AND WHAT HAPPENED.

A merchant carried wine across the sea in barrels with two dividers: below and above there was wine, and in the middle, water, so that half was wine and half water. Below and above there were taps, but not in the middle. He sold the water as wine and doubled his money above what he deserved; as soon as he had been paid, he embarked upon a ship and set off to sea with his money. Then, by God's decree, there appeared on that ship a large monkey which snatched the purse containing the merchant's money and climbed to the top of the mast. The merchant, fearing lest the monkey throw his purse into the sea, tried to entice it back.

The ape sat itself down, opened the purse with its mouth, and took out the gold coins one by one. It dropped one coin into the sea and let the next one fall into the ship; and it kept on until half the coins were in the ship, exactly the profit the merchant deserved.

Franco Sacchetti (c. 1335–1400)

Franco Sacchetti wrote his *Trecentonovelle* or *Three Hundred Tales* during the 1390s, near the end of a life of involvement in Florentine politics. After having spent his younger years traveling as a businessman, Sacchetti was elected to some of the highest offices in the Florentine government and also served as a mayor in various parts of Tuscany. He lost his property in the war against Milan and died a few years later of the plague. Besides *The Three Hundred Tales*, Sacchetti wrote poems and madrigals of a fashionable kind and an incomplete commentary on the New Testament. This biblical commentary reveals the author's developing interest in narrative through the exemplary tales which appear with increasing frequency in its later chapters.

As Sacchetti acknowledges in the preface to his *Three Hundred Tales*, Boccaccio's example inspired him to write his book of stories. Although there is no frame to Sacchetti's collection, one tale is often linked to another by topic or comment. They are "novelle" in the sense of "news," anecdotes from contemporary or nearly contemporary times, and many of the characters are historical. Sacchetti even tells a few anecdotes about himself and his friends as well as about more famous people. Needless to say, his book was never as successful as Boccaccio's and lacks the elegance of Boccaccio's style, but Sacchetti's simpler writing is nonetheless full of vitality.

There are gaps in the text, which, as we have it, contains over two hundred tales. Entire stories as well as story fragments are missing, and occasional phrases have become illegible in the manuscripts. Apparently, the book did not have wide diffusion, thanks partly to Sacchetti's refusal to lend it to friends for copying. There are only two extant MSS. upon which modern editions can be based: a sixteenth-century transcription of the original manuscript, plus a copy of that copy, made soon after. The text was first established by Vincenzo Pernicone (Florence, Sansoni, 1946). This early version of the text, together with that of Ettore Li Gotti (Milan: Bompiani, 1946), has since been used by Aldo Borlenghi for his edition of Sacchetti's *Opere* or complete works (Milan: Rizzoli, 1957), which includes notes, a brief bibliography, and an index of names. Further bibliography can be found in Porcelli's *Novellieri Italiani* (Italian Short Story Writers). Mary Steegman has translated a selection of eighty-three *Tales from Sacchetti* with prudish omissions. Translations of single tales can also be found in Morris Bishop, *A Medieval Storybook*, and in the anthologies by Clark and Lieber, Pasinetti, Pettoello, Roscoe, and Valency.

Introduction

Considering the present times and the condition of human life, which is frequently subject to pestilential illness and death by unknown causes; and seeing how many downfalls there are in life and how many wars, both within the city and on the battlefield; and thinking of the many people and families that are thereby brought to poverty and wretchedness, and with what bitter sweat they must bear their misery, when they feel that their lives are over; and furthermore imagining how eager people are to hear new things, and especially to read books which are easy to understand, and, better still, which give comfort by provoking laughter in the midst of so many sorrows; and considering finally the excellent poet Mister Giovanni Boccaccio, whose book of a hundred tales, although a lowly thing with regard to its author's noble intellect . . .[1] has spread and . . . they have translated it into their own languages as far as France and England . . . I, Franco Sacchetti, a Florentine, as one uneducated and coarse, proposed to myself to write the present work and to collect all the stories, both ancient and modern, of various kinds, which have existed through time, and some too concerning events which I witnessed or which happened to me.

And it is no wonder most of these tales are Florentine . . . for I have been closest to those events . . . the tales will tell about . . . conditions of people, such as marquises and counts and knights . . . and great and small, and also about every kind of woman, noble, middle class, and lowly; in magnificent and virtuous works their names will be told. As for the mean and blameworthy, it is better that their names go untold, and especially when they are men of great business or state; I will take example from the Florentine vernacular poet Dante, who set the praises and virtues of others in his own mouth, but blamed their vices through the words of the spirits of the dead.

No doubt many people, and especially those who are criticized to their displeasure, will say, as is often said, "These are made-up tales." I reply to this that perhaps there will be some of that sort, but I have tried to compose them true to life. It could well be, as one often finds, that a story will be told about John, and someone will say that it happened to Peter; this

*would be a small error, but it would not mean that the events of the tale
did not take place in real life. And others may say . . .*

FRIAR TADDEO DINI,[2] PREACHING AT BOLOGNA ON ST. CATHERINE'S
DAY, IS MADE TO EXHIBIT A FALSE RELIC OF THE SAINT AGAINST HIS
WILL, BUT QUIPS ABOUT IT TO THE CONGREGATION.

Relics are often found to be fraudulent, as happened a short time
ago among the Florentines. Having obtained an arm from Puglia
which had been given to them as the arm of St. Reparata, and
having welcomed its arrival with great ceremony, exhibiting it for several
years on the saint's day with grand solemnity, the people discovered in
the end that the arm was made of wood.[3]

Well then, Friar Taddeo Dini, a most worthy man of the order of preachers, was in Bologna on St. Catherine's day. As he was preaching at the
convent of St. Catherine for the holiday, it happened that, when he had
finished the sermon and before he could descend from the pulpit to hear
confessions, a crystal coffer was brought to him with many candles and
covered with clothes, and he was told to "exhibit this arm of St. Catherine."

Friar Taddeo, who was no fool, said, "How can this be the arm of St.
Catherine? I have been to Mt. Sinai, and I have seen her glorious body
whole with both arms and all her other limbs intact."

The old priests said, "It may be as you say, but we maintain that this is
truly her arm."

Friar Taddeo argued with clear reasons that the arm should not be exhibited. Upon hearing this the Abbess sent for him, begging him to display
the relic since if it were not exhibited, the convent would lose its holy reputation. Seeing that he had no choice in the matter, Friar Taddeo opened the
coffer and, taking the arm in his hand, said,

"Ladies and gentlemen, the sisters of this convent claim that this arm
which you see belongs to St. Catherine. I have been to Mt. Sinai and have
seen the body of St. Catherine whole, with both its arms; if St. Catherine
had three arms, then this must be the third." With that he began making the
sign of the cross with the arm, as one does, over the whole congregation.

Those who understood laughed, speaking among themselves; many simple men and women crossed themselves devotedly, as did those who could
not hear Friar Taddeo and never realized what he had said.

Faith is a good thing and saves everyone who has it; but the vice of avarice
is responsible for the existence of many fraudulent relics; which is to say that
there is no chapel which does not display some milk of the Virgin Mary! For

[handwritten margin note: 12 doesn't sum up rubrick very well. they seem like headlines "news"]

if it were as they say, how precious it would be to think that something of her glorious body remained on earth; but so much of her milk is exhibited around the world that the Virgin would have had to have been a fountain gushing for many days to make so much milk. If one could test the truth of the matter, as Friar Taddeo did with the said arm, all such claims would suddenly vanish. Now our faith saves us; but those who cook up schemes to take advantage of the faithful must pay the penalty for it in this or in the other world.

[handwritten margin note: But story is not about salvation]

[handwritten margin note: these people don't appear]

115

DANTE ALIGHIERI, HEARING AN ASS-DRIVER RECITE FROM HIS BOOK AND SAY "GEE-UP," STRIKES HIM SAYING, "I DIDN'T WRITE THAT"; AND WHAT FOLLOWS, AS THE TALE TELLS.

The story just told impels me to tell another which is brief and amusing. One day while the said poet, Dante, was walking for pleasure in some part of the city of Florence and wearing a gorget and a bracer,[4] as was the custom to do then, he encountered an ass-driver who had some sacks of garbage loaded in front of him; this ass-driver was walking behind the asses, reciting from Dante's book, and when he had recited a bit, he would poke the ass and say "Gee-up."

Coming up to him, Dante with his bracer gave him a big blow on the shoulder, saying, "I didn't put that 'Gee-up' in there."

The fellow knew neither who Dante was nor what he was talking about; so he poked the asses hard and said again, "Gee-up, gee-up." When he had moved away a small distance, he turned to Dante, stuck out his tongue and made the fig at him with his hands,[5] saying "Take that!"

[handwritten margin note: vulgar, unintelligible, more eloquent]

Dante seeing him said, "I wouldn't give you one of mine for a hundred of yours."

[handwritten margin note: Allowed Dante to maintain his composure]

O sweet words full of philosophy! For there are many who would have run after the ass-driver, shouting and screaming, and others who would have thrown stones; but the wise poet confounded the ass-driver, receiving praise from whoever had overheard him, with such a wise word as the one he had hurled against such a base fellow as that ass-driver.

[handwritten margin note: wise words]

[handwritten margin note: Sacchetti intends some motto effect]

169

BUONAMICO THE PAINTER, PAINTING SAINT ERCOLANO IN THE PIAZZA IN PERUGIA, DEPICTS HIM WITH A CROWN OF MULLETS[6] ON HIS HEAD, AND WHAT COMES OF IT.

As in the last tale, where Doctor Foolgod thoroughly duped Mr. Robust with a medicine which was never again to be prescribed, after which the bean came out of his ear unexpectedly because of a great jousting blow, so in this next story I will tell you a tale about Buonamico the painter previously mentioned in another story.[7] And this tale will show that as Doctor Foolgod cured Mr. Robust with great derision, so this Buonamico adorned a saint of the Perugians with great derision in such a way that he left them all stupified.

In the time of the said Buonamico, when Perugia was in a state of prosperity, it was decided by the Perugians that a Saint Ercolano[8] should be painted as magnificently as he could be painted in the piazza in Perugia. And as they sought which of the very best painters they could get, this Buonamico was proposed to them, and so they determined to send for him. When they had sent for him, and he had arrived in Perugia, and they had made a contract and given him the location and the space and the means, the said Buonamico, as is the custom of painters, wanted to be all closed about with planks and straw; and for several days he gave orders for plaster and paints; in the end he climbed upon the scaffold and began to paint. After eight or ten days the Perugians, who wanted their Saint Ercolano made quickly,[9] began to go up to the scaffolding where he was painting, as they went strolling in groups through the piazza, and one would say, "O Master, will this work ever be done?" Shortly another would come and say, "O Master, how far along is the work?" But the painter remained silent . . . as all painters do. Another group would come to him and say, "O Master, when will we see this patron saint of ours? He should have been finished six times by now, eh? Hurry up, we beg you."

And so all the Perugians, saying one thing or another, not once a day but many times, would go over to Buonamico to urge him on; until Buonamico said to himself, "What the devil is this? These fellows are all crazy, and I will paint as befits their craziness." It entered his head to make Saint Ercolano a crown, not of laurel as for poets, not of jewels as for saints, not of gold as for kings, but of mullets. And having arranged to be paid when the figure was almost complete, he waited until payment had been made for it, claiming afterwards that he still had to touch up the ornaments for the space of two days; and they were satisfied. The touching up which Buonamico did involved making a crown well stocked with mullets for the said Saint Ercolano; and when he had finished it, one morning early he got together with Giovanni . . . and left Perugia and returned towards Florence.

The Perugians went on in their accustomed manner, and some said, "O Master, surely you can begin to uncover it; show it to us just a little bit." The master was silent, for he was on his way to Florence. They had spent the whole day talking to him, some saying one thing and some another, and not hearing any reply, but by the second day they suspected he was not there, because they had not seen him; and asking at the hotel where he used to stay, they were told that it was nearly two days since he had settled with the innkeeper, and they believed he had left town.

When the Perugians heard this, some went off for a ladder and leaned it up to the scaffold to see what was there; and having climbed up, someone saw the saint wreathed with many mullets. At once he climbed down and went to the elders to tell them how the painter from Florence had served them well, and that in mockery, where he should have made the crown of a saint for Saint Ercolano, he had made a wreath full of the biggest mullets that ever had come out of the lake. When this news came to the palace, at once they sent a search party all over Perugia to find Buonamico, and they sent for certain horseback riders from outside town who could catch up with him. It was in vain, for Buonamico had come away safe and sound. The rumor of this deed spread throughout Perugia, and everyone ran to see this strangely painted Saint Ercolano. In a fury they tore down the planks and straw; and it was incredible to see and hear what they said, not only about Buonamico, but about all the Florentines, and they spoke ill especially of those Florentines who were in Perugia. In the end they got a painter to convert those mullets into a jeweled crown and published a bann for the person and property of Buonamico. When Buonamico found out about it, he said, "They with their bann and I with my mullets; as for me, even if they made me emperor, I wouldn't paint in Perugia ever again; for they are the strangest fools I have ever found."

So the matter ended there. Buonamico soundly demonstrated their ignorance to the Perugians, who believe more in Saint Ercolano than in Christ and maintain that he is superior to the greatest Saint in Paradise. If he were there with mullets on his head, maybe they would be saying the truth, for those Apostles who were fishermen, seeing him with mullets on his head, would do him great honor.

175

ANTONIO PUCCI[10] OF FLORENCE FINDS CERTAIN ANIMALS HAVE BEEN PUT INTO HIS GARDEN AT NIGHT AND INGENIOUSLY DISCOVERS WHO DID IT.

Now I don't want to say any more about the doings of Gonnella, because it suits me to make room for others; and also because Antonio Pucci, a good-humored Florentine and versifier on many topics, has begged me to record a prank that was played upon him which he bore patiently and with laughter, also figuring out who did it to him. There is still a bit of amusement to be had from this tale.

Antonio Pucci had a house near the kilns on Ghibelline Street, where he had a little vegetable garden which was barely big enough to produce one bushel of grain. In that small patch he had planted almost every kind of fruit and especially figs, and he had a large quantity of jasmine; and there was one corner full of oak trees which he called "the forest." Now the said Antonio had celebrated this garden, along with other property of his, in a poem where he had used the rhyme and canto scheme of Dante. And in this poem he described all the fruits and conditions of the garden as if it were as abundant as the Old Market Place of Florence, which he had also described thoroughly in another poem, magnifying it above all the piazzas of Italy. In those days there were certain practical jokers in Florence, one of whom was a Girolamo who is still alive, one Gherardo di . . . and Giovanni di Landozzo of the Albizzi, and one who was named Tachello, the dyer, and others, each one of whom was more full of new tricks than the other. They were as original a group as any at that time in the city.

Hearing Antonio say so much about this garden both in prose and in verse, they took it into their heads to lead some animals into it at night to eat it up and make Antonio go out of his mind. To make a long story short, late one evening in the field of Renaio they saw a mule and two asses, thin and old, at pasture. They found a way to get these beasts into a place behind Antonio's garden, where there was a small entry blocked up with timber, walled up outside without mortar, and locked on the inside with a bolt and a lock which had not been opened for a long time. As soon as folk were asleep, two of them went ahead to take down the wall from the outside while the others having entered over the wall, opened the said lock, either with a picklock or with some other instrument, so that the entryway stood unblocked and open. When this was done, they led the two asses and the mule inside. The mule had been decorated at Tachello's house, before they brought him over, with a leather collar and other astonishing things. And when he had been led into the garden, they made him a very fancy harness and bridle of jasmine, and tied him to the foot of a big round slab where Antonio was accustomed to eat outside in

the evenings; and on that slab they set many cabbages which they had
gathered in the said garden, so that the mule would have good prov-
ender. And having done this, they immediately locked the entry cleverly
so that it looked as if it had never been opened. Next they walled up the
outside as it had been before, and they went on their way.

Antonio slept in a bedroom which opened onto the said garden from
the other side where the house was. The following morning, his wife having gotten up before him, Antonio headed for the garden while buttoning
his clothes. There he saw the three strange animals and saw moreover
that they had chewed and ruined all the fruits of his hard labor, leaving
not a stitch. He was almost beside himself, saying, "What's all this?" Going
to the entry by which they had gotten in, he found it locked as before,
wherefore he was even more puzzled; and more still when he went outside and saw it all walled up as it had been.

In brief, his melancholy for the ruined garden was great; but greater was
his perplexity as to how the mule and the two asses could have gotten in.
And among other things, seeing the mule adorned and with cabbages in
front of him, he was even more bewildered, saying, "What sort of gar-
landing is this?"

Then Antonio Pucci exclaimed, "I believe that I was born from a legitimate marriage,"[11] and turning to his wife, he added, "And I believe that
you were too; this is such a strange state of affairs that I don't know what
to make of it! I could hit my head against the wall and not know any
more than I do now; yet I will endeavor as cunningly as I can to find out
who has done this to me; and then let us set our minds at rest."

Having said this, they tried to get the animals out of the garden; they
had to take them through the small bedroom where Antonio and his wife
slept, and they had to take the bed apart so that the animals could get
past. Having been put out into the street, the animals made their way
back to Renaio's to graze; and so the matter rested.

That same day the said Antonio thought up a subtle means of finding
out who had done the deed. Whenever he ran into someone he knew, he
greeted him by saying, "I've caught you." The innocent ones went on
their way without saying anything further.

That day he ran into Tachello the Dyer, who said, "Good day, Antonio."
And Antonio replied, "Good day, Tachello, I've caught you."
And Tachello replied, "By the gospels, Antonio, it wasn't me!"
Then Antonio drew close to Tachello and said, "Oh? Who was it then
if not you?"
And the other replied, "There was so-and-so and so-and-so."

And in this way he found out all who were involved; when he had complained to them one by one, it cost each of them a dinner and peace was made; then Antonio Pucci wrote a sonnet about all this which was no less enjoyable than the tale.

Someone else would have barked for three months and said at every corner, "Such and such has been done to me; by the body and the blood, there's going to be Rome and Tome."[12] But this Antonio was wise, for without letting on, he quietly learned who had put the animals in his garden with an "I've caught you," and had better food at the prankster's expense than the cabbages which they had given to the mule; and then as he told the story to many, they laughed about it for a long time.

211

GONNELLA THE CLOWN[13] AT THE FAIR OF SALERNO[14] SELLS DOG TURDS AS PILLS OF GREAT VIRTUE, ESPECIALLY FOR SEEING THE FUTURE; AND HOW, HAVING RECEIVED A HANDSOME PRICE FOR THESE PILLS, HE GOES FREE.

It still seems to me that certain people (in the last tale) did not come out of it very well when they tried to taste food which they had bought from a vendor, even though they did not have to cook it with millet stalks. Gonnella the clown, who had no peer in doing new tricks, as has been narrated in some previous tales, often traveled through the world to the most faraway places. He once landed in Puglia at the fair of Salerno. And seeing a number of young men who had full purses to buy merchandise, he dressed himself up in a gown so that he looked like a doctor come from overseas; and having found a box low and wide, he spread a white napkin inside it, upon which he placed about thirty little pills made of dog turds; and with the open box in hand, and a napkin draped over his shoulder, he arrived at the said fair. Setting himself apart at a table, with a servant at his side, he displayed the aforesaid merchandise; and speaking with his servant in a sort of gibberish as if he came from Torissi,[15] he attracted a diverse crowd.

Some would ask him, "Doctor, what merchandise is that?"

And he would say to them, "Go on your way; it's not your business; it's too valuable a thing, and it's not made for anyone who has no money to spend." And to some he said it one way and to some another, only to whet the appetites of those around him; at last certain young men, pulling him aside, said,

"Doctor, we beg you to tell us what sort of pills those are."

And he said, "You look to me like serious men to whom one can speak the truth," and speaking half German and half Latin, he said, "This merchandise is such that whoever learns about it will value it more than everything else at this fair, and if you saw me arrive, then you know that I carried it myself and didn't entrust it to my servant."

They went on asking him about it. He claimed that those pills had so much virtue that whoever ate even one of them would suddenly become a seer; and that with great difficulty he had gotten the recipe from the King of Sara, who ruled thirty-two pagan kingdoms; and it was because he often ate them, that he had become such a great ruler.

The young men said, "What is the price of one pill?"

Replied Gonella, "It can't cost so much that it isn't still very cheap; for you know what the proverb says: 'Make me a prophet and I'll make you rich.' I was a poor man, but through using these pills I am now so well off that I have grown rich and lack nothing; but because you seem to me gentlemen, I will give you one for five florins."

They said that for love and for grace they wanted to have four of them in exchange for twelve florins. Gonnella, hearing the offer, rejoiced inwardly, but outwardly he made a show of being a hundred miles from accepting such a deal, saying, "I wouldn't give them to anyone else for three times that much." Finally they agreed on fifteen florins; and he said, "Do one thing; say at the table that you got them from me for five florins apiece." And they said they would do that.

Gonnella, rascal that he was, was thinking ahead to the consequences. Since the fair lasted all Thursday, he said to them, "You must take them on a Friday, on an empty stomach, between the hours of nine and three, because that's the day and the hour when our Lord had his passion; otherwise you won't accomplish a thing." They said they would do it, and that it was easy enough to do. And he took fifteen florins in exchange for four pills made of dog turds. The others around, seeing the sale and hearing the rumor which was already spreading, that whoever ate one of those pills would suddenly become a seer, ran to buy at the best price they could, all receiving from Gonnella the prescription to take them on Friday on an empty stomach and at the said hour, until he had sold all thirty for about one hundred and twenty florins.

Early Friday morning, Gonnella jumped on horseback with his servant and his luggage, and set off without telling the innkeeper which way he was heading. When the hour arrived which the buyers had been waiting for, that is to eat the pills to become seers, two of the young men who had bought them first and were eager to be prophets, bit a big mouthful each from his pill. Suddenly one spit his out saying, "Ah me! they're dog turds!" And the other did likewise; and immediately they went to the inn to ask for the doctor who sold the pills.

The innkeeper said, "He must be six miles away by now, he left so long ago."

"And where did he go?"

He replied that he did not know, but indicated the direction in which the doctor and his servant were heading. The young men, quick on their legs, began to make their way on foot, going so swiftly that they caught up with him at . . . as he was on horseback about to leave an inn. When they reached him, they said,

"Doctor, you sold us those dog turds at too high a price. When we had them in our mouths, we spit them out."

Said Gonnella, "What did I tell you?"

"You said that suddenly we would be seers."

Replied Gonnella, "And so now you see," and being on horseback he spurred his horse, and he and his servant went on their way.

Left feeling foolish, and seeing that they couldn't hold him back, the young men turned to each other very sadly, saying, "We've certainly made ourselves a fine mess; the mockery is even worse than the damage." And having reached Salerno they found some others who had bought the same merchandise, looking for the doctor, some in one direction and some in another; and some were standing as if stunned, and each one was lamenting and feeling foolish from such a dirty joke. Others, learning the story, began to chant,

"May he who wants a seer to be, let dogs shit in his mouth and see." And so the buyers went on being mocked for a long time; and Gonnella went on his way towards Naples, where with an even more rascally trick he drew to himself more money than before, as the next story will tell.

I am sure that Gonnella said afterwards that he had earned the money; but one could say rather that he had stolen it with great deceit and fraud; for in such matters no one was ever as subtle and clever as he. And it seems to me a great wonder that in all his days he did not find someone who paid him for the light and the dice[16] as he deserved, although his tricks were a laughing matter to those who were not involved.

Ser Giovanni Fiorentino (Second Half of the Fourteenth Century)

Little is known about the author of the *Pecorone* or *Big Sheep*. We do not even know whether it was the author or someone else who appended the verses at the end of the book to explain its title:

> Thirteen hundred and seventy-eight years
> had passed when this book
> was written and put in order,
> as you see, by me ser Giovanni.
>
> And I had no trouble in baptizing it,
> for a dear lord of mine gave it its title:
> and it is called the Big Sheep
> because it contains strange dolts.
>
> And I am the chief of such a group,
> who go bleating like a sheep,
> making books when I don't know a thing about it.
>
> Let's say that I made it early in life,
> and so that my reputation might be honored,
> as it will be by boors.
>
> Don't marvel at that, reader,
> for the book is made just like the author.

The preface too dates the beginning of the work in 1378; but as the tales refer to events occurring in 1385, ser Giovanni must have composed his book over a number of years.

The author sets up a narrative frame in which a monk and nun, in love with each other, meet for twenty-five days to tell each other stories. The influence of the *Decameron* is visible not only in the division of story-telling into days and the use of fictional narrators who each tell one story a day, but also in the habit of following the stories with a song. At the end of each day of storytelling, the narrators shake hands or kiss and agree to meet again. It has been suggested that the monk's name, Auretto, is an anagram for Auttore or "author," especially as the author at the very end of the book claims to have been frequently present at these meetings. There is no resolution of the narrators' impossible love.

Ser Giovanni has mixed fantastic fables with the history of Florence and Rome. The last three-fifths of the book are almost entirely copied from Villani's chronicles of Florence. The collection ends with a very bawdy parody of the framing tale, followed by the narrators' chaste farewell.

I have included the opening tale and one full day, omitting the chronicles. The first tale, which I include, showed up again in Masuccio's *Novellino* (no.21). The second tale, not included, was later retold by Straparola (IV, 4), whose version I have used in this book. IV, 1 became a source for *The Merchant of Venice* and is ser Giovanni's most popular tale. Although the author's style is simple and inelegant, his book has appealed to readers throughout the centuries, as demonstrated by the fact that the collection was recopied in the fifteenth century, printed in the sixteenth, and has been printed at least a few times in every century since then. My translation is based on *Il Pecorone*, ed. Enzo Eposito (Ravenna: Longo, 1974), which includes notes, bibliography and an index of names. Bibliography can also be found in Carlo Muscetta's *Il Pecorone e la Novellistica del Quattrocento* (Catania: F. Castorina, 1966). *The Pecorone of Ser Giovanni* was translated by W .G. Waters (London: Society of Bibliophiles, 1897). IV, 1 can be found in the anthologies of Pettoello, Roscoe, Taylor, and Valency. There is one article in English about this writer: J. Hinton, "Walter Map and Ser Giovanni," *Modern Philology* 15 (1917), 203–9, on tale I, 1.

Introduction

Charity moves me to begin this book in order to offer a drop of comfort and cheer to those who feel what I myself have felt in the past.[1] By the grace of God and His most holy Mother, you will hear presently of a monk and a nun who were deeply in love with each other. But they knew so wisely how to behave and so well how to bear the yoke of sparkling love that they gave me material to write a book; for I heard their charming wit and gracious manner and the amorous conversations which they held in order to mitigate the flame of ardent love with which they burned beyond measure. So finding myself in Doadola,[2] blasted and exiled by Fortune, as you will hear later in this book, and having a subject matter and an occassion to speak, I began this work in the thirteen hundred and seventy-eighth year of Christ, when by divine grace Pope Urban VI, an Italian of ours, was elected the true and supreme apostle.[3] And this was during the reign of the Gesuatic, Charles IV, who by God's grace was king of Bohemia, and emperor and king of the Romans.

There was a convent in Romagna, in the city of Forlì, ruled by a prioress with ten nuns, all of whom lived a holy and perfect life. Among them was one named Saturnina, who was as young, well-mannered, wise and fair as Nature could make her; and so honest and angelic was her life, that the prioress and the other nuns bore her singular love and respect. And so perfectly had Nature endowed her, that the fame of Saturnina's beauty and goodness spread throughout the region. Wherefore a young man, whose name was Auretto, and who was wise, prudent, well-mannered, expert in all things, and who had spent much of what he possessed in courtly living,[5] found himself in Florence, and hearing the noble fame of this prized Saturnina, fell in love with her at once without ever having seen her. So much in love was he with Saturnina that he resolved to become a friar and to come to Forlì where he could set himself up as chaplain for the prioress so that he might see her more easily. Having decided this, he put his affairs in order, turned friar and came to Forlì, where, through the help of a mediator, he became chaplain in this monastery because he was very knowledgeable. And he knew to behave so wisely and prudently that in a short time he entered into the good graces and love of the prioress and all the other nuns, and especially of Sister Saturnina, whom he loved better than himself.

Now it happened that as the said friar Auretto kept looking honestly many times at the said Sister Saturnina and she at him, their eyes often met; and Love, which takes swiftly to the gentle heart,[5] bound them together in such a way that, smiling from a distance, they bowed to each other; and thus in pursuing Love, many many times they held hands and wrote and talked to each other. And this love increased so much that they decided to meet at a certain hour of the day in the parlatory, which was a remote and solitary place. And hither they arranged to come once a day in order to be able to talk at ease. And they established this rule, that each of the two of them should tell one little story every day to their comfort and pleasure. And so they did.

Day 1

Having arranged to meet in the said parlatory in the manner which we told above, and seeing the appointed hour arrive, the two lovers met and sat down with the greatest joy and happiness. And the said Friar Auretto began, and spoke thus: "My Saturnina, I want to tell you a little tale that happened in the city of Siena not long ago, about a lover and a noble lady." *And he spoke thus:*

[handwritten margin notes: Saturnina; virtue spreads; Courtly Lover hears of her; ✓; ✳ Love enters through the eyes; SUBLIMATE with story telling; Story of virtue over consummation (unlike Boccaccio's clergy)]

I

There was in Siena a young man whose name was Galgano, who was rich and of noble blood, able, experienced and generally expert in all things, valorous and strong, magnanimous and courteous and affable with everyone. This Galgano loved a noble lady of Siena named Lady Minoccia, the wife of a noble knight named Sir Stricca. Wherefore the said Galgano always used to dress well and to wear the emblem of this said lady-love, and often jousted and fenced and gave rich feasts for her love; but the said Lady Minoccia never cared either to hear or to see him. Wherefore the said Galgano knew not what to do or say, seeing how much cruelty ruled in the breast of this lady of his, whom he loved better than himself; and at parties and weddings he was always right behind her and felt unhappy on a day when he could not see her; and many many times he sent gifts and messages to her through a go-between, but the said lady would never accept them or listen to him, but was always more and more unresponsive each time. And so the said lover remained passionate for a long time, filled with the great love and loyalty he bore for this lady. And often he complained to the God of Love, saying, "Alas, my lord, how can you endure it that I love and am not loved? Don't you see that this is contrary to nature?" And thus many times, remembering her cruelty, he was ready to despair. And yet he wisely decided to bear this yoke for as long as it might please the God of Love, always hoping to find grace; and he always tried to do and say everything which he thought might please her. But she grew always colder to him.

Now it happened that Sir Stricca and his wife went to a place of theirs near Siena, and the said Galgano was passing through the countryside with a hawk on his fist, pretending to go hawking so that he might see this lady. And as he passed near the house where she was, Sir Stricca saw him and recognizing him, at once went out to meet him and familiarly took him by the hand, inviting him to dine with him and his wife. Whereupon the said Galgano thanked him greatly, but refused on the pretext that he had to be going somewhere else.

Whereupon Sir Stricca said to him, "At least stop in to have a drink."

Whereupon the young man replied, "I don't want to, thank you very much; God be with you, for I'm in a hurry."

Whereupon Sir Stricca, seeing it was his will, let him go and returned into the house. Having left Sir Stricca, Galgano said to himself, "Alas, wretched me, why didn't I accept? At least I would have seen her whom I love better than all the world." And while he was turning over this thought, a magpie took to flight; whereupon he loosed his hawk. The magpie flew into Sir Stricca's garden, fighting with the hawk. Sir Stricca and his wife, hearing this hawk, ran to the window overlooking the garden, and seeing the valor with which the hawk was catching the magpie, the wife asked to whom the hawk belonged.

Replied Sir Stricca, "That hawk takes after its owner, for he is the most valiant and the most accomplished young man in Siena."

Whereupon the lady asked who its owner was. To which the husband replied, "It is Galgano's who passed by here a little while ago, and I wanted him to dine with us, but he refused. Surely he is the most pleasing and the most honest young man that I have ever seen."

And so they left the window and went to dinner. Galgano recovered his hawk and went on his way. But the lady noted her husband's words and remembered them.

Now it happened that a few days later Sir Stricca was sent by the Council of Siena, that is by the Governors, as an ambassador to Perugia; whereupon the lady remained alone. And as soon as she heard that her husband had ridden off, she immediately sent a confidant to Galgano, asking him to come to her because she wanted to speak with him; and when Galgano heard the message, he replied that he would gladly come. Hearing that Sir Stricca had gone to Perugia, Galgano, as soon as it was a suitable hour of the evening, set out for the house of the woman whom he loved more than all the world. And when he stood before her, he greeted her with great respect; whereupon the lady with much joy took him by the hand and then embraced him, saying, "You are a hundred times welcome, my Galgano"; and without saying more, they gave each other the kiss of peace[6] many times. And then the lady had sweets and wines brought in; and when they had eaten and drunk together, the lady took him by the hand and said, "My Galgano, it is time to go to sleep, so let us go to bed."

Whereupon Galgano replied, "I am ready."

And when they had entered the bedroom, after much lovely and pleasant conversation, the lady undressed and got into bed, saying to Galgano, "It seems to me that you are fearful and shy; what's the matter? Don't I please you? Aren't you glad? Don't you have what you want?"

Replied Galgano, "My lady, yes; and God could not have given me more grace than to find myself in your arms."

And so as they were talking about this, he undressed and got into bed beside her whom he had so long desired. And when he had gotten under the covers, he said to her, "My lady, may it please you to answer one question."

Said the lady, "My Galgano, ask; but first I want you to put your arms around me."

Said Galgano, "My lady, I am much astonished that you sent for me this evening, unlike the other times when I so long desired and pursued you and you never wanted to see or hear me. What has moved you now?"

Replied the lady, "I will tell you. It is true that a few days ago you were passing by here with a hawk of yours; whereupon it seems my husband saw you and invited you to dinner, and you refused to come. Whereupon your hawk chased after a magpie; and seeing it fight so well I asked him whose it was; whereupon he answered that it belonged to the most valiant young man of Siena, and that it took after you because he had never seen anyone so accomplished as you in all things. And besides this, he praised you to me very highly; wherefore, hearing you praised in this way, and knowing that you loved me, I decided in my heart to send for you and not to be cruel to you any more; and this is the cause."

Responded Galgano, "Is this true?"

Said the lady, "Certainly, yes."

"Is there no other reason?"

Replied the lady, "No, truly."

Said Galgano, "May it not please God nor may it be His will that after your husband has done and said such courteous things about me, I should do him any evil"; and at once he jumped out of bed, got dressed again and took leave of the lady, and went on his way; and because of what had happened, he never again looked at that lady, while he always bore singular love and respect for Sir Stricca.

Day 4

Returning on the fourth day to the accustomed parlatory, the two lovers greeted each other with great respect, took each other by the hand, and when they had sat down, Saturnina began thus: "I will tell you a tale which will be queen and mistress of all the tales which we have told." And she spoke as follows:

I

There was in Florence in the firm of the Scali a merchant whose name was Biondo, who had been many times to Tanais, in Alexandria, and on all those great voyages that one makes with merchandise. This Biondo was very rich, and had three grown sons. And approaching death, he called the oldest and the middle son, and in their presence made his will leaving the two of them heirs to all that he had in the world, but to the youngest he left nothing.

And when he had made his will, and the youngest son, whose name was Gianetto, heard about it, he went to him where he lay in bed and said, "My father, I am much astonished that you have not remembered me in your will."

The father replied, "My Gianetto, there is no creature in the world that I love better than you; and therefore I don't want you to stay here after my death, rather I want you to go, when I am dead, to Venice, to your godfather, whose name is Lord Ansaldo, who has no son of his own; and who has written to me often that I should send you to him. And I can tell you that he is the richest merchant alive today among all Christians. Therefore I want you, when I am dead, to go to him with this letter; and if you know how to act, you will end up a rich man."

The son said, "My father, I am ready to do what you command."

Whereupon the father gave him his blessing; and a few days later he died. All the sons lamented greatly and gave his body the honors which befitted it.

And then a few days later these two brothers called Gianetto and said,

"Our brother, it is true that our father made his will and left us his heirs and made no mention of you; nevertheless, you are our brother, and therefore whatever we have is yours as well as ours."

Gianetto replied, "My brothers, I thank you for your offer; but my intent is to seek my fortune elsewhere, and that is my firm decision. You keep the inheritance, as assigned and blessed."

Thereupon the brothers, seeing his resolve, gave him a horse and money for expenses. Whereupon Gianetto took leave of them and went to Venice. Arriving at the warehouse of Lord Ansaldo, he gave him the letter which his father had entrusted to him before he died. Whereupon Lord Ansaldo, reading the letter, knew him to be the son of his dearest Biondo. When he had read it, at once he embraced Gianetto, saying, "Welcome, my son, whom I have so long desired." And he immediately inquired about Biondo; whereupon Gianetto answered that he was dead. Thereupon, with many tears he embraced and kissed him and said, "Lo, now I am much grieved for the death of Biondo because he helped me to gain a large part of what I possess; but I have such joy in you that it mitigates that sorrow." And he brought him home and ordered his business agents, his servants, his squires, and whoever was in the house, to obey and serve Gianetto more and sooner than himself. And he gave him the keys to all his money, saying, "My son, what there is, is yours; spend it freely, dressing yourself from now on as it pleases you, and give dinners

for the citizens, and make yourself known; for I leave this to your de-
vising, and I will love you the better the more you make yourself valued."

Thereupon Gianetto began to go about with the men of Venice, giving
dinners and suppers. And he began to give gifts, to take liveried servants, to
buy good horses, to joust, to practice arms, as one who was experienced
and expert and magnanimous and courteous in all things; and well he knew
how to do honor and courtesy where it was fitting, and he always rendered
honor to Lord Ansaldo, more than if he were a hundred times his father.
And he knew how to behave so well with all manner of people that almost
the whole community of Venice loved him, seeing him so wise, so pleasant
and courteous beyond measure. Therefore the ladies and gentlemen were in
love with him, and Lord Ansaldo had eyes only for him, so much did his
manners and behavior please him. And there was almost no party to which
the said Gianetto was not invited, so much was he loved by everyone.

Now it happened that two of his dear companions wanted to go to
Alexandria with their merchandise and with their two ships, as they were
wont to do each year. Therefore they asked Gianetto whether he wanted
to amuse himself by going with them to see the world, and especially
Damascus and the surrounding region.

Gianetto replied, "In good faith, I would gladly come if my father Ansaldo
gives me permission."

They said, "We will see to it that he gives it to you, and he will be willing."

And they went at once to Lord Ansaldo and said to him, "We pray it please
you to give Gianetto permission to come this spring with us to Alexandria,
and equip him with a ship or boat so that he may see a bit of the world."

Said Lord Ansaldo, "I am willing if it is what he wants."

They replied, "Sir, it is his wish."

Therefore Lord Ansaldo immediately had him furnished with a beautiful
ship, and had it loaded with as much merchandise and decked with as
many banners and equipped with as many arms as necessary. And when
it was ready, Lord Ansaldo commanded the captain and the others who
were serving on board to do whatever Gianetto ordered and to take care
of him, "For I am not sending him because I want him to earn a profit but
so that he may go at his pleasure to see the world."

And when Gianetto was about to leave, all Venice gathered to see, because for a long time no ship had left Venice so beautiful and so well furnished as this one. Everyone regretted his departure. And so he took
leave of Lord Ansaldo and of all his companions. They set off on the
sea, raised the sails and made their way towards Alexandria in the name
of God and good fortune.

When these three companions in their three ships had been sailing many many days, it happened that one morning before dawn the said Gianetto looked out and saw a beautiful port in a bay by the sea, and he asked his captain what the port was called.

Replied the captain, "Sir, that port belongs to a noble widow, who has ruined many lords."

Gianetto said, "How?"

He said, "Sir, it is true that she is a beautiful and charming lady, but she maintains this law: that whoever arrives there must sleep with her, and if he makes love with her, he must marry her and be lord of all this region; but if he does not make love with her, he loses all that he has in this world."

Gianetto thought about this for a while and then said, "Find any means you wish to set me down in that port."

Said the captain, "Sir, beware of what you say, for many lords have gone there who have ended up penniless and dead."

Gianetto said, "Don't worry about it, just do what I tell you."

And so it was done, and at once they turned the ship and dropped anchor in this port, so that his companions in the other ships did not perceive it. In the morning the news spread that this beautiful ship had arrived in port; whereupon all the people gathered to see it, and at once word was sent to the lady; whereupon she sent for Gianetto. He went to her immediately and greeted her with great reverence. She took him by the hand, asking him who he was, from whence he had come, and whether he knew the custom of the land.

Gianetto replied that he did, and that he had come for no other reason.

She said, "You are a hundred times welcome."

And so all that day they honored him greatly and invited many barons, counts and knights under her rule so that they might keep him company. Whereupon all these barons were pleased with the behavior of this youth, so well-mannered, pleasant, and eloquent that almost everyone fell in love with him; and all that day they danced and sang and feasted in the court for the love of him; and every one of them would have been glad to have him for his lord.

Now it happened that, when evening came, the lady took him by the hand and led him into her chamber saying, "It seems to me that it is time to go to bed."

Said Gianetto, "My lady, I am at your disposal."

Whereupon when they were in the chamber, two damsels came, one with wine and the other with sweets.

Said the lady, "I know that you have become thirsty, so drink."

Gianetto took some sweets and drank the wine, which was drugged to make one sleep, but he did not know it; and he drank half a cup of it because it tasted good. Immediately he undressed and went to bed. And as soon as he got into bed, he fell asleep. Whereupon the lady got in beside him, but he never felt a thing until morning, past the hour of nine. Whereupon the lady, when it was day, arose and ordered that they begin to unload the ship, and they found it full of much rich and good merchandise. Therefore when nine o'clock was past, the lady's chambermaid came to the bed and, waking him, told him to go on his way, for he had lost the ship and all that was in it; whereupon he was ashamed and thought he had done wrong. The lady had some money given to him for expenses and a horse. He mounted the horse, sad and mournful, and made his way to Venice. And having arrived in Venice, for shame he did not want to dismount at Lord Ansaldo's house but went to the house of one of his companions.

This companion of his was astonished and said, "Ah me, Gianetto, what's this?"

He answered, "My ship struck one night on a reef where it broke and was wrecked totally, and some of the men went one way and some another; I held on to a piece of wood which threw me up on a shore, and I have come by land the rest of the way here."

And so he stayed a few days in the house of this companion of his.

The companion went one day to visit Lord Ansaldo and found him very melancholy. He said, "What's the matter, why are you so melancholy?"

Said Lord Ansaldo, "I have such great fear that my son may be dead, or that the sea may have done him harm, that I find no relief and won't feel well until the day I see him again, so great is the love I bear him."

The young man said, "Sir, I can tell you some news: he has shipwrecked at sea and lost everything, except that he himself has escaped."

Said Lord Ansaldo, "Praised be God! As long as he has escaped, I am happy; for I care nothing about the goods which are lost." He immediately set out to see Gianetto. And as soon as he saw him, Lord Ansaldo ran to embrace him, saying, "My son, you needn't be ashamed before me, for ships are frequently wrecked at sea; and therefore, my son, don't be dismayed; as long as you yourself have come to no harm, I am happy." And he brought him home, always consoling him. The news spread through all of Venice, and everyone regretted the loss which Gianetto had sustained.

Now it happened that a short while after, these companions of Gianetto's returned from Alexandria quite wealthy. And when they arrived, they inquired after him and were told everything; whereupon they ran at once to embrace him, saying, "How did you part from us or where did you go, that we could never get any news about you? And we turned back all that day and never could see you or find out where you had gone. And we were so sad that we were inconsolable during the whole journey because we thought that you were dead."

Gianetto replied, "A wind arose in a bay of the sea driving my ship straight onto a reef which was near the land, so that everything went topsy-turvy, and I barely escaped."

And this was the excuse which Gianetto gave so as not to reveal his failure. And they rejoiced together greatly, thanking God that he had escaped, and saying, "With the grace of God, next spring we will recover all that you lost this time; and so let's have a good time without any melancholy." And thus they attended to amusing themselves as they had done before.

Gianetto, however, did nothing but think about how he could return to that lady, day dreaming and saying, "Certainly I must have her as my wife or I will die there." And he could scarcely take any delight.

Lord Ansaldo said to him many times, "My son, don't make yourself melancholy, for we have so much money that we can go on very comfortably."

Replied Gianetto, "My lord, I will never be content if I do not make this journey once again."

When the time came, seeing that it was his will, Lord Ansaldo equipped him with another ship with much more merchandise of even greater value. And he began preparations for this voyage a long time in advance so that when the time came, the ship was ready and furnished. He put into it a large part of his worldly possessions. The companions, when they had equipped their ships with what was necessary, set off on the sea and raised their sails and went on their way.

And as they sailed for many many days, Gianetto always watched for the lady's port, which was called the port of the lady of Belmont. And arriving one night at the mouth of this port, which was on a bay of the sea, Gianetto recognized it at once, and had the sails and rudder turned and dropped anchor within it.

The lady, rising in the morning, looked down to the port and saw the banners of his ship flapping in the wind. Recognizing them at once, she called one of her chambermaids and said, "Do you recognize those banners?"

Said the chambermaid, "My lady, they seem to be the coat-of-arms of that young man who arrived here a year ago, and brought us such wealth with that merchandise of his."

Said the lady, "Certainly you speak the truth; and truly this fellow must be of no small importance; truly he must be in love with me, for I have never yet seen anyone return here a second time."

Said the maid, "I never saw a man more courteous nor more gracious than he."

The lady sent many servants and squires for him, who went to meet him with great enthusiasm, and he was happy and merry with all of them; and so he came into the sight of the lady. And when she saw him, with great joy and enthusiasm she embraced him, and he embraced her with great respect. And so they spent the whole day in celebration and in joy, for the lady invited many barons and ladies to come to the court to feast for the love of Gianetto. And almost all the barons felt sorry for him; gladly would they have wished him for their lord on account of his grace and courtesy, and almost all the ladies were in love with him, seeing with what measure he could lead a dance. His face always looked happy, and everyone thought that he must be the son of some great lord.

When the time came to go to bed, the lady took Gianetto by the hand and said, "Let's go to rest." They went into her chamber and sat down, and there came the two damsels with wine and sweets, just as before; they drank and ate and then went to bed. As soon as he was in bed, he fell asleep. The lady undressed and got in bed beside him, and, in brief, he did not feel a thing all night. When morning came, the lady arose and at once ordered the ship to be unloaded. When it was past nine o'clock, Gianetto awoke and looked for the lady but did not find her; he raised his head and saw that it was late morning; he arose, feeling ashamed. Again he was given a horse and money for expenses and at once he left, sad and mournful, and did not stop until he got to Venice. That night he went to this companion of his, who, when he saw him, was more astonished than at anything in the world, saying, "Ah me! What's this?"

Replied Gianetto, "Woe is me; cursed is my fortune that ever I arrived in this country!"

Said his comrade, "You can certainly curse it thoroughly, for you have ruined Lord Ansaldo, who was the greatest and richest merchant among all Christians; and the shame is even worse than the loss."

And so he stayed hidden for several days in the house of this friend and did not know what to do nor what to say, and he almost wanted to return to Florence without saying a word to Lord Ansaldo; but then he decided to go to him after all, and so he did.

And when Lord Ansaldo saw him, he rose up and ran to embrace him saying "Welcome, my son"; and Gianetto, weeping, embraced him. Said Lord Ansaldo, "Now do you know what? Don't make yourself one bit melancholy; as long as I have you, I am content. We have still enough left to live on quietly."

The news of this event went all through Venice, and everyone said of Lord Ansaldo, "He was asking for it." And thus he had to sell many possessions in order to pay the creditors who had given him merchandise.

It happened that his two companions returned wealthy; and when they arrived in Venice, they were told how Gianetto had returned and how he had wrecked and lost everything. Whereupon they marvelled, saying, "This is the strangest thing we have ever seen." They went to Lord Ansaldo and to Gianetto, and greeting them joyfully, these two said, "Sir, don't be dismayed, for we intend to go next year to make money on your behalf, for we were in a way the cause of this loss. It was we who induced Gianetto to come with us the first time; and therefore don't worry, for while we have any money, treat it as your own."

Lord Ansaldo thanked them, and said he still had enough for them to live comfortably.

Now it happened that Gianetto, thinking about this night and day, was inconsolable. And Lord Ansaldo asked him many times what was the matter.

Replied Gianetto, "I will never be content if I don't win back what I have lost."

Said Lord Ansaldo, "My son, I don't want you to venture forth again, for it is better that we live here plainly with the little we have than that you put it anymore at risk."

Said Gianetto, "I am determined to do what I say, for I would consider it a great shame to live in this manner."

Whereupon Lord Ansaldo, seeing his determination, decided to sell all that he had in this world and equip for him another ship. And so he did, for he sold until he had nothing left, and equipped a beautiful ship full of merchandise. And because he was short 10,000 florins, he went to a Jew in Mestre and borrowed them from him on this condition: that if he had not returned the money between then and St. John's day the following June, the said Jew could take a pound of flesh from his body from whatever place he wished. To this Lord Ansaldo agreed, and the Jew drew up notarized papers about this with witnesses, and with those precautions and formalities that were necessary; and then he counted out for him 10,000 florins of gold. With this money Lord Ansaldo furnished the ship with whatever was still lacking; and if the other two were beautiful, this ship was much richer and better furnished. His companions also readied two ships, with the intention that what they earned should be Gianetto's. And when it was time to go, and they were about to leave, Lord Ansaldo said to Gianetto, "My son, you are going, and you see in what state you leave me; I beg of you one favor: should you come out badly, return to me so that I may behold you before I die, and I will go contentedly." Gianetto promised him, and Lord Ansaldo gave him his blessing. So they took leave and went on their way.

The two companions always kept watch over Gianetto's ship, and Gianetto was always looking for and eager to drop anchor in the port of Belmont. Therefore he arranged with one of his sailors to sail the ship into this lady's port at night. In the morning, when the day began to dawn, the companions looked around and did not see his ship anywhere. They said to each other, "This certainly is bad luck." And they decided to pursue their own course, more astonished than at anything in the world.

Now it happened that when this ship arrived in port, the whole city gathered to see it, hearing that Gianetto had come back; much astonished they said, "Surely this is the son of some very great man, considering that he comes here every year with so much merchandise and such beautiful ships; would God that he were our lord." And so he was visited by all the citizens, barons and knights of that city.

The lady was told that Gianetto had come; whereupon she went to the window and saw this beautiful ship and recognized the banners; whereupon she made the sign of the cross saying, "Surely this fellow is the man who has brought wealth to this country"; and she sent for him. Gianetto went to her; with many embraces they greeted and honored each other. And then they spent all that day in joy and celebrations; and for the love of Gianetto they held a beautiful tournament, and many barons and knights jousted that day; whereupon Gianetto wanted to joust, and that day he performed miracles for he handled his arms and horse so well; and his behavior so pleased all the barons that everyone wanted him for their lord.

When evening came and it was time to go to rest, the lady took Gianetto by the hand, saying, "Let us go to bed."

And when they were at the door of her chamber, one of the lady's chambermaids, feeling sorry for Gianetto, whispered in his ear, "Pretend to drink, but don't drink this evening." Gianetto heard her words and entered the chamber.

Said the lady, "I know that you are thirsty, and so I want you to drink before you go to sleep." And at once the two damsels came, who looked like two angels, with wine and sweets in the usual manner, and attended to giving them something to drink.

Said Gianetto, "Who would hold back from drinking, seeing these two damsels so pretty?"

Whereupon the lady laughed. And Gianetto took the cup and pretended to drink, but he tossed the wine down his chest. The lady, believing that he had drunk, said in her heart, "You will bring another ship, for you have lost this one." Gianetto went to bed feeling wide awake and lusty, and it seemed to him a thousand years before the lady came to bed. He said in his heart, "For certain I have caught her"; just so the hungry man reckons one way and the innkeeper another.[7] And so that the lady would come to bed sooner, he began to snore and pretend to be asleep. Whereupon the lady said, "You're all right." And at once she undressed and entered the bed beside Gianetto. Whereupon Gianetto did not wait a moment; as soon as the lady had gotten under the covers, he turned to her and embraced her and said, "Now I have what I wanted for so long." And with this he gave her the pax of holy marriage and held her in his arms all night long. Whereupon the lady was more than content. She arose quickly in the morning before daylight and sent for all the barons and knights and many other citizens, and told them, "Gianetto is your lord, and therefore prepare to celebrate." Immediately a shout rose through the land as they cried, "Long live the lord!" and the bells were rung and instruments sounded. And she sent for many barons and counts from the city and the surrounding country to see their lord. Then there began a grand and beautiful celebration. When Gianetto came out of the chamber, he was knighted and placed on the throne, and the scepter was put in his hand, and he was called lord for life with great triumph and glory. And when all the barons and ladies had come to court, he married this lady with such joy and such festivity that it is impossible to imagine or describe. Whereupon all the lords and barons of the land came to the city to celebrate with jousting, fencing, dancing, singing, playing instruments, and all those things which befit a celebration. Lord Gianetto, as a magnanimous man, gave away silk clothes and other rich things which he had brought, and began to take on authority and make himself respected, and so he maintained law and justice for all his people. Thus he lived in joy and festivity and did not think about or remember poor Lord Ansaldo, who had been left as a pledge for 10,000 florins to that Jew.

One day while Lord Gianetto was at the window with his lady, he saw an assembly of men crossing the piazza with candles in hand who were going to make offerings.

"What's that?" he asked.

Replied the lady, "That is an assembly of artisans who are going to make offerings at the church of St. John, for today is his holiday."

Remembering Lord Ansaldo, Lord Gianetto arose from the window, heaved a great sigh, completely changed his expression and began to pace the chamber, thinking over this event. The lady asked him what was wrong.

Replied Gianetto, "Nothing is wrong."

Thereupon the lady began to insist and to say, "Surely there is something wrong, but you don't want to tell me." And she insisted until Lord Gianetto recounted the whole story, telling her how Lord Ansaldo had been left as a pledge for 10,000 florins; and how that day was the final day, when he would have to lose of pound of flesh from his body. The lady said, "Mount on horseback at once, take whatever company seems proper to you, and carry 100,000 florins, and never stop until you are in Venice; and if he is not dead, bring him here."

Therefore he immediately had a trumpet sounded, mounted on horseback with more than a hundred companions, carried much money, and taking his leave, rode hard towards Venice.

Now it happened that when the allotted time had come to an end, the Jew, having had Lord Ansaldo arrested, wanted to take his pound of flesh. Whereupon Lord Ansaldo begged him to delay his death a few days so that if his Gianetto came, he might at least see him.

Said the Jew, "Regarding the delay, I am willing to grant it, but even if this Gianetto were to visit you a hundred times, I intend to take a pound of flesh from your body as we contracted."

As Lord Ansaldo agreed to the Jew's terms, all Venice was abuzz over this event, for everyone felt sorry about it, and many merchants got together and wanted to pay the money, but the Jew refused to accept it; rather, he wanted to perform that murder in order to be able to say that he had killed the greatest of all Christian merchants.

Now it happened that while Gianetto was riding hard, his lady, dressed in the manner of a judge, also set forth with two of her servants. When Lord Gianetto arrived in Venice, he went to the house of the Jew where he embraced Lord Ansaldo with much joy. Afterwards he told the Jew that he wanted to pay back what Lord Ansaldo owed, and more besides. The Jew replied that he no longer wanted the money, since he had not received it in time. Rather, he insisted upon collecting a pound of flesh from Lord Ansaldo's body. Thereupon there was a great debate, in which everyone said the Jew was wrong; but considering that Venice was a state run by law, and that the Jew's case was irrefutable on legal grounds, they could not confute him but only appeal to his sense of compassion. Whereupon all the merchants of Venice came to plead with this Jew, but he remained unmoved. Whereupon Lord Gianetto wanted to give him 20,000 florins, but he refused; he offered 30,000, then 40,000, then 50,000, and so on until he offered to give him 100,000 florins.

The Jew said, "You know how it is: if you were to give me more than the worth of this entire city, I could not be appeased; rather I prefer to carry out the terms of our contract to the letter."

And as the case stood thus, lo Gianetto's lady, dressed as a judge, dismounted at a Venetian inn. Whereupon the innkeeper asked one of her servants, "Who is this gentleman?"

To which the servant replied, "This gentleman is a judge who comes from Bologna[8] and is returning to his home."

The innkeeper did him much honor. And as they were at the table, the judge said to the innkeeper, "How is this city of yours run?"

Replied the host, "Sir, Venetian justice is too strict."

Said the judge, "How is that?"

Said the host, "Sir, I will tell you. A young man named Gianetto came to us from Florence, to live with his godfather, whose name is Lord Ansaldo, and he was so pleasing and so well-mannered that men and women were in love with him. And no one ever came to our city who was quite so well-liked as he. Whereupon this godfather of his furnished him with three ships of great value, and every time he ran into misfortune, because of which for the last ship he was short of money. This Lord Ansaldo borrowed 10,000 florins from a Jew with this condition: that if he hadn't returned them between then and St. John's day the following June, the said Jew could take one pound of flesh from whichever part of his body he wished. Now this blessed youth has returned, and wants to give the Jew 100,000 for the original 10,000 florins, but the false Jew refuses them. And all the good men of the land have gone to entreat him, but it is no use."

Replied the judge, "This case is easy to resolve."

Said the host, "If you succeed in resolving it so that the good man's life is saved, you will acquire the thanks and love of the most virtuous young man who was ever born, and what's more, of all the men of this land."

Thereupon the judge sent an announcement through the land that whoever had a case to resolve should come to him. Lord Gianetto was told that a judge had come from Bologna who would resolve any case.

Whereupon Lord Gianetto said to the Jew, "Let's go to this judge, who I hear has arrived."

Said the Jew, "I agree to it."

When they arrived before the judge and paid him his due respects, the judge at once recognized Lord Gianetto, but Lord Gianetto did not recognize him because he had transfigured his face with certain herbs. Whereupon Lord Gianetto and the Jew narrated their case in the proper manner before the judge.

The judge took the papers from the Jew and read them, after which he said to the Jew, "I want you to take these 100,000 florins and free this good man, and he and his godson will always be obliged to you."

Replied the Jew, "I won't do anything of the sort."

Said the judge, "It is best for you."

The Jew absolutely refused to comply.

Said the judge, "Then send for Lord Ansaldo so that you may take your pound of flesh from wherever you wish."

Whereupon the Jew sent for Lord Ansaldo. And when he had arrived, the judge said to the Jew, "Do your business." Whereupon the Jew had him stripped naked, and took a razor in hand, which he had had made for the occasion; and he went up to make the cut.

Lord Gianetto turned to the judge and said, "Sir, this is not what I asked you for."

Said the judge, "Don't interfere; leave it to me." Thereupon seeing that the Jew was going up to Lord Ansaldo, the judge said, "Watch how you do it; for if you take more or less than one pound, I will have your head cut off. And furthermore I say, that if even one drop of blood is drawn, I will have you put to death, for while your contract states that you are entitled to one pound of flesh, it allows neither more nor less than a pound, and it makes no mention of the spilling of blood. And therefore, as you are wise, do it as you think best." And immediately he sent for the executioner and had the block and the axe brought, saying, "As soon as I see a drop of blood drawn, I will have your head cut off."

The Jew began to be afraid, and Lord Gianetto to be gladdened. And after much talk, the Jew said, "Sir Judge, you have outwitted me; have them give me the 100,000 florins, and I will be content."

Said the judge, "You must take a pound of flesh as it says in your contract, for you should have taken the 100,000 florins when I wanted to give them to you."

And the Jew came down to 90,000 and then to 80,000, but the judge remained firm.

Said Lord Gianetto to the judge, "Give him what he wants, as long as he returns Lord Ansaldo."

Said the judge, "Leave it to me, I tell you!"

Said the Jew, "Give me fifty thousand."

Said the judge, "I will not give you the sorriest penny you ever had."

Replied the Jew, "At least give me back my 10,000 florins, and cursed be the anger and the air and the land!"

Said the judge, "Perhaps you haven't heard me? I won't give you a thing; if you want to cut, cut; if not, I will consider you to have defaulted and will annul your contract."

Whereupon everyone present rejoiced greatly at this, and mocked the Jew, saying, "He who thought to trap another has been caught in his own snare." Thereupon the Jew, seeing that he could not do what he wanted, angrily took his contract and tore it up. And so Lord Ansaldo was freed and led home with great rejoicing. And then Lord Gianetto took the 100,000 florins and went to the judge, and, finding him in his chamber preparing to ride onward, he said to him, "Sir, you have done me the greatest service that was ever done me; and therefore I want you to take this money home with you, for you have earned it well."

Said the judge, "My good Lord Gianetto, many thanks to you, but I don't need it; take it with you so that your wife won't accuse you of having made a bad bargain."

Replied Lord Gianetto, "By my faith, she is so magnanimous, so courteous and so good-humored, that if I spent four times this much, she would be content, for she wanted me to bring much more than this."

Said the judge, "How well do you like her?"

Replied Lord Gianetto, "There is no creature in the world that I love better than her, for she is as wise and as fair as nature could possibly make her. And if you want to do me such a favor as to come to see her, you will be astonished at the honor she will do you, and you will see whether what I say is true or falls short."

Replied the judge, "When you see her, give her my regards."

Said Lord Gianetto, "It will be done; but I wish you would take this money."

And while he was saying these words, the judge saw a ring on his finger, whereupon he said, "If you wish to pay me, give me your ring rather than money."

Said Lord Gianetto, "I agree, but I give it to you unwillingly, for my lady made me a present of it and instructed me to wear it always for her love; and if she sees me without it, she will think that I have given it to some other woman, and so she will be angry with me, and will believe that I love another; and yet I love her much better than myself."

Replied the judge, "I am sure that she loves you so well that she will believe you when you tell her that you gave it to me. But perhaps you wanted to give it to some old lover of yours here?"

Replied Lord Gianetto, "Such is the love and faith I bear her, that the world has no woman for whom I would exchange her, so perfectly beautiful is she in every way."

And so he drew the ring from his finger and gave it to the judge; then they embraced, paying respects to each other, and took leave.

Said the judge, "Do me one favor."

Replied Lord Gianetto, "You have only to ask."

Said the judge, "Don't linger here; go soon to see that lady of yours."

Replied Lord Gianetto, "It seems to me a hundred years until I shall see her again."

And so they parted; and the judge went his way, embarking upon the sea. Thereupon Lord Gianetto gave dinners, suppers, horses and money to his companions and thus for several days he held court in celebration. Afterwards he bid farewell to all the Venetians, taking with him Lord Ansaldo and many of his old companions. And almost all the men and women wept for affection at his departure, so pleasantly had he behaved to everyone during the time when he lived in Venice. And thus he departed and returned to Belmont.

Now it happened that the lady arrived several days before him, pretending to have been at the baths. Dressed again as a woman, she made great preparations, had all the streets covered with silk canopies, and had robes made for many groups of men-at-arms. And when Lord Gianetto and Lord Ansaldo arrived, all the barons and the whole court went to meet them, crying, "Long live the lord, long live the lord!" And as soon as they arrived within the city, the lady ran to embrace Lord Ansaldo, but looked a bit cross at Lord Gianetto, although she loved him better than herself. And as they were having a great celebration with jousting and fencing, with dancing, with singing, for all the barons, wives, and maidens who were there, Lord Gianetto, seeing that his wife did not show him her usual sweetness, went into their chamber and called for her saying, "What's wrong?" And he wanted to embrace her.

Said the lady, "You needn't make me these caresses, for I know very well that you looked up your old lovers when you were in Venice."

Lord Gianetto began to deny it.

Said the lady, "Where is the ring which I gave you?"

Said Lord Gianetto, "It is happening just as I expected! I said that you would think ill of it. But I swear to you by the faith which I bear to God and to you that I gave that ring to the judge who won the case for me."

Said the lady, "And I swear to you by the faith which I bear to God and to you that you gave it to a woman, and I know it; aren't you ashamed to swear so?"

Said Lord Gianetto, "I pray God that he take me from the world if I am not telling you the truth, and furthermore, I told him this would happen when he asked me for it!"

Said the lady, "You should have stayed there and sent Lord Ansaldo here, and you could have enjoyed yourself with those lovers of yours, for I hear they all cried when you left."

Thereupon Lord Gianetto began to weep and to suffer, saying, "You are making an oath about something which is not true and could never be."

Thereupon the lady, seeing him weep, felt that she had been knifed in the heart, and at once ran to embrace him, laughing more than anything in the world; and she showed him the ring, and told him everything, both what he had said to the judge and what the judge had said to him. Whereupon Lord Gianetto was more astonished by this than anything in the world; and seeing that it was true, he began to laugh about it. And leaving the room, he told it to some of his barons and companions. On account of this, love grew and increased between them. Then Lord Gianetto called for that chambermaid who had instructed him not to drink in the evening, and gave her as a wife to Lord Ansaldo. And so they lived always in joy and festivity, and had good fortune.

When the tale was finished, Brother Auretto spoke up and said: "Certainly this is one of the richest tales that I have ever heard, and truly this one can well be crowned as the most beautiful that we have yet told. But I wish to tell one that I think will please you, although I neither compose nor narrate as well as you."

2

There was in Provence a nobleman named Carsivallo, who was the lord of several castles. This Carsivallo was a man of great courage and intelligence, much loved and honored by the other lords and barons of the region because he was descended from the ancient and noble stock of the family Del Balzo of Provence, to which had belonged one of the three Magi who followed the star in the east to adore Christ in the city of Bethlehem in Judea, as Saint Matthew narrates in his gospel. This man had a daughter named Siletta, and she was the most noble and beautiful child to be found at that time anywhere in Provence. Many lords, counts and barons asked for her in marriage, and they were bold and young and handsome of body. But the aforesaid Carsivallo said no to all of them and refused to marry her to any of these men.

There happened to be a count in that region, who was lord of all the Venisi,[9] where he had many cities and castles. His name was count Adobrandino. He was an old man of more than sixty years, who had neither wife nor children, and was so rich that his wealth had neither edge nor bottom. This count Adobrandino, hearing of the beauty of this daughter of Carsivallo, fell in love with her and would gladly have taken her to wife, but he was ashamed to ask for her because he was old, hearing that so many valiant young men had asked for her hand and that Carsivallo had refused to give her to any of them. And so he was consumed with desire to have her but did not know how to attain her.

As he was giving one of his parties, it happened by chance that this Carsivallo, being his friend and servant came to the party to pay his respects. The count did him very great honor, giving him horses, chargers, birds and dogs and many other gifts. Thereupon the count decided to ask him privately for his daughter, and so he did; for one day when they were in the chamber together, the count began very pleasantly by saying, "My Carsivallo, I will tell you what is on my mind without making any exordium or preface, for I believe I can speak freely with you, except that I am ashamed to speak of one thing, even though I have seen the leek which stays underground and gets fat and old while the stalk outside always stays green;[10] but be that as it may, I will tell you anyway. If it pleases you, I greatly desire to have your daughter as my wife."

Carsivallo replied saying: "In good faith, my lord, I would gladly give her to you, but it would be too great a disgrace to me, considering that those who have asked for her are all young men of eighteen or twenty years who could become my enemies; and then her mother and brothers and my other relatives and companions would perhaps be displeased about it, and perhaps the girl would not be happy with you since she is able to have others fresher than you."

The count replied saying: "My Carsivallo, what you say is true; but you will be able to say that she is to be the lady of all that I have in the world. And therefore I would like the two of us to find some way to bring this marriage about."

Said Carsivallo: "I am very willing, and so let's think it over tonight, and tomorrow morning let each of us say how he sees it; and so let it be done."

The count did not sleep, but he made a very fine plan about this matter. The next morning he summoned Carsivallo and said: "I have thought of a way which will provide you with both an excuse and a great honor."

Said Carsivallo: "What is it?"

The count said: "Have a tournament announced, such that whoever wishes to marry your daughter shall come on such and such a day: whoever wins will have her as his wife. Leave the rest to me, for I will find a way to be the winner; and by this means you will be excused by everyone."

Carsivallo said: "I am willing."

And so he left and returned to his home. And when it seemed right, he summoned his wife and other relatives and friends and said to them: "It seems to me that the time has come to marry our Siletta; how do you think we should go about this, considering how many suitors we have for her and that they are all our neighbors and friends? If we give her to this one instead of to that other one, the latter will always be our enemy, because he will feel insulted and will say: 'Am I not just as good as he?' And so it will be with him and another and others too; and just where we thought we would acquire friends, we will acquire enemies. And therefore I thought that this spring we should announce a tournament, and whoever wins it may marry her with good fortune."

The mother and others replied that they were willing to do it this way; and so it was done. Carsivallo had the tournament announced in this way: that whoever wanted his daughter in marriage should come on the first of May to a tournament in the city of Marseilles, to compete for her hand. Thereupon the count Adobrandino sent a messenger into France begging the king to send him the boldest squire he had in feats of arms. The king, considering that the count had always been a servant of the crown and was even a relative, sent him a squire, whom he had raised since childhood, whose name was Ricciardo and who was descended from the ancient, noble and valiant house of Montalban. And the king commanded this squire to do whatever the count Adobrandino told him to do. This young man came to the count, who did him great honor. Then he told him the whole affair and why he had sent for him.

Said Ricciardo: "I was commanded by the king to do whatever you might command. Command me therefore, and I will do it well and boldly."

Said the count: "We will go to Marseilles to a tournament, at which I intend you to be the winner. Then, when I enter the field to fight with you, you must act so as to let me win, so that I may triumph at the tournament."

Ricciardo replied that he was ready. Thereupon the count made him stay hidden until it was time, and then he said: "Take whatever arms you wish and go to Marseilles. Pretend to be a passerby, take money and horses as you see fit, and see to it that you are a valiant man."

Said Ricciarcdo: "Leave it to me." With that he went to the stable where he saw a horse which had not been ridden for several years; whereupon he mounted this horse, took whatever escort seemed appropriate, and made his way to Marseilles. Great preparations had been made for the tournament. Many young men had arrived to fight; and happy was he who had been able to appear most handsome or honorable with so many trumpets and fifes that all the world was nothing but sounds. A great plaza had been fenced off where the said tournament was to be held, with many balconies around it where the lords, ladies and maidens might stay to watch. And on the day of the first of May, this noble damsel came, that is Siletta, who looked like a sun among the other girls, so perfectly beautiful and virtuous was she in every way. And so everyone who wanted to marry her came to the aforesaid tournament with diverse coats of arms and banners, and they inflicted the greatest blows they could upon each other.

This Ricciardo came to the tournament very boldly on this horse of his, making everyone else give way to him. The tournament lasted a great part of the day, and Ricciardo was always the winner because he was more expert at arms than any of the others, assaulting boldly and defending himself well with rapid turns, as a person who was experienced and practiced in this business. And as people asked one another who this fellow was, it was said that he was a foreigner who had arrived. And as everyone else was beaten, he remained the winner of the field, and many left the field because they could not bear his mighty blows. Shortly thereafter the count Adobrandino entered the field all covered with armor. He charged at Ricciardo and struck, and Ricciardo struck at him. And after many blows, as they had arranged, the said Ricciardo let himself be beaten; and he never did anything less willingly, for he had already fallen in love with Siletta; but he had to do it by order of the king, who had commanded him to do whatever the count told him. Thereupon as the count remained the winner and was running about the field with sword in hand, all his squires and barons came to meet him with much rejoicing. And when he took off his helmet from his head and was recognized, every man was astonished at his winning, and especially the girl. And so he married her and took her to his home; and in this way he got her as his wife, and on this account he made a very great festivity and rejoicing.

Now it happened that the said Ricciardo returned to France. The king asked him what he had done.

Replied Ricciardo: "Most holy Crown, I come from a tournament, in which your count cunningly made me take part."

Said the king: "How?"

Said Ricciardo: "I was the count's pander." And he told him the whole story, at which the king was astonished. Ricciardo said: "My lord, do not be astonished, for I never did anything which gave me greater pain than this, so immeasurably beautiful is she whom he has with cunning known how to obtain."

Thereupon the king was thoughtful and paused a while, and then he said: "Ricciardo, do not fear, for this will have been a good tournament for you; and let this suffice you."

Now it happened that shortly thereafter the said count Adobrandino died without an heir; and as Lady Siletta was left a widow, her father took her home, but he did not speak to her or show affection as he had been wont to do.

The girl began to wonder greatly at this; and one day, unable to bear it any longer, she said these words to her father: "My father, I wonder greatly at you, considering that I used to be as dear as one of the eyes in your head, and you loved me more than any of your other children. Every time you saw me your whole heart would be gladdened, that is while I was a maiden and a wife; now it seems, and I don't know why, that you cannot bear to see me."

Her father replied saying, "You are not so astonished at me but that I am even more astonished at you; for I thought that you were wise, considering why and with what cleverness I gave you in marriage and to whom, only in order that you might have sons so that you would be left as the lady and the mistress of that wealth; and I did it for no other purpose."

Replied the daughter: "My father, I did what I could about it."

Replied the father: "How can it be that in his court there was neither squire nor knight nor servant suitable for this purpose?"

Replied the daughter: "My father, don't be angry about this, for I swear to you that there was no squire nor knight nor servant to whom I did not speak of it, but no one ever wanted to believe me."

At that the father, hearing this pleasant reply, was completely gladdened again and said: "I am content, and I promise to give you a husband such that you will not have the trouble again of asking anyone else except him; and leave it to me."

Now it happened that the whole inheritance of the count Adobrandino's wealth went to the king of France; whereupon the king remembered the prowess and courtesy shown by Ricciardo. At once he sent word to Provence

to Carsivallo indicating to him that he wanted to give his daughter to one
of his own squires, who ought by right to be her husband. And Carsivallo
immediately understood the matter; he replied to the king that he would
do all that might please him. The king mounted on horseback with a huge
company of barons and came into Provence bringing with him Ricciardo
and made this match, that is he gave Siletta as a wife to this Ricciardo;
and then he made him a count and gave him all of Venesi with everything
that the count Adobrandino had left. This match pleased everybody, and
especially her. And she had no need at all to go begging any more servants or squires, for both of them were young and fresh and very valiant
in doing everything. And so they lived together a long time and had
wealth and good fortune.

   *When the tale was finished, Saturnina said: "Since today it is my turn
to recite a little song, I will recite you one which I am sure you will understand better than I will know how to perform." And she recited thus:*

> Will I ever find peace in you, lady,
>   who know that I love you much more than life?
>
> So much does love's fire heat me
>   from the sweet looks that issue from your eyes
>   that I cannot and dare not find rest;
>   so much do you with your beautiful rays touch my heart,
>   that truly the tasty manna which you give me
>   seems like falling snowflakes.
>
> Do you not remember with how much desire
>   I brought you faith and loyalty,
>   and gave you myself with heart and soul,
>   always hoping to find mercy in you?
>   Your discernment sees this very well;
>   then why have you no pity on me?
>
> You know already very well how much sweetness
>   your sweet words offered to my mind,
>   when you said without any maybe:
>   "Yes, I want you to be my loyal servant."
>   Then, lady, don't let slip from your mind
>   what your eyes and heart promised me.
>
> I have borne for you and bear you that faith
>   which every loyal lover ought to bear;
>   for I still believe that I will find mercy
>   from your precious and holy arms.
>   I can no longer bear so many pains,
>   unless you first grant me some grace.

Go, ballad, to her who has my heart,
  and who has become mistress of my soul:
  tell her from her servant
  that she would now be courteous
  to have for him a little pity,
  since he is hers and always will be.

Will I ever find peace in you, lady,
  who know that I love you much more than life?

When the song was over, the two aforesaid lovers took each other by
the hand, telling each other that this was a very great pleasure and consolation to them, considering their sweet conversations. And so they
took leave of each other, and each went away.

[handwritten annotations: effect of novelle; Decameron: to console women; No consummation]

writers get more complex

Giovanni Sercambi (1348–1424)

Sercambi was born in Lucca, where his father had a store that sold books and paper. He grew up with a good library at hand and was educated by private teachers for a government career. For supporting the successful rise to power of the Guinigi family against their rivals, he was rewarded with political success of his own and with a monopoly for selling paper and office supplies to the public offices. The Guinigi, who had obtained their victory by allying themselves with the small shopkeepers against other wealthy families, at first appreciated the public relations work done for them by a citizen like Sercambi. After 1400, however, they paid less and less attention to him, until he withdrew unhappily from public life and began to write a history of Lucca, pieces of which reappear in his tales. He also wrote a compendium of advice on finance and administration derived from his experiences in government. Addressed to the Guinigi, it advocates very strict control over citizens, who should be kept track of by census and forbidden to possess arms, and suggests creating a legislative council filled with one's friends and relatives. Like Sacchetti, he turned to writing stories at the end of a political life, probably in the early 1400s, and wrote over a hundred and fifty tales.

some historical context

The framing narrative, set in 1374, presents a group of men and women who travel about Italy trying to avoid the plague. Sinicropi has suggested in his notes to Sercambi's *Novelle* (p.782–84) that this frame may be based on a series of real pilgrimages in 1399 by the "Bianchi," folk who dressed in white and, with abstinence and sabbath fasting, followed ecclesiastical leaders in order to arouse the world to penitence. Sercambi's own brother went on one of these processions, and so did Paolo Guinigi, soon to become Lucca's lord. The influence of Boccaccio is clear in Sercambi's frame, in a number of the tales, and in the occasional insertion of poems; but instead of having the members of the group all contribute stories, he instead limits the narrating to one official storyteller who has been brought along to entertain the others on their way. Besides the *Decameron*, from which Sercambi took about two dozen stories, sometimes with modifications, he also drew upon books of

frame

pilgrimage (Chaucer)

Decameron – frame – some stories (?) one narrator

Roman mythology and history, popular *fabliaux*, and other medieval
tales such as those of the *Disciplina clericalis* and of the *cantari* or street-
singers. Many of his stories are contemporary or nearly contemporary
anecdotes and events. The tales are often linked by subject matter and related to the places where the group is traveling. Thus, for example, the
journey through southern Italy is full of stories of robbery; Roman
history is treated in ten tales at Rome; and Venetian customs are described in
half a dozen tales at Venice.

Betrayal is a recurring theme in Sercambi's stories. He is also very
interested in money matters, and many of the tales are concerned with
theft or fraud. In one tale Sercambi himself foresees how others are plotting to rob him. I find a mean streak in Sercambi, unusual among these
story writers, which I have attempted to represent in my selection.
Perhaps his political disappointments made him feel bitterly betrayed.

His style is certainly unpolished, and his tales were rarely mentioned
before the end of the eighteenth century when one of the two fifteenth-
century manuscripts which form the basis for modern editions turned up
in a private collection. The work first appeared in print in the early nineteenth century; since then it has been reprinted many times. There are
two good editions which I have used: *Il Novelliere*, ed. Luciano Rossi
(Rome: Salerno, 1974) and *Novelle*, ed. Giovanni Sinicropi, Scrittori
d'Italia 250–251 (Bari: Laterza, 1972). Both include biographical and
bibliographical notes. Rossi gives notes to the stories, and Sinicropi provides an index of names. The tales are numbered differently in the two
editions because Sinicropi counts the introduction as no.1; I have followed Rossi's numbers. No one has translated Sercambi's whole work,
and I have been unable to find even single stories in English. One of the
tales, however, seems to be a forerunner or analog of *King Lear* (no.57).
Despite the lack of translations, there are a few studies in English: James
W. Alexanders, "A Preparatory Study for an Edition of the Novelle of
Giovanni Sercambi," diss. University of Virginia, 1940. Peter Nicholson,
"The Two Versions of Sercambi's *Novelle*," *Italica* 53 (1976), 201–13.
R. A. Pratt, "Chaucer's Shipman's Tale and Sercambi," *MLN* 55 (1940),
142–45. Ann W. Vivarelli, "Giovanni Sercambi's *Novelle* and the legacy
of Boccaccio," *MLN* 90 (1975), 109–27.

Preface

T**he supreme and powerful God, from whom all blessings flow,
created human nature and made it in His image so that such
human nature, if it were not filled with sins, might possess the**

courts of heaven; and if through folly it lost the celestial paradise, one must blame nothing but that very human nature; and similarly if He sends us adversity on account of our committed sins. For we often see that on account of our sins God grants the angelic and malign spirits power over many people and over the heavenly bodies, which through the power of God have the function of guiding and leading the bodies below (that is us and all the plants and animals and everything made of the elements), and often, because of some committed sins, fire and water and blood have come from heaven to purge and punish the evildoers, and many cities and countrysides have been flooded and burned. And yet no one wants to heed the example of all these signs, whether those written about in the ancient scriptures or those which are seen every day, and not only do people not abstain from vices, but they even endeavor with all solicitude to do evil in as many ways as they know how; and he who cannot do so himself teaches others the way to do it. And in this way that creature which God made most blessed and created most like Himself departs most shamefully from God.

And so it is no wonder if sometimes human nature suffers afflictions and wars and plagues, hunger, fires, thefts, and extortions; for if he were to abstain from vices, God would give us that good which he promised us, that is in this world all grace and in the next his glory. But because human nature inclines to and follows what is contrary to the good, it has disposed God's power to send some of those signs which he sent to Pharoah, so that quitting our vices we may amend ourselves; but we are stubborn, and as our hearts are hardened like that of Pharoah awaiting the final sentence, He will place us in eternal torments. And it is no wonder if now in 1374 the plague has come and no medicine is of any avail, and neither wealth nor status nor anything else is sufficient to evade death but only goodness, which is what escapes all pestilences; and that is the medicine which saves the soul and the body. And if we do not take the path of goodness, we must necessarily go on the evil path . . . for, if one merely goes close to a sick person, even without fever death arrives; therefore there is no point in being valiant, therefore rank is worthless for one's parentage cannot defend one from such a blow.

And as there were a number of men and women, friars and priests and other members of the city of Lucca—the plague and pestilence being in that area—they decided to draw nearer to God through good deeds and to abstain from all vices; and if they did this, God in his mercy would put an end to the plague and the other evils which are expected now and in the future. Then as they, the men and women, friars and priests, saw the pestilence spread, first disposing themselves properly towards God, they thought to pass the time with some fine practice until the air of Lucca had been purified and cleansed of the plague.

And having gathered together, the aforesaid persons decided to leave Lucca and to make their way on foot through Italy in good order and with honest and holy manners. And in the month of February on a Sunday, having had a Mass said and having all taken Communion and made their wills, they gathered in the church of Santa Maria del Corso, talking about God. Then an excellent and very rich man named Aluisi rose to his feet and said, "Dear brothers and superiors, and you dear and respectable ladies of every condition who have gathered here to flee the death of the body and this pestilence, before I come to other matters, let me say that, since we have decided to save our lives and shun the plague, we ought also to think of shunning the death of the soul, which ought to be of more concern than the body. And so that both dangers may be shunned, it is necessary that we follow the path of God and his commandments and conduct ourselves with those wise manners which are due. And this cannot be done unless there is first some person whom all of us respect and are ready to obey in all honest things, and unless he as a most honest man commands nothing but that which pleases the group without sin. And when this is arranged, let him decide our route and the life and manners which we should keep, so that without offense or harm, and safe without shame to our city and our homes, we may return merry and joyful, having set good examples for all the lands."

When Aluisi had said these words, at once the members of the group said to one another, "Surely in this group we could find no one better than he." And at once they all said with loud voice, "We want Aluisi to be the leader of this group, and we beg him to accept this office, as we are all ready, both men and women, to obey his commandments, for in him we perceive such virtue that he will require of us nothing that is not honest, and by his great wisdom and foresight he will lead us safely back to Lucca in the name of God."

Aluisi, hearing the group and unable to demur, said, "Dearest brothers and superiors, and you most honest ladies, I know that in this group there are many more wise and understanding and provident than I who would do better at this office in an hour than I in a year, and you would have done well to elect someone else. But since it pleases you that I be called your leader, I am content, begging all of you to obey what I will command." Everyone said, "Command and it will be done."

The leader said, "Before we do anything else, we must make a pool of our money so that we can use the money to support ourselves with necessary *items." At once they put their hands to their money and, having made a heap of four thousand florins, gave them into the hands of the leader, saying, "When these have been spent, we will contribute more." The leader, seeing the quantity of money and the willingness to give more, said, "Now let us be glad, for the group will do well."*

Having the money, the leader spoke aloud saying, "Now that we are to save ourselves, I command you all, men and women, that while we are traveling, nothing dishonest be done either among ourselves or to others. And if anyone had thoughts of doing otherwise, before we set out, let him return to Lucca, and if he has paid any money, let him come forward and it will be returned to him." The group, hearing this, all replied, "O leader, be assured that we will live in such honesty while we are traveling that wives will not even sleep with their husbands let alone with anyone else; and so, quite on the contrary, during our voyage none will get together in a dishonest manner."

The leader, having made certain that nothing dishonest would be done, appointed a loyal treasurer, who would sooner have put his own money at the service of the group than have taken or embezzled one coin of that treasure which the leader gave him. And in this way the group hoped to have their needs well served.

Having appointed a treasurer, the leader arranged that there should be two purchasers: one at the service of the men and the other at the service of the women. And because such offices should always be given and assigned to persons suited to what they have to manage, the leader arranged that at the service of the men there be a young purchaser, wise and not full of avarice, and at the service of the ladies there be a man of mature age and moderate in spending, so that the whole group would have nothing to complain of.

Afterwards he ordered that each morning some of the priests in the group should say Mass, which he wanted the whole group present to hear; and each evening, without the group present, they were to say the hours and compline, so that no negligence could be imputed to them.

Having given this order, he gave orders to those who should entertain the men at dinner and supper by singing songs of chivalry and of morality and by talking, playing musical instruments and sometimes fencing with swords to amuse everybody; and some of them were to debate in the liberal sciences, and these were to be chosen by the group only from among the men and priests.

Also he ordered that with lutes and delightful instruments, with voices clear and low and also with boys' voices, songs of love and chastity be

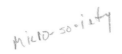
micro-society

recited to the ladies (because there were some elderly ladies, and some under vows, and married women and widows). He ordered some little boys who knew how to play the psaltery to play a psalm and a Gloria, and when Mass was being said and at the raising of the Host to play a "Holy, holy, holy, Lord God." And in this way he wanted there to be music in the morning during Mass and at dinner and supper a different music according to the conditions of the men, and so too of the ladies. Afterwards he ordered that such instruments and players after dinner and after supper should delight the group with pieces delightful and free of vainglory; and he put everything into effect as ordered.

Then, turning to the group and speaking through a riddle, the leader said, "To him who without cause has sustained many injuries, and they were done to him without his being guilty, I command that in this voyage of ours he be the author and maker of this book and of that which I will command him each day. And so that he cannot excuse himself by saying that I did not command him every time, and also to take away thoughts of revenge if he had any, I will recite a sonnet in which his name and surname will be found. And thus I command without further ado that every time I say, 'Author, tell us about such and such,' he will obey without further excuses." And speaking aloud, he said:

> Now I find that Pompey gave himself peace
> Imagining the grave betrayal,
> The cruel and violent homicide,
> Wished for by Caesar and Ptolemy.
> Hecuba too . . . the wicked
> Son of Antinor (may his name perish)
> Hid herself at the altar, and with great passion
> Converted him with thanks to God.
>
> Under the semblance of the kiss of peace Judas
> Betrayed our savior Christ,
> Giving himself from life to harsh death.
> Considering this, I give myself peace:
> Having always had a harsh spirit
> Moved to vengeance, I cancel my intention.
> Well I say that tongue and mind
> Do not misconform to each other in a faithful man.[1]

And as everyone in the group heard the pleasant sonnet and no one could guess to whom the leader was speaking except the man who, understanding the words and verses of the sonnet, found himself in it by name and surname, he understood without another word that he must be the author of this book; and without saying more, he stood silent like the others.

The leader, having delegated some of his duties and ordered who was to lead the group, . . .

I I

VANNI THE DYER OF SAN PAULINO, OR ON THE SHAMEFULNESS OF THE CLERGY.

(*anti-clergy*)

In the city of Lucca, in the neighborhood of San Paolino, was a dyer named Vanni. This Vanni had an honest young wife named Lady Margarita, who willingly delighted in hearing the word of God and went frequently to the church of San Paolino.

It happened that, as she made her daily trip to the said church, a priest of the church named Father Anfrione said to her, "O heart of my buttocks, how you make my heart die and my rod grow! Speak to me." The wife, hearing such words, said to herself, "I can no longer come here." And she thought of going to San Piero Macaiuolo, about twenty yards away, in which a chaplain of San Paolino named Father Bonzera officiated. Becoming desirous of her when he saw her coming alone to San Piero, this other priest said, "My soul, I pray you to lend your vessel[2] to my clergyman who is under me." Lady Margarita without speaking left the church, saying to herself, "From now on I cannot go to any of the churches in my parish!" And she thought of going to hear the service in Santa Maria Filicorbi, near by. And so the following morning she went to Santa Maria, Father Ronchetta of St. Angelo, who was the chaplain there, seeing the wife come to church, suddenly decided to tell her his thoughts. And seizing the opportunity, he said, "Lady, I would like to hook you,"[3] and other dishonest words; when the wife heard them, she decided she would tell her husband about the underhanded dealings of the said priests.

And returning home at once, she told Vanni that she had been insulted by the said priests. Vanni, who was displeased by such things and knew his wife to be pure, said, "I will pay them what they deserve"; adding, "Margarita, now we will see how you uphold your and my honor." His wife said she would do whatever was necessary, if she had to die for it. To which Vanni replied, "See to it that Sunday you go to San Paolino and if Father Anfrione says anything to you, listen to him and tell him that you are willing to have him come that evening around nine, telling him that I have gone out of town. And having made arrangements with him, go to San Piero Macaiuolo and say the same to Father Bonzera, and then do the same to Father Ronchetta. And when the hour of evening comes, you will put each of them in the shop and dine together; having dined, you will prepare three baths in three big tubs, one yellow, one red, and one blue, making them all wash at the same time. Then when you hear a noise, make them, naked as they are, enter the vat, and you pull the cover shut." The wife said she would do it all, and in the morning she arranged with each of the said priests that they should come that evening, one not knowing about the other.

When day was over, the wife had dinner prepared; and when nine o'clock had been rung, Father Anfrione was the first to enter; the wife put him in the shop. And soon after Father Bonzera arrived; the wife put him where Father Anfrione was. Finding themselves both there, they said, "Now we're in this together." And each told how he was invited. And a little later Father Ronchetta arrived; and shutting the door, she led him into the shop, where, as the three men all recognized each other, the wife said, "Since all three of you have requested my love, I saw no better time to serve you than this evening; and therefore be content, for there is enough for all. And afterwards, on other days, each of you will be able to take your pleasure with me." The priests were content, one day feeling like a thousand to them until they could come to it. As the wife had prepared good capons and drawn some wine, the group dined. And when they had dined, the wife said, "Before we go to bed, I want us all to wash." As the priests willingly stripped naked, she prepared for each a hot bath, and thus she put them into the tubs filled with dyes. The wife, to make it more credible, similarly undressed and washed herself in warm water.

And while they were washing, suddenly there was a knock at the door; the wife, putting on her shift, said, "Priests, enter this vat until I see who it is." The priests, naked as they were, entered the vat. And when the door was opened, Vanni said, "Now what does this mean that you are in the shop in your shift like this?"

The wife said, "I was about to go to bed." And having said this, she went at once to the vat and pulled the cover shut, saying, "I don't want Vanni to see you, so I'm closing you in this way as long as he is in the shop."

Vanni, seeing that the priests were in the vat, at once put the bar across so that they could not open it and said to his wife, "I have to work a bit this evening because tomorrow morning I must go out of town."

The wife said, "Didn't you go today then?"

Vanni said, "No." The priests heard all that they were saying.

The wife said, "It would be better if you went to rest while I stayed here to get the container boiling until you'd caught a bit of sleep."

Vanni replied, "As you've undressed, go to bed. I will do a bit of work and then I'll call you."

The wife replied, "Do as you wish."

The priests said to one another, "Certainly the wife wanted to help us and has helped us; and see how cleverly she tried to send Vanni to bed! But let's not worry about it, for at midnight she will return."

While Vanni was in the shop going about his business, he called certain shopboys of his who lived across the way, and when they had come, he made them work all night, and Vanni slept for a while in the shop until day. Then Vanni sent to the piazza for six porters. And when they had arrived, he told his shopboys and certain of his friends that some of them should go to the door of San Paolino and some to the door of Santa Maria Filicorbi, and if any odd-looking person arrived, they should hold him until Vanni returned.

Having set up guards, Vanni told the porters that he wanted them to carry that vat to Piazza San Michele.[4] The porters tied ropes to the vat—the priests, knowing nothing about what Vanni intended to do, felt the vat move and stayed silent for fear of death—and having tied the vat, the porters carried it into the piazza. Presently Vanni took an axe and began cutting the hoops that held the vat together, while people gathered around thinking Vanni had gone mad. In a little while, when the hoops were unfastened, the vat fell into a bundle of wood, and the priests, one red, one yellow, and one blue from head to foot, ran naked through the piazza, with people following after. Not knowing where to run, the priests headed towards their churches. And as Father Anfrione and Father Bonzera tried to enter San Paolino, and Father Ronchetta to enter Santa Maria, the guards set there saw them and caught them at once. And when Vanni arrived, the other people around said, "Those are our good priests who have returned from Jerusalem from the holy sites; and therefore it is well that with these pretty sanctities they be shown to my lord the bishop." And so they were led by the neighbors to my lord the bishop.

The bishop, seeing them and hearing who they were, at once had them put in prison; and taking away their benefices, he refurnished the churches with other, better priests; and those priests, naked as they were, were held in jail until the heat of their dishonest lusts had left them. And sent out of Lucca, they lived out their lives as wretches.

54

When the leader and the group had arrived at Iesi, they dined there, amusing themselves in their usual way. And turning to the author, the leader bid him compose a fine story for the following day for the entertainment of the group, because he intended to head towards Naples, going by the road which Vergil with his art made *easier for travel.*[5] *He was thinking of stopping at the end of the first day at the place where Medea was buried. The author, hearing Medea named, and feeling compassion because he knew how she had died and who was the cause of it, asked whether the leader would permit him first to recite some moral verse. With the leader's agreement, the author said:*

> *Medea was not so deceived by love*
> *for that cruel Jason*
> *when he left her sleeping on the island,*[6]
> *nor Dido by Aeneas,*
> *she who had been famous among other women*
> *for chastity before he came;*
> *as I have been deceived by one man*
> *seeing that he takes all my life from me; and once,*
> *at the time when he entered*
> *my thoughts, he loved me so well*
> *that in him was all my delight.*
> *Now he holds me in suspicion*
> *and does everything to hurt me;*
> *thus I see myself betrayed by him*
> *as one who trusts in another that kills her.*

Having said the verse, he decided to tell some story based on the example of Medea. And when they had slept through the night without waking and had all arisen at dawn, the author, turning to the group that was present, spoke out loud, saying:

ON THE CASTLE OF CASTRI IN SARDINIA, WHICH BELONGED TO ONE NAMED PASSAMONTE, WHO HAD A BEAUTIFUL DAUGHTER NAMED ZUCCARINA, OR ON FALSEHOOD AND BETRAYAL.

At the same time when Sismondo was judge of Arborea, there was a very bold young man named Gotifredi, who boasted that he could take by force the castle of Castri on the island of Sardinia, a castle which the Judge Sismondo had long coveted; and that castle belonged to a gentleman named Passamonte, a man of great courage and sixty years old. This Passamonte had a daughter of sixteen, beautiful in body and a wise virgin who had never had a husband; her father loved her more than himself, and he would not have entrusted the custody of the castle to anyone in the world except this daughter, whom he named Zuccarina because of his affection for her.[7] And it was she who had the whole governance of the castle and of Passamonte in her hands.

Sismondo, hearing the boast which Gotifredi had made about taking the castle, in order to inflame him to accomplish the deed, said, "O Gotifredi, I promise that if you manage by your force or wit to put the castle of Castri in my possession, I will give you my daughter Biancia for a wife and will make you a count."

Gotifredi, hearing this, said, "I will do it, certainly."

And having requested several trustworthy servants to go with him, he left Arborea and went in the guise of an ambassador to the castle of Castri. And when he had arrived there, he sent word to ask Passamonte to grant him an audience. Passamonte, who did nothing without his daughter Zuccarina, sent for her, saying, "An ambassador from the judge of Arborea wants to come to me, and I don't know why; perhaps it could be that the judge, who has a very handsome son, wants him to marry you. Or truly I hear that he has a pretty daughter, whom he might wish to give to your brother and my son, although my son is not as smart as he ought to be." Zuccarina, who heard her father, asked the man sent by the ambassador whether Gotifredi was a gentleman and how tall and how wise. The messenger said that Gotifredi was a very handsome and bold young gentleman of great courage, wiser and richer than any of judge Sismondo's men.

Zuccarina, who heard him describe Gotifredi's youth, beauty and prowess, said, "If these three things reign in one man, the woman who gets him may consider herself well satisfied, not to mention that besides his other virtues he possesses nobility and wealth. Therefore certainly if he comes here, and I see in him what I hear about him, my body will enjoy no man but him." And having replied thus, she said to her father, "Give him safe-conduct and let him come with as many men as he wishes." The father granted it at once, and told the servant to go and say that he would willingly hear his whole message.

Departing with safe-conduct, the messenger reported all the words and questions which Zuccarina had put to him. Gotifredi heard and understood; he remarked, "Since she certainly desires to see me, I wish to go to her as soon as I can." And having prepared his dress and his clothing so as to make an honorable appearance, he mounted his horse and rode towards the castle of Castri.

Zuccarina, after the messenger's departure, went up to the top of a tall house and from there she could see everything. Seeing people coming towards the castle, she guessed that it was Gotifredi; and leaving her place immediately, she entered her chamber, to make herself beautiful in order to please Gotifredi. Not caring about anything else, she got dressed. And when she came into the hall to her father, he said, seeing her dressed so well, "Oh, what's all this?"

To which Zuccarina replied, "Since this ambassador is coming, whatever his reason may be, whether on account of me of for something else, I want to appear the daughter of the great lord that you are."

Passamonte said, "Daughter, now more than ever I recognize how wise you are and provident before the event."

And while they were saying such words, Gotifredi came and presented himself before Passamonte in the presence of his daughter, greeting him warmly and telling him the wise message that the judge of Arborea wished to be in good accord with him. "And that he has many means of becoming your friend and kinsman, such as by joining your daughter to the son of judge Sismondo, and your son to his daughter." Passamonte, hearing this and weeping with joy, said to Zuccarina that she should give Gotifredi an answer. Zuccarina said, "Father, leave this matter to me." And she took Gotifredi by the hand and led him into a chamber.

And there when they were alone, Zuccarina said, "Gotifredi, I have heard of your nobility, prowess and wealth, and these things I cannot at present know for sure, except that your appearance makes me almost certain of them; for the youth and beauty which I have heard you possess are clear to me without any other proof, and they are just as I have heard; and these two things lead me to believe the other things I have been told about you. Therefore, before we come to other words, I pray you tell me the reason which has brought you to this region. Do not try to conceal it from me, whatever it is, for before you came here, I was yours in my heart, disposing myself to obey all that you might command me, even if you should ask for myself and all that my father possesses and this land, to do with everything as you would."

Gotifredi, hearing Zuccarina speak so firmly and with such love, decided to reveal to her why he had come; and told her all about his boast, saying, "I boasted that I would give this castle to Sismondo, judge of Arborea."

Zuccarina, hearing this, said, "O Gotifredi, if I were to satisfy you in this, would you take me as your wife and never abandon me? And I will give you the castle and all that my father possesses, and you may do with him and with the land whatever you wish." Gotifredi said yes, promising, and swearing to keep his promise.

And to be more certain of the matter, Zuccarina had herself betrothed to him with a gold ring which she received from him, and she gave him one of flesh with many kisses. Gotifredi, who thought he had what he wanted, said happily, "O Zuccarina, now we can speak in safety." Zuccarina said he should set forth what he wanted her to do and she would do it all.

Gotifredi said that she should give him the city, that is admittance into it, and he would send for the men of judge Sismondo to come for her: "Under the appearance that the son of Sismondo is to marry you. And he and I will come, and with the gates open we will enter; and you will come with me, and the land will remain in the possession of judge Sismondo, and we will have plenty from this and other lands."

Zuccarina, whom the rage of lust had so stupefied that she did not recognize her own undoing, gave orders as Gotifredi had told her. And leaving the chamber, she reported to Passamonte that she agreed to marry judge Sismondo's son, named Dragonetto.

Passamonte joyously gave gifts to Gotifredi, who, taking his leave, departed and returned to judge Sismondo, telling him all that had been agreed upon, but that he was not able to accomplish the deed without having promised to marry Zuccarina, saying, "You know that you promised me your own daughter; I would not like because of my promise to Zuccarina to forfeit yours."

Sismondo said, "What will you do, since you can't have two wives?"

Gotifredi said, "When we have the castle, and I have taken Zuccarina out of it, I will drown her in the sea." Sismondo, who coveted the castle, said he was content. Gotifredi said, "You must give out word that your son Dragonetto is going to fetch Zuccarina; and when the company is ready and I with them, the castle will be given to us by night." Sismondo said that Gotifredi had arranged things well. And he told Dragonetto that he had given him as wife Zuccarina, the daughter of Passamonte of the castle of Castri, and that he wanted him to go with Gotifredi to fetch her, and Dragonetto said that he was pleased.

Having armed the company, Dragonetto with Gotifredi set out on their way, and when they were near the castle, Zuccarina opened the gates, and the company, set in order, entered and took possession of the land. And with Passamonte dead, Gotifredi, leading Zuccarina away and taking her to the sea, there in the presence of several of Dragonetto's barons threw her into the sea. And so Zuccarina died.

Dragonetto, who did not find Zuccarina in the castle, asking about her, was told that Gotifredi had taken her out and drowned her in the sea. Hearing this, Dragonetto said, "Now have I been thus betrayed? Certainly I will avenge her." And calling for Passamonte's son, who was rather a fool, he asked him whether he wanted to avenge the death of his father and the loss of his land and of his sister and of his other dead kinsmen. Said Passamonte's son, "I don't want revenge for it except against the one who is responsible for it."

Dragonetto, who heard this, said, "Certainly you say well," and thought how to satisfy him.

And when Gotifredi had returned, he went merrily to Dragonetto, saying to him, "Now your father can call himself lord of this fortress, and for this he can thank me."

Dragonetto said, "It well pleases my father and me that the land is ours, but truly so many betrayals as you have committed do not please me"; saying to him, "The first betrayal was to Passamonte, the second to Zuccarina, the third to me who should have married Zuccarina, and you with deceitful means have killed her." And calling the idiot son of Passamonte, he bid that in his presence Gotifredi be killed.

And in this way he paid for the promise made to Zuccarina, whom, having done him so much honor that she gave him her father's land and herself, he so wickedly betrayed and drowned in the sea. And if Dragonetto had him killed, he well deserved it.

57
ON THREE DAUGHTERS FROM VENICE, OR ON EXCELLENT AND GREAT WISDOM.

I n the city of Venice there was a great and rich merchant named Lord Piero Sovranzo, who had three daughters, and being an old man without a wife and not having any sons (the hope of having any had been disappointed), he thought of marrying these daughters of his to three merchants and gentlemen of Venice, giving them each a dowry of six thousand ducats. And when he had married them off, the said Lord Piero kept one serving woman in the house to serve him, and in this manner he lived many years, being sometimes invited to the houses of his sons-in-law and daughters.

And living in this manner, the said Lord Piero thought he would divide the rest of his money among his daughters. One day he invited all his daughters and sons-in-law, saying to them: "My sons and my daughters, I have some money left, and I am no longer likely to engage in business any more as I am old, and I don't need to keep up a household. Thus if it pleases you to feed me in your homes while I am alive, I will give you what money I have; I don't need to ask you for clothing, because I have still many clothes. And I will return to my own house to sleep." The daughters and sons-in-law, hearing him mention money and eager to have it, said they were willing and that they would never fail him, making him great offers. Lord Piero, thinking they would keep their promises, drew from one of his chests 30,000 ducats, keeping a little money for himself (about a hundred ducats' worth, so that he might occasionally spend them on a luxury or a sweet), and having divided the said 30,000 ducats into three parts, he gave each daughter 10,000, for which the daughters and sons-in-law were very pleased and dined together merrily. Now they arranged among themselves that he should spend one month with one and another month with the next and so on, continuing in this way until his death.

Beginning with the oldest for the first month, and then going to the second daughter and then to the third, he finished out three months. When he returned to the first daughter, she received her father somewhat sadly. When her father asked her why she was melancholy, she replied, "Because my husband would like sometimes to eat earlier than you do."

The father, who saw that the oldest daughter was already sorry about his return to her, said to himself, "If the others make me a similar face, I will be in a bad spot."

Nonetheless he stayed his month. And when the month was over, he went to see the second daughter . . . [8] already in the same manner, saying, "My husband doesn't like to eat as early as you." The father, who heard this and could say nothing else, determined to stay the whole month. And when the month was up, he went to the youngest and found her in the same way as the other two, saying that her husband couldn't bear to eat pasta every day as the father liked to do. Lord Piero, who saw his daughters with new reasons inventing new excuses, sadly determined to try further.

And when the month was over, he returned to the first; when the oldest daughter saw him, she said, "Won't this old fellow ever die? O what a bore he is!" And she said this so loudly that a household servant heard her. Lord Piero, who had heard her mutter but had not understood what she was saying, asked the servant, "What did my daughter say?"

The servant said, "She said what a bore you are; won't you ever die?" Lord Piero, in order to see whether such dealings were instigated by his son-in-law, pretended not to have heard.

And when noon had passed, as he was waiting for dinner, the son-in-law, who knew that Lord Piero had come to his house again, did not go home but stayed out at the store. Lord Piero waited and said to his daughter, "What's your husband doing that he doesn't come home to dinner?"

The daughter, who knew the reason for his not coming home, replied, "He must have work to do."

Lord Piero said, "Let me eat, and he may come when he will."

The daughter said, "It wouldn't be proper for me to start dinner for you until my husband gets home."

Lord Piero said, "Let's wait for him some more." And when three o'clock in the afternoon had passed, old Lord Piero said, "Daughter, I can't wait so long. Let me eat. And since I see that your husband has much to do, tomorrow I will go to my other daughters, for I think their husbands won't be so busy." The daughter, hearing that he would leave, with effort gave him something to eat. And when he had eaten, Lord Piero left the house and returned to his own home, where he found his serving woman and told her to prepare an evening meal. The servant prepared him good food that evening without protest.

In the morning around nine o'clock, Lord Piero went to the house of his second daughter. And as he entered the front room, his daughter said, "Now why have you come here when you should be with my sister? For certain my husband won't endure it."

Replied Lord Piero, "Daughter, I believe you speak the truth, and I don't want you to get blamed by him for this." Whereupon he left and went to the third daughter.

The oldest son-in-law, returning home and seeing that Lord Piero had not come that morning, said, "Now we've gotten that old bore off our backs." The husband of the second daughter, returning to eat, heard from his wife how Lord Piero had come and how she had behaved. The husband said, "You did well, for when I see him, I think I'm seeing the devil from hell."

Lord Piero, who had gone to the house of his youngest daughter, finding the daughter and her husband at table, said, "God save you." The daughter and her husband asked what news he had. Lord Piero said, "I have come to eat with you."

Replied the daughter, "My husband bought nothing for you this morning because you know you should be going to your oldest daughter, and it seemed to us a thousand years until the month would be over so that we wouldn't have such a chore."

Lord Piero said, "Children, I thought it was still the same month, but since you say it's over, I will go where I will be received." And he turned and went downstairs and walked home, and he had his servant prepare some dinner, saying to her, "From now on, make dinner and supper for me and for you, for it's arranged that way."

The servant said, "It will be done." And when he had dressed in the morning, Lord Piero dined with great melancholy for what he had done for his daughters and sons-in-law, that is for having given them all he had left. And being a wise man, he thought he would avenge himself for the betrayal done to him by his daughters and sons-in-law. With that he went to a wise gentleman, to whom Lord Piero had often lent money, a man named Lord Marco da Ca'Balda, telling him everything he had suffered at the hands of his daughters and sons-in-law. Lord Marco, hearing what had been done to Lord Piero, said, "Command me, and I will do what you wish."

Lord Piero said, "I want you to come directly to my house and bring with you 50,000 ducats, and when it suits you, enter my bedroom (I will give you the keys to it now) and put those coins in my chest, you staying all the while at the foot of the bed." And he continued, "I will bring my sons-in-law and my daughters to the house, and when I have entered my room alone and shut the door, let me count the money, and then you can take it back with you and you will have done all I wish." Lord Marco said that he was ready.

Having arranged that the money be brought one Sunday morning, letting a few days pass without saying anything to his sons-in-law nor to his daughters, nor had they spoken to him lest it cost them something, Lord Piero went to all three inviting them for Sunday morning, both husbands and daughters. The sons-in-law gladly said yes, hoping to find another 10,000 ducats as they had the last time. Lord Piero, knowing that his sons-in-law and daughters would come, told his servant to prepare food for an honorable dinner, and when he had given her money, the servant put everything into effect.

When Sunday morning came, Lord Marco brought the 50,000 ducats and put them in a trunk in the bedroom, and he remained present in the room with some of his servants. When Lord Piero had dressed, and the meal was cooked, and the daughters and sons-in-law had arrived and come into the dining room with Lord Piero, he welcomed them, saying, "If you don't mind, I want to go into my bedroom briefly, but you stay here in the dining room." And opening his bedroom door with a key (Lord Piero had made some holes in the door so that one could see in) and having locked himself in, he went to the chest and drew out with lots of noise and clatter a large pouch of ducats; the daughters and sons-in-law, hearing the noise and putting their eyes to the holes where they could all peer into the room, saw Lord Piero by the trunk.

He had already pulled out a pouch of ducats and spilled them onto a cloth-covered table, and then he lifted out another pouch and then another until he had taken them all out. Then he began to count out loud, pushing the coins four by four and saying, "1, 2, 3, 4, 5, 6," and so on up to 125, which makes 500 ducats. And then he took a pair of scales, putting 500 on each side, and then 1,000; and in this way Lord Piero made fifty heaps of ducats with 1,000 ducats per heap. And having made all these heaps (the daughters and sons-in-law watched it all without saying a thing), Lord Piero put the ducats back into the chest; and pretending to lock it with a key, he arose, came to the bedroom door and opened it.

The daughters and sons-in-law had moved away and returned merrily into the dining room; and Lord Piero, locking the bedroom with a key, said, "Now it's time to eat." While they were washing their hands and sitting down at the table, Lord Marco took his ducats and went out by the back stairs.

Lord Piero dined with his daughters and sons-in-law, giving them good advice, and saying from time to time, "I will see truly which of you loves me, my children." And they would reply, "We all love you." And in this manner the dinner passed. When they had finished and risen from the table, Lord Piero spoke, saying, "I am now old and truly I wouldn't be able to bear the exertion that I have borne until now; and so I pray you, let it not displease you that I wish to stay at home without being a burden to you; and when God calls me to himself, all that I have will belong to whoever has loved me best."

The daughters and sons-in-law, having seen the treasure and heard the words of Lord Piero, each thought to himself how to honor the old man. And from then on, one asked him to dine with him in the morning, and another to sup in the evening, and each one said, "How now, I'm not like that other son-in-law of yours." And in this way, Lord Piero could not possibly eat as much as each one prepared for him as a proof of love, not for him, but for those new ducats which they had seen. (But it was to happen to them as to the dog who left a sure thing for an unsure one!)

Living this way for a long while, Lord Piero, who could no longer sustain his constitution, fell ill. At once his daughters and sons-in-law were beside him, telling him to make a will. Lord Piero, who knew very well what to do, said, "O my daughters and you my sons-in-law, I see that I can stay with you no longer; and so, before I do anything else, I want you to promise me that you will execute what I arrange." They replied that they were willing.

And in the presence of the above-mentioned Lord Marco and a very reverend friar, he made his will: that more than 18,000 ducats should be distributed to the poor, and 6,000 to priests and friars, and 2,000 to dress and honor the daughters and relatives and the corpse; so that all together they should distribute 26,000 ducats; furthermore, leaving his daughters equal heirs on condition that his chest, in which was his treasure, not be opened until the other bequests and legacies had been carried out by his sons-in-law, the keys being left with Lord Marco and the friar. And in case his sons-in-law did not do these things, he left the charity of San Marco heir with this obligation. Giving over the keys, and receiving extreme unction, he passed away.

The sons-in-law, united together, put everything into effect and paid for it all, thinking to have the 50,000 ducats they had seen. And when everything else was done, receiving the keys and opening the chest in presence of the friar and Lord Marco, they found nothing inside but a mallet on which was written: "Whoever abandons himself for others, let him be given a blow with this mallet."[9]

And in this manner the ingratitude of Lord Piero's sons-in-law was ultimately punished.

Masuccio da Salerno, or Tomaso Guardati (c. 1410–1475)

Masuccio's father was a secretary to the prince of Salerno and married a woman of nobility. Masuccio grew up learning Latin and reading Dante, Boccaccio, and the classics. Without any regular course of study, he became a secretary to the new prince, Robert Sanseverino, whose death in 1474 he laments elaborately at the end of his *Novellino* or *Little Storybook*.

It seems likely that he wrote his stories separately and later gathered them into a book, which, in imitation of Boccaccio's, is divided into five days of ten tales each; every tale, however, comes with its own dedication and concluding comments, and there is no narrative frame. Each day has its own topic: I, criticism of the clergy; II, amusing pranks or jests; III, criticism of women's lust; IV, an alternation of tragic and comic tales; and V, following the model of Decameron's final topic, examples of magnanimous virtue. The topics are mixed in accordance with the principle of variety. Masuccio's vituperations against fraudulent clerics and women are perhaps to be viewed within the context of his generally extreme style, his enjoyment of polemic going hand in hand with a love of contrasts which verges on the grotesque.

By the early 1460s the *Little Storybook* was circulating in manuscript form, and it was first printed in 1476, a year after the author's death. The seven Venetian editions printed between 1503 and 1539 show that the tales soon became popular in northern parts of Italy as well as in the Kingdom of Naples.

I have used *Il Novellino*, ed. Giorgio Petrocchi (Florence: Sansoni, 1957), which has an introduction and bibliography, but no notes. Bibliography can also be found in Porcelli's *Novellieri Italiani*. *The Novellino of Masuccio* was translated, with added flourishes, by W. G. Waters (London, 1895). A selection of tales can be found in Bishop's *Renaissance Storybook* and in Roscoe; single tales appear in Pettoello, Taylor, and Valency. There are several studies in English: O. H. Moore, "The Source of the Thirty-third Novella," *Italica* 15 (1938), 156–59; "Da Porto's deviations

Prologo

OME CHE io manifesta mente comprenda e per indubitato tē ga iclita e ex celsa madon na che al sono de la mia bassa e raucha lira nō si cōuē gha de libro comporre ne meno de proprio nome intitularlo : e che piu de temerita dignamente sero redarguito che dal cuna eloquentia ne molto ne pocho commendato : Nondimeno hauendo da la mia tenera eta saticato per exercitio del mio grosso e rudissimo ingegno e della pigra e roza mano scripte alcune nouelle per autentiche historie approbate negli moderni & antiqui tempi trauenute: e quelle ad diuerse dignissime persone per me mandate si come chiaro nelli loro titoli se dimostra . Perla cui chagione ho uoluto quelle cheran gia disperse congregare e de esse insieme unite sabricare il presente libretto & quello per la sua pocha qualita nominare il Nouellino . Et ad solo presidio e lume della nostra italica regione in from Masuccio," *PMLA* 55 (1940), 934–35; Howard K. Moss, "A Re-evaluation of Masuccio's Anticlericalism," *Italian Quarterly* 75–76 (1976), 43–61; J. V. Ricapito, "Lazarillo de Tormes (chap. 5) and Masuccio's Fourth Novella," *Romance Philology* 23 (1970), 305–11; and Janet L. Smarr, "Masuccio and the Irrational," *Romance Philology* 32 (1979), 315–20.

Preface

THE LITTLE STORYBOOK OF THE NOBLE VERNACULAR POET MASUCCIO GUARDATO DA SALERNO, DEDICATED TO THE ILLUSTRIOUS IPPOLITA OF ARAGON AND OF THE VISCONTI, DUCHESS OF CALABRIA; AND FIRST THE PROLOGUE HAPPILY BEGINS.

Renowned and sublime lady, though I clearly understand and know without doubt that it is unseemly to compose a book to the sound of *my lowly and hoarse lyre*, much less to dedicate it to your name, and that I will be justly blamed for temerity rather than praised at all for any eloquence; nonetheless, having since my tender age wearied my thick and rough wit with exercise, and with my lazy and untrained hand written certain tales confirmed as authentic histories which took place in modern and ancient times, and those tales having been sent by me to various most worthy persons, as is set forth clearly in their dedications, for this reason I wished to collect those which had already been dispersed and to make of the collection this little book, which I name the Novellino[1] on account of its poor quality, and to dedicate and send it to you, sole guardian and light of our Italian region; so that you, with the eloquence of your most beautified speech and the excellence of your far-reaching wit, cleansing the many rusty spots that are in it and taking away and pruning off the superfluities, might add it licet indigne[2] to your lofty and glorious library. And although very many reasons had almost restrained and dissuaded me from undertaking such a labor, yet having recently come upon a popular anecdote which not many years ago truly happened in our city of Salerno, I was comforted and spurred on by it to follow its example; before I go any further, I will narrate it.

I say, then, that in the time of the happy and bright memory of Queen Margarita,[3] there was in the above-named city a very rich Genoese merchant, named Mister Guardo Salusgio, from a very honorable family of this city, who had a huge business and was known all over Italy. As this man, then, was strolling one day in front of his stand, located on a street called the Drapparia,[4] where there were many other stands and shops of silversmiths and tailors, he happened to see a Venetian ducat at the feet *of a poor tailor. Although the coin was very muddy and battered, nonetheless the great merchant recognized it at once, as one familiar with its imprint, and bending down without delay, he said laughing, "By my faith, here's a ducat!"*

When the poor tailor, who was mending an apron in order to earn some bread, saw this, he was overcome with venomous envy, rage and grief, and because of his extreme poverty, he shook his fist at heaven and, much agitated, cursing God's justice together with His power, added: "It is well said, gold runs to gold, and the wretched lot of the poor never alters.

Woe is me! I, who have labored all day and not earned five pennies, find nothing but stones which break my shoes, and this fellow, who is lord of a treasure, has found a gold ducat in front of my feet, when he needs it as much as the dead need incense."

The wise and prudent merchant, who had meanwhile had the ducat returned to its pristine beauty with fire and other means at the silver shop across the way, turned to the poor tailor with an amiable face and said to him, "My good man, you are wrong to complain about God, for He has done justly to have me find this ducat; had it fallen into your hands, you would have thrown it away, and even if you had kept it, you would have put it in some vile rags and left it all alone and not in its proper place;

whereas with me it will be quite the opposite, for I will put it with its peers and in a great and pretty company."

And having said this, he returned to his stand, and tossed it on top of many thousands of florins that were there inside.

Having then, as I have already said, composed a very battered and muddy little book of my scattered tales, I wished to send it to you, most worthy silversmith and excellent connoisseur of this imprint, for all the aforesaid reasons and also because I knew how easily you might refurbish it and hoped that, thus beautified, it might find a small place among your ornate and elegant books. It will add further adornment to their beauty because, as the philosopher said, when opposites are joined together, their disparity appears with greater light. Moreover, I hope that when you find a little leisure it may please you to read my tales, because in them you will find many jests and jolly pleasantries which will continually bring you new pleasure. And if any of the listeners chance to be among the superstitious followers of hypocritical friars—whose wicked life and unspeakable vices I touch upon in the first ten tales—and should these same listeners wish to attack me by claiming that I, like a blasphemer with a venomous tongue, have spoken ill of the servants of God, may it please you not to lay my book aside because of them. For as regards such quarrels I ask only that Truth take arms in my defense and bear witness for me that my stories do not proceed from a desire to speak ill of others nor from any private or personal hatred that I might bear such people.

Yet rather than remain silent about the truth, I wanted to bring to the attention of a few great princes and other particular friends of mine certain events of relatively recent memory through which it will be understood with what diverse methods and wicked skills foolish laymen have been deceived by fraudulent friars in the past. Thus I hope that men may be more astute in the present and that in the future they may have the foresight to prevent such a base and corrupt race from cloaking itself under their faith in its false goodness. Moreover, as I know the friars to be very good persons, I believe I am necessarily constrained to imitate them, at least in part, and especially the majority of them who, as they have a cowl on their backs, think they have permission to speak ill of laymen both in private and in public, adding that we are all damned and other stupidities which make them worthy of stoning. And if perhaps they wish to object that by preaching they reproach the defects of the wicked, I easily answer that by writing I do not speak against the virtue of the good; and so without deceit or advantage we will go on, and we will all equally pierce each other with our fangs.

*So then, no one ought to feel annoyed at my following in their foot-
steps and truthfully writing down the wickedness and vitiated life of some
of them. Nonetheless, for those who have their ears plastered up with holy
paste so that they cannot hear evil spoken of friars, I think the best and only
remedy for their infirmity is that, without reading or listening to my
stories, they go on their way and follow the practice of the friars, which
they will find every day more fruitful to soul and body; for the friars, being
full of every charitable love, continually share it with their followers. And
you, most worthy and beautiful lady, reading with your accustomed kindness, will find among the many thorns some little flower which will cause
you to remember your humblest servant and most obsequious Masuccio,
who continually commends himself to you and prays to God for the increase of your happy and auspicious state. Farewell.*

*Now that the brief and inept exordium directed to your above-named
Serenity is finished, there will follow next my promised tales or histories;
the first ten of which, as I said, will recount some detestable doings of
certain clergymen; tales some of which will generate not only astonishment but deep grief to the hearers, and others of which are to be perused
with pleasant laughter and mirth. And among others the first is dedicated
to the unconquered and most powerful King our lord; after which I intend to tell of other matters, both delightful and moral, and sometimes
pitiful and lamentable, as you will find in the order that follows.*

TO THE SUPREME KING DON FERRANDO OF ARAGON.[5] EXORDIUM.[6]

*upreme and most glorious king, there have been and are so many
skilled poets, eloquent orators and other most worthy writers
who have composed and continue to compose writing both in
elegant prose and in worthy verse, both in Latin and in the mother
tongue, to the praise, glory and perpetual fame of your most serene majesty, that I am persuaded that next to them my rustic style will appear to
you not otherwise than as a black spot in the middle of a white ermine.
Nonetheless, since your highness with your usual kindness deigned to tell
me that you would be very pleased to have me set in memorable writing
the worthy history which took place in the kingdom of Castille between a
knight and a minor friar, I preferred to write faultily in obedience to your
wish than to fail to do you sufficient homage by remaining silent. For this
reason, and not for any boldness, I have even offered willingly to enter
into the toilsome labyrinth and to make my unworthy letters presump-
tuous of being read by so great a king. With due humility I beseech that*

you may be pleased to accept them with delight; and that, when you have
respite from other business, you will not find it tedious to read them
along with your magnificent children and zealous pupils. For besides the
fact that the story is in itself notable, you will find in it some amusing and
worthy doings of the clergy, which I do not doubt will cause you to in-
crease and augment continually your devotion to them, as is expected of
so high a majesty. At whose feet and to whose kind mercy your most
loyal Masuccio commends himself, and begs that he not be placed by you
among the ranks of the forgotten.

I

MASTER DIEGO IS CARRIED DEAD TO HIS CONVENT BY SIR RODERICO;
ANOTHER FRIAR, THINKING HIM ALIVE, HITS HIM WITH A STONE AND
BELIEVES HE HAS KILLED HIM; HE FLEES WITH A NAG, AND BY A
STRANGE CHANCE ENCOUNTERS THE DEAD MAN MOUNTED ON A
STALLION WITH LANCE AT REST, WHO PURSUES HIM THROUGHOUT THE
CITY; AND THE LIVING MAN IS CAUGHT; HE CONFESSES TO THE
HOMICIDE; HE IS TO BE PUNISHED; THE KNIGHT REVEALS THE TRUTH,
AND THE FRIAR IS EXCUSED FROM AN UNDESERVED DEATH.

I say then, most pious king, that in the time of the happy and bright
memory of the Lord King Don Ferrando of Aragon, your most
worthy grandfather, who was governing the kingdom of Castille
under his tranquil protection, there was in Salamanca, an ancient and
noble city of that kingdom, a minor conventual friar[7] named Master
Diego da Revalo; who, being no less knowledgeable of St. Thomas's doctrine
than of his own Scotus's,[8] earned a place among those who were elected and
commissioned with no small salary to lecture at the worthy schools of the
very famous university of that city; and there with a remarkable reputation he made his knowledge noted throughout the kingdom, and also occasionally made some little speeches more useful and necessary than
devout. And being young and very handsome, quite charming and subject to the flames of love, he happened to see one day, while preaching, a
young woman of wonderful beauty, whose name was Lady Caterina, the
wife of one of the foremost knights of the city, named Sir Roderico
d'Angiaia; when he had seen her and liked her very much at first sight, Sir
Love together with her image gave an amorous blow to his already sullied
heart. And having descended from the pulpit, he went into his cell and,
throwing aside all theological arguments and sophistic proofs, gave himself over completely to thinking about the pleasing young lady. And as he

knew the lady's lofty station and whose wife she was and what an insane undertaking it would be, although many times persuading himself not to get involved in that tangle, yet at other times he would say to himself, "Love applies his forces wherever he will and never looks for equality of blood; for if this were required, then great princes would not seek at every hour to play the pirate on our shores. Therefore, Love must have given us the same privilege of loving in high places as he gave them to incline themselves to low places. Love always wounds the lover unexpectedly; thus if this lord, against whose blows no defense avails, has found me disarmed, I, unable to resist, am deservedly overcome; and, come what may, I will enter the fierce battle as his subject. And if death is the result, besides my escape from pain, at least my spirit will go to the other side with a bold face for having set its hooks in so high a place."

And so saying, without returning to the previous negative arguments, he took a piece of paper and with many deep sighs and warm tears wrote a well-ordered and elegant letter to the beloved lady, first praising her more divine than mortal beauties, then describing how he had been so taken by her that he awaited either her favor or death, and finally, although he knew that because of her lofty status he did not deserve to be granted a hearing, nonetheless begging her piteously that she deign to concede him a time and means to speak with her in secret, or at least to accept him as her servant as he had elected her to be the sole mistress of his life. And ending it with many other ornate words and sealing it and kissing it many times, he gave it to a little clerk of his and told him to whom he should carry it. This fellow, well-trained in such services, hid the letter in a secret place, which they are wont to wear under the left arm, and went off whither he had been sent.

Arriving at the house, he found the noble lady with many of her women attendants around her, and greeting her properly, he said, "My master commends himself to you and asks you to give him a little refined flour for communion wafers, as is written in this letter at greater length."

The lady, who was most discreet, seeing the letter, felt sure of what he really meant; and taking it and seeing the gist of it, although she was very chaste, she was not displeased that such a man loved her, esteeming her more beautiful than any other woman. Reading, she thoroughly enjoyed hearing her beauties praised so highly, as one who had contracted along with original sin the innate passion shared by the rest of the feminine sex, who universally hold that all their fame, honor, and glory consist in nothing other than being loved, desired, and exalted for their beauty, and would sooner be considered beautiful and wicked than virtuous and ugly. Nonetheless, hating all friars fiercely and with reason, she decided not only not to satisfy the teacher in any way but also to refuse him the courtesy of an answer. And she also decided for the time being not to say anything about it to her husband. Firm in this conclusion, she turned to the clerk and, without showing herself agitated in the least, said to him, "Tell your master that my husband wants all my flour for himself, and so let him think about getting it somewhere else, and the letter doesn't need any further answer; but if he still wants it, let him notify me, and when my husband comes home, I will have him do what is appropriate for this request."

The teacher, receiving this stern reply, did not in the least diminish his ardor on its account, but rather his love grew together with his desire into a greater flame; and not to retreat a jot from the undertaking begun, as the lady's house was very near the convent, he began anew to woo her, with such importunity that she could not show herself at a window nor go to church nor to any other place outside her house without the solicitous teacher hanging constantly around her. Whereupon it happened that not only the people in the neighborhood noticed it, but even a large part of the city became aware of it. For this reason, she herself was convinced that she could no longer keep silent to her husband about such a matter, worrying that if he were to hear of it from someone else, besides the danger, he would consider her a less than honest woman. And having conceded to this thought, one night while she was with her husband, she told him all about it in detail. The knight, who was a man of honor and very spirited, was kindled with such wild rage that he was barely kept from going at that very hour to set fire and sword to the convent and all its friars. But having calmed down slightly, after having praised the honesty of his wife with many words, he bid her arrange an assignation with the teacher for the following night in whatever way she thought best, so that he might at once satisfy his honor and avoid the sullying of his dearly beloved wife; and she was to leave the rest to him. Although it was painful to the lady, thinking what would come of it, yet she said she would do it, to obey her husband's will; and as the little clerk kept returning with new ruses to hoe away her hard stoniness, she said, "Commend me to your master and tell him that the great love he bears me, along with the warm tears which, according to his letters, he is continually shedding on my account, has already found a place in my heart, so that I have become more his than my own. And as our good luck would have it, just today Sir Roderico has gone into town and will stay there tonight in a hotel; and so, when nine o'clock rings, let him come secretly to me, and I will give him a hearing as he wishes; and in any case ask him not to confide about this to any friend or companion no matter how intimate."

The little monk, marvelously happy, left and brought the gracious message to his master, who was the gladdest man that ever was, thinking it a thousand years until the shortly appointed time should draw near. When it came, having perfumed himself thoroughly so that he would not have the air of a little friar, and thinking that the race was to be won by trotting with good endurance, he dined that time on excellent and delicate confections. Wearing his usual clothing, he made his way to the lady's door and, finding it open, entered inside and was led by a maid like a blind man through the darkness into a room where, expecting to find the lady who would joyfully receive him, he found instead the knight with a trusty servant; and seizing him without any risk and without making any noise, they strangled him.

When Master Diego was dead, the knight, feeling somewhat contrite afterwards for having stained his powerful arm with the death of a minor friar, and seeing that repentance was no use as a remedy, thought that for the sake of his honor, and also in case of the king's wrath, he ought to get the dead man out of his house. And as he thought, it occurred to him to carry the dead man to his convent, and having placed him across the servant's shoulders, they brought him to the friars' garden; easily entering the convent from there, they carried him to the place where the friars go to relieve themselves; and by chance finding only one seat in order, for the others had fallen into ruin (because, as we see continually, most areas in convents look more like robbers' caves than dwellings of the servants of God), they sat him on that one just as if he were relieving himself, and there they left him. After they had returned home, as Mister Teacher sat there looking truly like someone eliminating the superfluities of his body, it happened that around midnight another friar, young and sturdy, felt an overwhelming need to go to the aforesaid place to do his natural business. And lighting a small lamp, he went swiftly to the very spot where Master Diego was sitting dead; recognizing him and thinking him alive, he drew back without saying a word because there was a mortal and fierce enmity between them on account of some friarly envy or hatred. And so he waited to one side until the teacher, as he thought, should finish what he too intended to do. Having waited in this way for quite a long time and not seeing the teacher move, he himself being drawn by the urgency of his need, said to himself many times, "By God's faith, this fellow is still sitting there and won't yield the place to me for no other reason than to show me even in this his enmity and the ill will he bears me; but he'll be the loser, because I will suffer it as long as I can, and if I see him remain fixed in his obstinacy, even though I could go elsewhere, I'll take the place from him against his will."

The teacher, who had already fixed his anchor in a hard rock, moved not the slightest; and the friar unable to endure it any longer, said in rage, "So then, may it displease God that you should do me such shame without my being able to do anything about it."

Picking up a large stone and drawing near, he gave him such a blow in the chest that it made him fall backwards without moving any of his limbs.

The friar, seeing first the fierce blow and then that the man did not get up, worried that he had killed him with the stone; and after hesitating between belief and disbelief, finally went up to him and inspected him with his lamp. Recognizing that he was certainly dead, as he was, the friar felt sure that he was responsible for his death. And dreadfully sorry, worrying that because of their enmity he would be suspected of the blow and therefore would lose his life, he decided several times to go hang himself by the neck. But thinking better of it, he resolved to carry the body outside the convent and throw it in the street in order to prevent anyone from suspecting him of murder. Moreover remembering the teacher's public and dishonest wooing of Lady Caterina, he said to himself: "Where can I more easily carry him and with less suspicion on me than in front of the door of Sir Roderico? For he is near by and moreover it will surely be believed that he had him killed as he was going to see the wife."

And so saying, without further deliberation, he took the corpse upon his shoulders with great effort, carried it in front of the aforesaid door, from which a few hours earlier it had been dragged out dead; and leaving it there, without having been perceived by anyone, he returned to the convent.

Although this action seemed sufficient to secure his safety, nonetheless he thought he had better absent himself from the convent for a few days under some feigned pretext; and having thought this, he went that very hour to the cell of the father superior to whom he said, "Father, the day before yesterday, lacking a beast of burden, I left a large quantity of our stuff near Medina in the house of one of our devotees; therefore I would like your blessing to fetch it and to take along the convent's nag and, God willing, to return tomorrow or the day after."

The father superior not only gave him leave but highly praised his handling of the matter. The friar, having this answer, arranged his few small possessions, got the horse ready, and waited for dawn in order to depart. Sir Roderico, who had slept little or not at all that night because of anxiety about what he had done, now that day was near decided to send his servant around to the convent to hear whether the friars had found the dead teacher and what they were saying about it. The servant, leaving the house to do as he was bid, found Master Diego settled in front of the door, looking as if he were engaged in an argument; which gave him no small scare. Going back in, he called his master at once and, hardly able to speak, showed him the teacher's dead body brought back to their house. The knight was much astonished at the event, and it gave him cause for greater worry. Nonetheless, comforted by the thought that his undertaking had been just, he resolved to await the outcome of the deed and, turning to the dead man, said, "So then, you are the thorn of my household which I can't pull out dead or alive. But to spite whoever brought you here, you will leave again mounted on the same kind of beast that you were yourself when alive."

And having spoken thus, he bid the servant bring a stallion from the stable of one of his neighbors, which the owner kept as a stud horse for the mares and donkeys of the city, and it lived there like the ass of Jerusalem. The servant went speedily and brought the stallion with saddle and bridle and everything else that was appropriate all in order. And as the knight had already decided to do, he put the aforesaid dead body on the horse, and propping him up and tying him on well, they set a lance at rest with the bridle in his hand as if they were sending him into battle; and having

arranged him thus, they led him in front of the door of the friars' church, where they tied the horse. And then they went back home.

The friar, thinking it time to start on his way, opened the convent door, mounted his nag, and came forth; and finding the teacher in front of him, who truly looked as if he were threatening to kill him with his lance, the friar was suddenly struck with such terror that he was in danger of dropping dead on the spot, and furthermore he had a wild and anxious thought that the soul of the man had reentered the body and had been condemned to pursue him everywhere, according to the belief of some fools. And while he stood there so stunned and frightened, not knowing which way he should go, the stallion caught scent of the nag, and unsheathing his iron club with a whinny, tried to approach her; these moves gave the friar an even greater fright. Nonetheless, coming to himself, he started to head the nag on her way, who, turning her rear towards the stallion, began to kick up her hooves; the friar, who was not the best rider in the world, was close to falling off; and to avoid a second such tossing, he clapped his legs hard to her side, pressing the spurs into her flanks and leaning with both hands on the pommel, and dropping the reins, committed the beast to fortune's sway; who, feeling the spurs prick her flanks, was forced to run for a while without guidance, and to take whatever street she first came to.

The stallion, seeing his prey depart, with fury broke his weak tie and began to follow her wildly. The poor friar, hearing his enemy behind him and turning his head, saw him bent over his lance like a fierce jouster, and this second fear overcame the first,[9] and as he fled he began to scream "Help! Help!"

Now that it was daylight, his screams and the sound of the two runaway horses brought everyone to the windows and to the doors, and they all nearly burst out laughing with astonishment, seeing such a new and strange chase of two minor friars on horseback, for one appeared no less dead than the other. The nag without guidance went running through the streets, now this way, now that, wherever the way was easiest; behind her the stallion did not pause from pursuing her furiously; and whether the friar was frequently near to being wounded by the lance there is no need to ask.

A large crowd kept following them with cries, whistles, and shouts; and everywhere they were yelling, "Watch out! Get him!" Some were throwing stones at them, and some were striking the stallion with sticks, and everyone was trying to separate them, not so much out of charity for the man fleeing, as out of desire to find out who they were, who could not be recognized because of the speed at which the horses were running. And so as they were thus working at it, by chance they came to one of the city gates where, caught in the enclosure, the dead and the live man were both taken hold of; and being recognized by everyone, with great astonishment, the two were led, on horseback as they were, into the convent and received with immeasurable dismay by the father superior and the friars. They had the dead man buried and prepared the strappado[10] for the live one; who, being tied up and not wanting to be tortured, readily confessed to the murder for the reason told above; but truly he could not guess who had set the dead teacher up on horseback in this way. For his confession he was exempted from the strappado but put in a harsh prison, and the magistrate was sent for to have the bishop of the city rescind his holy orders and give him over to the secular court, so that they could punish him for homicide as the laws required.

By chance, the story was told to the king Ferrando, who had come to Salamanca in those days. Although he had been a most temperate prince and was very sorry about the case and about the death of such a renowned teacher, nonetheless overcome by the amusing aspect of the event, he laughed with his barons so hard that they could not stand on their feet. And when the time came to proceed with the unjust condemnation of the friar, Sir Roderico, who was a most valorous knight and much favored by the king, incited by his zeal for truth and seeing that his silence would be the sole cause of such an injustice, resolved sooner to die, if necessary, than to hide the truth of the matter; and standing before the king, where many barons and people were gathered, he said, "My lord, the stern and unjust sentence given to the innocent minor friar together with the truth of the matter induce me to solve the riddle of the event. And therefore if your majesty will pardon him who justly killed Master Diego, I will have him come here before you and with confirmed truth tell you in detail how the event occurred."

The king, who was a most merciful ruler and eager to hear the truth, was very generous with the requested pardon; once it was granted the knight recounted to the king and the other bystanders all the details about how the teacher had fallen in love with his wife, and all the letters and messages he had sent, and everything else he had done up to that final hour.

The king, already having heard the friar testify, seeing that the tales confirmed each other in large part, and considering Roderico to be an upright and good knight, gave him entire credence without further investigation; yet with astonishment and grief, and sometimes with honest laughter, he pondered the nature of this strange and elaborate case. However, not to allow the undue sentence against the innocent friar to take effect, he sent for the father superior together with the poor friar; and in the presence of his barons and other nobles and people, the king explained to them how everything had really happened: whereupon he ordered that the friar not be condemned to suffer a cruel death but rather be set free at once. At this, with his good name restored, the friar went home a most happy man. Sir Roderico was commended with wonderful praises for everything he had done about the situation, and so was the pardon he had received. And thus this wonderful story with swift fame and great pleasure spread throughout the Castillian kingdom in a very few days; and as it penetrated into our Italian regions and was told with brief eloquence to you, most powerful king our lord, it pleased me, in obedience to your commands, to make it worthy of eternal memory, as is shown especially in its dedication.

Masuccio

I do not doubt that the quality and manner of the strange, new and unexpected event of the tale just told, my most illustrious lady, will, after some laughter, cause you and the listeners to say that our Master Diego was appropriately rewarded for his fervent love. And besides I think it certain that some will say that if he had been a spiritual or observant friar, he would not have pursued disordered lusts of this kind and not have come, as a consequence, to dark death. And although in another part of this little work of mine we will satisfy such birdbrains as these both by propounding and by replying, and by distinguishing the life and actions of conventual friars from those of observing friars, nonetheless I need to touch here somewhat briefly on this matter, saying that undoubtedly all Christendom would be better if we had no other religion than that which Christ left on earth through the glorious apostle St. Peter; and although that too has been in part corrupted, still its ministers and also those friars who are called conventual demonstrate clearly to us how and in what way we should guard ourselves against them, because all their appearances, in their dress and in their walk and in all their other actions, are nothing but frightful shouts and cries which say: "Do not trust us!" For this reason, anyone who has the slightest understanding can truly judge how much those clergy are to be praised who do not seek to deceive others through going about ill-clad, with bent head and hypocritical countenance.

But if it happened to all those who have the minds of wolves and yet show themselves to us covered with the fleece of mild lambs as happened to the above-named master, I do not doubt that they would guard themselves from *coming at all hours to contaminate our flocks. How God provides for the lack of sense of secular fools, who are incapable of realizing how many religious hypocrites there are who, like charlatans, go running about the kingdoms and countryside with new fraudulent tricks, living at ease, robbing, and indulging their lusts! And when all else fails them, they pretend to be saints and show how they can do miracles: and one goes with the tonsure of St. Vincent, others with the order of St. Bernard, and some with the ass's halter of the Capistrano, and with a thousand other diabolical manners they usurp the authority and honor of those orders. And as their doings resound and are told throughout the world, so too in the next tale, dedicated to the most serene prince your most worthy companion, you will hear about a remarkable trick played against the person of a very illustrious German lady by a diabolical Dominican friar, in the name of holiness. From its outcome we can draw the conclusion that the more erect and eminent the trees, the more boldly and impudently they are attacked by the woodsman's axe as he endeavors to send them crashing to earth.*

4

BROTHER JERONIMO OF SPOLETO WITH A BONE FROM A CORPSE MAKES THE PEOPLE OF SORRENTO BELIEVE IT IS THE ARM OF SAINT LUKE; HIS COMPANION DENIES IT; HE PRAYS GOD TO SHOW A MIRACLE; THE COMPANION PRETENDS TO DROP DEAD, AND HE BY PRAYING RESTORES HIM TO LIFE; AND BY THIS DOUBLE MIRACLE, HE COLLECTS LOTS OF MONEY WITH WHICH HE BECOMES A PRELATE AND LIVES AT EASE WITH HIS COMPANION.

To the magnificent Messer Antonello de Petruciis, the king's sole faithful secretary.

Exordium

I think, my magnificent superior, in wanting to begin writing to you, who are an ocean of every rhetorical style, that if I had the lyre of Orpheus or the eloquence of Mercury, it would seem to you no other than the lowly song of a blind man to the crude mob. This alone caused me up until now to defer writing the following tale. Yet, knowing it to be very amusing and clever, I decided to send it to you as unadorned and rusty as it is. It may be that because you receive frequent notice of events occuring in the world, you will find no profit in it; nonetheless, if you will read it to others, I have no doubt that they will take from it some very useful advice, and it will perhaps be an efficient cause to put them on guard against the strange fraudulent sect of holy men who, with most *treacherous skill and subtle deceit, while pretending to work miracles, manage to rob us of our honor, wealth, and felicity. And though I think no eloquence would be sufficient to speak fully of their wickedness, nevertheless to take one small flower from a vast field, I will tell you next of the devilish invention of a minor friar, against which, according to my humble judgment, no human sagacity would have been able to protect us.*

Narration

I n the time when King James of France, previously named count of the Marche, became husband of the last of the Durazzi women,[11] there arrived in Naples a minor friar named Brother Jeronimo of Spoleto; who, seeming almost saintly in appearance, continually went around preaching not only in Naples but through all the surrounding towns, and there won for himself a wonderful fame and following. Whence it happened that, finding himself in Aversa, at the monastery of some friar preachers, he was shown as a wonder the body of a renowned knight, dead long years; which, either because of having been well preserved or perhaps because of the even temperament which that body had during its life or for whatever other reason, was so whole and firm that not only was every bone in its proper place but even the skin was still so uncorrupted that one could move the lower end of the body by touching the head. Mister Friar, who had inspected it carefully, suddenly got the idea of obtaining one limb of the said body so that by calling it a relic he could draw forth hundreds and thousands of ducats, and with these not only could live at ease but also, as is the custom, could come by their means to a high rank in the Church. And if you took a good look around, you would see how many have become great prelates at the expense of poor and foolish laymen, this one becoming an inquisitor of heresies, that one a collector for the crusades; I won't mention some who with real or counterfeit papal bulls, remit sins and for a fee place anyone in paradise, by hook or by crook filling their guts full of florins, even though it is expressly forbidden by the rules of their holy orders.

To come back to our Brother Jeronimo, having gotten the idea and bribed the sacristan of the place, although he was a Dominican, with the favor of the prior of Santa Croce,[12] he obtained the arm and right hand of the said corpse; on which one could see not only the skin and some hairs but also the nails so clean and firm that they seemed almost those of a living person. And without delay Mister Friar set the holy relic, wrapped in many layers of silk with sweet perfumes in a box and made ready to depart. Returning to Naples, he found his faithful companion, Brother

Mariano of Saona, who was no less skillful an artist than he. And agreeing between them to go into Calabria, a province inhabited by crude and uneducated people whom they could easily fool with their tricks, they settled on a plan.

Brother Mariano, cautiously disguised as a Dominican, went to the port to find a passage to Calabria; Brother Jeronimo, from another direction, with three other companions of his, loaded with sacks, made their way to the seashore. There they chanced upon a boat from Amantea[13] about to sail right away; they all got on board, keeping separate from each other and showing little sign of friendship, just as cardsharks do at the fairs or sometimes when they arrive at an inn along the road; and with things thus arranged, the sailors put their oars in the water and spread their sails to the winds and attended to the voyage. And when they were not far from Capri, suddenly there broke upon them a squall so fierce and perilous that the sailors said there was no coping with it. In desperation they were forced to put in at a small beach near Sorrento, where with no little difficulty they pulled the boat ashore, everyone getting off and heading into town, intending to stay there until the weather improved. So among the others our Brother Jeronimo went to the local friars' convent with his companions, while Brother Mariano, who had become a Dominican, lodged with the other laymen at an inn. Realizing that the turbulent sea would not soon be calmed, the worthy friar, not to lose time, resolved to make here the first trial of his false relic. For he remembered having heard in his home county that the said city of Sorrento was not only one of the noblest but also one of the most ancient cities of the realm and that therefore the citizens still had some of that old rust of the ancients. Thus his devised plan would succeed no less easily with them than in Calabria.

And having secretly given notice to Brother Mariano, as the next morning was Sunday, he sent the father superior of the convent to announce to the archbishop that with his blessing he intended to preach a devout sermon on the following morning in the main church; and he begged them to let it be known both inside and outside the city so that if a large enough number of people came with such devotion as seemed appropriate, he might to the glory and praise of God show them a sacred relic, and the most holy ever seen in their time. The archbishop, himself one of the ancient Sorrentan race, gave his undoubting credence to everything and immediately sent a proclamation not only throughout the city but also into the surrounding countryside, that everyone for the said reason should come devoutly to hear the sermon and see the relic, which was to be shown to the people of Sorrento by a servant of God; and as the news spread at last over the whole region, so many people came running to the church that morning that barely half of them could squeeze inside. And when the hour came for the sermon, Brother Jeronimo, accompanied by many friars with their usual ceremonies, mounted to the pulpit and when the time seemed right to him, having made a long speech about deeds of charity and holy almsgiving, uncovered his head and began to speak in this manner:

"Most reverend Monsignor, and you other gentlemen and ladies, my fathers and mothers in Jesus Christ, I do not doubt that you have heard news of my preaching in Naples, where by the grace of God and not for my own merits or virtue, I have always had an exceptional audience. Hearing about the fame of this beautiful city of yours and about the kindness and devotion of its citizens, together with the beauties of the region, I resolved many times to come and speak the word of God before you, and to enjoy with you a bit this lovely climate of yours, which in truth I consider very good for my health. Receiving then an order from our father the general vicar that I should go at once into Calabria to fill some posts in certain cities which had called for us, I was constrained to turn my steps and go where I was ordered. Whereupon, as I believe you know, finding ourselves and our ship in this bay of yours, beset by opposing winds and stormy seas, against all the strength and will of the sailors, we arrived here almost having given ourselves up for lost. This arrival, I believe, was caused not by the opposition of the winds but by the divine operation of my Creator, who wanted in part to satisfy my longing; and so that you also may participate in the said divine grace, I want to show you a miraculous relic, for the strengthening of your devotion. It is an arm with the whole right hand of the excellent and glorious scribe of our redeemer Jesus Christ, my lord Saint Luke the Evangelist, which the patriarch of Constantinople gave to our father vicar, and he is sending it with me into Calabria for the aforementioned reason, because there was never the body or limb of any saint in that province. So then, my friends, may God bless you, let everyone with devotion take off his hat to see this treasure, which God has granted you to see more by a miracle than by my agency; and let me tell you first that I have a bull from our lord the pope which grants great indulgences and remission of sin to whoever will make some charitable offering to the said relic according to his means, so that with what is collected we may make a tabernacle of silver set with jewels as befits such a holy object."

And having said this, drawing out from his sleeve a bull counterfeited in his usual manner, without his even reading it he was immediately believed by everyone; and so they all approached in order to offer some charity, even when their means were very small. Brother Jeronimo, having delivered his made-up tale in a well-ordered manner, bid his companions hand him the box wherein was the holy arm, and having many candles lighted, kneeling down, and holding it in his hand with great reverence, first with tears in his eyes devotedly kissed the rim of the box in which he kept the relic to deceive people. Then, with solemnity, he turned to his companions and sang with them pontifically a pious hymn to Saint Luke. And seeing finally that the people were all watching with wonder, he opened the box, from which issued forth a marvellous fragrance. Then, removing the silk wrappings, taking hold of the relic and displaying the hand with a bit of the arm, he spoke thus:

"This is that blessed and holy hand of the most faithful secretary of the Son of God! This is that blessed hand which not only wrote such excellent things about the glorious Virgin Mary but also many times drew true portraits of her face!"[14]

And as he was about to go on recounting to them the praises of the said saint, lo from a corner of the church Brother Mariano da Saona in his new Dominican habit, making way for himself with great importunity and shouting with a loud voice to his fellow Brother Jeronimo, began to speak in this way:

"O base villain, coward, deceiver of God and of men, are you not ashamed to tell such a great enormous lie, that this is the arm of Saint Luke, given that I know for certain that his most holy body is in Padua quite whole? But you must have pulled this rotten bone out of some grave in order to deceive others. I am extremely astonished at Monsignor and these other venerable church fathers, who ought to stone you, as you deserve."

The archbishop and all the people, marvelling not a little at this new turn of events, rebuking him for his words, told him to be quiet; but for all that, he did not cease to shout, rather he became more and more fervent in persuading people not to believe that man. While things were in this state, Brother Jeronimo, thinking it was time to perform the premeditated and false miracle, showing himself somewhat disturbed, silenced the murmuring people with his hand, and seeing briefly that everyone was attentive to what he would say, turning towards the main altar, where there stood an image of the crucifixion, and kneeling to that image, with many tears he began to speak thus:

"O my Lord Jesus Christ, redeemer of the human race, God and man, you who have formed me and made me in your image and have brought me here, by the merits of your glorious body and by your immaculate human flesh, and by the bitter passion by which you redeemed us, I also pray you by the miraculous stigmata which you gave to our seraphic Francis, that it please you to show a clear sign in the presence of these your devoted people concerning this able friar who, as an enemy and rival of our religion, has come to repudiate my truthfulness; so that if I am lying, send at once your wrath upon me and make me die right here; and if I am speaking the truth, that this is the true arm of Saint Luke, your most worthy scribe, my Lord, not for vengeance but for the clear demonstration of truth, send your sentence down upon him so that despite his will he may be unable with tongue or hand to speak his error."

Brother Jeronimo had barely finished his entreaty when Brother Mariano suddenly, as they had planned, began to twist his hands and feet and to cry out loudly and to stammer with his tongue without getting out a single word, and with his eyes crossed and mouth twisted and every limb awry, he let himself fall helplessly backwards. Everyone in the church, having seen the manifest miracle, began to cry all together for mercy so that had it thundered no one would have heard it. Brother Jeronimo, seeing the people hooked as he wished, in order to kindle them further and perfect the deceit, began to shout loudly:

"Praise the Lord! Silence, my friends!"

And when his words had quieted them down, having Brother
Mariano, who had by all appearance looked dead, lifted up and placed in
front of the altar, he began to speak thus:

"My lords, gentlemen and ladies and all you other folk, I beg you by
the virtue of the holy passion of Christ, let everyone kneel down and devoutly say a paternoster in reverence to my lord Saint Luke, for the sake
of whose merits may God not only return this poor man to life but also
restore his maimed limbs and lost speech so that his soul may not go into
eternal perdition."

No sooner was it commanded than everyone got down to pray, while
he on the other hand, descending from the pulpit, took a small knife and
cutting a bit of the fingernail of the miraculous hand, put it in a glass of
holy water and opened the mouth of Brother Mariano, pouring the
precious fluid down his throat, and saying, "I order you in the name of
the Holy Spirit immediately to rise up and return to your former health."

Brother Mariano, who had with greatest difficulty held back his
laughter up till then, having received the mighty drink and having heard
the end of the false incantation, at once rose to his feet, opened his eyes
and, completely dazed, began to shout "Jesus! Jesus!" and some ran to
ring the church bells, and some to kiss and touch the clothing of the
preacher, so that everyone seemed so impelled by devotion that you
would have thought the last and universal judgment had come.

Brother Jeronimo, who wished to fulfill the purpose of his coming,
with no little difficulty remounted the pulpit, and commanded that the
relic be placed before the altar. Then he had his companions set
themselves all around it, some with lighted candles in their hands, some
laboring to clear a little space, so that everyone could pray and make offerings to the holy arm as much as he wished without impediment.
Besides the great quantity of money which was offered there with the
thickest crowd ever seen, there were some ladies assailed with unbridled
zeal who tore off their pearls and silver and other precious jewels and offered them to the holy evangelist. And so the friar, having left the holy
relic on display all that day and thinking it time to return home with the
booty he already had, gave a cautious sign to his companions, and swiftly wrapping up everything together with the arm in the box, they all set
off together towards the convent. The friar, esteemed and reverenced by
all no less than a saint, was honorably accompanied to his lodging by the
archbishop and all the populace. The following morning, after Brother
Jeronimo had been escorted back and had publically authenticated the
two remarkable miracles, seeing the weather suitable for his departure,

he boarded the ship with Brother Mariano, his other companions, and with no small quantity of loot. And sailing with a favorable wind, they arrived in a few days in Calabria, where with new and varied methods of deceit they filled their pockets full of money, traveling ultimately inside and outside Italy; having grown very wealthy by their innumerable deceits, and by the grace of the miraculous arm, they returned to Spoleto. Feeling safe there, Brother Jeronimo bought himself a bishopric through the aid of a lord cardinal, not by simony but, as they newly interpret it, by procuration, and there, living at ease together with Brother Mariano, they had themselves a good time as long as they lived.

Masuccio *(conclusion)*

The past story has shown something of the skill with which the fraudulent and rapacious wolves work zealously to manipulate our wits, without any human sagacity being sufficient to prevent it. Worse still, to spite us, they continually condemn and rebuke avarice in their preaching, not only as a mortal sin but as the irremissible sin of heresy; while at the same time we see clearly not only that Avarice is an innate passion in all friars but that they pursue and embrace her as a lover and sister of them all, as if by the express precept of obedience it were so ordered and commanded in their rules. And if I mentioned near the end of the said tale that our Brother Jeronimo bought a bishopric and that simony has changed its name, no one ought to be surprised. For it is evident that nobody, however virtuous he may be or however many years and abilities he may have used up in studies or in attendance at the Roman court, can ever reach a high rank in the Church without the favor of the master of the exchequer; and such offices must be purchased with competitive bidding like horses at a fair, together with the bribery of gifts and promised payments not only to those who do favors but also to the others to keep them from making trouble; nor is it surprising from this that an improperly acquired benefice is called a rightful annuity. From this, then, we can draw the conclusion that the friars and priests and monks have invented a foreign language with a strange idiom; for to all the most wicked vices they fit a new name, along with a few notable words from the holy Scripture; and so, eating and living at ease at the expense of the Crucifixion, or rather at our expense, they mock both God and men. And when in regard to the most execrable sin one can commit on earth in offense to God and nature they say "It's a secret of the order," and commit it without restraint, fear or shame, you can imagine what they do in regard to other sins which are not of such a horrible nature.

Wishing to speak further about what I hear of their doing both public and private, I am drawn to proceed with the tales I have begun; from which I will produce for my case another piece of confirmed evidence, and in the following fifth story will show how a ribald priest, besides singing "Let us rejoice" and "By the mystery of the Word incarnate" and "Come, Bride of Christ" and other infinite enormities, called his sword as he was going about "You are my salvation"; and also, transforming another name from its natural one, said he wanted to put the pope in Rome and pull the Turk out of Constantinople.[15]

24

A Youth Loves a Lady but Is Not Loved in Return; He Hides in Her House; a Blackamoor Has Carnal Knowledge of the Lady Where the Lover is Hidden; He Reveals Himself and with Many Insults Rebukes the Lady's Wickedness, and His Love Is Changed to Hatred.

To the excellent Count of Altavilla.

Exordium

Not to turn my pen with black color against those who have not given me cause, wishing to dedicate the present tale to you, excellent lord, I decided not only to keep silent the names of both the lady and the man in it but also to leave unnamed the city where the event occurred. In this story you will hear a strange and cruel case that befell a most unhappy lover, who was brought to such a point that he was forced to make a quick decision about something which would have been very difficult even for a lofty intellect with a long time for reflection. I pray you therefore, when you care to read of this event, if you were ever heated by the flames of love, judge aright, according to your pleasure, what the wretched lover ought to have done and whether in what follows he is to be commended. Farewell.

Narration

Not long ago, in a famous city of Italy, there was a handsome and powerful young man who was well-mannered and full of every virtue. It happened, as is often the case with young men, that he fell in love with a charming and pretty woman, the wife of one of the foremost knights of the city. Becoming aware of this and seeing his daily efforts to enter into her favor, the lady, as is the innate habit of her sex, decided from the first encounter to use all her wits and skills to entangle him in her deceitful net. And doing this very easily, she recognized that he was so captivated that he would not readily be able to disentangle himself; and so as not to allow him to be happy in love for long, after a few days she gradually began to withdraw her favors and continually showed him that she cared nothing for him and all his doings. Extremely unhappy, the poor lover bore this with insufferable pain; and seeing that the jousting, liberal spending and other noteworthy actions which he continually performed for her sake were of no avail to him but rather seemed to cause ever new disdain, he tried often to give up the whole undertaking and, if he could, to turn his thoughts in another direction. And while he set his mind to this with every effort, the lady, seeing that his ardour was somewhat cooled, made him return to his former game with new kinds of deceit; and when she saw that she had hooked him as she wished, she began to sail with contrary winds, reducing him to his former wretched state; and she managed this with the skill of a real master, both so that she might glorify herself as one of the chaste and beautiful because she had kept such a fine lover waiting so long, and also that he might bear witness to her feigned virtue so that no one would believe anything wicked of her even if it became public.

Being then in such cruel and evil torment for many many years without having once been given any true hope, the unhappy lover decided, though he should die for it, to enter secretly into the lady's house and to do as much as fortune allowed him. And when a time befell that the knight, the lady's husband, had gone out of town on business matters for several days, the lover cautiously entered her house late one evening and, hiding himself in a storage room used for fodder which was in the courtyard, he settled himself to stay the night behind certain empty barrels with the hope that when the lady went to church in the morning, he might have the opportunity to enter her bedroom and hide himself under her bed, in order later that night to try his ultimate fortune. But as luck would have it—and his luck had always driven him from bad to worse—the lady, because of some unexpected duty, did not leave the house that morning; whereupon he, who had waited until three in the afternoon in vain with his usual pain and patience, resolved to remain there until the next morning and, eating some food that he had brought with him for the occasion, stayed quietly in the said place with much regret and little hope. And when the day was nearly over, he heard a black moor arrive, who was the muleteer of the house, with two bundles of wood; as the moor was unloading them in the courtyard, the lady came to a window at the noise and with sharp words began to scold the moor for staying away a long

time and for having brought back so little wood and in such a sorry condition. The moor, replying little or nothing, attended to easing his mules
and to adjusting the packsaddles; and as he entered the place where the
young man was hidden in order to take some fodder, here came the lady
who entered after the moor, and taunting him with her usual words, she
began carelessly to play with his hand; and as she was proceeding from
one thing to another, the wretched lover, who was watching and because
of that fellow's luck could have wished himself worse than a moor if only
he had been granted what the moor was being granted without any efforts, saw the lady lock the door and without further ado seat herself on
the mules' packsaddles and pull the horrible moor down upon her, who
not waiting for a second invitation, putting his hand to the tools, began
to hump her like a dog.

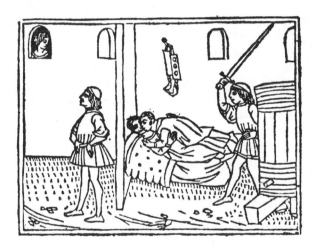

Ah, longing youths! Ah, loyal and perfect lovers, who at every hour
place your honor and ability together with your life in danger for the sake
of the faithless and rotten female sex! Step forward at this point and each
of you, considering for yourself, judge as rightly as you can what the unfortunate young man should have done in such an extreme situation; for
surely, according to my limited view, any revenge would have fallen
short of such a deed. But to go on with the story, I will tell you in truth

what the poor young lover suddenly thought to do about it. He, as I said, seeing all this and unable in any way to bear it, feeling his fervent love changed into fierce hatred, came forth from his hiding place with his drawn sword in hand, with the cruel intention of ending both their lives at one blow; yet, restraining himself in that brief moment for some reason, he thought he would be acting basely to stain his sword with the death of a cur and of such a vile bawd as she evidently was, whom until then he had considered most virtuous; and coming upon them with a terrifying shriek, he said:

"O wretched and unhappy is my life! What horrible and monstrous doings my evil fortune has led me to see!" And turning to the moor he said, "To you, wild dog, I don't know what else I should say but that, praising your actions, I remain obliged to you forever for having freed me from the power of that wild beast, devourer of all my joy and comfort."

Each of you can judge for yourself how stunned the lady remained and what were her thoughts when she saw the lover; she, who would have suffered death with much less dismay, and rightly so, had meanwhile in rage and intense grief thrown herself at his feet, not asking for mercy but begging him to give her the deserved death at once without delay.

Whereupon he, who had his answer prepared, said to her, "O wicked and libidinous wolf, o shame and eternal infamy of the rest of womankind, by what fire, by what lust have you let yourself be overcome that you subject yourself to a black hound, to an irrational brute, or to speak more correctly, to a monster of the earth, as is this biting dog to whom you have fed your infected and rotten flesh? And if you think you acted worthily to rack me for so many years on account of this fellow, should you not at least have had regard for your own dignity, for your honor in the world, for the love which your husband bears you and which you ought by right to bear for him, who seems to me without doubt the most handsome, virtuous, and worthy knight in our city? Surely I don't know what else to say, except that the majority of you, unbridled herd of women, when it comes to matters of lust are reined in neither by fear nor by shame nor by conscience to make any distinction between lord and servant, noble and base, handsome and ugly, but are guided only by your imperfect judgment of how well he knows or is able to beat the wool. It seems unnecessary for me to give you the death for which you so urgently plead, for you have it already, because with your reputation so blackened, defamed, and darkened, you can consider yourself henceforth and deservedly worse than dead; rather I want you alive in the world to bear witness to yourself of your unspeakable wickedness, and as many times as you see me, so many deaths will you suffer anew, remembering your misery and your past life. Now live on with your bad luck, for such is the canine stink coming from your rotten flesh that I cannot stay here any longer."

And as the hour was late by now, without being seen by anyone, he went outside and returned home, and the lady, who had not answered a word, grieving, weeping, and sad, returned to her chamber. The young man, setting aside the insignia which he used to wear when jousting and tourneying, made one of a fierce black hound that was holding and devouring a beautiful naked lady between its paws and teeth; whenever she saw it, she felt a cold knife in her heart; and so the evil woman, continually vexed by such a punishment, was every day bitten and torn.

Masuccio

T he enormity of the case just recounted moves me to wonder whether one ought more to praise the lover, who did what was right for a noble spirit to do, or to blame the scoundrel woman, given that she did what almost all women do or even worse when the opportunity arises, for we can maintain indubitably that rare are those women who, having the occasion, don't go running after the goods of every man, for which we see clear evidence every day, as the next story will also confirm. . . .

31

A COUPLE OF PRETTY LOVERS RUN AWAY IN ORDER TO CONVERT THEIR LOVE INTO MARRIAGE; LOST IN A SUDDEN STORM, THEY COME UPON A HOSTEL OF LEPERS, AND THERE, HER LOVER HAVING BEEN KILLED BY THE LEPERS, THE YOUNG GIRL WILLINGLY KILLS HERSELF OVER HIS BODY.

To the illustrious Infanta Lady Elionora of Aragon.

Exordium

I f our nature is gladdened by successful and joyful things adorned with wit and jolly pleasantries, and in listening to them becomes gracious and benevolent, I believe similarly, illustrious lady, that in reading or hearing the unfortunate, adverse, and horrible events befalling others, we are constrained by our humanity duly to accompany their miseries by weeping our most bitter tears. There having come to me news of the fierce, unlucky and lamentable fate which befell two most unhappy lovers, led and driven by their evil fortune to suffer a most cruel death, I

Violent story

Manual for
given for
for Ladies

decided to give particular notice of this frightful and tragic event to you,
who are more than any other woman robed with kindness and compassionate charity, so that as you read it and as other women listen, overcome with compassion you may shed a few little tears of pity, which I am
convinced will bring no small refreshment to the two young lovers' wretched
souls, which I think are tormented in the eternal flames. Farewell.

Narration

Fame, the truthful reporter of ancient deeds, has shown me how
in the time when the Maid[16] rose up in the kingdom of France,
in the city of Nancy, foremost and noblest among the cities of the
duchy of Loreno, there were two very liberal and vigorous knights, each
of them an ancient baron of certain castles and villas located around the said
city, of whom one was called the lord of Cundì and the other Sir Jannes of
Bruscie. And as fortune had granted to the Lord of Cundì an only daughter named Martina, full of singular virtue and praiseworthy manners for
one of her tender age, and beautiful in body and face beyond all the
others of her region, so too Sir Jannes, of the many sons which he had
begotten, was left with only one. Almost the same age as Martina, his
name was Loisi, and he was very handsome, of good courage, and full of
every virtue. Although between them there was a certain distant kinship,
nonetheless such an ever-increasing friendship and familiarity had been
contracted between their ancient grandfathers that, besides continually
visiting each others' houses, they appeared to hold their servants and
other goods in common, so that one could barely find any division between them.

And as Loisi was by now entering the age of manhood, it happened
that from his and Martina's continually seeing each other without any
suspicion or guard and from their great familiarity with each other, they
found themselves equally enamoured with each other and burned within
by such flames of love that neither one could or knew how to get any rest
unless they were talking and playing together, as they were drawn to do
by love and their blossoming age. And in such loving joy they spent many
years of their youth with happy fortune, without proceeding to any illicit
action. And although each one deeply desired to taste the ultimate and
sweetest fruits of love, nonetheless Loisi, whose passion was somewhat
more temperate, shunning the dishonor to the young girl and to her family,
had resolved within himself never to join with her carnally unless it were
allowed him by the laws of marriage; and he often revealed this virtuous
and unshakeable intention to his Martina; and as it pleased her very much,

she frequently urged him that this marriage be suggested to their parents
by some faithful advocate. Loisi, who wanted nothing else, had his father
make the request himself in a very proper manner to the Lord of Cundì;
who, having absolutely refused the alliance for many true reasons, requested Sir Jannes honestly and temperately that, for the preservation of
their common honor, the visiting between their children be henceforth
restricted and that Loisi not come to their house for any but the most
urgent necessity. Whereupon they were not only denied marriage but
also prohibited from seeing each other by everyone in every way.

When they heard this, it would be long and superfluous to recount
how great and of what sort were the loving laments, the bitter complaints,
and the fiery internal sighs of the two lovers, and the pain that most afflicted poor Loisi was the thought that such evil had befallen him as the
result of his acting with complete virtue, so that he himself did not know
by what chain his soul was still held to his body; yet he decided to visit
his Martina with letters sent by a faithful messenger of theirs, and to ask
her dearly to advise him if she knew of any means for their comfort; and
having written the letter, he sent it to her in a very discreet manner.

The girl, having resolved with intolerable grief to demonstrate the
greatness of her spirit, when she saw the messenger, took the letter with a
tear-streaked face, and having read it, hindered by grief and by her in-
ability to respond by letter, said to the secret bearer, "O you who alone
have knowledge of our hidden and fierce passion, commend me to him
who sent you to me, and tell him that either he will be my husband and
the only lord of my life or else truly I will gladly chase my soul from my
afflicted body with either weapon or poison. And seeing that his supreme
virtue in seeking rather the honor of my father than the love to which our
youth incited us has converted our greatest delights into the impossibility
of our seeing and speaking with each other, nonetheless, if he has the
heart to come, accompanied by a few of his men, to the foot of this castle
under the window of my bedroom with a rope ladder and anything else
necessary for lowering me down to him, I will come at once, and we will
go to the castle of some common relative, and there we will contract our
marriage. And when the deed is known, if my father is content, all will be
well; and if not, it will be done nonetheless, and he will have to use his
wisdom, converting his impotence into virtuous generosity. And if Loisi
is ready to do this, let him come to me this very night in the manner I
have said, without further delay."

Having carefully heeded the message and the signal she had devised to
safeguard them from mistaking one another for somebody else, the faithful

servant left her and, coming to his master, told him everything in detail. Loisi did not need much urging to pursue the deed; but having hastily sought out about twenty bold and spirited young men, his servants and faithful vassals, he made all the necessary arrangements. When night fell, he went quietly and noiselessly by a short road and in a few hours found himself with his companions under the designated window of his lady. And when he had given the established signal, she, who was waiting eagerly, hearing and recognizing it, immediately threw down a strong cord to which he tied the ladder; she, having pulled the ladder up to herself and having attached the iron hooks firmly to the window ledge, calmly, as if she had done it many times, climbed down and was received into the arms of her Loisi. After infinite kisses, they set off on their way, riding on two mares brought for the purpose, and bid their guide lead them where he was supposed to; and the servants, some in front and some in back, followed the way with great pleasure.

But their contrary fates, having perhaps decided otherwise, brought them to a bitter end, and I think none so horrible has ever been heard; for they had barely gone a mile when a rainstorm poured down upon them so heavily and so continually, with such a conflict of winds and thick hail, of frightening thunder and lightning, that it seemed the machine of the world was crashing to ruin about them. The darkness was so great and the tempest so irksome that not only those on foot, and for the most part in light jackets, lost their way together with the guide, some fleeing this way and others that way wherever they thought they might best find shelter, but even the two lovers, holding tightly to each others' hands, could barely see each other; and thoroughly frightened and terrified, lest this sudden manifestation be God's lash sent upon them for their rapine, not knowing where they were or which way to go, hearing none of their companions nor receiving any answer, though they called them many times aloud, the lovers commended themselves to God and, giving free rein to the horses, committed their path together with their life to the judgment of the horses and of fortune.

And having wandered many miles hither and thither like a ship without a navigator, beckoned by cruel death towards its final torment, they saw a little light in the distance and, taking some hope from it, directed their horses towards the said light without, however, the wickedness of the weather abating in the least. And after going a long way, arriving at the place where the light was shining, knocking at the door and having it answered and opened for them, they found it was a hostel of lepers. Some of the wasted members, coming forward, asked them with little

charity what had brought them there at such an hour. As the two youngsters were so chilled and weakened that they could barely speak, Loisi
answered as briefly as he could that the perversity of the weather and
their cross fortune had been the cause; and then he begged them for the
love of God to allow them a bit of the fire and a place to put their tired
horses. The lepers, who can be compared to the damned as destitute of
any hope of being saved[17], so that in them reigns no kindness or charity,
nonetheless moved by a weak compassion, they helped the couple to dismount and, putting the horses with their asses, brought them into their
kitchen by a big fire and sat down with them; and though the nature of
the two youngsters was somewhat repelled by the presence of such rotted
and ruined folk, yet, unable to go further, they did their best to make
their peace with it.

The fire worked its virtue upon Loisi and Martina, whose revived
beauty made them look like Diana and Narcissus; this then was the
reason for which one of the impious scoundrels of the said ruined folk,
who had been a mercenary in the last war and was more deformed and
rotten than the others, entered into an unbridled desire to have carnal
knowledge of the pretty girl and, assaulted by wild lust, resolved firmly
by means of her young lover's death to enjoy such a worthy prey. Without further ado, confiding in one of his companions no less scoundrelly
and inhuman than he, he went with him to the stall; and one of them, undoing the horses and making a lot of noise, called out, "O gentleman,
come and attend to your horses so that they don't bother our asses"; and
the other, standing behind the door with a big axe in hand, waited to perform the horrible murder.

Ah, scoundrel Fortune, always turning and never content with the long
happiness of any subject of yours, with what flattering hopes you
brought these two innocent doves into the ultimate net of their cruel
death! And if it did not please you that the wretched lovers should sail
successfully across tranquil and calm seas, did you not have infinite other
ways, both in life and in death, to separate them? Did you deliberately
choose this particular way because it was the cruelest? Surely I know not
what else to say about your detestable operations except woe unto him
who places his faith and hope in you!

Loisi, hearing himself called, although he was reluctant to leave the
fire, nonetheless, in order to take care of his horses, made his way with
weak steps towards the stall, leaving his lady in the company of many
others of the said lepers, both male and female; no sooner had he arrived
than the fierce scoundrel gave him such a blow on the head with the said

axe that before he could say "Alas!" he fell dead to the ground; and although they knew that he was dead indeed, they struck at his head with many other unmerciful blows. Leaving him there, they went to where the unhappy girl was and, being leaders among the others, ordered the rest of the group to go to their own places to sleep; and at once it was done.

Poor Martina, remaining alone and asking after her Loisi, received no reply, until at last the murderer, coming forward, with his hoarse and ruined voice said to her, "My girl, you must be patient, for we have now killed your man, and therefore don't have any more hope for him, for I intend as long as I live to enjoy your lovely body."

O pitiful and tearful ladies who have deigned to read and hear in my lowly tale the most cruel and unheard of case, if any of you ever loved your husband solely or were fiercely impassioned for some other lover, and you, young enamoured girls who are now in the flower of your life, if ever at any time love heated your breasts with equal flames, ah! I pray you, if any humanity reigns in you, accompany with your dolorous tears the weeping of my pen, which does not know how or cannot write the bitter and intolerable grief which that girl, more unfortunate than any other woman, felt at that moment. However, wishing to narrate some part of it, I picture to myself the fearful image of those lepers standing around the miserable girl, with their eyes bloodshot and brows peeled, their noses eaten away, their cheeks swollen and blotched with different colors, their lips twisted and rotten, their hands filthy, paralytic, and contorted, who, as we see, resemble more closely a diabolic than a human form; and such is the force of these figures that they impede my trembling hand so that it is no longer able to write.

You then who listen with pity, consider what thoughts were hers, and how much fear, besides grief, sprang from seeing herself between two most ferocious dogs, so inflamed that each seemed to want to be first in the race. She, besides uttering tremendous screams and beating her head many times against the wall, frequently fainting away and then coming back to herself, with her delicate face all scratched and bloody, recognizing that there was no escape or rescue for her safety, resolved without further fear to follow and accompany her Loisi in death as she had done in life; and turning to those rapacious brutes, she said:

"O pitiless and inhuman spirits, by the one God I pray you that since you have deprived me of the only treasure of my life, before you proceed to further action on my body, grant me the special grace to see briefly the dead body of my poor lord and to have the satisfaction of washing his bloody face a little with my bitter tears."

They, whose thoughts were far from what the lady intended to do, and also to please her, conceded to her request and led her to the place where the unfortunate Loisi lay dead. At seeing him, seized with fury like a madwoman, with a cry which reached heaven, without any restraint, she threw herself upon him; and after she had somewhat sated herself with weeping and kissing him, although she had a small knife ready to execute her cruel intent, nonetheless, looking at her lover's side and seeing the dagger that they had left there, she thought it a quieter and more expeditious means for success in her design; and secretly taking it and concealing it between herself and the dead body, she said:

"Before the ready blade pierces my heart, I call to you, gracious spirit of my lord, which a short time ago made a violent departure from this afflicted body; I beg you let it not irk you to wait for mine, which will gladly join itself with you; may the eternal love burning with equal flames hold us both tightly bound together; and if it was not allowed our corruptible bodies during their lifetime to enjoy living together in this world and to demonstrate to each other their unique love, I wish that our souls may be eternal only that they may enjoy being knitted together, and whatsoever place may be assigned to them, may both dwell there forever. And you, o noble and well-beloved body, will receive in sacrifice and marriage my body, which with such liberality hastens to follow where you go; it was reserved to you not in pleasure but as a victim; and the funeral offerings, which people are wont to give to complete the funeral rites, will be our blood commingled and befouled in this vile place, together with the tears of our stern fathers."

And having said this, although she desired at greater length to weep and lament and had other piteous words left to say, yet, thinking to execute her last and premeditated course, she carefully set the handle of the said dagger on the breast of the dead body and the sharp point right at her heart and, pressing herself upon it without reluctance or fear, let herself be run through by the cold blade, saying, "Ah! pitiless dogs, take the prey you so much desired"; and closely embracing her dead lover, she departed from this life of sorrow. They had barely heard the last words when they saw more than a palm-length of blade pushing out between her shoulders. At this they were nearly dead with regret and, fearing for their lives, immediately dug a big ditch in the stall and, without disturbing how they lay, buried the lovers.

Such a dolorous and cruel end, then, had the loving couple as I have with my tearful pen now told. After many fierce and mortal battles between their fathers and great slaughter among their people, the justice of

God did not want such an enormous crime to go unavenged but made punishment follow the murderers; and because of an enmity among the lepers which developed as time went on, one of the lepers from that hostel revealed truly what had been done. The said barons, hearing this, by mutual accord sent someone to the designated place in that hostel, and digging out the ditch, they found the bodies of the noble and unfortunate lovers. Although they were all rotted and ruined, the dagger bore witness of their cruel and pitiless death. And when they had been taken out of the vile place and put into a wooden coffin and carried away, the doors were locked; and fire being set inside and all around, the whole population there with their goods, their living quarters, and even their church, were all converted to ashes in a few hours. And the two corpses, carried into the city of Nancy, with the general grief, weeping, and mourning attire not only of the relatives, friends, and citizens, but also of all the foreigners, were buried in the same grave with a holy and solemn service; and a worthy inscription was written on the tomb in memory of the two wretched lovers: "Envious fortune and hostile fate brought to a cruel death the two lovers buried here, Loisi and Martina, who ended in bitter desire: offer tears; offer weeping, you who read."

Masuccio

We can consider this report no less abhorrent and cruel than lamentable and pitiful. I do not know whether its nature will do to others what it has done to me; and that is, that whenever I see a leper or recall this deed, then I always picture before my eyes the two poor youngsters closely embraced together in that stall and dead, rolled in filth and stained with their own blood. Wherefore not only have I lost all compassionate charity which I used to feel for that ruined folk, but I am now left with so great a hatred for them that nature has apparently granted me to proceed against all of them in revenge for the two unhappy lovers. And because I remember that I promised above to cover past grief with new pleasantness, withdrawing my pen from their miseries for now and leaving the poor lovers in peace, I will follow next with another case so different from the other just told that just as the one must always be read with weeping, so the other is to be perused to the end with frequent laughter.

Antonio di Tuccio Manetti (1423–1497)

T he long *novella sciolta* or single tale of "Fatso the Carpenter" is generally attributed to the Florentine Antonio Manetti, a mathematician, architect, and friend of other artists. He is also the supposed author of a *Life of Filippo Brunelleschi* and did certainly continue the execution of Brunelleschi's plans for the church of San Lorenzo after the famous architect had died. His admiration for Brunelleschi manifests itself in this tale, which celebrates the architect's cleverness in arranging an elaborate joke. Beyond that, it celebrates Florentine craftsmanship in general and the international demand for its products; for even the poor butt of the prank becomes wealthy and respected for his work at the royal court of Bohemia.

The story ends with an account of its own transmission through a series of retellings and mentions the existence of several versions of the tale. Three different versions still exist. The present translation is based on the text in *Prosatori volgari del quattrocento* edited by Claudio Varese, La Letteratura Italiana: Storia e Testi, vol. 14 (Milan: Riccardo Ricciardi, 1955), which includes notes and a very brief bibliography. Other notes to this long version can be found in the *Novelle del Quattrocento*, edited by Giuseppe Fatini (Turin: UTET, 1929). Two shorter versions have also been published, one by Domenico Maria Mani in the *Libro di novelle e di bel parlar gentile* (Florence, 1782), 2, p.248ff; and the other by Michele Barbi in *Studi di filologia italiana,* Bulletino della R. Accademia della Crusca I (1927), 133–44. It has been translated by Roscoe and Valency, but Roscoe's version is not full-length. There is very little written about this tale, and nothing that I know of in English.

Fatso the Carpenter

T he city of Florence has had many merry and pleasant fellows in times past, and especially in recent times, for one evening, in the year 1409, a certain group of many good fellows made up of government officials and masters of various arts and of wit, such as painters, goldsmiths, sculptors, and carpenters and similar artisans, gathered to dine together, as was their custom, at the house of Tomaso Pecori. Pecori was a very good fellow, merry and intelligent, who had invited them because he took greatest pleasure from their company. Having dined happily, and sitting down around the fire because it was winter, speaking separately and together of diverse and pleasant matters, they discussed among themselves for the most part their own arts and professions. And while they were conversing together, one of them said, "Why isn't Manetto the carpenter here this evening?"[1] (For this was the name of one of them who was nicknamed Fatso.) And it turned out that several of them had told him about the evening but had been unable to induce him to come for whatever reason. This carpenter had his shop on the Piazza San Giovanni and was at that time one of the finest masters of his art in Florence. Among other things he was reputed to be very good at making both ornamental toppieces and panels for altars and such things, at which not every carpenter is skilled. He was a very good-natured person, as are most fat people, and in truth he was a bit simple, about twenty-eight years old, large of build and stout, on account of which he was usually called Fatso by everyone. However, he was not so simple that his simplicity was recognized by anyone but sharp men, for he was no fool. And because he had always been in the habit of joining this group, his absence that evening gave them reason to try to imagine the cause; and unable to find any other, they concluded that some eccentricity, with which even he was slightly affected, had kept him away. As they were feeling somewhat scorned by him, because generally they were all of better status and circumstances than he, and as they were casting about merrily for how they could avenge this injury, the one who had spoken up first said, "We could play some trick on him to make him wiser the next time."

To which another replied, "What could we do to him except trap him into paying for a dinner without his taking part in it?"

There was among them Filippo di ser Brunellesco, a man of wonderful wit and intelligence, who is still renowned among most men.[2] This fellow, then, whose age at that time was about thirty-two and who, having spent much time with Fatso, had weighed his carats[3] and sometimes cautiously derived amusement from him, after thinking for a while, said, "What I'd like to do as vengeance for his not being here this evening is to play a merry prank on him of such a kind that we will long derive pleasure and amusement from it; if you would go along with me, that's what I'd like. Just now I had the idea that we could make him believe he had become someone else and is no longer Fatso the carpenter"; and he made a certain grin that was habitual to him and came from self-confidence.

And although the group knew Filippo to be very clever (for he is surely blind who does not see the sun), since thus he showed himself in his undertakings and in his work, nonetheless, even though they were not all unaware of Fatso's simplicity, the plan seemed to them all impossible to execute; but Filippo, explaining his reasoning and his careful and subtle arguments, as one who was very skilled at that, after much talk convinced them that it could be done. And having agreed on the method they should use so that the matter be kept secret, they concluded merrily that the vengeance should be enacted and that Fatso should be made to believe he had become someone named Matteo, who was known to some of them and to Fatso too but who was not one of the intimate group that dined together; and some of the group, having drawn slightly aside, formed their plot with the greatest laughter in the world and said that the sooner it was carried out the better.

The beginning of this merry history was not delayed, for it happened the following evening in this manner. At about the hour when such artisans close their shops to work inside by lamplight, Filippo, as the one who was most familiar with Fatso and knew everything about him as well as he knew himself, because he discussed everything with him good-naturedly (for otherwise he wouldn't have been able to do what he was planning), went to the carpenter's shop where he had been a thousand times before at that hour; and as he was chatting with him a bit, there arrived, as planned, a boy all breathless who asked, "Is Filippo di ser Brunellesco here?"

To whom Filippo, stepping forward, said, "I am he; what do you want?"

Answered the boy, "If you are he, you must come at once to your house."

Said Filippo, "God help me! What news?"

Replied the boy, "I was sent running to you, and the reason is that two hours ago your mother had a terrible attack and is almost dead; so come quickly."

Filippo, pretending to be much surprised at this event, commending himself once again to God, bid Fatso good-bye; but Fatso, being his friend, said, "I will come with you, in case I am more needed there than here; in cases like this one shouldn't spare one's friends; I will lock up the shop and come along."

Filippo, thanking him, said, "I don't want you to come right now; this matter can't be very important, surely; but if I need anything, I will send someone to tell you; do me a favor and stay a while in your shop and don't leave it for anything in case I need you; and if you haven't heard from me after a while, go do what you wish."

When Filippo left, having secured Fatso in his shop and pretending to go home, he went by an alleyway to Fatso's house, which was near Santa

Maria del Fiore; and having opened the door with a knife, as he knew how to do, he entered the house and locked himself in with the bolt so that no one could get in. Fatso had a mother, but she had gone into the country to Polverosa during those days in order to do laundry and to salt the meat and other such tasks, as it happens, and she was due back any day, according to Fatso's opinion; and that was why he had left the door unbolted, and Filippo knew it.

After Fatso had stayed in his shop for a while and then had locked it up, in order to satisfy more fully his promise to Filippo, he walked many times back and forth around the shop and finally said, "Filippo's affairs can't be going badly, and he won't need me." With these words he set off for home and, arriving at the door which was two flights up, tried to open it in his accustomed manner; and trying many times and not being able, he noticed that the door was bolted within. Therefore, knocking loudly, he said, "Who's up there? Open up," figuring that his mother had returned and had locked the door as a precaution or perhaps absentmindedly.

Filippo, coming to the top of the stairs, counterfeiting Fatso's voice so that he sounded just like him, said, "Who's down there?"

Fatso, although he thought the voice different from his mother's, said, "It's Fatso."

At which Filippo pretended to take the carpenter for Matteo whom they were going to make Fatso believe he had become, and he said, "Ah, Matteo, go away, for I have a mountain of troubles. A few hours ago, while Filippo di ser Brunellesco was at my shop, someone came to tell him that his mother was nearly dead; I've had a bad evening because of it." And turning away, he pretended to say to the mother: "Make me supper; you should have been here two days ago, and here you arrive at night too"; and he continued with further grumbling.

Fatso, hearing whoever was in the house grumble at his mother and noting that not only the voice but all the actions and manners seemed his own, said to himself, "What's all this? That fellow who's upstairs seems to be me, since he says that Filippo was at his shop and that someone came to tell him that his mother was ill; and besides he is shouting at Lady Giovanna and has my voice; could I be confused?"

And as he descended the two flights and was backing away in order to call up to the windows, Donatello the sculptor,[4] whose skill is famous to all, and who was a member of the dinner group and a friend of Fatso's, came by as planned; and passing him in the twilight, he said, "Good evening, Matteo, are you looking for Fatso? He went home just a short while ago." And he did not stop but went on about his business.

If Fatso had been surprised before, he was now much more surprised, hearing that Donatello called him Matteo. And remaining stunned and confused, for the yes and the no were debating in his head, as he went to Piazza San Giovanni, saying to himself, "I will stand here until someone passes by who knows me and will say who I am," adding, "Alas! could I be Calandrino⁵ to have so suddenly become another person without realizing it!"

And as he stood there, half beside himself, there arrived as planned six officers of the Court of Commerce and one bailiff, and among them was a man pretending that he was a creditor of that Matteo whom Fatso was beginning to believe himself to be; and coming up to Fatso, he turned to the bailiff and to the officers and said, "Take Matteo here away; he is my debtor; you see, I've been on your tail until I caught you."

And the officers and bailiff seized him and began to take him away. Fatso, turning to the man who had had him arrested and bracing his feet in front, said to him, "What do I have to do with you that you have me arrested? Tell them to let me go; you have mistaken me for someone else; I'm not who you think, and you do great wrong to embarrass me this way when I have nothing to do with you; I am Fatso the carpenter, and I'm not Matteo, and I don't know what Matteo you're talking about."

And he tried to scuffle, being large and strong; but they seized his arms at once, and the creditor, stepping forward, stared him hard in the face saying "What do you mean, you have nothing to do with me? As if I didn't know Matteo my debtor from Fatso the carpenter! I wrote your name down in my book; and what's more it's been there a year or more; what do you mean you have nothing to do with me? He claims he is not Matteo, the scoundrel! Take him away! This time you'll have to pay before you get out of it; we'll see whether you're he or not." And thus quarreling, they took him to the Court; and because it was about half an hour before dinner time and quite dark, they met no one who knew him either on the way or there.

When they arrived there, the clerk pretended to write Matteo's name in the register, for he had been informed about everything by Tomaso Pecori, who was a good friend of his; and they put him in jail. The other prisoners, having heard the uproar when he arrived and hearing him called Matteo several times, accepted that this was his name without asking him further when he was among them, there being by chance no one who knew him except perhaps by sight; and hearing and seeing himself called Matteo by everyone when they wanted him, with great agitation he thought he must surely be somebody else. And having been asked why he was arrested, he said, totally befuddled, "I owe someone some money, and so I'm here; but I'll clear this up early tomorrow morning."

And the prisoners said, "You see, we're about to have supper; sup with us and then tomorrow morning you'll clear this up; but we warn you that one always stays here longer than one expects; may God give you his grace so that it doesn't happen like that to you."

Fatso accepted the invitation but ate little; and when they had supped, one of them lent him one side of his narrow cot, saying, "Matteo, stay here as comfortably as you can for tonight, and tomorrow morning if you get out, fine, and if not, you can send for some bedding from home." Fatso thanked him and settled down to sleep as well as he could.

When the errand boy who had played the part of the creditor had accomplished whatever was necessary at the Court, Filippo di ser Brunellesco conferred with him and learned from him all the details about the arrest and their taking the carpenter to prison, and went away. Fatso, having lain down on that cot and thinking about all this, said to himself, "What should I do if I have become Matteo? For it seems to me certain by now, from so many signs that I've seen, and from everyone's agreeing about it; but which Matteo is this? Suppose I send home to my mother and Fatso is there, for I heard him there? Since that's how it is, they will laugh at me." And with these thoughts, sometimes affirming that he was Matteo and sometimes that he was Fatso, he lay until morning, scarcely sleeping at all but always full of foolish fancies that tormented him from all sides. And having arisen with the others, he stood by the little window in the prison door, judging that surely someone would come by who knew him, to draw him out of the doubts into which he had entered that night; into the Court came Giovanni di Lord Francesco Rucellai,[6] who was one of their group and who had been present at the dinner and merry plotting. He was well known to Fatso, who was at that time making him an ornamental top for a Madonna, and just the day before he had been with Fatso for quite a while at his shop to hurry him on and had promised to pay him in four days. This man, arriving at the Court, put his head inside the door across from the prisoners' window, where Fatso was standing, which at that time was on the ground floor; and seeing Giovanni, Fatso began to look him in the face and grin; and Giovanni, as if he were seeking something, looked at him as if he had never seen him, for Matteo was not an acquaintance of his or so he feigned, and said, "What are you laughing about, comrade?"

Fatso said, "Nothing, no"; and seeing that he didn't recognize him, asked, "My good man, would you happen to know someone named Fatso who has a place on the Piazza San Giovanni, behind there, and makes inlaid woodwork?"

"Are you speaking to me?" said Giovanni, continuing, "Why, I know him well; oh! he's my best friend, and I'll be going to him soon for some work that he's doing; were you arrested at his demand?"

Fatso answered, "No, Santa Maria!" then he continued, "Excuse me, but I will ask you something confidential; eh, do me a favor since you're going to him anyway, eh, tell him, 'A friend of yours has been taken to jail and asks as a favor that you stop by briefly for a word.'"

Said Giovanni, looking him continually in the face, barely able to keep from laughing, "Who is it I am to say is sending for him?" (So that he would confess to being Matteo, in order that Giovanni might tease him about it afterwards.)

Said Fatso, "Never mind, it's enough just to tell him that."

Then said Giovanni, "I will do it gladly, if that's all"; and he left; and finding Filippo, he informed him of everything, laughing.

Remaining at the prison window, Fatso said to himself, "Now I can be sure that I am no longer Fatso. Oh! Giovanni Rucellai never took his eyes off me; he doesn't know me, he who is in my shop all the time! Yet he hasn't lost his memory! I am certainly no longer Fatso but have become Matteo. Cursed be my lot and my misfortune! For if this event gets out, I will be shamed and considered mad; children will run after me, and I'll run a thousand dangers. Besides, what have I to do with another man's debts, I, and with troubles that I always kept myself out of? And with a thousand other errors that may endanger me? Moreover, I can't discuss this with anyone; I can't get any advice about this; and God knows whether I need any! In every way I'm badly off. But let's see whether Fatso comes, and then perhaps I'll understand what all this means: could he have become me?" Whereupon, having waited a long time for the other Fatso to come, and not seeing him arrive, Fatso drew back from the bars to make way for another man and stared now at the floor, now at the ceiling, clasping his hands together.

In those days there was a very worthy judge whose name is better left unsaid. This man, who was no less renowned for letters than for law, was being held for debt in the same prison. Having made arrangements for his own case, he was soon to be free and no longer felt troubled. Thus although he was not acquainted with Fatso and knew nothing about him, yet seeing him so melancholy and noting his gestures and thinking that it was because of the debt which was weighing on his mind, this man tried charitably to comfort him, as people sometimes do, saying, "Hey, Matteo, you are as melancholy as if you were going to lose your life or were in danger of some great shame; and according to what you say, it's a small debt. One mustn't get so discouraged by fortune; why don't you send for some friend or relative? Don't you have anyone? Eh! try to pay or to come to terms of some sort so that you get out out of jail, and don't make yourself so melancholy."

Seeing himself so lovingly comforted and with such kind words, Fatso did not say to him as he might have to someone else, "Why don't you look after your own business?" but thought more wisely, knowing him to be an honorable man; and he decided to speak to him with all respect, even though he was in jail, and to reveal to him completely the case that had befallen him. Drawing him into a corner of the prison, he said, "Sir, although you don't know me, I know you well and know that you are a worthy man; therefore your kindness to me is the reason that I have decided to tell you what is making me so melancholy, for I don't want you to think, neither you nor anyone, that for a small debt, even though I am a poor artisan, I would be in such distress; but it's something else which is bothering me, and perhaps something which has never happened to anyone else in the world." The judge was not a little surprised hearing him say these words and stayed to hear him with great attention.

Fatso began from the beginning and told all the way to the end what had befallen him, with effort holding back his tears, begging him heartily two things: one, that he never speak to anyone about this on his honor; the other, that he give him some advice and help, adding, "For I know that you have long read many things and both ancient and modern histories and the writings of men about many events; did you ever come upon anything similar?"

The worthy man, having heard him out, considering the matter at once, imagined that one of two things must be true: that is, either that this fellow as a man of small courage had lost his wits because of an overwhelming melancholy on account of the present case or for some other cause, or else that it truly was a prank, as it was. And in order to understand him better, he replied that he had read about many such cases, that is, where one person became someone else, and that it was nothing new; indeed there was worse, for some had become brute beasts, like Apuleius who became an ass, and Actaeon who became a stag.[7] "And one reads of many others which I don't recall right now"; for he thought to have a bit of amusement.

To whom Fatso said, "Oh! I would never have believed it!" and he gave it the same faith that one gives to every truth. Then he added, "Now tell me, if I who was Fatso have become Matteo, what must have happened to him?"

To whom the judge replied, "He must have become Fatso; this is a case of exchange, and it usually happens this way, according to what one reads and according to what I have seen up till now, which indeed has been several incidents; and it can't be otherwise; I would certainly like to see this fellow a bit, this is certainly a laughable matter."

"For those whom it doesn't touch," said Fatso.

"That's true," continued the judge, "it's a great misfortune, and God keep every man from it; we are all under the same threat. I had a worker once to whom this same thing happened." Fatso sighed loudly and did not know what else to say, since that's how it was. The judge added, "One reads the same about the companions of Ulysses and other men transformed by Circe. It's true, according to what I hear and have read, if I remember rightly, that some have returned to themselves, but it happens rarely if the case goes on for long." He said this to entangle him further, at which Fatso was stunned.

And he was still in this state at about three and had not eaten yet when two of Matteo's brothers came to the Court of Commerce and asked the clerk of the Treasury whether a brother of theirs named Matteo had been arrested and for how much debt he was there, because they wanted to get him out of jail. The clerk of the Treasury said yes and, pretending to look him up in the register, after turning a few pages said, "He's in for such an amount, at the petition of so-and-so."

"It's too much," said one of them; then they said, "We would like to speak with him briefly, and then we will arrange to pay for him"; and going to the jail, they said to someone who was at the little grating, "Tell Matteo that two of his brothers are here, and have come here briefly"; and looking in, they recognized the judge who happened to be talking with Fatso.

Receiving the message, Fatso asked the judge what happened afterwards to his worker; and hearing that he never recovered, Fatso, with his worries redoubled, came to the grating and greeted them; the older brother began to say to him, "You're still up to your old tricks, Matteo," always looking him in the face; "You know how many times we have warned you about these wicked ways of yours, and how many times we have bailed you out of this jail and others, but telling you does no good at all, for you always do worse. How we manage to do it, God knows better than anyone; for you have since recently consumed a treasure; and who ever saw any good for what you spent? Rather, you have thrown it away and wasted it. What's more, at every game they mock you: don't you have stolen money? And we bear these sufferings and even the shame is all ours, for you don't care a bit; rather you seem to do everything to insult your companion and think you have justified yourself when you've said, 'You've mistaken me for someone else.' Are you a child? You are surely by now beyond childhood. But be certain of this, that if it weren't for our honor and for the urgings of our mother, for whom we are more concerned than for you, for she is old and frail, this would have been the time—you've given us so many—that we would have left you to think about yourself; and we assure you once and for all that if you ever get in trouble again, come what may, you will stay in a lot longer than you'd like; and let this suffice you for now." And having paused a while without saying anything, he continued, "And so that we aren't seen every day going about these matters, we will come for you this evening at the hour of the Ave Maria, when there will be fewer people about, so that everyone doesn't have to know our miseries and make us ashamed for your doings."

Fatso turned to them with kind words, believing by now without doubt that he was Matteo (since they were paying for him and had both looked him continually in the face, and it was not dark), saying to them that for certain they would never again be troubled with his affairs and that he would no longer behave the way he had up till now and that if he ever again fell into similar errors, they should mock him and his mother and any other intermediary he might use, for he was now resolved entirely to be Matteo, begging them for God's sake to come for him at the assigned hour; and they said they would, and left; and he turned back and said to that judge, drawing him close, "It's even better, for two of Matteo's brothers, brothers of this Matteo in whose place I am here—how should I say it?" and he looked into the judge's eyes. "And they spoke with me face to face, both of them, as you saw, just as if I were Matteo, and after a long admonition, they told me that at the Ave Maria they would come for me and would take me out of jail"; adding, "Up till now I wouldn't have believed it, but now I'm convinced of what you say"; and then he said, "So that worker of yours never returned to his former self?"

"Never, poor fellow," said the judge.

Fatso let out a big sigh, then added, "Lo, they will bail me out of here; where will I go and where will I return? I can't go back home; but which is my home? This is the rub; listen to me," and he looked at the judge, "For if Fatso is there, as he certainly is, for I heard him with these ears, what shall I say so as not to be considered mad and deceived? Oh, you know, I will go into the house as if it were mine; Fatso will be there perhaps and will say, 'Is this fellow mad?' and if he's not there and comes home later and finds me there, what will happen? Who is to stay there and who is to go?" Then he added, "You know, oh, if I hadn't been at home, wouldn't my mother have had me searched for and found even if I were in the stars? But seeing him before her, she is unaware of my plight."

The judge with great effort kept from laughing and was amused no end and said, "Don't go there, but go with these men who say they are your brothers, and see where they lead you and what they do with you; what can you lose by this? In any case, they're paying for you."

"It's true," said Fatso.

And the judge added, "When you get out of prison and are received without doubt as their brother, who knows, maybe you'll be better off; maybe they are wealthier than you."

As they were thus conversing, evening began to fall, and it seemed a thousand years to the judge until he could get free of this man in order to laugh, and he couldn't hang on any longer. Those who played the part of Fatso's brothers had hung around the Court of Commerce laughing continually, waiting until it was time, and they had seen that judge's case arranged and saw him come out soberly, looking just as if he had been talking with the magistrate as they sometimes do for clients in a trial, and they saw him go on his way. And when the clerk had returned to his seat, they came forward pretending to have settled with the creditor and the treasurer.

The clerk rose from his seat again with the prison keys and, going over there, said, "Which one is Matteo?"

Fatso, having no further doubt about being Matteo, stepped forward and replied, "Here I am, Sir."

The clerk looked at him and said, "These brothers of yours have paid your whole debt for you, so you are free," and opening the prison door, he said, "Come this way."

Fatso, coming forth, now that it was already very dark, felt glad to be out of jail without having had to let go of a penny. And because he had gone all day without eating, he thought of going home as soon as he was out the door; then, remembering that he had heard Fatso's voice at his home the evening before, he changed his mind and decided to follow the judge's advice, and went with them, who lived by Santa Filicità at the bottom of the Hill; and while they were walking together, they scolded him on the way, but sweetly, not with that sternness that they had shown in prison, and they informed him of the distress he had caused his mother and reminded him of the promises he had made them previously not to keep on in this way. And when they asked him why he had kept saying he was Fatso, whether it was because he really thought so or whether it was in order to make them believe that they had mistaken him and let him go, Fatso did not know what to answer; he hesitated and began to regret having gone with them; it seemed hard to him to confess that he was Matteo; on the other hand, he said to himself, "If I say once again that I am Fatso, perhaps they won't want me and I will have lost both their house and my own." He promised them never again to behave that way; and to the part about his telling them he was Fatso, he did not answer but let time elapse in between.

And in this way they arrived at home; and having arrived there, they went with him into a room on the ground floor, telling him, "Stay here until dinner time," as if they did not want to present him to his mother in order to spare her the grief.

And as there was a fire going and a small table set, one of them stayed by the fire with him, and the other went to the priest at Santa Filicità, who was their parish priest and a kind person, and said, "I come to you with trust, as one neighbor ought to go to another, and also because you are my and our spiritual father. We are three brothers (so that you may be better informed of everything and may act more effectively) here very near by to you, as you have perhaps noticed."

"Yes," said the priest, who knew them slightly.

And he continued, "One of us is named Matteo, who was arrested yesterday at the Court of Commerce for a debt; and because this is not the first time that we have bailed him out of there, he has become so melancholy about it that he seems to have somewhat lost his senses and seems to us obsessed about this event, although in all other respects he is truly the same Matteo that he used to be or almost; and the thing that's different is that he has gotten it into his head that he has become someone other than Matteo. You never heard such a fantastic thing! Yet he says that he is a certain Fatso the carpenter, an acquaintance of his, indeed, who has his shop behind San Giovanni and his house next to Santa Maria del Fiore; and many ways have been tried to get this out of his head, but nothing has helped. Therefore we have taken him out of jail and brought him home and put him in a room lest his follies be heard outside; for you know that whoever begins to show these signs, even though later he is back in the best of mental health, is made fun of ever after. And also, if our mother became aware of it before he recovered, it could cause some problems; what do I know? Women are of small courage, and she is frail and old. And therefore, in conclusion, we beg you in charity that you come to our house (we consider you a worthy man and know that you are a kind person and would be conscientious about not revealing this disgrace;

and for this reason we did not want to use anyone else), to try to get this fantasy out of his head. We will remain eternally obliged to you, and it will win you merit in the eyes of God; not to mention that you are concerned with his salvation as he is one of your flock, and you have to give account of him; for if he were mad, being in mortal sin, in dying without returning to himself, he would perhaps be damned."

The priest replied that this was true and that it was his duty and desire to make every effort. And this is the truth for, besides the duty, he was by nature glad to be of service. Then, pausing a moment, he said, "His condition could be such that effort will not be wasted; bring me to him"; adding, "unless he is dangerous."

"No, Santa Maria," said the brother, "Oh! I understand you, you mean unless he is enraged."

"Well, you know," said the priest, "that people like this have no regard for their father let alone for the priest, for they think they're seeing something other than what it is."

"Mister Priest, I understand you," said the brother, "and you are right to ask about it; but this man, as I tell you, is more obsessed than enraged, and from the outside neither you nor anyone would notice his error; and truly, if he were enraged, we would be beyond hope and would not make this effort, because rarely or never do such people recover. One can say this man has lost his way slightly rather than entirely, and we would like our mother to know nothing about it. It's because we are hopeful that we are acting this way."

"If that's how he is, I will see him," replied the priest, "and will make every effort as duty bids in a case like this. I also recognize the danger about your mother, as you say, and it is good to spare her this trouble if possible." Therefore the brother brought him home to the room where Fatso was.

Fatso, who was sitting in thought, rose to his feet upon seeing the priestly habit; and the priest said, "Good evening, Matteo."

And Fatso replied, "Good evening and good year."

"Now you're speaking this way," said the priest thinking he had already cured him; then he took him by the hand and said, "Matteo, I have come to sit with you for a little while." And he sat down by the fire and pulled up a bench beside him; and seeing that he was not making any demonstration of insisting that he was Fatso, as he had been told, he began to have good hope, making a sign to the brother who had brought him there that so far all the indications looked good, and gesturing him to remain outside; and so he did.

Then the priest began to speak in this way: "You must know, Matteo, that I am your parish priest and spiritual father; and it is my duty to comfort all my people as much as I can both in spirit and in body. I hear things which make me very sorry, and among them that you have recently been in jail for debt. I want you to understand that this is nothing new either for you or for others, nor should it seem so; for this world strikes daily blows of this kind and lesser and greater ones too, and one must always be prepared for them and have patience; this I say because I hear that you have made yourself so melancholy about it that you have nearly gone crazy; and worthy men do not act this way, but with the shield of patience and of providence, as much as they can, whenever necessary, they protect themselves from it all; and this is wisdom. What folly is this, which I hear among other things, that you have done and do, to say that you are no longer Matteo and wish by all means to be someone else named Fatso, who is a carpenter, and to make yourself the butt of mockery by this insistence with little honor to you? Truly, Matteo, you are much to blame when for a small adversity you have set such pain in your heart that it seems you have lost your senses. For six florins! Oh! Is that really such a big deal? And even now after they've been paid! Matteo my friend," said the priest squeezing his hand, "I don't want you to be like this any more; and for my love (and also for your honor and that of your family, who seem to me honest folk) I want you to promise me that from now on you will put an end to this fantasy and will attend to your business, as honest folk do and other men who have any sense; and commend yourself to God, for whoever places his hope in Him does not place it in vain. What's more you will do good and honor to yourself and to these brothers of yours and to all who love you, and to me too. How now! Is this Fatso such a grand master forsooth or such a rich man that you would rather be him than you? What advantage do you see in it for yourself to behave this way? Moreover, let's even suppose that this man was an honorable man, and that he was richer than you (though according to what your family tells me, he is rather several degrees lower), by saying that you are he you won't thereby have his honors nor his riches, if he had any; do what I say in this, for I am advising you for your own good. Alas! among other things, if you earned notoriety because of this, you would be in danger of having the children run after you, whereupon you would be in trouble and shame all the rest of your life; and that's all you would have accomplished by this; and I promise you to report well of you to your brothers and to make them willing both to love you and to help you always as their good brother. Come now, Matteo, dispose yourself to be a man and not a beast, and let these follies go; what is this question of Fatso or not Fatso? Do as I say, for I'm giving you good advice." And he kept looking him sweetly in the face.

Fatso, hearing with how much love this man was speaking to him and the fitting words he was using, not doubting in the least that he was Matteo, replied at once that he was ready to do whatever he could of what the priest had told him; and because he realized that the priest was saying it all for his own good, he promised him from then on to make every effort never again to try to persuade people that he was Fatso as he had done up till then, unless he became Fatso again; but he wished to ask one favor of him if possible, and this was that he wanted to talk to Fatso briefly for a good reason; and that by speaking with him, he thought he would easily put an end to his error; but if he didn't confer and talk with him, he doubted that he would be able to fulfill his promise.

And the priest grimaced and said, "Matteo my friend, all this goes against your business, and I see that you still have this idea in your head; what do you mean 'unless I become Fatso again'? I don't understand it; why do you need to talk with Fatso? What do you have to do with him? For the more you speak about him and the more people you talk to, the more you will reveal this matter; and the worse it will be, for you and your family." And he spoke so much about this that he made Fatso agree that he ought not to talk with the other Fatso, but he agreed very unwillingly.

In leaving, the priest told the brothers what he had said and what Fatso had replied and promised in the end, although he had agreed to it only with great reluctance; and from something that he said, which the priest did not understand very well, the priest was not at all certain that he would keep his promise, but he had done what he could. One of the brothers put a silver coin in his hand to make the matter more credible, thanked him for his labors and begged him to pray to God to make him sane again. The priest opened and shut his hand and, having taken leave of them, returned to the church.

While the priest had been talking with Fatso, Filippo di ser Brunellesco had arrived laughing heartily and, keeping his distance from the room where Fatso was, had one of the brothers inform him of everything concerning Fatso's exit from jail, of their conversation on the way home, and so on; and in informing him of all this, the brother told him about the judge they had seen talking with Fatso in prison, and how they had seen him go free; and Filippo had carefully noted and remembered everything, adding it to what had been said by the creditor that had him arrested. And having brought a beverage in a medicine bottle, he said to him,

"While you are having dinner, see that you give him this to drink, either in wine or in whatever manner seems best to you, so that he is not aware of it. This is an opiate which will make him sleep so soundly that even if he got a beating, he wouldn't feel it for several hours." And making this pact with them, he went away.

The brothers, reentering the room, sat down to dinner with Fatso, as it was already past nine-thirty; and as they were thus dining, they gave him the beverage, which was neither foul-tasting nor bitter, in such a way that he was not aware of it. And when they had dined, they sat for a while by the fire, talking all the while about these wicked ways of his and begging him that by his faith he would agree to abstain from such behavior, and especially that for their love and for their mother's love he would put off this madness of believing himself to have become someone else; and that it was too great an error, and that he shouldn't be surprised if they begged him, since it hurt them almost as much as it did him; for just today it had happened that as they were passing through the New Market in order to get the money for him, one of them had heard someone say behind him, "See there the fellow who has lost his memory, who has forgotten who he is and thinks he has become someone else;" although someone else said, "That's not the fellow, it's his brother." And while they were talking about this, the opiate began its work so that Fatso could not keep his eyes open.

They said to him, "Matteo, it looks as if you're falling asleep. You must have gotten little sleep last night." And they were right.

Fatso replied, "I swear to you that I have never felt so sleepy since I was born."

They said to him, "Go to bed if you wish." With difficulty he managed to undress and get into bed before he fell asleep so soundly that, as Filippo had said, he could have been beaten and not felt a thing, and he was snoring like a pig.

At the arranged hour, Filippo di ser Brunellesco returned with six companions, because Fatso was large and stout. All six of them had been to the dinner at Pecori's house and were sturdy, merry wags who wanted to take part in the joke, having begun to hear partly about it from Filippo who had been informing them all about everything with the greatest merriment in the world; and they entered the room where he was and, hearing him soundly asleep, took him and put him in a hamper with all his clothes and carried him to his own house, where by chance his mother had not yet returned from the countryside; and they knew it, for they were watching out for everything. And having put him in his bed, they put his clothes where he usually put them, but they placed his feet where he usually laid his head; and having done this, they took the key to the shop, which was hanging on his belt, and went to the said shop and, entering in, moved all his tools about from one place to another; and so they did too to his planes, turning the blades upside down, and so too the handles on his hammers, and on his saws they put the teeth towards the inside, and thus they worked on all the implements of his shop that they could, and they turned the whole shop upside-down so that it looked as if devils had been there; and having disordered everything, they relocked the shop, brought the key back to the house and hung it where it usually hung; and going outside and relocking the door, they went home to sleep.

Fatso, drugged by the beverage, slept all that night without coming to. But late in the morning at the hour of the Ave Maria at Santa Maria del Fiore, when the beverage had done all its work, he awoke, and recognizing the bell and having opened his eyes and taken a peep at the room, he recognized that he was in his own home, and suddenly a great joy came into his heart, believing he had returned to being Fatso and in control of everything; and thinking that he had previously been worse than in danger, he nearly wept for happiness; yet he was annoyed and surprised to have his feet where he usually put his head; and remembering the past events and where he had gone to bed the night before and where he now found himself, he suddenly fell into a mood of uncertainty as to whether he had dreamed it or was dreaming at present; and sometimes the past seemed surely true and sometimes the present, and he looked about the room saying, "This indeed is my room from when I was Fatso, but when did I enter here?" And he touched his arm with the other hand and vice versa, and his chest, assuring himself that he was Fatso. But then he reflected, "If it is thus, how was I taken for Matteo? For I remember indeed that I was in jail and that no one recognized me ever as anyone but Matteo, and that I was taken out by those two brothers; that I went to Santa Filicità and the priest talked to me so long and I dined and went to bed there, because I felt so sleepy." And he was again in the greatest confusion as to whether it had been a dream or whether he was dreaming now; and he began anew to feel anxious, but not so much that there wasn't always a bit of joy gleaming inside him, remembering what the judge had told him in jail and thinking that he must have turned back into Fatso rather than otherwise; and although he remembered very well from the event of his arrest until the whereabouts of his going to bed the night before, it did not bother him now that he was Fatso again, but it seemed to him to have come about quite naturally. Then he turned over in his mind the preceding events and said to himself again, "Who knows whether I dreamed it or am dreaming now?" And after a heartfelt sigh, he said, "God help me." And getting out of bed as in the past and dressing himself, he took the shop key and went there and, opening it, saw all his tools turned topsy-turvy, both generally and individually. And being still tangled in the thoughts of his bedroom, upon seeing this he was at once assailed by new thoughts, blotting out all the old ones with an inky brush.

And while he was pondering these events, unable to make up his mind whether he was doing or dreaming but glad to have become Fatso again and in possession of his things, here came Matteo's two brothers, and finding him so perplexed, pretending not to recognize him, one of them said, "Good day, master."

Fatso, turning and recognizing him, without replying to the greeting and without thinking about what to reply or taking council with himself, said, "What are you looking for?"

One of them answered, "It's true that we have a brother named Matteo who a few days ago, on account of being arrested for his debts, somewhat lost his wits with melancholy. It's a shame to us but that's how it is nonetheless; and among the other things which he says is that he is no longer Matteo, as he is named, but the master of this shop, who seems to be named Fatso; and although we have admonished him at length and had him spoken to, neither one means nor another will remove him from this silliness or foolishness, however we ought to call it. And just yesterday evening we brought our priest to him from Santa Filicità (for we're in that parish and he's a kind person), and he promised the priest to get this idea out of his head; he dined with us in the best possible mood and went to sleep in our presence; but this morning, without anyone hearing him, he left the door open and, perhaps long before dawn even, left the house; where he has gone, we don't know; and therefore we came here to see whether he happened by here, or whether you can tell us anything about him."

When Fatso heard them, who the day before had taken him out of jail at their own expense and received him into their home to eat and sleep and now did not recognize him as their brother, he thought it completely certified that he had become Fatso again, seeing too that he had come from his own house, and he decided to joke with them, bursting his seams with joy, and said to them, "I would look to see if he's at the Misericordia[8] if he's a child." But he did not follow up on this idea, for having a plane in his hand, of which he was turning the blade around, holding the blade thus in his hand (for he had a big hand), he looked them in the face; whereupon they, not finding him in the mood they expected, were afraid that he might attack them and decided to get out of his way and retreat.

In truth Fatso had no such intention; nonetheless, when they had left, being unable to imagine how this matter had come about, he decided to leave the shop for a while and go to Santa Maria del Fiore in order to think through his affairs at leisure and to assure himself further whether he were Fatso or Matteo by his encounters with other men; although since he had slept in his own house and since the two brothers did not recognize him as Matteo, he thought he was almost sure of it. And turning this uncertainty about in his head again, whether it had been a dream or truth, and what he was now, he was reaching for the hammer, then forgetting it and turning elsewhere, and then turning back for the hammer, full of confusion; but he worked until he became dejected, and pulling the shutter down and heading towards the church, behaving as he had done with the hammer, he walked four steps towards it and then turned three steps back. In the end he arrived there, saying to himself the while, "This has been a strange event; let the judge say what he will, I don't know how this happened." Then he said, "Everyone mistaking me, not just one person, surely that must mean something." And seeking to free himself from these thoughts and to find out only whether he had truly become Fatso again, he still couldn't get them off his mind; and with regard to his case, he worried all the while that he might turn back into Matteo or into someone else. And with all these thoughts crossing his mind, he wanted at once to find out (to clarify whether it was as the judge had said) what had happened in the meantime to Matteo; and not being seen by anyone who took notice of him, he walked up and down, as was later reported by someone who met him, so that he looked like a wounded lion.

It was a working day and few people were there; no one was looking and it seemed to him the right place to let off steam to himself; and while he was in this condition in church, he ran into Filippo and Donatello, who were talking to each other as was their habit; this time they had gone there on purpose, for they had been on the lookout and saw him enter. Filippo knew that Fatso had heard nothing about whether it was a joke or not, nor could he have any suspicion of them; and they thought that all they had done they had done very carefully and secretly. Filippo, looking happy and starting far off in order to dissimulate well, said, "It's going to be all right about my mother; it was an attack which by the time I got home had already almost passed, and therefore I didn't send for you; she's had it before; old people are like that. I haven't seen you since then; what happened to you last night? Did you hear about Matteo Mannini?"

And as Fatso was embarrassed, looking back and forth at Donatello and at him, Donatello said, "What's that?"

Replied Filippo, "Don't you know?" and turning to Fatso said, "It seems that on the evening when we were together, between eight and nine, he was arrested here on the piazza; and the man who was having him arrested (I don't know who it was, but that has nothing to do with the story) was there with the agents, and he kept saying to the bailiff and even to the officers, 'What do you want? You have mistaken me for someone else, I don't have debts with anyone, I am Fatso the carpenter, do you want *me*?'"

Fatso thought that what Filippo was saying was natural and beyond any suspicion of his knowing about anything; and Filippo continued thus, "The man who was having him arrested went up to him, because the bailiff said, 'Be sure of what you're having us do; we're putting on you the responsibility for this arrest; if this is not the man, you will lose the expenses; for we will want to be paid; not to mention that we too, without our fault, could get in trouble for it.'

"The man who was having him arrested, who was the collector for a bank, came up to him and looked at him hard and said, 'He's disguising his face, the scoundrel!' Then considering again, he said, 'It's Matteo all right, take him away, he'll pay for it this time forsooth!'

"And while they were leading him away, he kept saying on the way that he was Fatso the carpenter, affirming, 'Here's evidence that I just locked up the shop' and showing a key" (and these were all things that Fatso had in fact done, which had happened just the way the boy had reported them to Filippo), continuing, "And I hear that there was an amusing incident at the Court of Commerce too. Can it be that you haven't heard about it? For it has caused the biggest laugh in the world."

Donatello pretended that he too knew nothing about it and said, "I remember just now that yesterday someone was talking about it in the shop; but I was distracted and busy and didn't pay attention. But I heard, now I recall, these names 'Matteo' and 'Fatso' and 'arrested' and didn't think to ask about it later, not having Fatso in mind. Eh, tell me a bit, Filippo, what's this about, since you know? Oh this is certainly a good laugh, yes sir, that he was being arrested and didn't want to be Matteo; how did it turn out?"

Said Filippo, to hit him right in the face, "Oh it can't be that Fatso doesn't know about it! Where were you yesterday? Can it be that no one came to the shop to tell you? For I hear that they were talking about it in a hundred circles of gossip throughout Florence. I was about to come to your shop three or four times yesterday to discuss this; I don't know why it turned out that I didn't get there."

Fatso was looking now at Filippo and now at Donatello and wanting to reply now to one and now to the other, and was swallowing his words, tugged now one way and now the other, so that he looked like a thing possessed, as one who did not well understand whether they were speaking the truth or joking. And after a great sigh, he said, "Filippo, these are certainly strange events!"

Filippo immediately knew what he meant and with difficulty kept from grinning; then he said, "You said you hadn't heard anything about it; how is that possible?" and they wanted him to sit down with them in order that they might hear him at leisure. Fatso regretted having replied those words and did not know what to do. He was all embarrassed because sometimes he thought they were speaking seriously and sometimes he thought the opposite.

Meanwhile here came Matteo, who joined them before they had noticed him, as one who had also been on the lookout (all by Filippo's orders); and fortune aided Fatso, for he couldn't have arrived more opportunely; and he greeted them. Fatso turned towards, him, completely bewildered, and was about to say "Your brothers were just now at the shop and are looking for you," but then he stopped himself.

Then said Filippo, "Where are you coming from, Matteo? We want to hear about this matter; we were just talking about you, and now we're all here."

Said Donatello to Matteo,"Were you arrested, the other evening? Tell the truth, for Filippo tells me . . ."

"Has no one else ever been arrested?" said Matteo; then he said to Filippo, who was looking him in the face, "I'm coming from home."

"Oh," said Filippo, "it was said that you had been arrested."

"Sure I was arrested and was paid for and am out; here I am indeed; what the devil is this? Do people never have anything to talk about but my affairs? All morning my mother's been harrassing me about it, from the moment I got home; and those brothers of mine are surly and look at me as if I were growing horns since I came back from the country, and they were just asking me when they ran into me here, 'At what time this morning did you go out and leave the door open?' They seem to have gone crazy along with my mother; I don't understand them; and they say I don't know what's what about my being arrested and that they paid for me, craziness indeed."

Said Filippo, "Where have you been? It's several days since I've seen you."

Said Matteo, "To you, Filippo, I'll tell the very truth; it's true that I had a debt to a bank for six florins of good quality, and that I put them off for a while with words because I too was being held up, for I was supposed to get eight from someone in Empoli, and I should have had them several days ago according to what he had promised me last time, and I had marked the florins for this debt with a bit left over for me. I promised my creditors on Saturday that I would get them to them on Tuesday, without fail, as that fellow had promised me; and having the law on his side (for in truth it was already a while since I was supposed to give them to him, for I've been short of cash), in order to avoid his doing me harm, I decided to go away from here to our place in Certosa and stayed there two days, and that's why you haven't seen me, for it's barely an hour since I got back, and the funniest thing happened to me that you ever heard. I went to the country Tuesday after dinner; and since I had nothing to do and haven't been there for a thousand years and there's nothing there except a bed (for we send for the wine from the harvest and the other things too in their season), I went strolling along the way to kill time, drank two draughts at Galluzzo so as not to bother our worker with supper, arrived at the house at nightfall and asked him for a bit of light and went to bed. It's really funny what I'm about to tell you; everyone seems crazy to me, I'll say it again; and maybe I'm crazier than anyone; I got dressed this morning in the country and had opened a window, I'll tell you the truth. I don't know whether I'm dreaming now or whether I dreamed what I'm going to tell you; I feel like a different person this morning, Filippo, it's a funny thing, but let it go. Says my worker, who had given me the lamp, 'Where were you yesterday?'

"Says I, 'Didn't you see me last night?'

"Says he, 'Not I; when?'

"Says I, 'Forgetful fellow! didn't you light the lamp for me, for you know that it wasn't burning before?'

"Says he, 'Yes, the evening before; but yesterday evening I didn't see you, nor all day yesterday; I thought you had gone back to Florence, and I was surprised that you hadn't said anything since I assumed you had come here for some purpose.'

"Did I sleep all day then yesterday? And I asked the worker, 'What day is today?' and he tells me it's Thursday. Indeed, Filippo, I find that I have slept an entire day and two nights without waking up; I only went to sleep once."

Filippo and Donatello pretended to be very surprised and kept listening attentively. Said Filippo, "Whatever you ate must have gone down by now."

Said Matteo, "I can tell you that I have such a hunger I can see it."

"It wouldn't be a good idea to board with you," said Donatello.

But his having slept through the whole time that everything was happening to Fatso made Fatso wonder, and he said to himself, "I have no help, I am certainly going crazy; I wouldn't have believed any of this three days ago, and yet it's true . . . ."

And Matteo continued what he was saying, "But I dreamed the craziest things that I ever heard of."

Said Filippo, "You're head's empty and you need to eat."

"I just ran into a boy," continued Matteo, "from the bank where I owe those six florins, who apologized to me and said it wasn't he who had me arrested, for he's the one who usually comes around asking for the money, a good boy, and he says, 'I'm sorry for all the expense you had because of it'; and from what I see, it's been paid. And with these words I understood what my mother was saying indeed and my brothers, who seemed crazy to me. As I was just telling you, it's been paid, but how I don't yet know; I wanted to find out from this boy. It seems that during the time that I thought I was asleep, however it happened, I spent most of the time in jail; Filippo, you figure it out, for I for my part don't know how this happened, and I couldn't wait to see you in order to tell you and laugh with you about it." Then he turned to Fatso and said, "I spent most of the time between your house and your shop; I have something that will make you laugh. I find that I have paid a debt of several florins, and I thought while I was sleeping that I was somebody else, just as surely as I see myself here among you; but who knows whether I was dreaming then or now?"

Says Donatello, "I didn't understand you very well, tell me again; I was thinking of something else. Oh, you're driving me crazy. You just said you were in the country."

To whom Matteo replied. "I know very well what I said."

Says Filippo, "He must mean in his dream."

Then Matteo said, "Filippo understood me."

Fatso never said a word; he stood like one possessed and very attentive to hear, in order to find out whether Matteo had been him during that time. Filippo was like a scratched pig,[9] and as people were beginning to gather around because now one and now another of them could not help laughing a little (except for Fatso who was lost in thought), Filippo, taking Fatso by the hand, said to everyone, "Let's walk a bit in the choir so people won't gather around us; for this is one of the finest stories I ever heard in my life; I want to hear this one. Eh, tell me a little, Matteo, this story; and you'll hear another from me in another place, which everyone

in town is telling; for what you're telling me doesn't quite jibe with it."
And they sat down in a corner of the choir where they could easily see
one another; that choir in those days was between two large pillars which
stand just before the entry to the pulpit; and the men were silent a while
because Filippo was waiting for what Matteo would say, and Matteo
was waiting for Filippo.

Filippo began talking first, and turning more towards Matteo, who was
holding up his end well, than towards Fatso so that Fatso wouldn't be offended, he said laughing, "Listen to what they're saying all over Florence (I
just told these others what it is), and then we will hear you, since you want
me to speak first. It is said that Monday evening you were arrested."

"Arrested, I?" said Matteo.

"Yes," said Filippo, "for that debt you mention"; and turning to
Donatello he said, "You see that indeed something was going on."

Said Donatello to Matteo, "And where were you when I saw you
knocking on Fatso's door the other evening?"

Said Matteo, "When? I don't know that I was ever knocking on his door."

"What do you mean you weren't knocking on his door?" said
Donatello. "Didn't I speak to you at the door?"

Matteo looked surprised, and Filippo continued addressing Matteo,
"And that you kept saying on the way both to the agent and to the man
that was having you arrested, 'You have mistaken me for another, I'm
not the one you want, I don't have debts with anyone,' and were defending
yourself as much as you could with saying that you were really Fatso
here. You say you were in the country, and according to what you declare
you were at that hour in bed and asleep; how is this possible?"

"Let them say what they will," said Matteo, "but you are joking; I was in
the country as I told you, in order not to be arrested, for in truth I was afraid
of that. And what Donatello said just now, I would swear on the altar that I
didn't knock then or ever on Fatso's door. Listen to how it happened, for it's
a hundred miles different from that. I asked a notary friend of mine in
Palagio to issue me a bulletin of debt[10] and to send it to me in the country,
and I thought I would have it by yesterday. The notary wrote me a voucher
early this morning and sent a messenger expressly to tell me that the assembly
had not met, that some of them were in the country and that as there was no
other urgent business, the magistrates did not want to make them return just
for a bulletin, adding that I could stay in the country for a few days if I was expecting arrest; however I came back and am and have been on guard; but
since it's paid, everything's all right, Filippo and Donatello, this is the real
truth. But what I dreamed in the mean time is truly funny, Filippo, no joking;

nor have I ever dreamed anything that seemed so true to me while I was dreaming. It seemed to me that I was in this fellow's house," and he tapped Fatso, "and that his mother was my mother; and so I was chatting familiarly with her as if she were my own, and I was eating there and talking about my business and she was answering me; and I remember all sorts of things that she said; and I went to sleep in that house and got up and went to the carpenter's shop, and it seemed to me that I was going to work as I have a thousand times seen Fatso do when I drop into his shop at times; but it seemed to me that no tool was in its right place and I reorganized all of them."

Fatso was looking at him like a madman, for he had just had the tools in his hands. And Matteo continued, "And then when I tried to work, they wouldn't function right and they were all alike in this, and it seemed I was putting them in places other than where they usually are with the intention of reorganizing them when I had time, and I was taking others, but they were all the same; and I seemed to be answering people who came to ask me questions, as if I were really he, for so it seemed to me indeed; and I went to eat and came back to the shop and in the evening I locked up and went home to bed, as I said, and the house looked just the way it does and the way I've seen it; for I've been there with Fatso as you know."

Fatso had been silent for an hour, he couldn't think of what to say that wouldn't cause him trouble with Filippo, who, he knew, could see a hair in the egg;[11] but this dream had convinced him completely that he was in an inextricable tangle; the telling of that dream of one day and two nights seemed to him to have filled in the whole duration of his own travails. And Filippo and Donatello were acting as surprised as anything at this dream.

Then said Filippo, "From this it seems that it wasn't you who was arrested, Matteo; and yet you say that the debt was truly paid, and that you were in the country; this is a snarl that not even Aristotle could untangle."

Said Fatso, clearing his throat and shaking his head and thinking perhaps of what Matteo was saying, that he seemed to have become Fatso, and of what the judge had told him at the Court of Commerce, "Filippo, these are strange events, and from what I hear, they have happened before; Matteo has spoken, you have spoken, and I too have something to say, and perhaps it is such that you will think I'm crazy; I'd better keep quiet, Filippo, eh, let's not talk about it any more." And then truly he believed that what the judge had told him was the express truth, having so many confirmations; and most certainly he believed that he had been Matteo during that time and that Matteo had been him, but with respect to that sleep, he thought that Matteo's troubles had been fewer, less important and less annoying than those that he, Fatso, had undergone.

But now he believed that he had truly returned to being Fatso, seeing and hearing the story of Matteo, who was not Fatso any more; and as his mother had not yet returned from Polverosa, it seemed a thousand years till he could see her to ask whether she had been in Florence during that time, and who had been at home with her when he knocked that evening, and who had opened the shop in the meantime. And he took leave of them, who could by no means make him stay, although they made only a gentle and polite effort so as not to offend him yet and also because they wanted to have a chance to laugh because they couldn't hold it in any more. Still, Filippo said, "We must have dinner together one of these evenings," whereupon Fatso left without responding.

If Filippo and Donatello and Matteo laughed then among themselves you needn't ask; for whoever saw and heard them thought them crazier than Fatso, and especially Donatello and Matteo who couldn't stop laughing for anything. Filippo was grinning and looking from one to the other. Fatso decided to lock his shop and go all the way to Polverosa, as they learned afterwards, where, finding his mother, he learned that she had not been in Florence, having decided by chance to prolong her stay in Polverosa. Therefore, thinking over and over about this fact and returning to his senses and to Florence, he concluded that it had been a prank, not understanding however how it had been arranged; but he thought it must be so as his mother had not been meanwhile in Florence, and the house had been empty. He couldn't figure it out, and he did not feel like defending himself for having been tricked, should anyone talk to him about it. He was especially pained that Filippo had been involved in it, for he did not see how he could get out of it.

Therefore he decided to go away to Hungary, recalling just then that he had been asked to go, and he decided to find the person who had invited him, a former acquaintance of his, with whom he had studied inlay under Master Pellegrino of Terma Street; that young man had gone to Hungary several years before where he had done very well with the help of Filippo Scolari, nicknamed Spano, one of our citizens who was then captain general of the army of Gismondo; and this Gismondo was the son of King Carl of Bohemia and was King of Hungary, a wise and shrewd king who was later elected emperor in the time of Gregory XII and was crowned as Caesar by Pope Eugenio IV. And this Spano welcomed all Florentines who came there with any intellectual or manual skill, because he was a very good lord who loved his own people very much, as they must have loved him; and he did good for many of them. Now the young man had come to Florence to find out whether he could bring any masters of his craft back with him for the many works he had contracted to do, and he had spoken of it many times with Fatso, begging him to go and showing him that in a short time he would be rich. Fatso ran into him by chance and going up to him, said, "You have often talked to me about coming with you to Hungary, and I have always said no; now, because of a certain thing which has happened to me, and because of a difference of opinion that I've had with my mother, I have decided, in case you will wish it, to come with you; but if you are ready, I would like to get going tomorrow morning because if I stay here longer, my departure will be hindered." The man answered that he was very pleased but that he couldn't leave the next morning because he had not yet accomplished all his duties; but Fatso should leave whenever he wished and wait for him in Bologna, for he himself would be there within a few days; and Fatso was content. Having agreed about their plans, Fatso returned to his shop, took some of his tools and implements and some money to carry with him, and having done this, he went to Borgo San Lorenzo where he rented a horse to be turned in at Bologna, and the following morning he mounted and made his way thither without saying a word to his relatives or anyone else, as if he were being hunted; and he left a letter at home addressed to his mother, which said that she should take for herself whatever was left in the shop, and that he had gone to Hungary with the intention of staying there for a few years. And while he was walking through Florence (letting himself be seen as little as possible in that short time, but still he had to do it that way), and before he got on horseback, he happened by a place where he heard people talking about his case, everyone laughing and joking about it; and he heard one of them say indirectly that it had been a prank. The matter had been leaked first by the boy who had him arrested and then by the judge; for Filippo had merrily conferred with him and asked him what Fatso was saying in jail and had disclosed the plot to him, at which the judge with the greatest laughter in the world had informed him of everything; and everyone in Florence was saying that only Filippo di ser Brunellesco could have known how to do this; which fit very well with Fatso's suspicion, since he knew what Filippo was like, and too well since he saw that he had been mocked and realized that it was by him; and this conversation greatly encouraged Fatso to pursue his plan.

Thus Fatso left Florence and went with his comrade from Bologna to Hungary. The dinner group kept up its habit of getting together from time to time; the first time they reassembled, it was in the same place, at Tomaso Pecori's house. And because of the joke, in order to laugh about it all together, they invited the judge who had been held at the Court of Commerce, who, hearing who they were, went gladly both to become better acquainted with some of them and also to get better informed of all the details, and because he saw that they wished it as well; and they invited also that errand boy together with the agent, Matteo, and those two brothers who had led the dance in jail, at home and by the fire. They invited the clerk of the Treasury too, but he could not come. The judge with great pleasure heard what had happened and similarly answered their questions and told what he had replied to him about Apuleius and Circe and Actaeon and about his worker in order to make it more plausible, saying, "If I had thought of anyone else, I would have mentioned him too"; and they had the biggest laugh in the world, jumping from one event to another as they came to mind. And seeing how the matter had turned out, and how much fortune had aided them both through the priest and through the judge and in general through all the events, the judge said this fine speech to them: that he did not remember ever having been in all his life to a dinner where there was more and better food; and that most of it had been so good that rarely or never did kings and emperors eat so well, not to mention other lesser princes and private men such as themselves. And he thought there was no one so clever that he could have defended himself from the prank had it been played on him, such was the carefulness and organization of Filippo.

Fatso and his companion, arriving in Hungary, set to work and had good fortune; for in a few years they became rich, relative to their status, through the favor of the so-called Spano, who made Fatso a master engineer, and he was called Master Manetto of Florence and had a good reputation there, and Spano took him with him to the camp when he was with the army and gave him good provisions and sometimes fine and rich presents when occasion allowed; for Spano was as generous and magnanimous as if he had been born a king, to every man but especially to Florentines, a manner which, besides his other virtues, had been the reason that drew Fatso there; and Fatso could do whatever he needed, either with his companion or without him, even when Spano was not in the camp. And later he came back to Florence over one span of many years for several months at a time; and at his first arrival, being asked by Filippo why he had left Florence so suddenly and without saying a thing to any of his friends, he told this story, laughing all the while, with a thousand fine details in it which had taken place within his head and couldn't be known to others, and about being Fatso and not being he, and whether he had dreamed or was dreaming when he remembered the past events; so that Filippo had never before laughed so heartily as then. Fatso looked him in the face saying, "You know it better than I, for you made so much fun of me in Santa Maria del Fiore."

Said Filippo, "Let it be; this will bring you much more fame than anything you ever did for Spano or Gismondo, and people will be talking about you a hundred years from now."

Fatso laughed, and Filippo no less; and with all this, he was never with anyone but Filippo when he had spare time, even when he had been told the whole truth; and Filippo would joke with him when they were together and say, "I knew all along that I would make you rich; and there are plenty of people who would have liked to be Fatso and be tricked like this; you've gotten rich from it, and have become acquainted with the emperor of the world and with Spano and many other great princes and barons."

And indeed this return or arrival of Fatso's, and the others afterwards, as he always stayed with Filippo, gave Filippo occasion and leisure many different times to examine him about the information he had received from the judge and from the boy and to question him in minute detail; for the best part of the laughing matter had been in Fatso's mind, as I said; and this is how it came about that the novella could be written in detail and full information given, because Filippo repeated it afterwards many times in detail, and this text was later derived from those who heard it. And everyone who heard it from Filippo declares that it is impossible to tell every detail as it happened without leaving out one of the delightful parts. Therefore after Filippo died it was gleaned from several persons who had heard it many times from him; for example from one named Antonio di Matteo dalle Porte, from Michelozzo, from Andreino da San Gemignano, who was his pupil and heir, from Scheggia, from Feo Belcari, from Luca della Robbia, from Antonio di Migliore Guidotti, and from Domenichino di Michelino,[12] and from many others; although something was written down at the time, it was not a third of the matter, and in many spots fragmented and with gaps. And perhaps it has accomplished this good: that because of it the story was not entirely lost. Thanks be to God. Amen.

Luigi da Porto (1485–1529)

O rphaned early, Luigi da Porto was raised by his uncle, a count of Vicenza, and was sent as a youth to the court of Urbino, one of the cultural centers of its time. He took up the profession of arms and fought for the Republic of Venice until at the age of twenty-six he was so badly wounded that he was forced to retire from the army. Returning to Vicenza, he began to write, producing sonnets in the Petrarchan style, a volume of historical letters about the Italian wars of his day, and *La Giulietta* or the *Newly Rediscovered History of Two Noble Lovers*.

Like Manetti's story of *Fatso the Carpenter*, *Giulietta* appeared by itself rather than as part of a collection; however, the dedicatory epistle and introduction to the story do provide a traditional kind of frame in which the author asserts the similarity of his condition to that of the characters he is writing about. Although da Porto presents the "history" as true, it has been suggested that earlier narratives such as Ovid's "Pyramus and Thisbe" or Masuccio's thirty-third tale were possibly models for the plot.

When the author died in 1529, Cardinal Bembo (the same patron who had urged publication of *The Hundred Old Tales*) asked the author's brother for his writings. *Giulietta* was first published in 1530 and soon reprinted several times. The story was retold somewhat differently by Bandello (II, 9); from this version it was translated into French by Boistuau and in turn into English by Arthur Brooke, William Painter, and others. It was dramatized most famously by Lope de Vega and Shakespeare. The many narrative, poetic and dramatic versions by various lesser-known Italian, French, English, Spanish and German writers attest to the immediate and widespread popularity of the tale. Despite the availability of this story in other translations, such a popular and influential tale deserves a place in this anthology.

I have used the Italian text edited by Giambattista Salinari in *Novelle del Cinquecento*, Classici italiani 44 (Turin: UTET, 1955), which includes notes. Numerous translations exist in English. *The Original Story of Romeo and Juliet,* trans. G. Pace-Sanfelice (London, 1868) has the Italian text on facing pages. The story is included in the anthologies of Bishop, Pasinetti, Roscoe and Valency. Translations have also been published separately, such as *Romeo and Juliet*, trans. Maurice Jones (London: Davis and Orioli, 1921) and *Juliet and Romeo*, trans. Jessie B. Evans (Portland, Maine: The Mosher Press, 1934). Thanks to Shakespeare's play, there are also studies in English dealing with the history of the tale: W. E. A. Axon, *Romeo and Juliet before and in Shakespeare's Time* (London: Allard, 1905), and Olin H. Moore, *The Legend of Romeo and Juliet* (Columbus: Ohio State University Press, 1950). Also of interest in this regard: Mariella Cavalchini, "Bandello, Shakespeare, and the Tale of Two Lovers from Verona," *Italian Quarterly* 70 (1974), pp.37–48; A. H. Diverres, "The Pyramus and Thisbe Story and its Contribution to the Romeo and Juliet Legend," in H. T. Barnwell et al., eds., *The Classical Tradition in French Literature: Essays Presented to R. C. Knight* (Edinburgh, 1977), pp.9–22.

To the very beautiful and charming Lady Lucina Savorgnana.[1]

*S*ince, when talking with you many days ago, I said that I wanted to write a piteous story which I had already heard many times and which took place in Verona, it seemed to me that I ought to set it forth in these few pages so that my words would not seem empty to you, and also because the cases of <u>wretched</u> lovers, of which this tale is full, suit me who am <u>wretched</u> myself; and I thought afterwards that I ought to address it to your worthiness so that, although I know how prudent you are for a beautiful woman, you might see more clearly from reading it to what ruinous straits, to what cruelest death wretched and unhappy lovers are usually led by Love. And furthermore, having decided for myself that it will be my last labor in this art, as I am now weary and sick of being the talk of the crowd, I send it gladly to your beauty so that my foolish poetizing may end in you; and as you are the harbor of worth, of beauty, and of charm, so may you also shelter the little boat of my wit, which, loaded full of ignorance and blown by Love through the shallower seas of poetry, has long ploughed the ocean; and so that, reaching you and realizing how far it has wandered, giving its tiller, oars and sail to others who sail this aforesaid sea with more learning and a better star, it may tie up safely unrigged at your shores. Take it then, my lady, in your customary manner and read it gladly both for the subject, which I think is very beautiful and pitiable, and also for the close bond of kinship and sweet friendship which exists between yourself and the author, who always with all reverence commends himself to you.

Giulietta

As you yourself see, before the heavens turned all their scorn against me, in my earliest youth I gave myself to the profession of arms, and following many great and valorous men in this profession, I spent several years in your delightful land of Friuli, through which I had to go now here and now there, according to my business, which was sometimes private. When riding I used constantly to take with me one of my archers, a man of perhaps fifty years, skilled in his art. Peregrino, as he was called, was very pleasant and, like almost everyone from Verona (where he was born) he was also very talkative. Besides being a bold and experienced soldier, this man was charming and, perhaps more than suited his years, always found himself in love, which added a double measure to his courage; he delighted in telling the prettiest tales, and especially those that spoke of love, with better order and grace than anyone I ever heard. For this reason, as I was departing from Gradisca, where I had been lodged, and was coming with him and two other of my men, driven perhaps by love, towards Udine on a road which at that time was very desolate and totally burned and ruined by the war, heavy with thought and distant from the others, I drew close to the said Peregrino, who, guessing my thoughts, spoke to me thus: "Do you want always to live your life in melancholy because a cruel beauty with feigned demonstrations cares little for you? And though I often speak contrary to what I do, yet because it is easier to give advice than to follow it, I will tell you, my captain, not only is it unbecoming for you who are in the army to spend a long time in the prison of Love, but also so wretched are almost all the ends to which Love leads that it is perilous to follow him. And in witness of this, if it should please you, I could tell you a story that happened in my city, which would make the road less lonely and less tedious; in which you will hear how two noble lovers were led to a wretched and pitiful death." And as I had already given him a sign that I would gladly hear him, he began thus:

In the time when Bartolomeo della Scala, a courteous and kind lord, tightened and loosed as he pleased the reins of my lovely homeland,[2] there were, as my father heard it said, two noble families, one named Cappelletti, the other Montecchi, which were enemies either because of opposing factions or because of personal hatred. It is considered certain that those who live in Udine are descended from one of the two families; Lord Niccolo and Lord Giovanni, now called the

Monticoli of Verona, came here to live by strange chance although they brought with them to this place little else of their ancient possessions except their gentlemanly manners. And although while reading some old chronicles I found that these two families used to give united support to the same party, nonetheless, I will tell you the story as I heard it, without changing it in any way.

There were, then, as I say, in Verona under the already-mentioned lord, the aforesaid noble familes, equally endowed by heaven, nature, and fortune with valorous men and wealth. Between whom, as is usually seen between great houses, there reigned for whatever reason a most cruel enmity; because of which many men, as well on one side as on the other, had been killed, so that from weariness, as often happens in these cases, and also because of the threats of the ruler, who beheld their enmity with the greatest displeasure, they had withdrawn from doing each other further injury, and without any other truce, they were in time so calmed that many of their men conversed with each other. While they were thus pacified, it happened during Carnival season that Lord Antonio Cappelletti, a jolly and mirth-loving man, who was head of his family, gave many parties in his house both by day and by night, at which almost everyone in the city gathered; to one of these parties one night (as is the habit of lovers, who follow their ladies not only with their hearts but also with their bodies if possible wherever they may go) came a young man of the Montecchi, following his lady. He was very young, very handsome, tall, charming, and very well-mannered; therefore, when he took off his mask as everyone else was doing, being in the costume of a nymph, there was no eye that did not turn to admire him, both for his beauty, which surpassed that of any woman who was there, and also for astonishment that he had come into that house (especially at night). But he struck a daughter of the said Antonio more than anyone else. She was Antonio's only child, a girl of supernatural beauty who was both bold and very charming. She, seeing the youth, received his beauty in her mind with such force that at the first meeting of their eyes she seemed to be no longer her own. He stood apart from the festivities with little mirth, all alone, and seldom mixed with anyone in dancing or in conversation, as one who, led there by Love, remained in that place with much misgiving; which painfully grieved the girl because she had heard that he was very pleasant and jolly.

And when midnight was past, and the party was coming to an end, they began the dance of the torch or of the hat, as we call it, and which we still see in use at the end of parties; in which, all standing in a circle, the men change women and the women change men at will. In this dance the young man was taken by some woman and placed by chance next to the already enamoured girl. On her other side was a young nobleman named Marcuccio Guertio, who by nature always had very cold hands, in July just as in January. As Romeo Montecchi (for that was the young man's name) was on the lady's left side and, as one does in that dance, took her beautiful hand in his, the girl said to him almost at once, perhaps desiring to hear him speak, "Blessed be your coming here beside me, Lord Romeo."

To whom the young man, already aware of her gazes, surprised at her speech, said, "How! Is my coming blessed?"

And she replied, "Yes, blessed is your coming here beside me, because you keep at least this left hand warm whereas Marcuccio freezes my right hand."

Taking courage he continued, "If I with my hand warm yours, you with your beautiful eyes burn my heart."

The lady after a brief smile, trying to avoid beeing seen or heard talking with him, said again to him, "I swear to you, Romeo, by my faith, that there is no woman here who appears to my eyes as beautiful as you are."

To whom the young man, already quite inflamed by her, replied, "However I may be, I shall be a faithful servant to your beauty, if that will not displease you."

Leaving the party soon after, and returning to his house, thinking over the cruelty of his first lady, who gave him small thanks for much languishing, Romeo decided, if it should be pleasing to her, to give himself entirely to this new lady, although she was of his enemies' family. On the other side, the girl, thinking of little else but him, after many sighs judged within herself that she would be happy forever if she could marry him; but because of the enmity that existed between the two houses, she had much fear and little hope to reach so joyful a pass. Wherefore, continually torn between two opinions, she said to herself many times, "Oh fool that I am! by what desire do I let myself be led into so strange a labyrinth? where, left without a guide, I shall not be able to get out at will even though Romeo Montecchi doesn't love me; for, because of the enmity between him and my family, he can be seeking nothing but my shame; and even granted that he wanted to marry me, my father would never consent to give me to him." Then, entering the other opinion she would say, "Who knows, perhaps the better to make peace between these two houses, which are already tired and weary of warring on each other, it could happen to me to get him in the manner that I desire!" And fixing herself on this, she began to grace him with a look. Both lovers then, burning with equal fire, both carrying the beautiful name and image of the other carved in their hearts, began to gaze wooingly at each other, sometimes in church and sometimes at a window; until neither the one nor the other had any joy except when they were seeing each other.

And he especially found himself so inflamed by her charming manners that almost the whole night, with greatest danger to his life, he would stand alone before the house of his beloved lady; and sometimes pulling himself with strength up to the window of her bedroom, there, without her or anyone else knowing it, he would sit to hear her pretty speech, and sometimes he would lie upon the street. It happened one night, as Love willed, with the moon brighter than usual, that while Romeo was about to climb up to the said balcony, the girl, either by chance or because she had heard him on other evenings, came to open that window and leaning out, saw him. He, thinking that not she but someone else was opening the balcony window, wanted to flee into the shadow of a wall; where-upon, recognizing him and calling him by name, she said, "What are you doing here at this hour thus alone?"

And he, recognizing her now, replied, "What Love wills."

"And if you were caught here," said the lady, "couldn't you easily be killed here?"

"My lady," replied Romeo, "yes, I could easily be killed here; and I shall certainly die here one night, if you don't help me. But as I am just as close to death in every other place as here, I am trying to die as near to your person as I can; with whom I would desire to live forever, if it pleased heaven and you alone."

To which words the girl replied, "From me will never come hindrance to your living honestly with me; if only hindrance did not come rather from you or from the enmity which I see between your house and mine!"

To which the youth said, "You may believe me that no one can desire anything more than I continually desire you; and therefore, if it pleases you alone to be mine as I long to be yours, I will do it gladly; nor do I fear that anyone may ever take you from me." And having said this much, making arrangements to speak another night at more leisure, they departed from the place where they were.

After the young man had gone many times to speak with her, one evening when much snow was falling, he found her again at the desired place and said to her, "Ah! why do you make me languish like this? Are you not moved by pity for me, who wait for you every night in this sort of weather on these streets?"

To which the lady said, "Certainly yes, I pity you; but what would you have me do if not beg you to go away?"

To her the young man replied, "That you let me enter into your room, where we will be able to speak more comfortably."

Then the lovely girl, almost indignant, said, "Romeo, I love you as much as a person may be permitted to love, and I grant you even more than is suitable to my honesty; and this I do, overcome by love for your worth. But if you thought either by long wooing or by any other means to enjoy my love further as a lover, put that thought aside, for in the end you will find it all in vain. And not to keep you any more in the perils by which I see your life threatened as you come every night to this neighborhood, I tell you that if you are pleased to accept me as your wife, I am ready to give myself to you completely and to go with you anywhere you wish, without reserve."

"This is all I desire," said the young man; "Let it be done now."

"Let it be done," said the lady; "but let it be confirmed afterwards in the presence of Friar Lorenzo of Saint Francis, my confessor, if you want me to give myself to you completely and willingly."

"Oh!" said Romeo to her, "is Friar Lorenzo da Reggio then the one who knows every secret of your heart?"

"Yes," said she, "and let us for my satisfaction wait to resolve our matter in his presence." And here, arranging discreet means for their business, they parted from each other.

This friar was of order of Minor Observants,[3] a great philosopher and experimenter with many things, both natural and magic; and he was such close friends with Romeo that perhaps at those times a closer friendship between two people could not have been found anywhere. For the friar, wishing simultaneously both to keep his good reputation with the common people and to enjoy a few of his pleasures, was obliged perforce to trust in some gentleman of the city; among them he had chosen this Romeo as a young man respected, courageous and prudent; and to him he had laid bare his heart, which by dissembling he kept hidden from all others. Therefore Romeo, finding him, told him freely how he desired to have the beloved girl as his wife, and that together they had decided that he alone should be the secret witness to their marriage, and afterwards the intermediary to bring about her father's consent to this union. The friar agreed to this, partly because he could not have denied Romeo anything without his own great harm, partly also because he thought that perhaps by his means the matter might turn out for the good, which would be a great honor to him in the eyes of the ruler and of everyone else who had been wanting to see these two houses at peace. And as it was Lent, the girl pretending one day that she wanted to go to confession, went to the monastery of Saint Francis and, entering one of the confessionals used by those friars, asked for Friar Lorenzo. He, hearing that she was there, entered through the convent into the same confessional together with Romeo, and locking the door and removing an iron grate that was between them and the girl, he said to her, "I am always glad to see you, but now you are more dear to me than ever if it is true that you want to take my friend Mister Romeo as your husband."

To which she replied, "I desire nothing more than to be legitimately his; and therefore have I come here into your presence, in whom I have great confidence, so that you, together with God, may be witness to that which I, constrained by love, have come to do." Then in the presence of the friar, who said he was accepting it all in the secrecy of confession, Romeo forthwith married the lovely girl with the proper words; and arranging between them to be together the following night, kissing each other only once, they parted from the friar; who, putting the grate back into the wall, remained to hear confession from other women.

The two lovers, having become husband and wife in the manner which you heard, happily enjoyed their love together for many nights, expecting in time to find a way of placating the lady's father, whom they knew to be opposed to their desires. And as things were thus, it befell that fortune, the enemy of all worldly delight, sowing I don't know what evil seed, revived between the two houses the enmity which had already nearly died away, so that with everything turned topsy-turvy, neither the Montecchi wishing to yield to the Cappelletti nor the Cappelletti to the Montecchi, they once attacked each other in the street; there Romeo, fighting but having regard for his wife, refrained from striking anyone in her family; yet in the end, as many men on his side had been wounded and almost all of them had been driven from the street, overcome by anger, he ran upon Tebaldo Cappelletti, who seemed the fiercest of his enemies, and with one blow laid him dead on the ground; and the others, who were now dismayed by his death, turned in hasty flight. Romeo had already been seen striking Tebaldo, so that he could not conceal the homicide; thus, bringing their grievance before the ruler, all the Cappelletti cried out only against Romeo; therefore he was perpetually banished by the court of justice from Verona.

Anyone who has loved well can readily imagine how the wretched girl felt at these events. She wept so bitterly that no one could console her;

and her sorrow was all the more bitter because she did not dare reveal her
ill to anyone. On the other side, the young man lamented his departure
from his homeland only because he had had to abandon her; not wanting
for all the world to depart without taking a tearful leave of her but unable to go to her house, he had recourse to the friar, who informed her
through a servant of her father's, one very friendly with Romeo, that she
should come to him; and she came there. And going together into the
confessional, they wept at length together over their misfortune. Finally
she said to him, "What shall I do without you? I no longer have the heart
to live. It would be better for me to come with you wherever you may go.
I will cut my hair short and follow you as a servant, nor could you be
served better or more faithfully by anyone else than by me."

"May it not please God, my dear soul, that when you come with me, I
should take you in any way but as my wife," Romeo said to her. "But
since I am certain that things cannot go on this way for long, but that
peace between our houses must soon follow, whereupon I will easily entreat the ruler for mercy, I think it better that you stay here for a few days
without my body; for my soul stays with you always. And if things do
not turn out the way I imagine, then we will make some other plan for
how we are to live." And having thus resolved between them, kissing
each other a thousand times, both weeping, they parted; the lady greatly
begging him to stay as near as possible and not to go, as he had said, to
Rome or Florence. A few days later Romeo, who had until then stayed
hidden in the monastery of Friar Lorenzo, departed and went like a dead
man to Mantua, having first told the lady's servant to inform the friar at
once of all that he heard said at home concerning her and to perform
everything faithfully that the girl might command him to do, if he wanted
to receive the rest of the reward promised to him.

When Romeo had been gone for many days and the girl still appeared
tearful, which was diminishing her great beauty, her mother who loved
her tenderly, often asked her sympathetically to tell the cause of this
weeping, saying, "O my daughter, whom I love as much as my own life,
what is this grief that recently torments you? Whence comes it that you
are not without tears for even a brief while? If perhaps there is something
you want, make it known to me alone; for I will do all that is permissible
to console you." But the girl always gave her only weak reasons for such
weeping. Thereupon, the mother, thinking that she desired to have a
husband and that this desire, concealed out of shame or fear, was the
cause of her tears, believing that she was seeking her daughter's well-
being when she was procuring her death, said to her husband one day,

"Lord Antonio, for many days now I have seen our daughter do nothing but cry, so that, as you can see for yourself, she no longer looks the way she used to. And although I have tried hard to find out the cause of her weeping, yet I have been unable to draw it from her. I cannot imagine what the cause of it might be if not perhaps the desire to marry which, as a good girl, she dares not reveal. Therefore, before she consumes herself further, I suggest that it would be good to give her a husband; for in any case she will be eighteen this St. Euphemia's day; and women, when they get much beyond this age, lose rather than gain in beauty. Moreover, they are not a merchandise to be kept long at home; although truly I have never known ours to act other than most honestly. I know you have already prepared the dowry; let us then see to giving her a suitable husband."

Lord Antonio replied that it would be well to marry her; and he greatly commended his daughter who, having this desire, would rather suffer by herself than make any request about it to him or her mother; and within a few days he began to discuss marriage with one of the counts of Lodrone. And when he was almost ready to conclude the discussion, the mother, believing that she would be giving her daughter great pleasure, said to her, "Cheer up now, my daughter, for within a few days you will be married worthily to a fine gentleman, and the cause of your weeping will cease; even though you did not want to confide in me, yet by the grace of God I understood; and I have managed things with your father so that you will be contented."

At these words the lovely girl could not hold back her tears. Whereupon her mother said to her, "Do you think that I am telling you a lie? Before eight days have passed, you will be the wife of a handsome young man from the Lodrone family."

The girl at these words more vehemently redoubled her weeping. For which reason the mother caressing her, said, "Come now, my daughter, won't you be pleased with that?"

She replied to her, "No, mother, never shall I be pleased with that."

At this the mother added, "What then do you want? Tell me, for I am disposed to do anything for you."

Said the girl then, "I want to die, and nothing else."

At this Lady Giovanna (for such was the mother's name), who was a wise lady, understood that her daughter was burning with love; and replying I know not what to her, she left her. And in the evening, when her husband came home, she reported to him what her daughter, weeping, had replied. This mightily displeased him; and he thought it would be well, before the wedding arrangements went any further, in order to avoid falling into some disgrace, to hear what was her opinion on the matter. And bidding her come before him one day, he said to her, "Giulietta (for that was the girl's name), I am ready to marry you nobly; will you not be pleased with that, daughter?"

To which the girl, having remained silent for a while after his words, replied, "My father, no, I will not be pleased."

"How! do you want then to enter a nunnery?" said the father.

And she, "Sir, I don't know"; and with these words out came tears at the same time.

Her father said to her, "This I know you don't want. Therefore set yourself at peace, for I intend to marry you to one of the counts of Lodrone."

The girl, weeping vehemently, replied to him. "May this never be."

Then Lord Antonio, getting very angry, threatened her physically if she ever again dared to contradict his will and, moreover, if she did not make clear the reason for her weeping. And unable to draw from her anything but tears, irate beyond measure, he left her with Lady Giovanna; nor was he able to discern what were his daughter's thoughts.

The girl had repeated everything that her mother told her to the father's servant, Pietro, who knew about her love, and in his presence she had sworn that even if she were single, she would gladly drink poison sooner than marry any man but Romeo. Whereupon Pietro, according to his orders, informed Romeo in detail by means of the friar, and Romeo wrote to Giulietta that she should not consent to the marriage under any circumstances, much less reveal their love; for doubtlessly within eight or ten days he would find a way to take her from her father's house. But as Lord Antonio and Lady Giovanna together could neither by persuasion nor by threats understand her reason for not wanting to marry, nor could her mother find out by any other means with whom she was in love, and as Lady Giovanna had often said to her, "Look, my sweet daughter, don't cry any more now; for we'll give you the husband you want, even if you wanted one of the Montecchi, which I am sure you don't"; and as Giulietta had never responded with anything but sighs and tears, they both entered into a more grave suspicion and decided to conclude the wedding they had planned between her and the count of Lodrone as soon as possible.

Hearing this, the girl became stricken with extreme grief; and not knowing what to do, wished for death a thousand times a day. However, she decided to make known her grief to Friar Lorenzo as the person in whom, after Romeo, she had more hope than in any other, and who, she had heard from her lover, knew how to do great things. Therefore one day she said to Lady Giovanna, "My mother, I don't want you to be surprised that I don't tell you the reason for my weeping, for I myself don't know it; but I only feel in myself such a continual melancholy that it makes me weary not only of others but of my own life; nor can I imagine from whence this comes, much less explain it to you or my father, unless it has come upon me for some committed sin which I do not recall. And because the last confession helped me very much, I would like, with your leave, to go again to confession so that on this Pentecost, which is near, I may be able in remedy of my griefs to receive the sweet medicine of the sacred body of our Lord."

Lady Giovanna replied that she was willing. And taking her two days later to the church of Saint Francis, she set her before Friar Lorenzo, whom she first heartily exhorted to seek out in confession the cause of her daughter's tears. As soon as she saw her mother withdraw some distance from her, the girl at once, with mournful voice, narrated all her troubles to the friar; and for the love and dear friendship which she knew existed between him and Romeo, she begged him to offer her some aid in this her greatest need. The friar said to her, "What can I do, my daughter, in this case since there is such enmity between your family and that of your husband?"

The sorrowful girl said to him, "Father, I know that you know many rare things, and that you can help me in a thousand ways if you want to; but if you do not want to do anything else for me, at least grant me this. I hear that my wedding is being prepared at a palace of my father's which is two miles outside the city towards Mantua; they will bring me there so that I may feel less bold to refuse the new husband; and no sooner will I be there than he who is to marry me will also arrive. Give me enough poison that I may simultaneously free myself from such grief and Romeo from such shame; if not, then with more pain to me and more grief to him, I will stab myself with a knife."

Friar Lorenzo, hearing that she was of this mind, and considering how much he was still in Romeo's power, who would without doubt become his enemy if he did not provide for this matter in some way, spoke thus to the girl, "Look, Giulietta, as you know, I confess half the people in this city and have a good reputation with them all; no last will or reconciliation is made without my involvement; therefore I would not like for all the gold in the world to incur any scandal or to have it become known that I was involved in this affair. Yet because I love both you and Romeo, I am ready to do something which I never did for anyone else, if you promise me truly to keep it always secret."

The girl replied, "Father, give me this poison with assurance, for no one but me will ever know of it."

And he said to her, "I will not give you poison, daughter; for it would be too great a sin that you should die so young and beautiful; but if you have the courage to carry out what I suggest, I may boast that I will bring you safely to your Romeo. You know that the tomb of your Cappelletti is located in the cemetery outside this church. I will give you a powder which when you drink it, will make you sleep for about forty-eight hours in such a way that every man, no matter how great a doctor he may be, will judge you dead. You will doubtlessly be buried in the said tomb as if you had passed from this life; and I, when it is time, will come to take you out and will keep you in my cell until I go the chapter meeting which we are having in Mantua, which will be soon; thither I will lead you disguised in one of our habits, to your husband. But tell me, won't you be afraid of the body of Tebaldo your cousin, who was buried there not long ago?"

The girl, already quite happy said, "Father, if by such means I could come to Romeo, I would without fear dare to pass through Hell."

"Well then," said he, "Since you are thus disposed, I am willing to help you; but before you do anything, I think you should write the whole matter in your own hand to Romeo lest he, believing you dead, run to some wild act of desperation, for I know that he loves you beyond measure. I always have friars going to Mantua, where he is, as you know. Let me have the letter, which I will send to him by a trusted messenger."

And having said this, the good friar (we see that without the means of friars no great matter comes to a successful conclusion), leaving the girl in the confessional, went to his cell and immediately returned to her with a small vial of powder, saying, "Take this powder, and when you think it the right moment, at nine or ten at night, drink it in cold water without fear; for at about midnight it will begin to work, and without fail our plan will succeed. But do not forget, however, to send me the letter which you must write to Romeo; for it is very important."

Giulietta, taking the powder, returned all happy to her mother and said to her, "Truly, my lady, Friar Lorenzo is the best confessor in the world. He has so comforted me, that I no longer remember my past sorrow."

Lady Giovanna, gladdened by her daughter's joy, replied, "Soon, my daughter, you will offer him some comfort in return with our alms; for they are poor friars." And speaking thus, they came home.

Giulietta was so completely happy after this confession that Lord Antonio and Lady Giovanna lost all suspicion of her being in love;

and they believed that she had wept by some strange and melancholy chance; and they would willingly have left her for now as she was without further talk about giving her a husband. But they had already gone so far into the matter that they could no longer turn back without great trouble. Therefore, as the count of Lodrone wanted someone from his family to see the girl, and as Madam Giovanna was slightly indisposed, it was arranged that the girl should go, in the company of two of her aunts, to that place of her father's which we mentioned, slightly outside the city; which she did without resistance. Thinking that her father had so unexpectedly bid her go there in order to give her at once in marriage to this second husband, and having brought with her the powder which the friar had given her, that night at about ten she called a servant of hers, who had been brought up with her and whom she regarded almost as a sister, and asked her for a cup of cold water, saying that she was thirsty from the food eaten earlier that evening, and putting in it the powerful powder, she drank it all. Afterwards, in the presence of the servant and one of the aunts who had awakened with her, she said, "My father will surely not give me a husband against my will, if I can help it." The women, who were thick-headed, although they had seen her drink the powder, which she said she was putting in the water to refresh herself, and had heard these words, still did not understand them, nor did they suspect anything, but went back to sleep. Giulietta, putting out the light and pretending to get up for a natural need when the servant had left, got out of bed and dressed herself again in all her clothes; and returning to bed as if she thought she would die, she arranged her body on the bed as well as she could and, with her hands crossed on her lovely breast, waited for the drink to take effect; which in little more than two hours rendered her as if dead.

When morning came and the sun had risen high, the girl was found on her bed in the manner I told you; and wanting to wake her and being unable, and finding her already almost entirely cold, the aunt and servant remembered the water and powder which she had drunk at night and the words she had said; and seeing moreover that she had dressed herself and arranged herself in that manner on the bed, they judged without doubt that the powder was poison and that she was dead. A great noise went up among the women, and a weeping, especially by her servant, who often called her by name, saying, "O my lady, this is what you were saying: 'My father will not marry me against my will!' O wretched me, you asked me deceitfully for the cold water which brought your cruel death. O woe is me! Of whom shall I first complain? Of death or of myself? Alas!

Why did you when dying scorn the company of your servant, whom while living you seemed to hold so dear? For as I have always gladly lived with you, so too I would gladly have died with you. O my lady! Did I with my own hands bring you the water, so that I — woe is me! — might be in this manner abandoned by you? I alone have killed at once both you and me, and your father and your mother." And so saying, getting onto the bed, she tightly embraced the girl who lay as dead.

Lord Antonio, who had heard the noise not far away, ran trembling to his daughter's chamber, and seeing her lying on the bed and hearing that she had drunk poison in the night and what she had said, sent swiftly to Verona for a doctor whom he considered learned and experienced, to assure himself that she was really dead as she seemed. When the doctor had arrived and seen and touched the girl a bit, he said that she had already passed from life six hours before from the poison she had drunk; at which knowledge, the sorrowful father burst into most bitter weeping. The doleful news, passing from mouth to mouth, soon reached the unhappy mother, who, bereft of all warmth, fell into a dead faint. And coming to with a womanly cry, almost out of her mind, beating herself, calling her beloved daughter by name, she filled heaven with her laments, saying, "Do I see you dead, o my daughter, only comfort of my old age! And how could you have left me so cruelly without allowing your wretched mother to hear your last words? At least I might have been there to close your lovely eyes and to wash your precious body! How can you let me hear this of you! O dearest ladies who are present with me, help me to die; and if any pity lives in you, let your hands (if such service suits them) sooner than my grief extinguish my life. And you, great Father in heaven, since I cannot die as soon as I wish, take me with your thunderbolt from my hateful self." As she was lifted up by some of the women and placed on her bed, and comforted by others with many words, she never ceased to weep and lament in this manner. Afterwards the girl, being taken from where she was and brought to Verona, with grand and very honorable funeral rites, mourned by all her relatives and friends, was buried as dead in the said part of the cemetery of Saint Francis.

Friar Lorenzo, who had gone a short distance out of the city on some necessary business of the monastery, had given Giulietta's letter, which she was supposed to send to Romeo, to a friar who was going to Mantua. Arriving in the city, and having been two or three times to Romeo's house but never, to his great misfortune, finding him at home, and not wanting to give the letter to anyone but him personally, this friar still had it in hand when Pietro, believing Giulietta dead and not finding Friar Lorenzo in Verona, decided in desperation to bear the dreadful news himself to Romeo. After returning in the evening to his master's place outside the city, the following night he set out on foot towards Mantua with such determination that he reached the city early in the morning. And finding Romeo, who had still not received his wife's letter from the friar, he reported to him, weeping, how he had seen Giulietta dead and buried; and he set forth to him all that she had previously done and said. Hearing this, Romeo turned pale and deathlike and, pulling out his sword, wanted to kill himself. But being held back by many men, he said, "My life can in any case not last much longer since the life of my life is dead. O my Giulietta! I alone was the cause of your death because I did not come as I had promised to take you from your father's; you, in order not to abandon me, preferred to die, and shall I for fear of death live on alone? Let this never be!" And turning to Pietro, and giving him dark clothing which he was wearing, he said, "Go, my Pietro."

When he had left, and Romeo had shut himself in alone, nothing seeming drearier to him than life, he thought at length about what he should do; and in the end, dressing himself as a peasant, and taking a glass vial of serpent water which he had long ago stored in a chest in case of need, and putting it into his sleeve, he set out towards Verona; thinking to himself that either he would be deprived of life by the hand of justice if he were found, or else he would close himself into his lady's tomb and die there.

In this latter thought fortune was so favorable to him that on the evening of the next day after the lady had been buried, he entered Verona without being recognized by anyone. Waiting until night, and hearing now that everything was silent, he made his way towards the place of the minor friars where the tomb was. This church was in the Cittadella, where these friars lived at that time; although later, I don't know why, they left it and came to live in the borough of Saint Zeno, in the place which is now called Saint Bernardino although it was once inhabited by Saint Francis himself. Certain tombs were set against the outside walls of the church, as we see in many places on the outside of churches; one of these was the ancient sepulchre of all the Cappelletti, and in it was the beautiful girl. To this one Romeo drew near (it was perhaps about ten at night), and as the man of great courage which he was, raising the cover by force, and propping it open with certain pieces of wood that he had brought with him so that it would not shut against his will, he entered inside and closed it after him. The unhappy young man had brought a dark lantern with him in order to see his lady somewhat; which, when he was shut into the tomb, he immediately pulled out and opened. And there he saw lying as if dead his beautiful Giulietta among the bones and shreds of many dead men; whereupon at once, weeping bitterly, he began to speak thus: "Eyes, which to my eyes were shining lights while it pleased heaven! O mouth, kissed by me a thousand times so sweetly! O lovely breast, which lodged my heart in such joy! Where, blind, mute and cold, do I now find you? How without you do I see, speak, and live? O my poor lady, where has love led you, that wants this little space to extinguish and contain two wretched lovers! Alas! this is not what hope promised me, and that desire which first kindled me with your love. O my unhappy life, why do you continue?" And so saying, he kissed her eyes, her mouth, and her breast, at each moment pouring forth even more abundant tears; meanwhile exclaiming, "O walls which stand above me, why do you not by falling upon me cut short my life? But as death is within the free power of everyone, it is surely most cowardly to desire it and yet not to take it." And so, pulling out the vial of poison liquid which he had in his sleeve, he continued speaking: "I do not know what fate leads me to die upon my enemies and by my own hand in their tomb. But since, o my soul, it pleases me to die thus beside our lady, now let us die." And putting to his mouth the cruel liquid, he swallowed it all. Then taking the beloved girl in his arms, embracing her tightly, he said, "O beautiful body, final end of all my desire! If any sentiment remains with you after the departure of your soul, or if your soul sees my cruel dying, I pray that it not displease you that not having been able to live with you in joy and in public, at least I will die with you in secret and in sorrow." And holding her tightly, he awaited death.

Now the hour had arrived when the girl's warmth should overcome the cold and potent strength of the powder, and she should awake. Therefore, held and stirred by Romeo, she awoke in his arms; and coming to, after a great sigh said, "Alas, where am I? Who is holding me so tightly? Woe is me! Who is kissing me?" And thinking it was Friar Lorenzo, she cried out, "Is this the way, friar, that you keep faith to Romeo? Is this the way you will lead me in safety?"

Romeo, feeling the lady alive, was greatly astonished; and perhaps recalling Pygmalion, he said, "Don't you know me, o my sweet wife? Don't you see that I am your sorrowful husband, come here alone and secretly from Mantua to die beside you?"

Giulietta, seeing herself in the tomb and in the arms of one who she heard say was Romeo, was almost beside herself, and having pushed him slightly away from her and gazed into his face, she gave him a thousand kisses and said, "What folly made you enter here and with such peril? Wasn't it enough for you to have understood from my letter how I with the help of Friar Lorenzo would feign to be dead, and that soon I would be with you?"

Then the young man, aware of his great error, began, "O most wretched my lot! O unhappy Romeo! O much more dolorous than all other lovers! I never received your letter about this." And here he told her how Pietro had reported her feigned death as true; whereupon, believing her dead, he had taken poison right there beside her to keep her company; which, as it was very keen, he felt beginning to send death through all his limbs.

The unfortunate girl, hearing this, remained so overwhelmed by grief that, other than tear her lovely hair and beat her innocent breast, she did not know what to do; and kissing him often, she poured an ocean of her tears over Romeo, who was already lying back, and having turned paler than ashes, she said trembling, "Then must you die in my presence and because of me, my lord? And will heaven permit that I live after you even briefly? Woe is me! If only I could give my life to you and die alone."

To whom the youth with fainting voice replied, "If my faith and my love were ever dear to you, my living hope, I pray you by these not to dispatch your life after my death, if for no other reason at least in order that you may think of him, who, all burning for your beauty, died before your lovely eyes."

The lady replied to him, "If you die for my feigned death, what should I do for your unfeigned one? I am only grieved that I have no means to die before you; and I hate myself for living so long! But I hope surely that before much time has passed, as I have been the cause of your death, so I will be its companion." And when she had with great effort finished these words, she fell into a swoon; and coming to, she gathered wretchedly with her lovely mouth the last breaths of her dear lover, who was hastening towards his end.

Meanwhile Friar Lorenzo, hearing how and when the girl had drunk the powder and that she had been buried as dead, and knowing that the time was come when the said powder would lose its force, came to the tomb with a trusted companion, about an hour before dawn. Arriving there, and hearing her weep and cry, peering through the slit along the cover and seeing a light within, he was much astonished, and thought that the girl had somehow brought the lantern in with her, and that having awakened, for fear of the dead or perhaps of being shut in forever in that place, she was lamenting and weeping in this way. And quickly opening the tomb, with the help of his companion he saw Giulietta, who all dishevelled and mournful had risen to a sitting position and had taken the almost dead lover in her lap. To her he said, "Did you fear, then, my daughter, that I would leave you to die in here?"

And she, hearing the friar and redoubling her tears, replied, "Rather I fear that you will drag me out of here with my life. Alas! for the pity of God, close up the tomb again and go away so that I may die; or give me a knife that by stabbing myself in the breast I may free myself from sorrow. O my father! O my father! well did you send the letter! well shall I be married! well will you lead me to Romeo! Behold him here in my lap already dead." And telling him the whole matter, she showed him to him.

Friar Lorenzo, hearing these things, remained stunned; and looking at the young man, who was about to pass from this life to the other, he said, "O Romeo! What misfortune has taken you from me? Speak to me a little; raise to me your eyes a bit. O Romeo! see your darling Giulietta, who beseeches you to look at her! Why do you not respond at least to her, in whose lap you are lying?"

Romeo, at the dear name of his lady, slightly raised his heavy eyes weighed down by approaching death, and having seen her, closed them. Shortly thereafter, with death coursing through his limbs, in convulsions, he gave a brief sigh and died.

When the wretched lover had died in the manner which I told you, as dawn was already approaching, the friar said to the girl, after much weeping, "And you, Giulietta, what will you do?"

She readily replied, "I will die in here."

"How? My daughter," said he, "don't say this; but come out, for although I do not know what to do or to say, yet you will not lack some holy monastery to enclose you, and there you may pray God continually for yourself and your dead husband, if he is in need of prayer."

To him the lady said, "Father, I ask you nothing but this favor which, for the love that you bear to the happy memory of this man (and she showed him Romeo), you will do for me gladly; and that is never to reveal our death so that out bodies may remain always together in this tomb; and if by chance our death should become known, by the already mentioned love I beg you to beseech our poor fathers in both our names that it may not seem ill to them to leave in one tomb those whom Love burned in one fire and brought to one death." And turning to the limp body of Romeo, whose head she had placed on a pillow that had been left with her in the tomb, closing his eyes and bathing his cold face with her tears, she said, "What should I do longer in life without you, my lord? and what else is left me to do for you except to follow you with my

death? Nothing else, certainly; so that from you, from whom only death
could separate me, death shall have no power to keep me away." And
having said this, bringing to mind her great misfortune and recalling the
loss of her dear lover, resolving to live no longer, having drawn in her
breath, she held it a while and then with a great cry let it out, falling dead
over his dead body.

When he knew that the girl was dead, Friar Lorenzo was quite bewildered
by great pity and did not know what to do. Together with his companion,
pierced to the heart by grief, he was weeping over the dead lovers when
some officers of the police, who were running after a thief, came upon
him here; and finding him weeping over this tomb, in which they saw a
light, they almost all ran over there and, surrounding the friars, said,
"Masters, what are you doing here at this hour? Would you perhaps be
performing some witchcraft over this sepulchre?"

Friar Lorenzo, seeing the officers and hearing and recognizing them, could
have wished himself dead. But he said to them, "None of you draw near me,
for I am not your man;[4] and if you want anything, ask it from a distance."

Then said their chief, "We want to know why you have thus opened
the tomb of the Cappelletti, where just the day before yesterday a girl of
theirs was buried; and if I did not know you, Friar Lorenzo, as a man of
good character, I would say that you came here to rob the dead."

The friar, putting out the light, replied, "I will not tell you what we are
doing here, for it is not your business to know it."

Answered he, "That is true; but I will report it to the ruler."

At which Friar Lorenzo, made bold by desperation, added, "Report it as
you wish"; and closing the tomb, he entered the church with his companion.

The day was almost light when the friars disengaged themselves from
the police, one of whom went at once to the Cappelletti to bring this
news about the friars. They, knowing also perhaps that Friar Lorenzo
was a friend of Romeo's, were soon before the ruler, begging him to find
out from the friar by force if not otherwise what he was seeking in their
tomb. The ruler, setting guards so that the friar could not get away, sent
for him. When he came perforce before him, the ruler said to him, "What
were you seeking this morning in the Cappelletti's sepulchre? Tell us, for
we want by all means to find it out."

The friar replied to him, "My lord, I will very willingly tell your lordship. When she was alive I confessed the daughter of Lord Antonio
Cappelletti, who died so strangely the other day; and because I loved her
dearly as a spiritual daughter, having been unable to attend her funeral, I
had gone to say certain kinds of prayers over her which, when said nine

times over the dead body, release the soul from the pains of Purgatory; and because few people know them, or do not understand such matters, the fools say that I had gone there to rob the dead. I don't know if I am such a robber as to do these things; for me this bit of cloak and this cord are enough; nor would I take anything from all the treasures of the living, much less the clothing from the dead; and they do ill who accuse me in this manner."

The ruler would easily have believed this if not that many friars who wished Friar Lorenzo ill, hearing how he had been found above that sepulchre, wanted to open it; and having opened it and found the body of the dead lover inside, they reported at once with great commotion to the ruler, while he was still talking with the friar, how Romeo Montecchi was lying dead in the Cappelletti's tomb over which the friar had been caught that night. This seemed impossible to everyone and brought extreme astonishment to all. Friar Lorenzo, seeing this and realizing that he could not hide what he desired to conceal, kneeling down before the ruler, said, "Pardon me, my lord, if I told your lordship a lie about that which you asked me; for I did it not for wickedness nor for any gain but in order to keep my promised pledged to two poor dead lovers." And thus he was constrained to recount the whole story to him in the presence of many.

Bartolommeo della Scala, hearing this, moved almost to tears in great pity, wanted to see the dead bodies himself, and with a very numerous throng of people went to the sepulchre; and taking out the two lovers, he had them placed on two carpets in the church of Saint Francis. Meanwhile their fathers came into the church, and weeping over their dead children, overcome by a double pity (even though they were enemies), they embraced each other so that the long enmity between them and their houses, which neither the prayers of friends nor the threats of the ruler nor the injuries received nor the passage of time had been able to extinguish, came to an end through the wretched and pitiful death of these lovers. And in a few days, a beautiful monument having been prepared, on which the cause of their death was carved, the two lovers were buried with great and solemn pomp, mourned and escorted by the ruler and by their relatives and by the whole city.

Such a wretched end had the love of Romeo and Giulietta, as you have heard, and as Peregrino of Verona narrated to me.

O faithful compassion which reigned in women in olden times, where have you gone now? In what breast do you lodge? What woman today would have died as did the faithful Giulietta over her dead lover? When will it ever be that this lovely name will not be celebrated by the most eloquent tongues? How many women are there now who would no sooner have seen their lover dead than they would have thought about finding themselves another lover instead of dying at his side? For I see some women, against all justice forgetting all faith and all good services, abandon those lovers whom they once held most dear, who are not dead but only slightly knocked by fortune; what must one think they would do after their death? Poor are the lovers of this age, who cannot hope either by a long proof of faithful service or by dying for their ladies that their ladies will ever die with them; rather they are certain to be dear to the ladies no longer than they can effectively serve their interests.

Giovan Francesco Straparola da Caravaggio (1480–1558?)

W e know nothing about the life of Straparola; he survives only through his stories and a few poems. The *Piacevoli Notti* or *Entertaining Nights* are tales told on thirteen nights by a group of men and women who gather at the Venetian palace of Ottaviano Maria Sforza, former bishop of Lodi and ruler of Milan, who has fled with his widowed daughter Lucrezia from political upheavals and persecution by his enemies at home. Ottaviano in fact became bishop of Lodi in 1497, and a French invasion led to the dispersal of the Sforza family from Milan in 1499–1500. Thus Straparola has set the frame for his book during his own lifetime. The narrators who assemble at Lucrezia's palace include ten romantically named ladies and a number of well-known, historically identifiable men, one of whom is the very Pietro Bembo who showed such interest in the publication of the *Hundred Old Tales* and da Porto's "Giulietta." Each evening five of the ten young ladies are chosen by lot to tell stories, though occasionally some of them are replaced by men. On the thirteenth and final evening, thirteen stories are told alternately by men and women, making seventy-three stories in all. Songs and riddles also form part of the entertainment, which is set during the Carnival season and comes to an end as church bells ring in the beginning of Lent.

In the preface to his second volume, Straparola notes that he has been accused of stealing others' stories; he confesses that they are not his own, but claims that he has written down just what the narrators at Lucrezia's palace were telling. IV, 4, included here, was previously told by Giovanni Fiorentino; VIII, 4, not included, is a retelling of *The Hundred Old Tales* no.97; VII, 2 seems to be a variation on the classical story of Hero and Leander. A few tales are borrowed from Boccaccio; others are similar to ones told by Sacchetti, Sercambi, et al., but may have come from a common oral tradition rather than from direct borrowing. Straparola called his stories *favole* or fables and was the first to include a number of fairy tales. Therefore, after a decline in its initial popularity, the book was rediscovered by the French in the eighteenth century when folktales and fairy tales became a subject of major interest.

The two volumes of tales were first published in 1550–1553; within twenty years of their first appearance, fifteen editions had already been published. The work was quickly translated into French; Jean Louveau's translation appeared in 1572 in Lyons, and Pierre de la Rivey Champencis's in 1585 in Paris. Painter's *Palace of Pleasure* (1566) included one of the stories (II, 2; Painter's I, 49). Basile seems to have drawn half a dozen of his stories from Straparola's collection.

I have used the edition by Giuseppe Rua, *Scrittori d'Italia* 100–101 (Bari: Laterza, 1927), which has some bibliography but no notes. It has been translated by W. G. Waters as *The Facetious Nights of Straparola* (London, 1894), also reprinted as *The Merry Nights of Straparola* and as *The Most Delectable Nights of Straparola of Caravaggio*. Select translations can be found in the anthologies of Crane, Pettoello, Roscoe, Taylor, and Valency. I know of no studies in English about these tales, but Carl Gustav Jung's "Phenomenology of the Spirit in Fairy Tales," in *Four Archetypes*, trans. R. F. C. Hull, Bollingen Series (Princeton University Press, 1973) and Sigmund Freud and D. E. Oppenheimer's *Dreams in Folklore*, trans. A. M. O. Richards, ed. V. Strachey (New York: International University Press, Inc., 1958), especially pp.29–30, contribute to an understanding of the fairy-tale elements in Straparola's tales.

Preface

In Milan, the ancient and chief city of Lombardy, filled with charming ladies, adorned with proud palaces, and abundant in all those things which befit a glorious city, lived Ottaviano Maria Sforza, the elected bishop of Lodi, to whom by right of inheritance, after the death of Francesco Sforza duke of Milan, belonged the government of the state. But because of the onset of wicked times, because of fierce hatreds, because of bloody battles and because of the continual changing of conditions, he departed thence and went secretly to Lodi with his daughter Lucrezia, the wife of Giovan Francesco Gonzaga, who was the cousin of Federico marchese of Mantua, and there he stayed for some time. His people, having anticipated this, pursued him not without great danger to him. The wretched fellow, seeing the harrassment of his family and the ill feelings against him and his daughter, who had by then become a widow, took what little jewels and money he had at hand and went to Venice with his daughter; finding there Ferier Beltramo, a man of high lineage, of a benevolent, affectionate and kind nature, Ottaviano and his daughter were honorably received by him into his own house with cordial welcome. And because too long a stay in someone else's house usually causes regret, he said wisely that he wanted to depart from there and to find lodgings of his own elsewhere. Therefore he embarked one day with his daughter on a small boat and went to Murano. And seeing there a palace of marvelous beauty which was empty at the time, he entered inside; and having considered the delightful location, the spacious courtyard, the proud loggia, the pleasant garden full of laughing flowers and well-supplied with various fruit trees and abundant with green grass, he praised it highly. And having ascended the marble stairs, he saw the magnificent hall, the comfortable bedchambers, and a balcony over the water with a view over the whole area. The daughter, enraptured with the desirable and lovely site, with sweet and gentle words so begged her father that to please her he rented the palace. Whereupon she felt very happy, for morning and evening she would go onto the balcony and gaze with wonder at the scaly fish which swam in many groups and schools in the clear sea water, and she took great delight in watching them flash hither and thither. And because she had been abandoned by the maidens who once formed her court, she selected ten other ladies, no less gracious than beautiful, whose virtues and charming manners would take long to recount. [There follows a description of the beauty and charms of each] . . . These ten lovely maidens, then, all together and each by herself served the noble Lucrezia as their lady. With them she chose also two matrons of venerable appearance, of noble blood, mature in age and much esteemed, so that with their wise counsels they might always stand by her, one on her right and one on her left. One of these two was the signora Chiara, wife of Girolamo Giudiccione, a gentleman of Ferrara; the other was signora Veronica, once the wife of Santo Orbat, an old and noble man from Crema. To this sweet and honest company there gathered many noble and very learned men, among whom Casal of Bologna, a bishop and ambassador of the king of England, the learned Pietro Bembo, knight of the grand master of Rhodes, and Vangelista de Cittadini of Milan, a man of great influence, held the place of honor near the lady. After them there were Bernardo Cappello, a fine versifier among other things, the amorous Antonio Bembo, the familiar Benedetto Trivigiano, the facetious Antonio Molino called Burchiella, the ceremonious Ferier Beltramo, and many other gentlemen, whose names would be tedious to list.

All of these, or the majority of them, returned almost every evening to the house of signora Lucrezia; and there they entertained her, now with amorous dances, now with pleasant conversations, and now with music and songs; and so in one way or another they passed the swift and fleeting time. In this the noble lady and her wise maidens took great delight. Moreover they often proposed puzzles, of which the lady alone gave the solution. And because by now the last days of carnival were approaching, days dedicated to entertainments, the lady commanded everyone to return to her assembly the following evening on pain of her disfavor so that they might devise the manner and order which they should use.

When the shadows of the next night had fallen, all came according to the command they had received; and when they had seated themselves according to rank, the lady began to speak thus: "My very honored gentlemen, and you lovely ladies, we are united here as is our custom in order to establish some rule for our sweet and delightful entertainments so that in this carnival season, of which now only a few days remain, we may have some pleasant amusement. Each of you therefore will propose whatever pleases you most, and that which appeals to the majority will be chosen."

The ladies and likewise the men unanimously replied that it was fitting that she determine the question herself. The lady, seeing such a burden placed upon her, responded to the pleasant company saying: "Since it so pleases you that I determine the order to be followed for your pleasure, I would like that every evening, as long as the carnival lasts, we dance; then that five maidens sing a song of their choosing; and then each of the five maidens to whom the lot falls must tell some fable, posing at the end a riddle to be solved most cleverly by the rest of us. And when we have come to the end of such talk, then each of you will go home to rest. But if my opinion does not please you (for I am disposed to follow your will), each of you may say what you prefer." This proposal was much praised by everyone. So then, a golden vase having been brought and the names of five maidens placed within, the first name to come out of the vase was that of the lovely Lauretta, who for modesty became as red as a morning rose. Then, as they followed the manner begun, the second to come out was the name of Alteria, the third of Cateruzza, the fourth of Eritrea, the fifth of Arianna. After this the lady ordered instruments to come; and having been brought a garland of green laurel, she placed it on Lauretta's head in sign of her preeminence, commanding her to begin the storytelling on the following evening. Then she bid Antonio Bembo along with the other men to lead a dance. And, ready at the lady's commands, he took Fiordiana by the hand, with whom he was somewhat in love; and the other men similarly chose partners. When the dance was finished, with slow steps and amorous talk the young men and maidens moved into a

smaller room where sweets and precious wines had been prepared. Having
somewhat refreshed themselves, the ladies and gentlemen turned to
banter; and after some amusing banter, they took leave of the generous
lady and all departed with her good grace.

Come the following evening, when all had reassembled in the most
honest company and had danced a few dances in the usual manner, the
lady made a sign to lovely Lauretta to begin the singing and storytelling.
And Lauretta, without awaiting further word, rising to her feet and making
the proper curtsy to the lady and to those present, mounted onto a slightly
raised area where there was a pretty chair all covered with silk cloth; and
when she had summoned her four selected companions, all five sang the
following song with angelic voices in praise of their lady thus:

> *Your actions, noble lady, modest and pleasing,*
> *with charming and wandering welcomes,*
> *make you rise among the souls divine.*
> *Your regal state which surpasses every other,*
> *at which I sweetly swoon,*
> *and your adornment full of every praise,*
> *as I feed myself on your nourishing appearance,*
> *keep my spirits so accustomed to you*
> *that if I wish to utter a word of anything else,*
> *I speak perforce of you, in all the world of you alone.*

I, 3

FATHER SCARPACIFICO, DUPED ONLY ONCE BY THREE ROGUES, DUPES
THEM THREE TIMES; AND FINALLY VICTORIOUS, LIVES HAPPILY EVER
AFTER WITH HIS NINA.

The end of the fable which Alteria has just told gives me material for
another one, which I hope will be no less amusing than pleasing to
you; but it will be different in one respect; for in the former tale
Father Sanseverino was tricked by Cassandrino, but in this one Father
Scarpacifico tricked several times those who intended to trick him, as you
will hear fully in the course of my tale.

Near Imola, a city full of feuds and in our times almost reduced by factions to final extinction, there was a village called Postema, in the church
of which there officiated in past times a priest named Scarpacifico, a man
truly rich but extremely miserly and stingy. He kept a shrewd and clever
woman named Nina to manage his household; and she was so sharp that
there was no man to whom she did not dare say what was needed. And

because she was faithful and prudently managed his affairs, she was very dear to him. The good priest while he was young was one of those sturdy men that one finds in the region of Imola; but having reached extreme old age, he could no longer endure the fatigue of walking on foot. Therefore the good woman tried many times to persuade him to buy a horse so that he would not die before his time on account of so much walking.

Father Scarpacifico, convinced by the prayers and persuasions of his servant, went one day to the market; and having looked over a mule which seemed to suit his needs, he bought it for seven gold florins. It happened that at that market were three close companions who enjoyed living at the expense of others rather than at their own, as occurs in modern times too. And having seen Father Scarpacifico buy the mule, one of them said, "My comrades, let's make that mule ours."

"But how?" said the others.

"Let's go to the street which he must pass along, and let one of us be a quarter of a mile from the next, and each of us separately will tell him that the mule he bought is an ass. And if we maintain it firmly, the mule will easily be ours."

And so, leaving in agreement, they disposed themselves along the street as they had planned; and as Father Scarpacifico passed by, one of the robbers, pretending to be coming from a direction other than the market, said to him, "God save you, Sir."

Father Scarpacifico answered, "Welcome, my brother."

"And where are you coming from?" said the robber.

"From the market," answered the priest.

"And what nice thing did you buy?" said the comrade.

"This mule," answered the priest.

"What mule?" said the robber.

"The one I'm riding on," answered the priest.

"Are you speaking in earnest or are you joking with me?"

"Why?" said the priest.

"Because that looks to me not like a mule, but like an ass."

"What do you mean an ass?" said the priest. And without another word he hastily pursued his way.

He had ridden hardly more than two bowshots when the next of the comrades came to meet him and said to him, "Good day, Sir; and where are you coming from?"

"From the market," replied the priest.

"Is there good merchandise?" said the comrade.

"Yes, very," replied the priest.

"Did you make some good purchase?" said the comrade.

"Yes," replied the priest, "I bought this mule which you see."

"Are you speaking in earnest?" said the comrade. "Did you buy that as a mule?"

"Yes," replied the priest.

"But in truth it is an ass," said the good comrade.

"What do you mean an ass?" said the priest. "If anyone else tells me that, I will give it to him as a present."

"And as he continued on his way, he encountered the third comrade, who said, "Welcome, my good Sir; are you by chance coming from the market?"

"Yes," answered the priest.

"And what nice thing did you buy?" said the good comrade.

"I purchased this mule which you see."

"What do you mean mule?" said the comrade; "Are you speaking in earnest or are you joking with me?"

"I'm speaking in earnest and not joking," answered the good priest.

"Oh, poor man!" said the robber; "Don't you realize that it is an ass and not a mule? Oh the greedy fellows, how they have duped you!"

Hearing this, Father Scarpacifico said, "Two other men a little while ago said the same thing to me too, and I didn't believe it." And getting down from the mule he said, "Take it, for I give it to you as a present." The comrade, taking it and thanking him for his liberality, caught up with his companions, leaving the priest to go on foot.

When Father Scarpacifico arrived at home, he told Nina how he had bought a mount and, thinking that he was buying a mule, had bought an ass; and because many men on the way had told him so, he had made a present of it to the last one. Said Nina, "O you little Christian, don't you realize that they played a trick on you? I thought you were shrewder than you are. By my faith, they wouldn't have deceived me."

Then Father Scarpacifico said, "Don't fret about it, for if they have played one on me, I will play two on them; and don't doubt it, for they who deceived me will not be content with this but will come with a new wile to see if they can take something else out of my hands."

In the village lived a farmer, not very far from the priest's house, and he had among other things two goats which looked so much alike that one could not easily tell them apart. The priest bargained for the two of them and bought them at a certain price. And on the next day he ordered Nina to prepare a fine dinner because he wanted some friends to come and eat with him; and he bid her take a certain cut of veal and boil it, and to roast some chickens and a loin of beef. Afterwards he handed her some spices and ordered her to make a tasty confection and a cake, the way she was accustomed to do. Then the priest took one of the goats and tied it to a bush in the courtyard, giving it some fodder; and the other he tied to a halter and went with it to market. As soon as he arrived at the market, the three comrades of the ass trick saw him; and approaching him, they said, "Welcome, Sir! And what are you doing? Do you want to buy something nice?"

To them he replied, "I have some shopping to do because some of my friends will come to dine with me today; and if you wanted to come too, you would give me pleasure." The good comrades very gladly accepted the invitation.

Father Scarpacifico, having shopped for what he needed, put all his purchases on the goat's back, and in the presence of the three comrades he said to the goat, "Go home and tell Nina to boil this veal and to roast the loin and the chickens; and tell her to make with these spices a good cake and some confection such as she is used to make. Have you understood everything? Now go in peace." The goat, laden will all those goods and set at liberty, took off; and into whose hands she fell, I don't know. But the priest and the three comrades and several other friends of his went on around the market, and when it seemed time, they went to the priest's house; and entering the courtyard, the comrades at once caught sight of the goat tied to the bush, which was ruminating some chewed grass, and they believed that it was the same goat which the priest had sent home with the goods; and they were much astonished. And when they had entered the house all together, Father Scarpacifico said to Nina, "Nina, have you done as I sent word to you by the goat?"

And she, being shrewd and understanding what the priest meant, replied, "Yes, Sir; I have roasted the loin and the chickens and boiled the veal. Besides that I have made a cake and a confection with the spices in it, as the goat told me."

"Fine," said the priest.

The three comrades, seeing the roast, the boiled meat, and the cake in the oven, and having heard Nina's words, were much more astonished than before; and they began to think among themselves about how they could get that goat. At the end of dinner, having thought hard about stealing the goat and duping the priest, but not seeing how they could do it successfully, they said, "Sir, we want you to sell us that goat."

The good priest replied that he did not want to sell it because there was not enough money to pay what it was worth; and yet if they insisted they wanted it, he would price it at fifty gold florins. The good comrades, believing they were getting a steal, at once counted out to him fifty gold florins. "But be warned," said the priest, "so that you don't complain to me later; for the goat, not recognizing you for the first few days and not being used to you, may perhaps not do what she ought."

But the comrades without further answer very happily led the goat home and said to their wives, "Tomorrow don't prepare anything for dinner until we send something home to you." And going to the piazza, they bought chickens and other things necessary for a meal; and setting it on the back of the goat, which they had brought with them, they instructed it about everything they wanted it to do and to tell their wives. The goat, loaded with victuals, being set free, took off and went where it pleased, for they never saw it again. When dinnertime had come, the good comrades returned home and asked their wives whether the goat had come home with the victuals, and whether they had done as it told them to.

The women replied, "Oh you fools and senseless men, do you believe that an animal will run your errands? Surely you have been deceived, for you want every day to dupe someone else and in the end you have been duped yourselves."

The comrades, seeing that they had been mocked by the priest and that they had paid out fifty gold florins, became so incensed with anger that they wanted absolutely to kill him; and taking their weapons, they went to find him. But the prudent Father Scarpacifico, who was not without concern for his life and who had the comrades always in mind lest they do him some harm, said to his servant, "Nina, take this bladder full of blood and put it under your petticoat; because when these robbers come, I will lay all the blame on you; and pretending to be angry with you, I will strike you a blow with this knife into the bladder, and you, just as if you were dead, fall to the ground; and then leave the rest to me."

Father Scarpacifico had barely finished his words with the servant when the robbers arrived, who ran up to the priest to kill him. But the priest said, "Brothers, I don't know why you want to harm me. Perhaps this servant of mine has done you some wrong which I don't know about." And turning to her, he grabbed the knife and struck her a blow with the point and stabbed the bladder which was full of blood. And she, pretending to be dead, fell to the ground, and the blood rushed out in all directions like a river. Then the priest, seeing the strange event, pretended to repent and began to cry out in a loud voice, "Oh wretched and unfortunate me! what have I done? Oh how foolishly I have killed her who was the support of my old age! How will I ever live without her?" And taking a pipe made in a certain way, he raised her dress and placed it between her buttocks and blew into it until Nina came to, and healthy and well she jumped to her feet. Seeing this, the robbers were struck with astonishment; and setting aside all their anger, they bought the pipe for two hundred florins and went happily back home.

It happened one day that one of the robbers had an argument with his wife, and in his indignation he stabbed her in the chest, a blow from which she died. The husband took the pipe bought from the priest and put it between her buttocks and did as the priest had done, hoping to bring her back to life. But in vain he labored to waste his breath; for the poor soul had departed this life and gone to the next. The second comrade, seeing this, said, "O you fool, you don't know how to do it right; let me do it a bit." And seizing his own wife by the hair, with a razor he cut her throat; then taking the pipe he blew into her rear; but for all that, the poor thing did not revive. And the third comrade did likewise; and so all three remained deprived of their wives. Whereupon in indignation they went to the priest's house and did not want to hear any more of his lies, but seized him and put him in a sack intending to drown him in the nearby river; and while they were carrying him to dump into the river, something—I don't know what—happened to the robbers which forced them to put down the priest tied securely in the sack and to run away.

While the priest was left shut in the sack, by chance there passed by a shepherd with his flock, grazing the tender grass; and as they were grazing, he heard a mournful voice saying, "They want to give her to me, but I don't want her; for I am a priest and can't marry her." And he was quite dismayed for he could not tell where that utterance was coming from which was repeated so often. And turning this way and that, he saw at last the sack in which the priest was tied; and approaching the sack, the priest shouting loudly all the while, he untied it and found the priest. And when asked why he was shut in the sack and why he was shouting so loudly, he replied that the lord of the city wanted to give him his daughter as wife, but that he did not want her because he was old and also because he could not marry her, being a priest.

The shepherd, who fully believed the priest's feigned words, said, "Do you think, Sir, that the lord would give her to me?"

"Yes, I think so," answered the priest, "if you were tied into this sack as I was." And when the shepherd had gotten into the sack, he tied it tightly and moved away from that place with the sheep. Not yet an hour had passed when the three robbers returned to the place where they had left the priest in the sack, and without looking inside it, they took the sack on their shoulders and threw it into the river; and so the shepherd, instead of the priest, ended his life miserably. Leaving the scene, the robbers headed towards home; and as they were conversing together, they saw the sheep grazing not far away. Whereupon they decided to steal a pair of lambs; and approaching the flock, they saw that Father Scarpacifico was the shepherd, and they were much astonished, for they thought he had been drowned in the river. Whereupon they asked him how he had gotten out of the river.

The priest replied to them, "Oh you crazy men, don't you know anything? If you had sunk me deeper, I would have come up with ten times as many sheep."

Hearing this, the three comrades said, "O Sir, would you do us this favor? Put us in sacks and throw us in the river, and from robbers we will turn into shepherds."

Said the priest, "I am ready to do whatever you wish and there is nothing in the world I wouldn't willingly do." And finding three good sacks of strong and tight canvas, he put them inside and tied them tightly so they couldn't get out and threw them into the river; and thus they went unhappily to the dark places where they feel eternal pain; and Father Scarpacifico, rich both in money and in sheep, went home and lived happily several years more with his Nina.

II, 1

GALEOTTO, KING OF ANGLIA, HAS A SON BORN AS A PIG, WHO MARRIES THREE TIMES; AND PUTTING OFF THE PIGSKIN AND BECOMING A HANDSOME YOUNG MAN, HE IS CALLED THE PIG KING.

Gracious ladies, there is no tongue so skilled nor so eloquent that in a thousand years it could sufficiently express how beholden man is to his creator for bringing him into the world as a man and not as an ugly beast. However I remember a fable, which occurred in our time, about someone who was born a pig and afterwards, having become a handsome young man, was called by everyone the pig king.

You must know, then, my dear ladies, that Galeotto was king of Anglia, a man no less rich in the goods of fortune than in those of the spirit; and he had to wife the daughter of King Matthias of Hungary, called by name Ersilia, who surpassed every other matron of her time in beauty and virtue and courtesy. And so prudently did Galeotto rule his kingdom that there was no one who could truly complain about him. Although the couple, then, had lived together a long time, fate willed that Ersilia never became pregnant, which discontented them both very much. It happened that Ersilia was walking in her garden, gathering flowers; and being already slightly tired, she eyed a place full of green grass and going over to it, sat herself down; and invited by drowsiness and by the birds, which were singing sweetly up in the green branches, she fell asleep. At that time to her good fortune three proud fairies passed by through the air; who, seeing the young lady asleep, stopped and, considering her beauty and grace, decided among themselves to make her inviolable and enchanted. The fairies then agreed all three. The first said, "I wish that she may be inviolable; and the first night that she will lie with her husband, let her become pregnant; and let there be born from her a son who for beauty has no equal in the world."

The second said, "And I wish that no one may be able to harm her, and that the son who will be born from her may be endowed with all those virtues and gentle manners which can be imagined."

The third said, "And I wish that she may be the wisest and wealthiest lady that one can find; but may the son that she will conceive be born all covered with the skin of a pig, and may his gestures and manners all be those of a pig; nor may he ever be able to emerge from this state until he will have married three times."

When the three fairies had departed, Ersilia awoke and, getting up at once, took the flowers which she had gathered and returned into the palace. Not many days later Ersilia became pregnant; and arriving at the time of the desired birth, she brought forth a son whose limbs were not human but porcine. When this came to the ears of the king and queen, they felt inestimable grief. And so that such a birth would not redound to the shame of the queen, who was good and pious, the king often thought he should have it killed and thrown in the sea. But yet turning the matter over in his mind and reflecting prudently that the son, however he was formed, was generated by him and was his own blood, he set aside every cruel intention that he had previously had in mind, and embracing mercy mixed with sorrow, he willed that it be raised and brought up not as a beast but completely as a rational animal. The child then, brought up carefully, would often come to his mother and, raising himself on his hind feet, put his snout and forefeet in her lap. And the loving mother would in turn caress him, putting her hands on his bristly back, and hug and kiss him, no otherwise than if he were a human creature. And the child would curl his tail and show with obvious signs that the maternal carresses pleased him very much. The piglet, being somewhat grown, began to speak like a human and to go about through the city; and where there was garbage and filth, as pigs do, he would thrust himself into it.

Afterwards, all dirty and stinking, he would return home; and running up to his father and mother and rubbing himself around on their clothes, he made them all filthy with dung; but because he was their only son, they suffered everything in patience.

One day among others the piglet came home, and, setting himself, as dirty and filthy as he was, on his mother's clothing, said to her, grunting, "Mama, I would like to get married."

Hearing this, the mother replied, "O you crazy fellow, who do you think will take you for a husband? You are stinking and filthy; and you think that a baron or knight will give you his daughter?"

To which he replied, grunting, that he absolutely wanted a wife.

The queen, not knowing how to deal with this, said to the king, "What should we do? You see in what condition we find ourselves. Our son wants a wife, and no one will want to take him as husband."

The piglet, returning to his mother, grunting loudly said, "I want a wife, nor will I cease till I have that young girl that I saw today, because I like her very much." This was the daughter of a poor woman who had three daughters, and each of them was beautiful.

Hearing this, the queen at once sent for the poor woman with her oldest daughter and said to her, "My beloved mother, you are poor and burdened with daughters; if you will consent, you will soon become rich. I have this pig son, and I would like to marry him to this your oldest daughter. Do not consider him, who is a pig, but consider the king and me; for in the end she will be the owner of our entire kingdom." The daughter, hearing these words, was very perturbed and, reddening like a morning rose, said she would in no way consent to such a thing. However, so sweet were the words of the poor woman that she persuaded her daughter to agree.

The pig, returning home all dirty, ran to his mother, who said to him, "My son, we have found you a wife, and one to your liking." And having the bride come in, dressed in most honorable royal clothes, she presented her to the pig.

He, seeing her pretty and graceful, was quite delighted; and stinking and dirty as he was, he ran all around her, caressing her with his snout and forefeet as much as any pig ever did. And she because he was dirtying all her clothes, pushed him away. But the pig said to her, "Why do you push me away? Wasn't it I who made you this clothing?"

To which she, being proud, answered loftily, "Neither you nor your kingdom of pigs ever made it for me." And when the hour came to go to bed, the girl said, "What do I want to do with this stinking brute? Tonight, as soon as he falls asleep, I will kill him."

The pig, who was not far away, heard the words and said no more. Going then at the proper hour all plastered with dung and garbage to his splendid bed, with snout and forefeet he lifted the very fine sheets and, dirtying everything with foul-smelling manure, lay down beside his bride. She lost no time in falling asleep. But the pig, pretending to sleep, with his sharp tusks struck her so strongly in the breast that she died immediately. And arising early in the morning, he went off, according to his habit, to feed and roll in the mud. The queen thought it fitting to visit her daughter-in-law; and going in and finding her killed by the pig, she was extremely grieved. And when the pig came home, being fiercely reproached by the queen, he responded that he had done to her what she wanted to do to him, and left indignantly.

Not many days passed when the pig urged his mother all over again that he wanted to marry the second sister; and although the queen spoke much against it, nonetheless he obstinately wanted her by all means, threatening to ruin everything if he couldn't have her. Hearing this, the queen went to the king and reported everything to him; and he said that it would be less harm to have him killed than to have him do a lot of damage in the city. But the queen, who was his mother and loved him greatly, could not endure to be deprived of him, even though he was a pig. And calling the poor woman with her second daughter, she talked with them at length; and after they had spoken together a great deal about marriage, the second daughter agreed to accept the pig as her husband. But the matter did not turn out the way she wished; for the pig killed her like the first daughter, and left home early. And returning at the proper hour to the palace with such dirt and dung that no one could get near him for the stink, he was much denounced by the king and queen for the outrage he had committed. But the pig boldly responded that he had done to her what she was intending to do to him.

Nor was it long before Sir Pig again approached the queen about wanting to remarry and to take to wife the third sister, who was much more beautiful than the first and the second. And as the request was absolutely denied, he importuned all the more to have her, threatening with frightening and brutal words the death of the queen if he did not have her for a bride. The queen, hearing his foul and shameful words, felt such torment in her heart that she nearly went mad. And setting aside all other thoughts, she bade come to her the poor woman and her third daughter, named Meldina, and said to her, "Meldina, my daughter, I want you to take Sir Pig for your husband; and do not have regard for him, but for his father and me; for if you will know how to make yourself comfortable

with him, you will be the luckiest and happiest lady that one can find."
To which Meldina with a calm and clear face replied that she was very
pleased, thanking her greatly for having deigned to accept her as
daughter-in-law. And if she had nothing else, it would be plenty for her
to turn in one instant from a poor girl into the daughter-in-law of a
powerful king. The queen, hearing this gracious and lovely reply, could
not for its sweetness keep the tears from her eyes. But she was afraid lest
it happen to her as to the other two.

The new bride, dressed with rich clothes and precious jewels, waited
for her dear husband to come home. When Sir Pig arrived, muddier and
dirtier than ever, the bride received him kindly, spreading her precious
robe on the ground, praying him to lie down beside her. The queen told
her to push him away; but she refused to push him, and said these words
to the queen:

> Sacred Majesty, of old
> Three wise lessons I've been told:
> First, don't waste your effort, please,
> To seek impossibilities;
> Second, don't go trusting quite
> In things that are not fair and right;
> Third, the precious gift you hold
> Value as the rarest gold.

Sir Pig, who was not sleeping but heard everything clearly, rising to his
feet, licked her face, her throat, her breast, and her shoulders; and she in
turn caressed and kissed him, so that he was totally kindled with love.
Come the hour of repose, the bride went to bed, waiting for her dear husband to come; and it was not long before the husband, all filthy and
stinking, went to bed. And she, raising the cover, bid him come near her,
and set his head on the pillow, covering him well and closing the curtains
so that he wouldn't get a chill. Sir Pig, come daylight, having left the mat-
tress full of manure, went off to feed. The queen in the morning went to
the bride's chamber and, thinking to see what she had seen the last two
times, found her daughter-in-law happy and content, although the bed
was all fouled with filth and garbage. And she thanked God on high for
such a gift, that her son had found a wife to his satisfaction.

Not much time passed before Sir Pig, having a pleasant conversation
with his wife, said to her, "Meldina, my beloved wife, if I were sure that
you would not disclose my deep secret to anyone, I, not without your

great joy, would reveal to you something which until now I have kept
hidden; but because I know you to be prudent and wise, and I see that
you love me with perfect love, I would like to have you share it with me."

"Safely reveal to me any secret of yours," said Meldina, "for I promise
you not to tell it to anyone without your will." Assured therefore by his
wife, Sir Pig pulled off his stinking and dirty skin, and was left an attractive and handsome young man; and all that night he lay embraced with
his Meldina. And bidding her to keep silent about it all because he was
soon to put off such wretchedness, he arose from the bed and, donning
his porcine apparel, gave himself to filthiness as he had done in the past. I
leave it to each of you to think what and how great was the joy of
Meldina, seeing herself joined to such a lovely and clean young man.

It was not long before the girl became pregnant and arriving at the time
of birth, brought forth a most handsome son, which was a great pleasure
to the king and queen, and especially because he had the form not of a
brute but of a human creature. Meldina felt much burdened by keeping
secret so deep and wonderful a thing; and going to her mother-in-law she
said, "Most prudent queen, I thought I was joined to a brute; but you
have given me for a husband the most handsome, the most virtuous, and
the best-mannered young man that nature ever created. When he comes
into the chamber to lie down beside me, he takes off his stinking rind
and, dropping it on the ground, is left as a tidy and lovely young man.
Which no one could believe, if she didn't see it with her own eyes."

The queen thought that her daughter-in-law was joking; but she kept
saying it was true. And asked how one could see this, the daughter-in-law
replied. "Come to my chamber tonight as soon as everyone is asleep, and
you will find the door open, and you will see that what I tell you is true."
When night and the awaited hour had come, when all had gone to rest,
the queen had some candles lit and went with the king to her son's
chamber; and entering in, she found the pig skin which had been dropped
on the floor on one side of the room; and approaching the bed, the
mother saw that her son was a handsome young man and was holding his
wife Meldina tightly in his arms. Seeing this, the king and queen greatly
rejoiced; and the king ordered that, before anyone left the room, the skin
should be all torn into tiny shreds; and such was the joy of the king and
queen for their new-made son that they nearly died of it. The king
Galeotto, seeing that he had such a son and from him such grandsons,
took off his crown and royal mantle, and in his place with greatest
triumph his son was crowned, who, called the Pig King, ruled the kingdom

to the great satisfaction of all his people, and lived very happily for a long time with Meldina, his beloved wife.

III, 3

BIANCABELLA, DAUGHTER OF LAMBERICO THE MARQUIS OF MONFERRATO, IS SENT OFF BY THE STEPMOTHER OF FERRANDINO, KING OF NAPLES, TO BE KILLED. BUT THE SERVANTS CUT OFF HER HANDS AND BLIND HER; AND SHE IS MADE WHOLE AGAIN BY A SERPENT AND RETURNS HAPPY TO FERRANDINO.

I t is very praiseworthy and necessary that a lady, of whatever status and condition, use prudence in her doings, without which nothing is well-managed. And if a stepmother, about whom I now intend to tell you, had used it with modesty, then perhaps, while thinking to kill someone else, she would not by divine justice have been killed herself at another's hand, as now you will hear.

There ruled a long time ago in Monferrato a marquis powerful in status and in wealth but deprived of children, and his name was Lamberico. Although he was very desirous to have children, the grace of God was denied him. It happened one day that while the marchioness was amusing herself in the garden, overcome by drowsiness, she fell asleep at the foot of a tree; and as she lay softly sleeping, a small serpent came and approached her and, slipping under her clothes, without her feeling a thing, entered her natural way and, gently ascending, settled itself in the lady's womb, remaining there quietly. Not long after, the marchioness, with no small pleasure and joy to the whole city, became pregnant and, arriving at the time of birth, brought forth a daughter with a serpent wound three times around her neck. Seeing this, the godparents who lifted her up were much frightened. But the serpent, unknotting itself from the baby's neck without doing any harm, curving and stretching itself along the ground, went into the garden. When the baby had been washed and made pretty in a clear bath and wrapped in the whitest cloths, there began little by little to reveal itself a necklace of gold most finely wrought, which was so beautiful and lovely that it showed through between the flesh and skin not otherwise than do precious things through the finest crystal. And it was wound around her neck as many times as the serpent had been. The little girl, who was named Biancabella for her beauty, grew up with such virtue and gentleness that she seemed not human but divine.

When Biancabella had reached the age of ten, having gone out on a balcony and seen the garden all full of roses and lovely flowers, she turned to the nurse who was taking care of her and asked her what that was which she had never seen before. She was answered that it was a place which her mother called *garden*, in which she sometimes amused herself. Said the girl, "The prettiest thing of all I never saw before, and I would gladly enter there." The nurse, taking her by the hand, led her into the garden and, withdrawing slightly from her, set herself down to sleep under the shade of a leafy beech, letting the girl enjoy herself in the garden.

Biancabella, quite charmed by the delightful place, went here and there gathering flowers; and being tired by now, she sat down in the shade of a tree. The girl had not yet settled herself on the ground when a serpent approached her. Seeing it, Bianacabella was much frightened; but as she was about to scream, the serpent said to her, "Ah, be quiet, and don't move, nor be afraid; for I am your sister and was born with you on the same day and in the same birth, and my name in Samaritana. And if you will be obedient to my commandments, I will make you blessed; but if you do otherwise, you will become the most unfortunate and unhappy lady ever to be found in the world. Go therefore without any fear, and tomorrow have brought into the garden two vessels, one full of pure milk, and the other the finest rosewater; and then come to me alone without any company." When the serpent had left, the girl got up from where she was sitting and went to her nurse, whom she found still napping; and waking her, without saying a word, she went with her into the house.

On the following day, as Biancabella was alone with her mother in her room, her expression looked very melancholy. Wherefore her mother said to her, "What's the matter, Biancabella, that I see you looking so unhappy? You used to be happy and merry, and now you seem to me all sad and sorrowful."

To whom her daughter replied. "There's nothing the matter, except that I would like two vessels to be carried into the garden, one full of milk and the other of rosewater."

"And for such a little thing do you grieve, my daughter?" said the mother. "Don't you know that everything is yours?" And having two large beautiful vessels brought, one of milk and the other of rosewater, she sent them into the garden.

Biancabella, when the time had come according to the arrangement made with the serpent, without being accompanied by any maids, went to the garden; and opening the gate, shut herself in alone and sat down by the vessels. No sooner had Biancabella sat down when the serpent approached and bid her undress immediately and to enter thus naked into the white milk; and bathing her with it from head to foot and licking her with her tongue, the serpent cleaned her all over wherever any defect might appear. Afterwards, drawing her out from the milk, she put her into the rosewater, giving her a fragrance which offered her great refreshment. Then she dressed her again, commanding her expressly to keep silent and to reveal this to no one, not even her father or mother, because she wanted no other lady to exist who might equal her in beauty and gentleness. And endowing her finally with infinite virtues, the serpent departed from her.

Coming out from the garden, Biancabella returned to the house; and her mother, seeing her so beautiful and lovely that she surpassed all others in beauty and loveliness, was astonished and did not know what to say. Yet she asked her what she had done to come into such extreme beauty. And the girl replied that she did not know. Then the mother took a comb to comb her hair and arrange her blond tresses, and pearls and precious jewels fell from her head; and as she washed her hands, there came forth roses, violets, and laughing flowers of various colors with such a sweet fragrance that it seemed that here was the earthly paradise. Seeing this, the mother ran to Lamberico her husband and with maternal joy said to him, "My Lord, we have the most gentle, the most beautiful, and the most lovely daughter that nature ever made. And besides the divine beauty and loveliness which are clearly seen in her, from her hair come pearls, gems and other precious jewels, and from her white hands, oh wonderful! come roses, violets, and every kind of flower, which render to all who see her the sweetest fragrance. I would never have believed it if I hadn't seen it with my own eyes." The husband, who was by nature incredulous and did not easily give faith to the words of his wife, laughed at what she said, and teased her; but being vehemently urged by her, he wished to see what was going on. And bidding the daughter come to his presence, he found it to be even truer than the mother had said. Wherefore he became so joyful that he judged assuredly there was no man in the world worthy to be joined to her in marriage.

The glorious fame of the charming and immortal beauty of Biancabella had already spread throughout the whole world; and many kings, princes and marquises came running from every direction in order to win her love and marry her. But none of them was of such virtue as to be able to obtain her, because everyone was imperfect in some way. Finally there arrived Ferrandino, king of Naples, whose prowess and illustrious name shone like the sun among the tiny stars; and going to the marquis, he asked for his daughter in marriage. The marquis, seeing that he was handsome, charming, and well-formed, and very powerful both in status and in wealth, concluded the betrothal; and when the daughter had been called in, they gave each other their hands and kissed. The marriage was no sooner contracted, than Biancabella remembered the words which her sister Samaritana had lovingly told her; and withdrawing from her spouse and pretending that she wanted to do certain things for herself, she went into her room; and closing herself in, through a little door she secretly entered the garden alone and in a low voice began to call Samaritana. But the serpent no longer presented herself as before. Seeing this, Biancabella wondered greatly; and neither finding her nor seeing her anywhere in the garden, she remained very sorrowful, knowing this had happened because she had not been obedient to her commandments.[1] Wherefore lamenting to herself, she returned to her room and opening the door, went to sit beside her groom, who had been waiting for her a long time. Now when the wedding was over, Ferrandino moved his bride to Naples, where with great pomp and glorious triumph and sounding trumpets she was honorably welcomed by the city.

Ferrandino had a stepmother with two dirty and ugly daughters; and she wanted to couple one of them to Ferrandino in marriage. But losing all hope of fulfilling this desire, she was kindled against Biancabella with such anger and disdain that she wished not only never to see her, but also never to hear her, feigning however to love her and cherish her. Fortune willed that the king of Tunisia made great preparations by land and by sea to wage war on Ferrandino; I don't know whether this was because of the wife he had taken or for some other cause; and already with his mighty army he had entered across the borders of the kingdom. Therefore it was necessary that Ferrandino take arms to defend his kingdom and confront the enemy. Wherefore, arranging whatever was necessary and commending Biancabella, who was pregnant, to his stepmother, he left with his army.

Not many days had passed when the wicked and insolent stepmother decided to make Biancabella die; and calling certain of her faithful servants, she bid them go with her to some place for amusement, and not to leave the place without having killed her, and for assurance of her death to bring back some sign. The servants, ready to do evil, were obedient to their lady; and pretending to go to a certain place for amusement, they led her into a forest where they prepared to kill her; but seeing her so beautiful and so gracious, they took pity on her and decided not to kill her, but they lopped off both her hands from her body and cut out both eyes from her head, carrying them to the stepmother as clear evidence that they had killed her. Seeing this, the impious and cruel stepmother was satisfied and very happy. And thinking to carry out her evil plan, the wicked stepmother spread word throughout the kingdom that her two daughters were dead, one of a continuous fever, the other from an abcess near the heart that had smothered her; and that Biancabella, in grief at the departure of the king, had aborted her child, and a tertian fever had seized her which was greatly consuming her, but that there was rather hope of life than fear of death. But the wicked and evil woman instead of Biancabella kept in the king's bed one of her daughters, pretending she was Biancabella oppressed with fever.

Ferrandino, who had already defeated and dispersed the army of his enemy returned home with glorious triumph; and expecting to find his beloved Biancabella all merry and joyful, he found her thin, discolored, and disfigured, lying in bed. And drawing close to her and gazing fixedly at her face and seeing her so ruined, he remained quite stunned, unable to imagine in any way that this was Biancabella; and when he had her combed, instead of the gems and and precious jewels that used to fall from her blond locks, there came forth fat lice which kept eating her; and from her hands, which used to bring forth roses and fragrant flowers, there came a filth and nastiness which sickened those who stood near. But the wicked woman comforted him, and told him this happened because of the long illness which produced such effects.

The poor Biancabella, then, with her hands chopped off and both eyes blinded, remained in a solitary place alone and out of the way in great affliction, always calling and calling her sister Samaritana to help her; but there was no one to reply except the resonant echo heard throughout the air. While the unhappy lady remained in such suffering, seeing herself completely deprived of human aid, lo there entered into the woods a very aged man, kind in appearance and very compassionate; who, when he heard the woeful and dolorous voice, following it by ear and slowly slowly approaching on foot, he found the girl blind and with her hands chopped off, who was fiercely lamenting her cruel lot. The good, old man, seeing her, could not bear to leave her among brambles, stumps, and thorns but, overcome by fatherly compassion, brought her home and commended her to his wife, bidding her strictly to take care of her. And turning to his three daughters who looked like three bright stars, he commanded them warmly to keep her company, treating her always affectionately and never letting her want for anything. The wife, who was more coarse than compassionate, kindled with raging anger turned impetuously against her husband and said, "Ah, husband, what do you want us to do with this woman, blinded and maimed not for her virtues surely but in reward for her desserts?"

To whom the old man replied with indignation, "Do as I tell you; and if you do otherwise, don't wait for me at home."

The sorrowful Biancabella, then, dwelling with the wife and her three daughters and talking with them about various things, and thinking to herself about her misfortune, prayed one of the daughters please to comb her hair a little. Hearing this, the mother was full of disdain because she did not want her daughter to become in any way this woman's servant. But the daughter, more dutiful then the mother, bearing in mind what her father had bid her, and seeing I don't know what in Biancabella's appearance which gave sign of greatness in her, untied the freshly laundered apron which she had been wearing and, spreading it on the ground, lovingly combed her hair. And she had barely begun to comb her when from her blond tresses showered pearls, rubies, diamonds, and other precious jewels. Seeing this, the mother, not without fear, remained astonished; and the great hatred which formerly she had felt for her was converted into true love. And when the old man returned home, they all ran to embrace him, rejoicing much with him for the good fortune that had befallen them in their poverty. Biancabella had a bucket of fresh water brought to her and had them wash her face and her maimed stumps, from which, while everyone was watching, roses, violets and flowers showered in abundance. Whereupon they all considered her not a human being but divine.

It happened that Biancabella decided to return to the place where the old man had found her. But the old man, the wife and the three daughters, seeing what great profit they had from her, made a fuss over her and begged her insistently in no way to leave them, alleging many reasons to dissuade her. But she, firm in her will, wanted absolutely to leave, promising them, however, to return. Hearing this, the old man without delay brought her back to the place where he had found her. And she bid the old man depart and return to her in the evening, when she would go back home with him. When the old man had left, the unfortunate Biancabella began to go through the woods, calling Samaritana; and her cries and laments reached the heavens. But Samaritana, although she was near and had never abandoned her, did not wish to respond. The poor girl, seeing that she was throwing her words to the wind, said, "What should I do any more in the world, since I am deprived of eyes and hands and ultimately lack all human aid?"

And kindled with a madness that took from her all hope of being saved, in desperation she wanted to kill herself. But having no other means to end her life, she made her way towards the water, which was not far off, to drown herself; and having now reached the bank to throw herself in, she heard a thundering voice say, "Alas! Don't do it, don't wish to be your own murderer! Save your life for a better end."

Then Biancabella, dismayed by such a voice, felt almost all her hair stand up on end. But thinking she recognized the voice, becoming a little bolder, she said, "Who are you who go wandering through these places, and with your voice show yourself sweet and pitiful towards me?"

"I am," replied the voice, "Samaritana your sister, whom you call so insistently."

Hearing this, Biancabella with a voice interrupted by fervent sobs, said to her, "Ah! my sister, help me, I beseech you; and if I departed from your council, I beg your pardon. For I erred, I confess to you my fault, but the error was through ignorance, not through malice; for had it been through malice, divine providence would not long have sustained me." Samaritana, hearing the piteous lament and seeing her so ill-treated, somewhat consoled her; and gathering certain herbs of marvelous virtue and placing them over her eyes, and joining two hands to her arms, at once she healed her. Afterwards Samaritana, laying down the wretched snakeskin, was left a beautiful young girl.

The sun was already hiding his shining rays and the shadows of night were beginning to appear, when the old man with hasty steps reached the woods and found Biancabella sitting with another nymph. And staring at her cleared sight, he remained astonished, almost thinking it was not she. But when he had recognized her, he said to her, "My daughter, this morning you were blind and maimed; how are you so soon healed?"

Answered Biancabella, "Not by myself, indeed, but by the virtue and courtesy of her who sits with me, who is my sister." And both of them arising, with supreme joy they went home together with the old man, where they were lovingly welcomed by the wife and daughters.

Many many days had now passed, when Samaritana, Biancabella, and the old man with his wife and three daughters went to the city of Naples to live; and seeing an empty place just opposite the king's palace, they sat down there. And when dark night had come, Samaritana, taking in hand a wand of laurel, three times struck the earth while saying certain words; which she had scarcely finished saying, when there burst forth a palace, the most beautiful and splendid ever seen. King Ferrandino, coming early in the morning to his window, saw the rich and miraculous palace and remained totally astonished and thunderstruck. And he called his wife and stepmother, who came to see. But to them it was most displeasing because they worried that something sinister might happen to them. As Ferrandino stood contemplating the said palace and looking it over in every part, he raised his eyes and saw through the window of a chamber two women whose beauty made the sun envious. And as soon as he had seen them, a fury entered his heart, for one of them seemed to him to look like Biancabella. And he asked them who they were and whence they had come. They answered him that they were two ladies who had left Persia and come with their possessions to live in this glorious city. And asked whether they would be pleased to receive a visit from him and his ladies, they answered that it would be very dear to them, but that it was more suitable and honorable that they, as subjects, go to visit him than that he and his wife, being king and queen, come to visit them. Ferrandino, calling for the queen and the other ladies, went with them, although they resisted going, in strong fear of their imminent ruin, to the palace of the two women; who with kind welcomes and honest manners received them most honorably, showing them the spacious loggias and ample halls and well-adorned chambers, with walls of alabaster and fine porphyry, where there were pictures that looked alive.

When they had seen the splendid palace, the beautiful girl, approaching the king, sweetly prayed him that he and his wife might deign one day to dine with them. The king, who did not have a heart of stone and was by nature magnanimous and generous, graciously accepted the invitation. And thanking the ladies for their honorable reception he departed with the queen and returned to his palace. Come the day appointed by invitation, the king, the queen, and the stepmother, royally dressed and accompanied by various matrons, went to honor the magnificent dinner already sumptuously prepared. And when they had washed their hands, the seneschal set the king and queen at a table somewhat higher than but close to the others; afterwards he seated all the others according to their degree, and everyone dined merrily and in great comfort. When the splendid dinner was finished and the tables cleared, Samaritana rose to her feet and, turning towards the king and queen, said, "Lord, so that we do not sit here wrapped in idleness, let someone propose something which may be entertaining and pleasing." Everyone agreed it was a good idea. However, there was no one who dared make a suggestion. Whereupon, seeing them all silent, Samaritana said, "Since no one has moved to say anything, with your

Majesty's leave I will summon one of our damsels who will give us no little delight." And calling for a damsel named Silveria, she commanded her to take a cittern in hand and sing something worthy of praise and in honor of the king. She, most obedient to her lady, took the cittern; and standing before the king, with sweet and delightful voice, touching the sonorous strings with a plectrum, she recounted in order the story of Biancabella, not however mentioning her by name. And when she had come to the end of the story, Samaritana arose and asked the king what suitable punishment, what fitting torture, would one deserve who had committed such an outrage.

The stepmother, who thought with a swift and ready reply to cover up her own fault, did not wait for the king to answer but said boldly, "A hotly blazing furnace would be little pain compared to what such a person deserved."

Then Samaritana, her face flaming like a coal afire, said, "And you are that wicked and cruel woman who caused such a crime to be commited. And you, evil and accursed, with your own mouth have now condemned yourself." And turning to the king, Samaritana with a joyful expression said to him, "This is your Biancabella! This is your wife so beloved by you! This is she without whom you could not live!" And as a sign of the truth, she commanded the three damsels, daughters of the old man, in the king's presence to comb her blond and curly hair, from which, as is told above, there came forth precious and delightful jewels, and from her hands showered morning roses and fragrant flowers. And for greater certainty, she showed the king the pure white neck of Biancabella encircled with a chain of finest gold, which appeared between her flesh and skin as naturally as through a crystal. The king, recognizing through true indications and clear signs that she was his Biancabella, tenderly began to weep and to embrace her. And he did not depart from there before he had had a furnace kindled and the stepmother and her daughters put inside, who, late repenting their sin, wretchedly ended their lives. After this, the three daughters of the old man were honorably married; and Ferrandino with his Biancabella and Samaritana lived a long time, leaving after them legitimate heirs of the kingdom.

IV, 4

NERINO, SON OF KING GALLESE OF PORTUGAL, IN LOVE WITH GENOBBIA, THE WIFE OF DOCTOR RAIMONDO BRUNELLO THE PHYSICIAN, OBTAINS HER LOVE AND TAKES HER TO PORTUGAL; AND DOCTOR RAIMONDO DIES OF GRIEF.

There are many men, delightful ladies, who because they have spent a long time in the study of fine writings, think they know many things, and then turn out to know little or nothing. And while men like these think they are crossing themselves on the forehead, they poke out their own eyes, as happened to a doctor very learned in his art who, thinking to fool another, was to his own grave harm ignominiously fooled, as you will fully understand through the present fable, which I intend to tell you.

Gallese, king of Portugal, had a son named Nerino; and he brought him up in such a manner that, until he came to his eighteenth year of age, he was unable to see any woman other than his mother and the nurse who took care of him. When Nerino had come then to the age of adulthood, the king decided to send him to study in Padua so that he might learn his Latin letters and the Italian language and manners. And as he had decided, so he did. Now while the young Nerino was in Padua, having made friends with many students who daily courted him, it happened that among them was a medical doctor named Doctor Raimondo Brunello the physician; and often talking together about different things, they began, as is the manner of young men, to talk about the beauty of women; and some said one thing and some another. But Nerino, because he had previously seen no woman except his mother and his nurse, said spiritedly that to his judgment no woman in the world could be found more beautiful, more lovely, and better dressed than his mother. And although many women were shown to him, he considered them all as garbage in comparison to his mother. Doctor Raimondo, who had as wife one of the prettiest women that nature ever made, entering into this idle chatter said, "Lord Nerino, I have seen a lady of such beauty that if you saw her perhaps you would not consider her less but instead more beautiful than your mother."

Nerino replied to him that he couldn't believe she was as pretty as his mother, but that he would like very much to see her.

To him Doctor Raimondo said, "If you would like to see her, I offer to show her to you."

"This," replied Nerino, "will please me very much, and I will be obliged to you."

Then said Doctor Raimondo, "Since you wish to see her, come tomorrow morning to the cathedral; and I promise you will see her."

And going home, he said to his wife, "Tomorrow rise early from bed, and arrange your hair, and make yourself beautiful and dress very elegantly, because I want you to go at the hour of high Mass to hear the service in the cathedral." Genobbia, such was the name of Doctor Raimondo's wife, not being in the habit of going now here and now there but for the most part staying at home to sew and embroider, was much surprised at this; but because he wished it so and it was his desire, she did it, and dressed up smartly and adorned herself so that she seemed not a lady but rather a goddess.

When Genobbia was gone to the sacred temple, as her husband had bidden her, Nerino, son of the king, came into the church; and seeing Genobbia, he judged her within himself most beautiful. After the fair Genobbia left, Doctor Raimondo arrived and, coming up to Nerino, said, "Now what do you think of that lady who just left the church? Do you think she has any rival? Is she more beautiful than your mother?"

"Truly," said Nerino, "she's a beauty; and nature couldn't make a more beautiful woman. But tell me, please, whose wife is she and where does she live?" Doctor Raimondo did not reply to this because he did not want to tell him.

Then said Nerino, "Doctor Raimondo, my friend, if you don't want to tell me who she is and where she lives, at least satisfy me in this, that I may see her another time."

"Gladly," answered Doctor Raimondo, "tomorrow come here to church, and I will arrange for you to see her as today."

And going home, Doctor Raimondo said to his wife, "Genobbia, make yourself ready for tomorrow morning, because I want you to go to Mass in the cathedral; and if ever you made yourself beautiful and dressed splendidly, see that you do it tomorrow." Genobbia was much surprised at this as before. But because her husband's command was important, she did all that he bid. Come morning, Genobbia, richly dressed and much more adorned than usual, went to church. And not long after came Nerino, who, seeing her extremely beautiful, was inflamed with such love for her as ever man felt for any woman. And when Doctor Raimondo arrived, Nerino begged him to tell who she was that looked so beautiful to his eyes. But Doctor Raimondo, pretending to be in a hurry because of his business, refused to say anything to him at the time; but leaving the young man to fry in his own grease, he went away delighted.

Thereupon Nerino, somewhat kindled with anger because of the small regard that Doctor Raimondo had shown him, said to himself, "You don't want me to know who she is and where she lives; but I will find out despite you." And leaving church, he waited until the beautiful lady also came out of church; and bowing to her, with modest manners and a happy face he accompanied her home.

Having thus learned clearly in which house she lived, he began to woo her; nor did a day go by without his passing ten times in front of her house. And desiring to speak with her, he tried to imagine by what way he could keep safe the lady's honor, while he himself obtained his aim. And having considered and reconsidered without finding any remedy that would help him, still he mused on until it occurred to him to obtain the friendship of an old woman who had her house across the street from Genobbia's. And having given her certain small presents and sealed a close friendship, he secretly went into her house. The house of this old woman had a window which looked into a room of Genobbia's house, and from it he could at his leisure see her go up and down through her house; but he did not want to reveal himself lest he give her cause for not letting him see her any more. So then, as Nerino was spending every day in this secret gazing, unable to resist the hot flame which burned his heart, he decided within himself to write her a letter and throw it into her house at a time when it seemed her husband was not at home. And so he threw it to her. And he did this a number of times. But Genobbia, without even reading it, nor thinking twice about it, threw it into the fire and burned it. And after she had done this many times, she thought she might just once open and see what was contained in it. And opening it, and seeing that the author was Nerino, son of the king of Portugal, ardently in love with her, she thought it over a bit; but then considering the sad life her husband gave her, she made good cheer and began to show Nerino a glad face; and having arranged things well, she brought him into the house. And the young man recounted the supreme love which he bore her, and the torments which he felt for her at every hour, and similarly the manner in which he had fallen in love with her. And she, who was beautiful, pleasant, and compassionate did not deny him her love.

So then, both of them being joined in reciprocal love and in the midst of amorous conversation, here came Doctor Raimondo knocking at the

door. Genobbia, hearing it, made Nerino lie down on her bed and stay there with the bed-curtains pulled shut until her husband left. The husband, entering the house and taking a few things of his, left without noticing anything. And so did Nerino. On the following day, as Nerino was strolling in the Piazza, by chance he passed Doctor Raimondo, to whom Nerino made a sign that he wanted to speak with him; and coming up to him, he said, "Sir, don't I have a bit of good news to tell you!"

"What's that?" said Doctor Raimondo.

"Don't I know," said Nerino, "the house of that beautiful lady? And haven't I had delightful conversations with her? And because her husband came home, she hid me in her bed and pulled the curtains so that he couldn't see me, and he left immediately."

Said Doctor Raimondo. "Is this possible?"

Replied Nerino, "It is possible, and it's true; and I have never seen a more merry nor a more gracious lady than she; if perchance, Sir, you go to her house, commend me to her, praying her to keep me in her good graces."

Doctor Raimondo promised him to do so and parted from him in a bad mood. But first he said to Nerino, "Will you go there again?"

To whom Nerino replied, "What do you think!" And going home, Doctor Raimondo decided not to say anything to his wife but rather to wait for a time when he could find them together.

The following day Nerino returned to Genobbia; and while they were in the midst of amorous pleasures and delightful conversation, home came the husband. But she at once hid Nerino in a chest, on top of which she put many clothes that she was cleaning so that they wouldn't get moth-eaten. The husband, pretending to look for certain things of his, turned the house upside down and even looked on her bed; and finding nothing, he left with a calmer mind and went about his practice. And Nerino similarly departed. And encountering Doctor Raimondo again, he said to him,

"Sir Doctor, did I not return to that gentlewoman? But envious fortune disrupted all my pleasure; for her husband arrived and disturbed everything."

"And what did you do?" said Doctor Raimondo.

"She," answered Nerino, "opened a chest and put me in it; and on top of the chest she put many clothes that she was taking care of so they would not get moth-eaten. And he, turning the bed upside down and every which way and finding nothing, left." How tormenting this was to Doctor Raimondo, he can imagine who has experienced love.

Nerino had given Genobbia a pretty and precious ring in the gold setting of which were carved his crest and name; and when day came and Doctor Raimondo was gone about his practice, Nerino was brought into the house by the lady; and as he lay with her in pleasure and sweet conversation, here came the husband back home. But Genobbia, naughty girl, perceiving his arrival, immediately opened a large letter cabinet that was in her room and hid Nerino in it. And Doctor Raimondo, entering the house, pretending to look for certain things of his, turned the room upside down; and finding nothing, neither in the bed, nor in the chests, quite bewildered, he took a brand and set fire to all four corners of the room with a determined intent to burn down the room and everything in it. Already the walls and beams were beginning to burn when Genobbia turning to her husband said, "What does this mean, husband? Have you perhaps gone crazy? If you want to burn down the house, burn it as you wish; but by my faith don't burn that letter cabinet which holds the documents pertaining to my dowry," and calling for four strong porters, she had them carry the cabinet out of the house and set it in the house of her neighbor the old woman; and Nerino opened it secretly, so that no one noticed, and went home. Out of his wits, Doctor Raimondo still stood there to see whether anyone was coming out whom he didn't like; but he saw nothing except the intolerable smoke and hot fire that was burning up the house. Already the neighbors had come running to extinguish the fire; and they worked at it until they put it out.

The next day Nerino, going towards Prato della Valle, ran into Doctor Raimondo, and greeting him, said, "Doctor, my friend, don't I have something to tell you that will amuse you greatly?"

"What's that?" replied Doctor Raimondo.

"I have escaped," said Nerino, "the most fearful danger that ever a living man escaped. I went to that gentlewoman's house; and as I was with her in pleasant conversation, her husband arrived; who, after he had turned the house upside down, set fire to it in all four corners of the room, and burned everything that was in the room."

"And you," said Doctor Raimondo, "where were you?"

"I," answered Nerino, "was hidden in the letter cabinet that she sent out of the house."

Hearing this and recognizing that what he was telling was true, Doctor Raimondo felt like dying from grief and passion; but still he did not dare reveal himself because he wanted to catch them in the act. And he said, "Sir Nerino, will you ever go back there again?"

To whom Nerino answered, "Having escaped the fire, what more do I have to fear?" Now putting these matters aside, Doctor Raimondo asked Nerino to deign to come the next day and dine with him; and the young man gladly accepted the invitation.

The following day, Doctor Raimondo invited all his relatives and the relatives of his wife and prepared a splendid and sumptuous dinner, not in the house which was half burned out but elsewhere; and he ordered his wife to come too, but she was not to sit at the table but stay hidden and prepare whatever was necessary. So then, when all the relatives and the young Nerino had assembled, they were placed at the table; and Doctor Raimondo with his blockheaded science tried to get Nerino drunk so that he could then do what he had in mind. Therefore after Doctor Raimondo had many times brought him a glass full of wicked wine, and Nerino had drunk it down every time, Doctor Raimondo said, "Say, Lord Nerino, tell these relatives of ours some little story good for a laugh."

The poor young Nerino, not knowing that Genobbia was Doctor Raimondo's wife began to tell them his story, holding back, however, the names of all the characters.

It happened that a servant went to the room where Genobbia was and said to her, "My lady, if you were hidden in a corner, you would hear the best story that you ever heard in your life; come, I pray you." And going into a corner, she recognized that it was the voice of Nerino her lover and that the story he was telling was about her.

And the lady, prudent and wise, took the diamond that Nerino had given her and, putting it in a silver cup full of a delicious drink, said to the servant, "Take this cup and give it to Nerino, and tell him to drink it so that afterwards he'll talk better."

The servant, taking the cup, carried it to the table; and as Nerino wanted something to drink the servant said, "Take this cup, lord, for afterwards you will talk better."

And he, taking the cup, drank down all the wine; and seeing and recognizing the diamond that was in it, he let it slip into his mouth; and pretending to clean his mouth, he slipped it out and put it on his finger. And realizing that the beautiful lady about whom he was talking was the wife of Doctor Raimondo, he did not want to go on any further; and being urged on by Doctor Raimondo and by the relatives to continue the story he had begun, he replied, "Oh yes, oh yes! The rooster crowed, I ceased to snore, and in the day I heard no more." Hearing this the relatives of Doctor Raimondo, who had first believed that everything Nerino told them about the wife was true, treated both of them as big drunks.

After several days Nerino met Doctor Raimondo, and pretending not to know that he was Genobbia's husband, he told him that he was about to leave in a few days because his father had written him to return to his kingdom. Doctor Raimondo in reply wished him a speedy journey. Nerino, having made secret arrangements with Genobbia, ran off with her and took her to Portugal, where with supreme joy they lived a long time. And Doctor Raimondo, going home and not finding his wife, died a few days later of despair.

VII, 2

MALGHERITA SPOLATINA FALLS IN LOVE WITH THE HERMIT TEODORO, AND BY SWIMMING GOES TO MEET HIM; DISCOVERED BY HER BROTHERS AND DECEIVED BY A BURNING LAMP, SHE WRETCHEDLY DROWNS IN THE SEA.

L ove, as I find most prudently described by wise men, is nothing other than an irrational will, caused by a passion that enters the heart through lustful thinking, of which the evil effects are the dissipation of worldly riches, the wasting away of bodily strength, the misdirection of the mind, and the loss of liberty. In it there is no reason, in it there is no order, in it there is no stability. It is the father of vices, the enemy of youth, and the death of old age; and rarely or never is it granted a happy and glorious end, as happened to a lady of the Spolatina family, who, subjected to love, wretchedly ended her life.

Ragusa,[2] worthy ladies, the most famous city of Dalmatia, is situated by the sea and has not far away a little island commonly called Midway Island where there is a strong and well built castle; and between Ragusa and the aforesaid island is a little rock where nothing is to be found save a very small church with a bit of a hut half-covered with planks. No one lived there, because the place was sterile and the air was bad, except for a hermit named Teodoro, who as a penance for his sins devotedly served at that chapel. This man, not having any way to support his life, went sometimes to Ragusa and sometimes to Midway Island to beg. It happened one day as Teodoro was on Midway Island and begging for his bread according to his habit, he found what he would never have dreamed of finding. For a charming and lovely girl named Malgherita came by him; who, seeing him look handsome and attractive, reflected to herself that he was a man rather to exercise himself in human pleasures than to devote himself to solitude. Whereupon Malgherita so wildly embraced him in her heart that day and night she thought of nothing but him. The hermit, who was not yet aware of this, continued his practice of begging and often went to Malgherita's house to ask her for alms. Malgherita, burning with love for him, gave him alms; however, she did not dare reveal to him her love. But love, which is a shield to whoever willingly follows its laws, nor ever fails to teach the way to arrive at the desired end, gave Malgherita some boldness; and going up to him, she spoke in this manner, "Teodoro, brother and sole comfort of my soul, such is the passion that torments me that if you do not help me, you will soon see me lifeless. I, inflamed with love for you, can no longer resist the amorous flames.

And so that you may not be the cause of my death, help me at once"; and having said these words, she began to cry copiously. The hermit, who had not noticed before that she was in love with him, was dumbfounded. But slightly reassured, he talked with her; and such was their conversation that, leaving aside celestial matters, they entered into matters of love; nor did anything remain for them but the means to find themselves together and to fullfill their yearning desire. The girl, who was very shrewd, said, "My love, don't worry; for I will show you the means we must take. The means will be this: you this evening at ten o'clock at night will put a burning lamp in the window of your hut; and I, seeing it, will immediately come to you."

Said Teodoro, "Ah! how will you manage, my girl, to cross the sea? You know that neither you nor I have a boat to ferry across; and to entrust yourself to the hands of another would be very dangerous to the honor and life of us both."

Said the girl, "Don't worry at all; leave the burden to me, because I have found a way to come to you without danger to life or honor. I, seeing the burning lamp, will come to you by swimming; and no one will know of our doings."

To whom replied Teodoro, "There's danger of your drowning in the sea, because you are young and of little endurance, and the way is long, and you could easily lose your breath and go under."

"I'm not afraid," replied the girl, "of maintaining my endurance; for I would swim in contest with a fish." The hermit, seeing her firm will, agreed; and when dark night had come, according to their arrangement, he lit the lamp and, preparing a very white towel, with greatest joy awaited the desired girl. She, seeing the light, rejoiced; and taking off her clothes, barefoot and in a shift, went alone to the seashore, where, pulling off the shift and wrapping it in their manner about her head, she threw herself into the sea; and she applied her arms and feet to swimming so hard that in less than a quarter of an hour she reached the hut of the hermit, who was waiting for her. Seeing the girl, he took her by the hand and led her into his ill-covered hut and, taking the towel white as snow, with his own hands dried her all over; then bringing her into his little cell and placing her on a small bed, he lay down beside her and took the ultimate fruits of love. The two lovers stayed for two long hours in sweet conversations and close embraces; then the girl very satisfied and pleased left the hermit, having made, however, good arrangements to return to him.

The girl, who had become habituated to the hermit's sweet food, every time that she saw the lamp lit went swimming to him. But cruel and blind fortune, changer of kingdoms, juggler of worldly things, enemy of every happy person, did not suffer the girl to enjoy her dear lover for long but, as if envious of another's good, intervened and broke up all their plans. For while the air was thickened all around by a troublesome fog, the girl, who had seen the burning lamp, threw herself in the sea; and as she swam, she was discovered by certain fishermen who were fishing near by. The fishermen, thinking her to be a fish swimming there, began to watch her intently, and recognized that it was a woman, and saw her emerge and enter the hermit's hut. At this they were very astonished. And setting their hands to the oars, they reached the hut where having placed themselves to spy, they waited until the girl came out of the hut and

swimming made her way towards Midway Island. But the poor thing did not know to hide herself well enough that she might not be recognized by the fishermen. Having thus discovered the girl and found out who she was, and seeing the perilous trip made several times, and having understood the signal of the burning lamp, they decided among themselves to keep the matter secret. But then, thinking of the dishonor which could come to her honest family and the danger of death which the girl could run into, they changed their minds and decided to lay open the whole matter to her brothers; and going to the house of Malgherita's brothers, they told them the whole story point by point.

The brothers, hearing and learning the sad news, could not believe it before seeing it with their own eyes. But after they were certain of the fact, they decided that she must die; and making a careful plan among themselves, they carried it out. Therefore the youngest brother, as evening grew dark, got into a little boat and quietly went alone to the hermit; and he asked him not to refuse him shelter for the night because something had occured for which he was in great danger of being arrested and sentenced to death. The hermit, who knew that it was Malgherita's brother, kindly welcomed him and treated him affectionately; and all that night he spent with him in varied conversation, declaring to him the miseries of this world and the grave sins which kill the soul and enslave it to the devil. While the youngest brother was staying with the hermit, the other brothers inconspicuously left their house and, taking pole and a lamp got into a boat and went towards the hermit's hut; and when they had arrived, they set the pole upright, and on top of it they put the burning lamp, waiting for what would happen. The girl, seeing the lamp burning, took to the sea as was her habit and bravely swam towards the hut. The brothers, who were keeping quiet, hearing Malgherita's movement in the water, took their oars in hand and quietly with the lamp still burning moved away from the hut; and without being heard by her, or seen because of the dark night, they began slowly slowly without making any noise to row. The girl, who through the dark night could see nothing but the burning lamp, kept following it; but the brothers rowed so far that they led her into the open sea; and lowering the pole, they put out the light. The poor girl, not seeing the lamp any more nor knowing where she was, already tired from her long swim, was dismayed; and seeing herself beyond all human aid, she gave herself up completely and, like a broken ship, was swallowed by the sea. The brothers, who saw that there was no longer any way for her to be saved, leaving their unfortunate sister in the middle of the ocean waves, returned home. The youngest brother at daylight thanked the hermit properly for his welcome and left him.

Already the sad report was spreading through the whole castle that Malgherita Spolatina was not to be found. At which the brothers pretended to feel great sorrow, but within their hearts they were supremely glad. The third day had not passed when the dead body of the unfortunate lady was thrown by the sea onto the hermit's shore. He, seeing it and recognizing it, was close to killing himself. But taking her by one arm, with no one noticing, he dragged her out of the water and carried her into his house; and throwing himself upon the dead face, for a long while he wept and flodded her white breast with abundant tears, many times calling her in vain. But after he had wept, he thought to give her a worthy burial and to help her soul with prayers, with fasts, and with other good deeds. And taking the spade with which he sometimes dug his little vegetable patch, he made a grave inside his little church and with many tears closed her eyes and mouth; and making her a garland of roses and violets, he set it in on her head; then giving her a blessing and kissing her, he put her in the grave and covered her with earth. And in this way was preserved the honor of the brothers and of the lady, nor did anyone ever find out what became of her.

Conclusion

Because rosy dawn was beginning to appear, and already the carnival time was over and the first day of Lent had arrived, the lady, turning to her honorable company with a pleasant expression spoke thus: "You know, magnificent lords and loving ladies, that we are at the first day of Lent, and now all around we hear the bells which invite us to holy prayers and to do penance for the wrongs we have commited. Therefore I think it honest and right that in these holy days we put aside delightful conversations and amorous dances and sweet music, angelic singing and ridiculous fables, and attend to the salvation of our souls." Both the men and women, who did not desire otherwise, highly praised the lady's wish. And without having torches lit, because by now it was daylight, the lady commanded each of them to go to rest, nor any more to return for company to their usual consistory until she bid them. The men, taking proper leave of the lady and her damsels, and leaving them in holy peace, returned to their lodgings.

The end of the thirteenth and final night.

Matteo Bandello (1485–c.1561)

Raised since the age of twelve in Dominican schools and convents, Bandello became a friar of that order, of which his uncle was a chief administrator. He traveled all over Italy, living both at convents and at courts, and moved to France when the Spanish invaded Milan, his home town. In France he served as secretary to the Venetian general Cesare Fregoso and in 1550 became bishop of Agen. He became acquainted with Marguerite de Navarre, sister of the French king and patroness of literary men; her own book of stories shares a few tales with Bandello's, although it is not clear who borrowed from whom.

His collection of 214 tales has no frame, and the author claims to have put them together in no particular order. Undoubtedly the stories had circulated separately before their publication. The letters of dedication which accompany all the tales refer to many of the famous writers, artists, statesmen, and clergymen of his time; and the historian Jacob Burkhardt used them to document sixteenth-century life. However, as the dedications were sometimes composed long after the death of the addressee, they must be viewed as part of the fiction, an evocation rather than transcription of historical situations.

Bandello emphasizes the historical truth of his stories and describes his role as writer in the dedication to III, 24: to record deeds and sayings worthy of memory and to reward the good with fame. The preface to the reader in volume III asks us "to take all my stories in the spirit in which I wrote them, which was no other end certainly but to delight and warn all kinds of people to leave indecent things and attend to living honestly, seeing that for the most part sorry and wicked doings are sooner or later punished, remaining in memory with eternal infamy; whereas things well done and honest live forever in glory and are praised and celebrated." His tales, however, are often less moralizing than his stated intent; and some readers thought it indecent that a bishop should write such things.

The first three volumes of tales were published in 1554 in Lucca, the fourth At Lyons in 1573. One of the tales (I, 8) had been told by Castiglione in his *Book of the Courtier,* and several others were used (either before or after

Bandello) by Marguerite of Navarre in her *Heptameron*. Boistuau translated six *Histoires Tragiques* in 1559; Belleforest translated others in 1560; and these two translations, separately or together, were reprinted many times before 1660. The French translations became in turn the source for a Spanish *Historias trágicas exemplares* (1589), for Geffraie Fenton's *Certain Tragical Discourses of Bandello* (1567), and for George Turberville's *Tragical Tales* (1582). Painter devoted nearly half of his *Palace of Pleasure* (1566) to Bandello and became a source for plays such as Webster's *The Duchess of Malfi* and Marston's *The Insatiate Countess*. Bandello is really the culmination of the Italian novella; through him more than anyone else, Italian narrative exploded into France and England.

I have used Bandello's *Tutte le Opere*, ed. Francesco Flora (Milan: Mondadori, 1934) which has notes, bibliography, and an index of names. Bibliography can also be found in the incomplete edition of *Novelle* by Giuseppe Ferrero, Classici Italiani 30 (Turin: UTET, 1974) and in Porcelli's *Novellieri Italiani*. The sixteenth-century translations are not at all accurate. *The Novels of Matteo Bandello*, trans. by John Payne (London: The Villon Society, 1890) includes 166 tales. There are *Twelve Stories selected and Done into English* by Percy Pinkerton (London: J. C. Nimmo, 1895). A few stories may also be found in the collections of Bishop, Clark and Lieber, Hall, Pasinetti, Pettoello, Roscoe, and Valency. There are a number of studies in English: T. G. Griffith, *Bandello's Fictions* (Oxford: Blackwell, 1955). K. Hartley, *Bandello and the Heptameron* (Melbourne: Melbourne University Press, 1960). R. Pruvost, *Matteo Bandello and Elizabethan Fiction* (Paris: H. Champion, 1937). Nancy D'Antuono, "The Italian Novella and Lope de Vega's Comedies," *DAI* 36 (1975) 1552A (University of Michigan) deals especially with Bandello.

From Bandello to his pure and kind readers.

Many years have already passed since I began to write some stories, spurred by the commandments of that virtuous lady of perpetually regretted and honored memory, the late Ippolita Sforza, consort of the very kind lord Alessandro Bentivoglio, may God keep her in glory. And while she lived, although some of the tales had been dedicated to others, nonetheless I presented the whole collection to her. But as the world was not worthy to possess so elevated and glorious a spirit on earth, our Lord God took her to Himself in heaven by an early death. After her death it happened to me as is wont to happen to a turning millstone, *which, having been spun by a strong hand, even when that hand is taken away, yet the wheel, by virtue of its earlier motion, continues to spin a good while without being touched. So after the death of the said most noble lady, my mind, always desirous of obeying her, did not cease moving my weak hand so that I persevered in writing now this and now that tale, according as the occasion was offered to me, until I had written many.*

Now, as some of my friends want to see my tales, and since they have seen many of them already, they continually urge me to publish them. I consigned a number of the tales to Vulcan; then I collected together those which knew how to protect themselves from the devouring fire, and not observing any order, but taking them just as they came to my hands, I made three groups of them, dividing them into three books so that they might be in the slimmest volumes possible. I neither invite nor force anyone whosoever to read them, but I beseech all those who may be pleased to read them that they deign to do so in the spirit in which they were written by me: I affirm assuredly that I wrote them to benefit and delight others. Whether I have accomplished that, I leave, my kind readers, to your benevolent and honest judgment.

I do not want to say, as did the noble and most eloquent Boccaccio, that these tales of mine are written in the Florentine vernacular because I would be manifestly lying, as I am neither Florentine nor Tuscan, but Lombard. And although I have have no style, which I confess, I emboldened myself to write these tales because I believe that history and stories of this sort can give delight in whatever language they may be written. Farewell.

I, 8

From Bandello to the most illustrious and most reverend Lord Monsignor Pirro Gonzaga, Cardinal.

I f in our times, my most honorable lord, we used as much care and diligence as were used for a long time by the Greeks and Romans in writing down all the events worthy of memory, I firmly believe that our age would be found no less praiseworthy than the ancient times which writers praise and commend so much. For when we consider painting and sculpture, if our painters and sculptors are not to be placed ahead of those much celebrated ancients, they are at least their equals. The good writers of our day are unequalled and need not yield one jot, I believe, to the ancient orators, poets, philosophers, and other writers, Latin as well as Greek. When was the military ever in greater esteem than now? Certainly *if Alexander the Great, Pyrrhus, Hannibal, and Philopomene, Quintus Fabius Maximus, those thunderbolts in battle the Scipios, Marcellus, Pompey the Great, and Caesar, with all the other famous heroes, were alive today and saw today's methods of warfare and what is done with sulfur, nitre, and carbon, they would be left in dismay. They would yield to many of our captains and would see in the privates as much courage, as much industry, and as much valor as they ever saw in their own soldiers. But the trouble is that in our times there is no one who takes pleasure in recording the events of his day; wherefore we lose many fine and witty sayings, and many generous and memorable deeds remain buried at the bottom of deep oblivion. And yet every day fine things are happening worthy of being consecrated to the memory of posterity. Wherefore I will now select some things that happened in these past years at Gazuolo.*

When I had come to pay my respects to my valorous Sir Pirro Gonzaga your uncle, and we were talking about various events, Sir Pirro commanded my honest godfather Lord Gian Matteo Olivo, who is something of a poet, to narrate this brief history. You too were present when my godfather narrated it, and you said that if it had happened in ancient times, one would see Giulia of Gazuolo no less celebrated and sung than the Roman Lucretia, who is so famous; except that Giulia was of too low a blood.

Now as I was putting together my tales, I wished to see this one, which I had written down at the time, among the others, armed with your lordly and virtuous name so that you might know that I am mindful of you. And how could I be otherwise, seeing that you have always loved me and paid me more respect than I merited? But I hope to have an occasion other than a tale to make known to you my gratitude towards you and the sincerity of my service to you and to your entire illustrious household for the many pleasures and honors which I have received and daily receive from you. Keep well.

GIULIA OF GAZUOLO, BEING FORCIBLY RAPED, THROWS HERSELF IN THE OGLIO, WHERE SHE DIES.

Our Sir Pirro Marquis of Gonzaga and Lord of Gazuolo—the town which you see set here on the banks of the Oglio on the side towards the Po, and which has belonged through many generations to the lords of the Gonzaga family—wishes that I narrate, kind lords and you courteous gentlemen, the memorable event of the death of a Giulia of this land, which happened not long ago. This illustrious lord himself could tell much better than I how it happened. There are many others too who would have satisfied his wish on this subject as well as I and narrated everything precisely. But since he commands me to be the narrator, it is my wish and duty to obey. Indeed I regret that I am not capable of praising the generous and manly spirit of Giulia as much as her unusual deed deserves.

You must know, then, that while the liberal and wise prince, the illustrious and most revered Monsignor Ludovico Gonzaga, Bishop of Mantua, lived here in Gazuolo, he always held a most honored court with many and virtuous gentlemen, as one who delighted in virtues and who spent money very generously. In those days there was a girl seventeen years of age named Giulia, the daughter of a very poor man of this land, of very humble birth, who had nothing but what by laboring and toiling all day with his hands he earned as a living for himself, his wife and his two daughters. The wife too, who was a good woman, labored to earn something by spinning and doing other similar domestic services suitable for women. This Giulia was very pretty, endowed with charming manners, and much lovelier than befitted such low blood. Now with her mother and now with other women she went into the country to hoe and to do other work, according to what was needed.

I remember that one day, when I was with the excellent Lady Antonia Bauzia, mother of these illustrious lords of ours, and going to San Bartolomeo, we met the said Giulia, who with a basket on her head was returning homeward all alone. Lady Antonia seeing such a pretty girl who looked about fifteen, stopping her carriage, asked her whose daughter she was. She respectfully replied with the name of her father and satisfied my lady's questions very properly, as if she had not been born and raised in a hovel and hut of straw, but had been brought up her whole life in court, so that Antonia told me she would like to take her into her house and raise her with the other maids. Why she never did it, I couldn't tell you.

Returning then to Giulia, I tell you that in all the days she was working, she never wasted time, but whether alone or in company was always busy. Then on holidays, as is the custom of the region, she went after dinner with other girls to the dances and honestly entertained herself. It happened one day that, when she was about seventeen, a chamber servant of the said Monsignor the bishop, who was from Ferrara, set greedy eyes on her upon seeing her dance, and thinking her indeed the most attractive and pretty girl he had seen in a long time, and one that, as I said, seemed to have been brought up in the most polite houses, he fell strangely in love with her so that he could think of nothing else. When the dance was finished, which had seemed very long to the valet, and they were beginning to play another tune, he asked her to dance a galliard with him for she performed a galliard very well and so neatly in time that it was a great delight to watch her as she gracefully moved. The valet returned to dance with her, and, if not for shame, he would have taken her for every dance, thinking that when he held her by the hand he felt more pleasure than he had ever felt before. And although she worked all day, nonetheless her hand was white, slender and very soft. While the poor lover, so suddenly kindled by her and her beautiful ways, thought by gazing at her to allay the newborn flames which were already consuming him and making him miserable, without realizing it, he gradually made them greater, with his gazes adding brush to the fire.

During their second and third dance, the youth spoke many little words and phrases to her such as new lovers are wont to say. She always answered wisely, saying he ought not to speak to her of love, because for a poor girl like her it was not suitable to lend an ear to fables of the sort, nor could the importunate Ferrarese ever get more out of her. When the dancing was over, the Ferrarese followed her to learn where she lived. Afterwards he often had opportunity both in Gazuolo and outside to speak with Giulia and reveal to her his fervent love, always trying to win her with his words and to heat her cool breast. But regardless of what he said, she never moved a jot from her chaste intentions; rather she begged him warmly to leave her alone and not to bother her. But the more she showed herself firm and reluctant, the more the wretched lover burned, whose heart was being cruelly gnawed by the worm of love; the more he pursued her, and the more he labored to make her yield to his appetites, although it was in vain. He bid an old woman, who looked like Saint Zita, go talk to her, who did this service for him very diligently, trying with flattering chatter to corrupt the stony affection of chaste Giulia. But the girl was so firm that never a word which the old bawd said could pierce her breast. Hearing this, the Ferrarese found himself the most desperate man in the world, unable to imagine leaving her, still hoping that by begging, serving, loving, and persevering, he must soften Giulia's cruel hardness, thinking it impossible that in the long run he could not obtain her. As the proverb says, he reckoned his account without the innkeeper.

Now seeing that from day to day she showed herself more reluctant and that whenever she saw him she fled as from a basilisk, he decided to see if he might accomplish through gifts what words and services were unable to effect, reserving force as a last resort. He returned to speak to the wicked, old woman, giving her some trinkets of small value to bring to Giulia on his behalf. The old woman found Giulia all alone at home; and seeking to speak of the Ferrarese, showed her the gifts which he had sent her. But the honest girl, taking those trinkets which the old woman had brought, threw them all out the door onto the public street and chased the old traitress out of the house, telling her that if she ever came back to say a word, she would go to the castle to tell it to Lady Antonia. The old woman, picking up the things that were lying on the street, returned to talk with the Ferrarese telling him that it was impossible to bend the girl, and that she did not know what more to do in this case. The young man found himself in the worst humor imaginable. He would gladly have withdrawn from the enterprise; but whenever he thought of leaving her, the wretch felt like dying. Finally unable to suffer any longer seeing himself so unwanted, the poor, blind lover decided that, come what may, if he saw a good opportunity, he would take from her by lively force what she was unwilling to give him.

There was in court a footman of Monsignor the bishop who was great friends with the Ferrarese, and if I recall rightly, he too was from Ferrara. The valet disclosed to him the whole of his very fervent love, and the extent of the effort he had made to arouse a little compassion in the girl's breast, complaining that she had always shown herself more and more rigid like a rock in the sea, and that he had never been able to soften her either with words or with gifts. "Now," said he, "seeing that I cannot live if I do not satisfy my desires, knowing how much you love me, I pray you to take my side and help me carry out what I desire. She often goes alone in the countryside, where, as the grain is already quite high, we shall be able to accomplish our intent." The footman, without giving it further thought, promised always to be on his side and to do all that he wished.

And so the valet, spying on her continually, heard one day that she was going out from Gazuolo alone. Thereupon, calling the footman, he went with him to where she was doing I don't know what in a certain field. Arriving there, he began as he was wont to beg her now to have pity on him. She, seeing herself alone, prayed the young man not give her any more trouble and, apprehensive of some ill, started towards Gazuolo. The young man, not willing to let the prey slip from his hand, pretended that he wanted to accompany her with his companion, all the while affectionately praying her with humble and loving words to have pity on his pains. She, hurrying on her way, was heading hastily homewards. And walking without her giving a reply to anything the young man said, they arrived at a large field of grain which it was necessary to cross.

It was the next to the last day of May, and could have been almost noontime; the sun was very hot according to the season, and the field quite remote from any habitation. When they had entered into the field, the young man, putting his arm around Giulia's neck, tried to kiss her; but she, trying to flee and screaming for help, was seized by the footman and thrown to the ground; he immediately stuffed a gag in her mouth so that she could not scream; both of them lifted her up and carried her forcibly a long way from the path that crossed the field; and there, with the footman holding her hands, the unbridled young man deflowered her who was gagged and unable to resist. The poor girl cried bitterly and with groans and sobs made manifest her inestimable grief. The cruel valet made love to her a second time against her will, taking all the pleasure he wanted. Afterwards he ungagged her and began with many loving words to try to pacify her, promising that he would never abandon her and that he would help her get married so that all would be well. She said nothing other than that they should set her free and let her go home, crying bitterly all the while. The young man tried anew with sweet words, with great promises, and with attempts to give her money to calm her down. But it was all singing to the deaf, and the more he tried to console her, the more violently she cried. Seeing that he was still multiplying words, she said to him, "Young man, you have done your whole will with me and sated your dishonest appetite; I beg you now to free me and let me go. Let what you have done be enough for you, which indeed was too much." The lover, anxious lest he be found out by Giulia's violent crying, since he saw that he was laboring in vain, decided to leave her and go off with his companion; and so he did.

Giulia, after having cried bitterly for a long time over her violated virginity, pulling back together her unfastened clothes and drying her eyes the best she could, came soon to Gazuolo and went to her home. Neither her father nor her mother were there; at that moment there was only her sister about ten or eleven years old, who because she was somewhat unwell had not been able to go out. When Giulia arrived at home, she opened a coffer of hers where she kept her few things. Then, taking off all the clothes which she was wearing, she took a freshly laundered shift and put it on. Then she put on her finewoven dress of snow white and a collar of white crape all embroidered, plus an apron of white crape which she was wont to wear only on holidays. She also put on a pair of white silk stockings and red shoes. Afterwards she arranged her hair as prettily as she could, and around her neck she put a string of yellow amber. In sum, she adorned herself with the prettiest trinkets she could find, as if she were going to show herself off at the highest holiday in Gazuolo.

Afterwards she called her sister and gave her all the other things which she had, and taking her by the hand and locking the door of the house, she went to the home of their neighbor, a very aged woman who was gravely ill in her bed. To this good woman crying all the while, Giulia narrated the whole event of her misfortune, and said to her,

"May it not be God's will that I remain alive after I have lost the honor which was my reason for living. Never will it happen that anyone points me out by finger or says to my face, 'Here's the nice girl who has become a prostitute and shamed her family, who if she had any intelligence ought to hide herself.' I do not want anyone in my family ever to have it cast in their teeth that I willingly satisfied the valet. My end will make clear to the whole world and will give more certain faith that if my body was violated by force, my spirit always remained free. These words I wanted to say to you so that you can report the whole thing to my unhappy parents, assuring them that there was never in me any consent to satisfy the dishonest appetite of the valet. Peace be with you."

Having said this, she went outside and walked a long way towards the Oglio, and her little sister followed behind crying, not knowing what it was about. When Giulia arrived at the river, she threw herself headfirst into the depth of the Oglio. At the sister's cries, who was sending screams up to the heavens, many came running hither but too late, because Giulia, who had willingly thrown herself into the river to drown herself, abandoning herself at once, was suffocated there.

The Lord Bishop and Lady Antonia, hearing of the miserable event, had her fished out. At this point the valet, calling the footman to himself, ran away. The body was found, and as the reason that she had drowned herself became known, she was honored with universal weeping by all the women and also with many tears by the men of the region. The illustrious and most reverend Lord Bishop, being unable to bury her in holy ground,[2] had her set on the piazza in a tomb which is still there, resolving to bury her in a sepulchre of bronze and to have it set on that column of marble which one can still see in the piazza.

And in truth, to my judgment, this Giulia of ours deserves no less praise than did the Roman Lucretia; and perhaps, if one considers the whole matter well, she ought to be placed ahead of the Roman woman. One can only accuse nature for not having endowed such a magnanimous and noble spirit as Giulia's with nobler birth. But one is noble enough who is a friend of virtue and who places honor above everything in the world.

I, 26

From Bandello to the very courteous and magnificent lord, the lord Count Bartolomeo Ferraro, greetings.

H ow good it would be if some of the customs which exist in those new worlds that the Spanish and Portuguese are said to be finding daily (although the way to them was first opened by the Italians) existed in these countries of ours, so that all the evil done would cease and one wouldn't hear all the time, "So and so has killed his wife because he feared she was making him vicar of Corneto;[2] someone else has smothered his daughter because she had secretly married; and that fellow had his sister killed because she did not marry as he would have liked." This is certainly a great cruelty, that we men want to do everything which comes to mind, and yet we do not want poor women to be able to do as they wish, whatever it may be, and if they do anything we don't like, we turn at once to nooses, blades, and poisons. But how good it would be for us if the wheel were to spin and women ruled men! You can imagine indeed that they would take vengeance for all the injuries and wrongs that have been done to them by cruel men. At least there would be this comfort for us, that as they are naturally compassionate and kind-hearted, and because their pitying nature is not too fond of blood, poison, deaths, and tears, they would be pliable and easily placated by our prayers.

And in truth, it seems to me a grave foolishness on the part of men to base their own honor and that of their entire household on one woman's sexual appetite. If a man makes an error, no matter how enormous, his family does not lose its nobility on this account. If a son falls away from the ancient virtue of his grandfathers, who were upright men, they do not lose their dignity on this account. But we make the laws, we interpret them, we gloss them, and we set them forth as we see fit. Take that count, for instance, whose name I won't say, who married the daughter of one of his bakers, and why? Because she had plenty of money, and yet no one reproached him for it. Another, he too a very noble and rich count, took to wife the daughter of a muledriver without any dowry for no other reason than that he felt like doing it, and she now holds the place and rank of a countess and yet he is still a count as before. Recently a daughter of Enrico of Aragon and sister of the Aragonese cardinal, after the death of her husband who had been the Duke of Malfi,[3] married Sir Antonio Bologna, noble, virtuous, and rich by honest means, who had served King Federico of Aragon as steward. And because they thought she was marrying beneath her, they raised a crusade against her

and never ceased until she had been cruelly killed, together with her hus-
band and several children, a thing truly worthy of the greatest pity.

Now as it has not yet been a year since Sir Antonio was wretchedly
murdered here in Milan, and as Sir Girolamo Visconti recently narrated
the course of their marriage and death in the presence of many at his
magnificent palace of the White House outside Milan, I, who had
already heard the whole thing in detail from the valorous Sir Cesare
Fieramosca, composed a tale on the subject, which I now give to you so
that at some time when you have retired from public duties, although
your leisure is always filled with honest business, you may read it and
keep it in memory of me, who am your debtor for much greater things.
And to you I commend myself. Keep well.

SIR ANTONIO BOLOGNA MARRIES THE DUCHESS OF MALFI AND BOTH OF THEM ARE MURDERED.

Antonio Bologna, a Neapolitan, as many of you know, stayed at the house of Sir Silvio Savello while he lived in Milan. After Sir Silvio had left, he became close to Francesco Acquaviva, Marquis of Bitonto, who, taken in the rout at Ravenna, remained in the hands of the French as a prisoner in the castle at Milan and, giving bail as a security, came out of the castle and lived for a long time in that city. It happened that the said marquis paid a heavy fine and returned to the Kingdom of Naples. Therefore this man Bologna remained in the house of the knight Alfonso Visconti with three servants, and dressed and rode honorably around Milan. He was a very gallant and virtuous gentleman; besides being good-looking and quite strong of body, he was very gentlemanly rider. He was also adorned with a better than average knowledge of letters, and used to sing very sweetly with a lute in hand. I know there are some people here who heard him sing one day, or rather through pitiful singing bewail the state in which he found himself, having been pressed by Lady Ippolita Sforza and Bentivoglia to play and sing.

Now having returned from France, where he had continually served the unfortunate Federico of Aragon, who being chased from the Kingdom of Naples had put himself in the hands of Louis, the twelfth king of this name in France, and had been kindly received by him, Bologna returned to his home in Naples where he remained. He had served King Federico as steward for many years. Therefore, not long after, he was asked by the Duchess of Malfi, daughter of Enrico of Aragon and sister of the Aragonese cardinal, whether he wanted to serve her as steward. He, who was accustomed to courts and very devoted to the Aragonese faction, accepted the offer and went there.

The duchess had been left a widow very young and was in charge of the Duchy of Malfi and one son, whom she had borne from her husband. And finding herself young, bold, and pretty, and living in comfort, nor judging it well to marry and put her son under the charge of another, she thought that if she could she would find herself some worthy lover and enjoy her youth with him. She saw many men, both among her subjects and among others, who seemed to her well-mannered and gentlemanly, but giving detailed considerations to the manners and habits of all, she saw no one equal to her steward because in truth he was a very handsome man, large and well-proportioned, with fine and charming manners and gifted with many talents. Whereupon she fell ardently in love with him, and from day to day praising him more and commending his good manners, she felt herself so aflame for him, that she thought she could not live without seeing him or being near him. Bologna, who was neither a simpleton nor asleep, although he knew he was not the equal of such a high-ranking lady, being aware of her love, had so received her into the secret places of his heart that he could think of nothing save his love for her. In such a manner, then, they lived, loving each other.

Overtaken by a new turn of thoughts, wishing to offend God as little as possible and to bar the way to any blame which might spring from it, the duchess decided to become not the lover but the wife of Bologna, without letting anyone else know about it, so that they might secretly enjoy their love until they were constrained to make manifest their marriage. Having deliberated thus within herself, she called Bologna into her room one day and set herself with him at a window, as she often did when making plans with him for the care of the household, and she began to speak to him in this manner:

"If I were to speak with anyone other than you, Antonio, I would be very hesitant to say what I have decided to reveal to you. But because I know that you are a discreet gentleman and gifted by nature with deep understanding, and you have been raised and brought up in the royal courts of Alfonso II, of Ferdinand, and of Federico, my kinsmen, I hold the firm opinion and am pleased to believe that, when you have heard my honest reasons, you will find yourself in agreement with me. For finding you otherwise, I would be forced to think that you did not have that perspicacity of mind which everyone judges you to have.

"I, as you know, through the death and blessed memory of the lord duke my husband have been left a widow very young, and up to now I have lived in such a manner that no one, no matter how censorious and severe a critic, can in any way reproach me, even so much as the point of a needle, in what pertains to my honesty. Similarly the management of the duchy has been attended to by me in such a way that when the lord my son will come of age to take charge of it, I hope he will find things in better shape than when the lord duke left them. For besides having paid off more than fifteen thousand ducats of debt, which that blessed memory had piled up during the past wars, I have since then bought a barony in Calabria with a good income; moreover I find myself without a penny of debt, and the house is very well provided with everything it needs. Now, although I had thought to keep living a widow's life as I have done up to now, passing the time by visiting sometimes this piece of land, sometimes that castle, and sometimes Naples and attending to the management of the duchy, it now seems to me that I ought to change my plan and lead a different life. And in truth I judge it much better to get myself a husband than to do as some other women do, who with offense to God and with the eternal blame of the world give themselves in prey to lovers. I know very well what people are saying about a duchess of this realm even though she loves and is loved by one of the foremost barons, and I know you understand what I am talking about.

"Now to return to my own case, you see that I am young and neither squinting nor lame, nor do I have the face of the Baronzi,[4] which cannot show itself among others. I live, moreover, in comfort as you see every day, so that contrary to my will I necessarily give way to thoughts of love. I wouldn't know how to find a husband equal in status to my first, unless I intended to marry some young boy, who when he was sick of me would chase me from his bed and bring prostitutes there. For there is at present no baron of an age suitable to mine who is unmarried. Therefore, after my going over this matter many times, it has occurred to me to find a well-qualified gentleman and to take him as husband. But to avoid the murmurs of the crowd, and also in order not to fall into disgrace with the lords my kinsmen, and especially Monsignor the cardinal, my brother, I would like to keep the matter hidden until an occasion comes when it can be made public with less danger to me. He whom I intend to take as husband has an income of about one thousand ducats, and I from my dowry, with the increase that the lord duke left me at his death, have more than two thousand besides the furnishings of the house, which are mine. And if I shall not be able to maintain the rank of duchess, I shall be content to live as a gentlewoman. I would like now to hear what you advise me about this."

Antonio, hearing this long speech from the duchess, did not know what to say because, believing firmly that she loved him, and loving her not a little himself, he would not have wished her to marry on account of his own hope of bringing their love to a happy conclusion. He remained silent, therefore, all changed in his face, and instead of answering her he fiercely sighed. She, guessing her lover's thoughts and not displeased to recognize by this sign that she was fervently loved by him, in order not to keep him any longer in displeasure nor with his mind in doubt, spoke to him in this way:

"Antonio, be of good cheer and do not be dismayed, for if you wish it, I have decided that you are to be my husband."

At this speech the lover returned from death to life, and praising the duchess's opinion, with suitable words offered himself not as a husband but as a most faithful and humble servant. Having given each other their pledge, they talked at length together, and after many words, they arranged to be together in the best and most secret manner possible. The duchess had already made her thoughts known to a daughter of the nurse who had raised her since she was in the cradle. Therefore she called for her, and with no one there but the three of them, she wished in the presence of her maid to be married as wife to Bologna.

Their marriage remained a secret for many years, during which almost every night they slept together. And while this was going on to the greatest pleasure of both parties, the duchess became pregnant and in time brought forth a male child, but she knew so well how to manage it that no one in the court was aware of it. Bologna had the child brought up with good care and at its baptism named it Federico. After this, continuing their loving relationship, she became pregnant a second time and brought forth a beautiful daughter. At this second birth, she was not able to do things so covertly, and thus it became known to many that the duchess had been pregnant and had given birth. And as the event was murmured about by various people, the fact came to the ears of her two brothers, that is to the Cardinal of Aragon and another brother who, hearing that their sister had given birth but not knowing who the father was, resolved not to bear this shame thrown in their faces, and with great diligence began by many means to spy on every action and every movement that the duchess made.

As this rumor was going about the court and every day her brothers' men were coming to the duchess's with no business but to spy out this fact. Bologna, worrying lest on some occasion the maid reveal how matters were, said one day to the duchess, "My lady, you know the suspicion which the lords your brothers have of this second birth of yours and the extreme diligence they are using to obtain complete information about it. I am very worried that they may get some indication about me and one day have me

killed. You know their nature better than I and know how they can
strike. But because I think that they will never be cruel to you, I believe
firmly that, when they have had me murdered, they will go no farther.
Therefore I have decided to go away to Naples and, having arranged my
affairs there, to continue on to Ancona, where I will find means for my
income to be sent to me. I will stay there until we see that this suspicion
has left the minds of the lords your brothers. Time will then be our ad-
viser." The words between the couple were many. In the end, to his
wife's greatest grief he departed, and arranging his affairs and giving
charge of them to a close cousin of his, he went on, as he had planned, to
Ancona, where having rented an honorable dwelling, he lived with an
honest household. He had brought with him his son and daughter and
had them reared with great care.

The duchess, who had been left pregnant for a third time and could
not bear to live without her dear husband, was so unhappy with her
situation that she was ready to go mad. And after she had considered her
case over and over again, anxious that if this third birth came to light,
her brothers would play her a mean trick, she decided rather to go to her
husband and live with him as a private gentlewoman than to remain
without him as a duchess. There will be some who claim that love is not
so powerful. But who can truly say that love is not of extreme might?
Certainly his forces are much greater than we can imagine. Doesn't one
see that love all day long causes the most unusual and astonishing effects
in the world, and that it conquers all? Therefore it is said that one cannot
love in a measured way. For when love wants, he makes kings, princes,
and the noblest men become not only the lovers but the slaves of the low-
liest women. But let us return to our history rather than stop to argue.

When the duchess had decided to go to Ancona to find her husband,
she secretly informed him of everything. Meanwhile she saw to the sending
of as much money and things to Ancona as possible. Then she let it be
known that she had made a vow to go to Loreto. And so, arranging everything and leaving good provision for the care of her son, who would remain a duke, she set out on her way with a numerous and honorable
company, and with a large train of mules arrived at Loreto. Having had a
public Mass sung and having offered rich gifts in that venerable and reverend temple, as everyone was expecting to return to the Kingdom of
Naples, she said to her people, "We are only fifteen miles from Ancona
which we hear is an ancient and beautiful city. Thus we will do well to go
there and stay for a day." Everyone agreed to the duchess's wish. Therefore,
sending the mule-train on ahead, the whole group took the road to Ancona.

Bologna, who had been notified of everything, had had his house most honorably prepared, and made ready for the company an honorable, sumptuous, and abundant dinner. His palace was on the main street, so that they would have to pass his door. His steward, who had come early in the morning to give orders for the dinner, was brought into the house by Bologna and was told that he had prepared to invite his lady the duchess. At this the steward was pleased because although Bologna had left the court, no one knew what the reason was, and he was well thought of by all. Bologna, when the time seemed right, mounted on his horse with a fine group of gentlemen of Ancona and went about three miles outside the city to meet the duchess. When the duchess's people saw him, they began to say happily, "Lady Duchess, here is our Sir Antonio Bologna"; and they all gave him a big welcome. He, dismounting and kissing the hands of his consort, invited the company to his house. She accepted the invitation, and he led her home not as his wife but as his employer.

There, after everyone had eaten, the duchess, wishing to take off her mask and knowing that she would have to come to it, called her people into the hall and spoke to them thus:

"It is high time, my gentlemen and you other servants, that I make manifest to the whole world what has been done in the sight of God. Being a widow I thought of marrying and of taking such a husband as my judgment had elected. Therefore I tell you that several years ago, in the presence of this maid of mine, who is here, I married Sir Antonio Bologna whom you see, and he is my legitimate husband, and with him, because his I am, I intend to remain. Up to now I have been your duchess and your employer and you have been faithful vassals and servants to me. For the future you will attend to the good care of the lord duke my son, and you will be faithful and loyal to him as is fitting. You will accompany these maids of mine to Malfi, whose dowries I deposited at the bank of Paolo Tolosa before I left the kingdom, and the written accounts for everything are in the monastery of Saint Sebastian with the mother superior. For of my maids I now want only this chamber maid of mine. Lady Beatrice, who until now has been my maid of honor, is, as she will attest, satisfied with everything. Nonetheless in the written accounts which I mentioned she will find a good dowry for one of her daughters whom she has at home. If of the servants there is anyone who wishes to remain with me, he will be well treated by me. As for the rest, when you will be in Malfi, the steward will provide for you as usual. And to conclude, I prefer to live privately with Sir Antonio my husband then to remain a duchess."

The entire company were left astonished and dismayed and almost beside themselves upon hearing such things said. But after each one saw that it was indeed true, and after Bologna had called in the son and daughter whom he had engendered in the duchess, and she had embraced and kissed them as her and Bologna's children, everyone agreed to return to Malfi except the maid and two footmen who remained with their accustomed employer. Great was the gossip, and everyone had something to say. Then they left the house and went to an inn because no one dared to stay with her once they understood how things were for fear of the cardinal and his brother; rather they decided among themselves that on the following morning one of the gentlemen should go to Rome posthaste to find the cardinal and inform him of everything; the other brother was there too. And so it was done. The others all took their way towards the Kingdom of Naples. Thus the duchess remained with her husband and lived with him in greatest happiness. Not many months later, she gave birth to another male child, whom they named Alfonso.

While they were living in Ancona, loving each other more every day, the cardinal of Aragon with his aforesaid brother, who by no means intended to tolerate that their sister had married in such a manner, effected by means of the cardinal of Mantua, Sir Gismondo Gonzaga, who was ambassador to Ancona from Pope Julius II, that Bologna with his wife be evicted by the Anconians. They had been in Ancona about six or seven months, and although the ambassador insisted on having them sent away, Bologna had made so many connections that the matter took a long time. But knowing that in the end he would be evicted, Bologna, in order not to be caught unprepared, obtained through a friend of his in Siena from that government a safe-conduct and the right to stay there with his whole family. Meanwhile he sent his sons away and arranged his affairs so that on the same day that he received the order from the Anconians to leave within fifteen days, he with his wife and others of his men mounted on horseback and went to Siena. Hearing this and seeing themselves deceived, the two Aragonese brothers, who had thought to catch him unawares on the way, worked on Alfonso Petrucci, the cardinal of Siena, until Sir Borghese, brother of the cardinal and head of the Sienese government, acted to have Bologna sent away from Siena. Therefore, thinking hard about where he could go, he decided to go with his whole family to Venice.

So they set on their way taking the Florentine road towards Romagna in order to put to sea and sail to Venice. And having already reached Forlì, they became aware of many horses following them, of which they were notified by spies. Therefore, full of fear and needy of counsel, not seeing any escape for their lives, they felt more dead than alive. Nonetheless, impelled by fright, they began to proceed as quickly as they could in order to reach a little village not far away, with the hope of saving themselves therein. Bologna was on a Turkish horse, a willing runner and of good stamina, and he had put his first son on another excellent Turkish horse. The other little son and daughter were both in a litter. The wife was on a good mare. He with his son could easily have saved themselves, because they were on good horses, but the love he bore for his wife would not let him leave her. She, who believed firmly that those who were coming would not harm any but her husband, exhorted him, weeping all the while, to save himself, saying to him, "My lord, go away, for the lords my brothers will not harm either me or our children; but if they get hold of you, they will be cruel to you and will kill you." And

giving him forthwith a large purse full of ducats, she did nothing but beg him to flee, for later with time perhaps God would permit the lords her brothers to be appeased. The poor husband, seeing that those who were pursuing them were so close that there was no way to save his wife, grieving extremely, with infinite tears took leave of her and, giving spur to the

Turkish horse, told his men to look to their own safety. The son, seeing his father flee with loose reins, boldly followed him, so that Bologna with his oldest son and four servants who were on good horses escaped, and changing their plan to go to Venice, all six went to Milan.

Those who had come to kill him took the lady with her little son, her daughter, and all the others. The chief of the troop, either having orders for this from the lady's brothers, or else acting on his own in order to cause less uproar and so that the lady might go along without screaming, said to her, "Lady Duchess, the lords your brothers have sent us to conduct you into the Kingdom of Naples to your house, so that you may take up once again the management of the lord duke your son and not go wandering any more, here today and there tomorrow; for Sir Antonio was a man who, after he had wearied of you, would have left you deprived of everything and gone off on his way. Be of good cheer and do not let anything trouble you." It seems that the lady was much calmed by these words and thought that what she had said was true, that her brothers would not be cruel to her and her children. And with this belief she went on for several days until they arrived at one of the castles of the duke her son, and when they were there, she with her two little children and the maid were taken and put in the main tower of the fortress. What became there of the four of them was not soon found out. All the rest were set at liberty. But the lady with the maid and her two children, as afterwards became clearly known, were wretchedly killed in that tower.

The unhappy husband and lover with his son and servants came to Milan, where they spent a few days under the protection of Sir Silvio Savello, in those days when Sir Silvio was besieging the French in the castle of Milan in order to seize it in the name of Massimigliano Sforza, as afterwards by treaty he did. From there Savello went to bring his army to Crema, where he stayed several days. And meanwhile Bologna took himself to the Marquis of Bitonto, and when the marquis had left, he stayed in the house of the lord knight Visconti. The Aragonese brothers had worked so at Naples that the State Treasury took possession of Bologna's property. Bologna attended to nothing but the pacification of these brothers, not willing in any way to believe that his wife and children were dead. He was occasionally warned by certain gentlemen that he should pay good heed to his affairs and that he was not safe in Milan. But he listened to nobody, and I believe, from some indications that I had of it, that underhandedly, in order to assure that he would not leave, he had been given to understand that he would get his wife back. Full therefore of this vain hope and growing weary from one day to the next, he remained in Milan more than a year.

At this time it happened that a lord of the kingdom, who had men-at-arms in the Duchy of Milan, narrated this whole history to our friend Delio, and moreover affirmed that he had been commissioned to have Bologna murdered but that he did not want to become a butcher for others, and that he had in a kind manner warned Bologna not to proceed further in the case and that for certain his wife together with the children and the maid had been strangled. One day while Delio was with Lady Ippolita Bentivoglia, Bologna played his lute and sang a mournful ballad about his own case which he had composed and set to music. When Delio, who had not known before who he was, found out that this was the husband of the Duchess of Malfi, moved by pity, he called him aside and assured him of the death of his wife and that he knew for certain that there were men in Milan out to murder him. He thanked Delio and said to him, "Delio, you are deceived, for I have a letter from Naples from my family that the State Treasury will soon release my property, and from Rome too I have good hope that Monsignor my illustrious and most reverend lord is no longer so angry, and even less so the lord his brother, and that without fail I will get back the lady my wife." Delio, knowing that he was being tricked, said what he thought appropriate and left him.

Those who sought to have him killed, seeing that the result was not forthcoming, and that that lord in charge of the men-at-arms showed himself cool towards this undertaking, gave the commission to one of the lords of Lombardy, begging him warmly to do anything necessary to have him murdered. Delio had told Sir Lucio Scipione Attellano the whole history up to that point and said that he wanted to put it in one of his tales, knowing for certain that poor Bologna would be murdered. And one day while Lucio Scipione and Delio were in Milan, across from the main monastery, there came Bologna on a very pretty jennet, on his way to Mass at San Francesco, and he had two servants in front of him, one of whom carried a lance and the other a book of hours of Our Lady. Delio said then to Attellano, "Here's Bologna."

It seemed to Attellano that Bologna looked completely lost, and he said, "By God, he would do better to have another spear carried instead of that book of hours, living in peril as he is." Attellano and Delio had not yet reached San Giacomo when they heard a great noise; for before he arrived at San Francesco, Bologna was attacked by Captain Daniele da Bozolo with three other well-armed companions and run through and through and miserably killed, without anyone's being able to help him.[5] And the men who killed him went at their ease wherever they liked, there being no one who wanted to take on himself the burden of pursuing them through the system of justice.

I, 53

From Bandello to the very generous lord the lord Pietro Margano.

Not long ago I had a letter from Rome from my father, who writes me about the very pleasing welcome you gave him with so many proffered courtesies, the day he had come to pay respects to the illustrious and most reverend lord, Cardinal Pompeo Colonna, my lord and patron. I was well acquainted by experience with your courtesy, great liberality and generosity when you were in Milan with our common patron the excellent Sir Prospero Colonna, which made me infinitely obliged to you. But now what you have done for my father—who, banished from his home without any fault of his, is staying in Rome—has so entered my heart and has added such a bond to the other obligations, that I confess it is impossible for any man in the world, whatever beneficence he may have received, to find himself more obliged than I am to my generous and most noble Margano. And because, as I said to you on other occasions in Milan, I have not the power to make up for so many and such large debts, I do not know what else to do in order to avoid the abominable vice of ingratitude except to confess myself your debtor, and where the ability is lacking, to show at least that my spirit is ready and grateful, which I hereby do. Now if I were not acquainted with the greatness of your spirit, I would try with fine and suitable words to thank you as much as possible. But I know that you esteem it much better to give pleasure and help to others than to receive it from others. Nonetheless, so that you may see that I am thinking of you, I have written you this letter which I accompany with one of my tales, not having forgotten how much you enjoyed reading my stories when we were together.

This tale which I send you was told not long ago in an honorable company, as they were talking about the tricks which women play on their husbands, by Lord Scipione Pepolo, descended from Lord Giovanni Pepolo, from whom Sir Bernabò Visconti bought Bologna for many thousands of ducats in those times when the Roman church resided in Avignon. This tale, then, I write and dedicate to your name as the fruit sprung from one who is wholly yours. Stay well.

THE TRICK PLAYED BY A PEASANT ON HIS BOSS'S WIFE AND BY HER ON HER OLD HUSBAND, WHO WAS JEALOUS, WITH CERTAIN LAUGHABLE MATTERS.

Infinite truly are the means which women use when, not well pleased with what they have at home, which seems to them insufficient, they look for an outside way to provide for their cases; infinite, I say,

are the means by which husbands find themselves deceived. And although
you may already have heard what I am now about to tell you, nonetheless
perhaps you never heard where it happened, which I intend to tell you
now if you will listen to me, as I have faith that you will, believing firmly
that my tale will offer you delight.

You must know, then, that in the time of the glorious duke of Milan,
Duke Filippo Visconti, there lived in Pavia a young lady of the Fornari
family, who was married to a Lord Giovanni Botticella, a doctor of law
over fifty years old; although he was very wise in his studies, for he was a
famous and most learned lawyer, I think that in common sense he showed
himself to be quite a fool, because at that age he entered into the mad
idea of taking a wife and picking a young one of less than twenty. But if
wise men did not occasionally err, fools would despair. The young lady,
whose name was Cornelia, was very attractive, with a pretty and well
shaped face, even if it was not the most angelic in the world; but she was
pleasant and spirited and as bold as could be. Shortly becoming aware of
this, the doctor of law repented too late having taken a wife so young,
and knowing himself to be old and not in condition to satisfy her, became so jealous about her that he did not know where to begin. He was
much called upon in the city affairs by the citizens, and often elected by
the community council to serve as ambassador to Duke Filippo,[6] whom
the doctor saw gladly because he had known him privately when Filippo,
under the title of count, ruled Pavia while his brother the Duke Gian
Maria was alive. Moreover, when the doctor was staying in Pavia, he
spent all his time on behalf of his clients, now giving them hearings, now
appearing with them before the magistrate, and now at the tribunal of
the ducal commissary and governor. The love which he bore for his wife,
or to put it better, the fierce jealousy which bitterly gnawed at his heart,
forced him continually to keep watch like a new Argus, staying near her
day and night to observe her actions carefully. On the other hand, the
pride and bold ambition which had wonderful power over him constrained
him to attend to the affairs of his city and not to fail various persons who
came to him all day long for counsel, favor, and help. More powerful in
him were pride and ambition than all the rest. Nonetheless, as the sharp
and piercing prick of jealousy never ceased to sting him and miserably
torture him and afflict him with the most biting thoughts, in order to assure himself of his wife when he went out of town or out of the house, he
arranged to fix all the windows which overlooked the street so that it was
no longer possible to see out of them. And because the house was full of
people all day, he ordered a passage made between the back gate and the

door of his office on the ground floor so that no one would have occasion to enter the courtyard of the house. Then he ordered his wife absolutely not to come downstairs, not wanting her to frequent the ground floor rooms; on this account the ill-married Cornelia lived in such boredom that she was ready to go mad. She went to Mass only on holidays, and according to the doctor's orders she had to go early in the morning to the first Mass of the day in the company of a servant. As for sermons, vespers, and other divine offices, there was no point in even mentioning them, much less going to parties and weddings even when she was invited. But what tormented the unfortunate and desperate young lady more than anything else was seeing herself with an old husband at her side, who made her observe so many fasts and vigils that he covered her barely once a month, and especially after the birth of their first son, which she bore in the first year of her unhappy marriage. She would have liked to have been well covered every night and not to have wasted her youth so wretchedly. But the doctor was so weak and short of endurance that on those few times when he engaged in battle with Lady Cornelia, even though he engaged in it very seldom, it took him many many days afterwards before he could recover his lost strength; and yet he believed he could appease her with excuses and trifling reasons. It was in vain, for the ill-fed young lady would have liked deeds rather than words.

Now when she had spent about four years in this wretched life, she saw that she could in no way make good with what there was at home, and having considered the matter at length she decided to take to the street to hunt for someone who might provide what she most needed. But such was the careful and continual guard upon her that it was very difficult to do anything to further her plan. Seeing therefore the extreme difficulty which she had in finding a Pavese gentleman or student who might water her ill-cultivated garden, she thought to provide herself with a waterer by some other means.

The doctor had certain properties at Selvano, a village belonging to Pavia, where he constantly kept a superintendant with farmers to work the lands. Among the laborers there was a young man of about twenty-seven, very big of body, attractive in face and well-mannered for a peasant, and stronger and more robust than all the others. Although he was shrewd and knew his business very well, this fellow nonetheless played the simpleton and the clown. He used to bring whatever was in season—eggs, butter, cheese, poultry, fruit—at least twice a week from the village to Pavia. He was generally well regarded by everyone in the doctor's house on account of his joking ways; nor did he ever stay idle at the house, for now he was splitting wood, now drawing water, and doing other similar services willingly and gladly; and he went freely throughout the house, downstairs and even upstairs wherever he wished. The doctor much enjoyed this fellow's wit and joking manner and gladly conversed with him, especially in the evening after dinner when there were no outsiders. Similarly Lady Cornelia delighted in having him tell her things about the village. Whereupon, being glad to see him, she began to cast eyes on him, and since she had no better means to fulfill her needs, she resolved to herself that this man would be the one who, as he worked the doctor's lands at Selvano, should work his little garden in Pavia too; and that the first time he came again from the village, she would try her luck, come of if what might. She was so discontent with the life she led with her husband that for a little bit more she would have thought nothing of dying.

One morning not long afterwards the peasant arrived in Pavia as was his custom with fruits from the village and letters for the boss, and not finding his boss at home, for he had gone to the palace to plead on behalf of other peoples' quarrels, he went upstairs where the wife was all alone in a room doing some of her work. When she saw him, she said, "Welcome, Antonello," for that was the laborer's name; "what are you up to?"

"My lady," he replied, "I have brought some of our fruits, and I have also carried a letter for the doctor which the superintendant sends on account of certain orders that the ducal officer had delivered to Selvano."

The lady then called for a boy of the house and sent him to the palace with Antonello to find the doctor. He went there and gave the doctor his letter. When he read it, the doctor said, "Antonello, go to the house, have a drink and wait for me there."

While the peasant was at the palace, the lady decided to herself that if he came back now, she would carry out her intentions, for she was quite sure that as she had often been seen talking with Antonello, no one would find their being together suspicious. So when he returned, she called him upstairs and came to meet him, showing him good cheer, giving orders for breakfast to be brought for him. And when whatever was necessary had been brought, she busied all the servants of the household with errands except an old woman whom she trusted, so that no one else was around. He, having walked for a good part of the night and worked up an appetite, ate heartily. Lady Cornelia, who wanted to feed herself too, in order not to lose the opportunity started a conversation with Antonello and asked him about various things at the village, and among other things whether he were in love. To this he replied grinning, "My lady, o what a good time you have! You sure have it good."

"And why?" took up the lady. "What kind of answer is that? It is quite off the point; what does my good time have to do with your being in love?"

"By the body of Saint Perpisto!" said he then, "Ever since these gentlemen of Pavia and our neighbors from Caselli have stuck their noses in, I can tell you our girls have become proud and don't want to see the rest of us anymore. They like their lovers well dressed and rich enough to bring them from the city, now a pretty border to put on their aprons, now striped silk bonnets, now ribbons of different colors, and one thing today and another tomorrow. They also often want *ambruogini, grossetti, brustie*[7] and other such coins, and without the security in hand they won't give you a loan, if you understand my meaning. And I who am a poor servant, a son of servants, what the devil do you think I can give them or bring them from the city? If I don't give them what I have, which I won't name, I don't know what else to give them. It would sooner suit me to find someone who would give me something of hers in exchange for what I can give her of mine"; and all the while that he was making this speech, he was laughing.

"Now tell me," said the lady, "if you found someone who would give you something of hers, what would you give in exchange?"

"My lady," answered the peasant laughing heartily like a country person, "I'd give it to her, and plenty. You understand me I'm sure. By the body of bloodpisser, I would content her so well with my doings that she wouldn't trade me in for another. I can tell you that I do a good job when I set to it, and I'm not easily tired."

"And what would you do in a thousand years," said the lady, "who are so brave with words and seem to me as weak as I don't know what?"

"Weak, my lady?" replied he. "You would find out if you had to do with me. You don't know me well nor what I'm worth. Watch and see if this seems to you the way of a lame man or a cripple." And so saying he jumped to his feet and made a somersault high in the air, for indeed he was daring, dextrous, and robust of body. At this the little son of the doctor and lady came in, to whom she paid no mind.

The lady was pleased that Antonello spoke with her so familiarly, thinking it much to the point; and she too began to joke with him familiarly, now pulling his hair, now his nose, and now playfully giving him a light cuff and other similar teasing things. He still attended to his eating and, realizing that she wanted the leg of Marcone, said to her, "My lady, if you don't want to give me something of yours, leave me alone; otherwise, by the body of whom I won't say, you will make me get angry, and then it will go the way it will. Be still." But as she laughed and did not cease molesting him, he, who felt something on him growing, rose to his feet and taking her in his arms, kissed her two or three times and then said to her, "If you don't leave me alone, I'll give it to you; just you wait and see."

She, warming to the deed and dying to essay his vigor in serving the needs of women, said to him, laughing, "By God's faith I'll have you castrated."

"Castrated?" replied Antonello. "You won't do that a bit. What the devil! Castrated? O bloodshit! And what would I be good for if I were castrated? What would you do with me after that? I know that you would want to repair me for another time. Go castrate the roosters to make capons and leave me with all my members. I would sooner give you the cart and oxen and all my father has in the world than ever let myself be castrated. And what would I do then with the hawk without his bells? Come now, go on, go on; leave me alone."

But she drew closer to him and kept molesting him, showing all the while that she was pleased by his joking with her. Near the head of the table where Antonello was eating in the salon was the door to the lady's bedroom. Withdrawing that way and pausing at the doorway, she looked precisely as if she were inviting him to enter the bedroom. And throwing at him now a little pebble, now a bit of straw, and now other such things, she did not cease to work him over in a thousand ways. The lady's little son, as small children do, was laughing, and in imitation of his mother he too was throwing at the peasant whatever came to his hands, and running away and turning back, while Antonello pretended sometimes that he wanted to catch him and sometimes let him go. And so all three looked just as if they were playing in a comedy.

Antonello, who clearly understood the lady's intentions since she had not shown any repugnance when he kissed her nor had scolded him with an angry face, said to himself, "This woman has an old husband who must be unable to satisfy her greatest needs, because in bed he must always be colder than ice, and for this reason she is looking around for someone instead of her husband who can prove himself a valorous knight at jousting. I will try my luck and see if I succeed. And by the devil, what harm can it do me? Here there is no one who can bear witness of what we do, because, from what I see, that old woman must know all about the forbidden things that lady does with these devil incarnate students who, when they ought to be studying, are making love with these women of Pavia, going about at night, and then making their parents believe that they are wearing themselves out over their books. I know very well what Lord Girolamo Sacco of Caselli used to say when he came from Pavia to Selvano. So I don't need to fear the old woman, because the lady would not joke in this manner with me if she did not have confidence in her. Of the little son there is no need to have fear because he doesn't yet know what this world is all about." While Antonello was making these calculations to himself and was scheming about how he might be able to get the boss-lady on the hook, she did not cease giving him trouble and teasing him.

Seeing then that the annoyance of the trouble which the lady was giving him did not diminish, but rather increased more and more, he took his knife and freely drew a line between himself and the lady, as if he wanted to make a boundary which should not be crossed. The lady stood in surprise to watch what he was doing and could not guess the reason. After Antonello had drawn the line, turning to the mistress with a solemn face he said proudly, "My lady, by the body of the knight Mister Saint Buovo, I swear to you and pledge my faith on it: if you pass this mark that I have made with my knife, I will play you a trick with another knife which may please you better than the foolish little games you are playing now. I'll give it to you if you don't stay on that side. Yes indeed, yes indeed, you will say afterwards, 'I wouldn't have thought it.' Step over, step over, and you'll see a good one. I've told you, and it's enough. Don't complain to me afterwards."

The lady, who wanted more than Antonello to come to grips and do some wrestling, approached the line slowly, slowly, pretending to be about to step over it and almost putting her foot on it; then she drew back and said, "Antonello, tell me a little by your faith what you have in mind to do now if I step over your established boundary. Come on, please tell."

Antonello, who was watching intently like a hawk when it sees a quail, said laughing, "My lady, pardon me, for this time I won't tell you. I want you to find out for yourself what it is when I have done it. At present I intend to do as Uncle Pedrone has often told me the nuns of Genoa do, who go wherever they please to amuse themselves inside and outside the city and who, when they return to the monastery, say to the abbess, 'Mother, with your permission we went to have some recreation and to get a bit of air.' And I too will do as they do. I've already told you more than a thousand times and I say it again and repeat it, that if you step over, I will by no means forgive you, but I will make you pay your way and the tariff on it at a stiff rate. Go ahead and step over if you want to, and you'll see what the miller does, and whether I know how to get my pay, and what part I can play."

Whereupon the lady, pretending to be afraid of what Antonello was saying, two or three times put her foot almost across the line and suddenly saying "Oh oh!" pulled it back. Antonello was laughing, waiting only for her to step across. The lady finally, eager to test how much Antonello weighed, with a little jump crossed over the established boundary saying, "Here, here, I'm across; what happens now?"

The good Antonello feeling his conscience rise up wonderfully, not waiting for the lady to finish her words nor to be invited a second time, said, "By God's faith, I'll give it to you"; and grabbing the lady who desired to be overcome in his arms, kissing her amorously he carried her into the bedroom and lay her down over a large chest, where although she gave a show putting up a little resistance, he played with her as much as he pleased and she with him, and they hoisted the sail twice to her great pleasure, who had never before tasted similar food; for when her husband lay with her, he did not have any endurance and was usually dull.

When the dance of Treviso[8] was finished, Antonello returned to the salon and sat back at his place; and as the lady came out of the room, all happy and merry from the milling she had done, he said to her laughing, "My lady, if the game we played together has pleased you at all and you want to try it again, you know what to do, because if you step over that line I'll do as before. And if perhaps in some way I was lacking, the second time I will amend it from good to better."

"Oh!" replied Lady Cornelia; "that's all right with me, brother. You want to play the braggart too much. I don't know what more you could do for you have run three relays, and I think you must be quite worn out and that whatever you tried to do would be a flop. My husband, who very rarely jousts with me, can barely break one lance, and he is left so weak that he spends the next half hour panting."

"Enough," replied Antonello," if you step over the line, you will realize your error." The child who did not know what all this meant, was playing by stepping over the line.

Now the lady, who had gotten a taste for it and had proven how hard of sinew Antonello was and how much better than her husband he could water the garden, thinking that she had opportunity and time because the servants she had to worry about were downstairs, and not caring about the old woman and her own son, boldly crossed over the line anew. Antonello, who was feeling ready, took her in his arms another time and entering the bedroom turned her over the same chest and, beginning to dance, soon completed three dances and so wonderfully satisfied the lady that she resolved not to seek farther for another lover, but to stick with the valiant Antonello because she knew that when he came to Pavia or when she went to Selvano they could play together without suspicion or scandal.

Therefore, having come back into the salon, she talked with him a long while and remained very content, because besides having proven him a valorous knight, she thought him also a man of wit.

While they were plotting together arranging how they should manage their affair for the future, her husband arrived from the palace and came upstairs. The little son, when he saw his father coming, ran to meet him and began, as little children do, to welcome him exuberantly. And as the doctor was heading towards the bedroom, when he was near the mark which Antonello had made with his knife, the boy said in a half-garbled manner as little tots do,

"Father, don't step over this line, because the farmer will do to you as he did to mother."

At these words the lady and Antonello both were struck with consternation; but luck was on their side, for the doctor paid no attention to his son's words, but called Antonello and began to talk with him about what the superintendent had written in regard to the orders from the officer. Meanwhile Lady Cornelia, who had had an extreme fright, took the little boy by the hand and, leading him into a room far away from the salon, gave him many spankings and scolded him severely, threatening worse if ever he said anything of the sort again.

Now the lady and the lucky Antonello knew so well how to weave their designs thereafter that they enjoyed their love together for a long while and had the best time in the world; and Lady Cornelia often became pregnant and bore children, while the doctor, thinking he was their father, felt very pleased about it. The mother, however, was careful to keep her son from seeing what she did, who in fear from the beating and his mother's threats never again repeated what he had said. Except that, keeping the matter in mind, he told the whole story when he had grown up, having gotten into a quarrel with his other brothers after their father and mother were dead.

II, 52
From Bandello to the very noble lord, Sir Angelo dal Bufalo.

W hile we were recently at Casalmaggiore, as you know, the valorous heroine, Lady Antonia Bauza, Marchioness of Gonzaga, having bought that castle from the most Christian king with her dowry money, held there a sumptuous wedding for her very noble daughter Lady Camilla Gonzaga to the Marquis of Tripalda, of the honored and royal family of the Castrioti, who have ruled Epirus for many years. The three brothers of the bride, three truly magnanimous heroes, Sir Lodovico of

Sabioneda, Sir Frederico of Bozolo, and the most kind and loving man in
the world Sir Pirro of Gazuolo were there with an honorable company of
many lords and gentlemen. After dinner was over, because it was extremely
hot, everyone gathered in a large hall on the ground floor which was quite
cool for the season, or at least less hot than the other rooms, and got into a
delightful conversation on the liberality and magnificence of several great
princes, and especially of those who, having their personal enemies in their
grasp, not only pardoned them and granted them their lives, but even
reestablished them in the kingdoms and dominions they had lost or gave
them help in recovering them. From the ancients we turned to the
moderns, and with the general praise of everyone commended most
highly Filippo Maria Visconti, the third duke of Milan, who, having in
his hands in prison Alfonso of Aragon with other kings and as many
princes, barons, and lords, not only did not make them pay any ransom,
but honorably lodged each one according to his rank, and with rich and
succulent banquets entertained them for many days, giving them every
pleasure of feasts and games that was possible. Then he liberally let them
all go home and helped Alfonso to recover the kingdom of Naples.

The great Lorenzo Medici, father of Pope Leo the Tenth, who was the
wisest moderator and chief of the Florentine republic, which he always
ruled so notably, was also greatly celebrated. The aged Ferrando of
Aragon, King of Naples, had made an alliance with Pope Sixtus the
Fourth to remove Lorenzo de' Medici by any means from the government
of Florence. And having assembled a huge army with which he attacked
Tuscany, and having already occupied many lands and castles in the
Florentine domain, Alfonso Duke of Calabria, with shrewdness and the
support of several citizens, had entered Siena with part of the army all the
while fighting the Florentines. After having given much thought to the freeing of his country, Lorenzo, who saw himself abandoned by the Venetians
and had no hope for aid from Milan because of the death of the Duke
Galeazzo Sforza and the strife among the regents of the ward, decided,
since the enemies were saying that they sought only an end to Lorenzo's
rule, to go in person to Naples to find Ferrando. And arranging things in
Florence as well as he could, he went down the Arno to Pisa where, taking a brigantine, he sailed to Naples. Arriving there with easy sailing and
disembarking onto land, he went without delay to King Ferrando in his
castle; finding him in the hall with his barons, he made the proper bow and
said, "Sacred king, I, Lorenzo de' Medici, come before you as to a most
just tribunal, and I beg you deign to grant me a kind hearing." Ferrando
was filled with extreme astonishment at the name of Lorenzo Medici, and

could not imagine how he had been so daring as to come unexpectedly, without safe-conduct or any security, into his hands. However, moved by I don't know what, he received him kindly and, withdrawing to a window, told him to say whatever he wished for he would listen patiently. The great Lorenzo was not only gifted with wide learning but was also a fine and most eloquent speaker. He set his case before the king in such a manner and demonstrated his reasons so well that after they had discussed the affairs of Italy together several times, and Lorenzo had discoursed on the mood of the Italian princes and people, and how much there was to hope for in peace and to fear in war, Ferrando marveled much more than before at the greatness of spirit and keenness of mind and seriousness and solidity of good judgment in Lorenzo, and esteemed him to be one of the outstanding persons of Italy. Therefore he concluded within himself rather to let Lorenzo go as a friend than to hold him as an enemy. And so, keeping him with him for some time, with every kind of beneficence and demonstration of love he succeeded in establishing between them perpetual accords for the common protection of their states. And so Lorenzo, if he had left Florence a great man, returned to it a very great man.

In our conversation, just as Duke Filippo and Ferrando were praised, so on the contrary the lack of liberality which Louis the Twelfth used with Ludovico Sforza, whom he let die in prison, was noted.

Lord Bartolomeo Bozzo, a man from Genoa, was also present at this conversation, and apropos of the topic of discussion he told a pretty story which happened in our time. And because it seemed to me worthy of memory and little known among the Latins, I wrote it down. As I was thinking afterwards to whom I should give it, you suddenly came to my mind, as one of the courteous and liberal gentlemen whom I know in these times. And because I know, from the long acquaintance we have had with each other, that you are opposed to ceremony, I will say no more. The story then I dedicate and consecrate to your name, merely beginning indeed to acknowledge the many courtesies and pleasures received from you.

MAOMET, THE AFRICAN LORD OF DUBDÙ, WANTS TO STEAL A CITY FROM SAICH, KING OF FEZ, BUT THE KING BESIEGES HIM IN DUBDÙ AND SHOWS HIM GREAT GENEROSITY.

Your conversation, my lords, has moved me to tell you, apropos of the courtesies of the duke and of the king, a story which happened in Africa during the time that I was trading in those parts. I have done business in all the provinces and kingdoms of Africa for

at least twenty years, and I believe that there are few cities which I have
not seen, and I have observed many of their customs. And among other
things that I found there, experience has shown me the great courtesy
and loyalty in those African merchants. Similarly it is very safe to do
business with the gentlemen of the country, given that they are ordinarily
good people, well-mannered, and live very civilly and dress cleanly according to their fashion. I can confess to you that I have found much
more affection and charity in many areas of Africa than—and I am
ashamed to say it—I have found among Christians. They observe their
Mohammedan laws much better than we do our Christian ones, and are
for the most part great alms-givers and true observers of all the contracts
one makes with them. And I say this of the majority of them because one
also finds cheaters and sorry characters among them, and especially if
one deals with the Arabs, who are scattered all over.

Now, coming to what I have decided to narrate to you, I tell you that
not far from the great kingdom of Fez is a city which the Africans call
Dubdù, an ancient city situated on top of a high mountain abundant with
many fresh streams, which run through the city for the convenience and
use of the inhabitants. Since long ago the rulers of this city have been
gentlemen of the house of the Beni Guertaggien, who possess it to this
day. When the house of Marino, who lost the kingdom of Fez, was
almost destroyed, the Arabs made every effort to seize Dubdù; but Musè
Ibnù Camnù, who was its ruler, valiantly defended himself, so that he
forced the Arabs to make several concessions and not to attack that city
any more, nor his other lands. After his death Musè left a son of his named
Acmed as ruler of Dubdù. This son was very similar to his father in
manners and in valor and preserved his state in great peace until his
death. To Acmed there succeeded as ruler, because he had no sons, a
cousin of his named Maomet, a young man of truly high courage, excellent in military matters and personally valiant. He acquired many
cities and castles at the foot of Mount Atlante, towards the south, within
the borders of Numidia. He also adorned Dubdù with many beautiful
buildings and made it even more civilized than it had been. He showed
such liberality and courtesy to foreigners and to those who were passing
through his city, honoring all according to their worth and spending
without measure, that the fame of his courtesy flew through all the surrounding regions. I once happened to go there in the company of several
gentlemen of Fez and was lodged in the palace with my companions,
where we were treated as honorably as possible. And because Acmed
heard that I was Christian and Genoese, he spoke with me at length about

the affairs of Italy and our manner of living, always using such kindness towards all that it was a wonderful thing. He offered many favors to me in particular.

Now because a man often can't see or recognize his own good, and blinds himself in prosperous fortune, and because there is no greater plague in the courts of lords than flattery, Maomet got the desire to seize Tezà, a city about five miles from Mount Atlante, which belonged to the King of Fez. He communicated this idea of his to some of his men, who, not considering the might and vast dominion of the King of Fez, to whom Maomet could in no way be compared, persuaded him with vain flatteries to undertake it. And because every week at Tezà it is the custom to hold an impressive market of grain at which many people gather and especially the mountain people, they induced Maomet to dress himself as one of the mountain folk to go to the market, and they would attack the captain of Tezà with men that they would bring with them, and without doubt they would take the city, because a great part of the population within, hearing the name of Maomet and seeing him present, would rise up in his favor. But however it happened, this plot came to the ears of Saich, of the family of Quattas, King of Fez and father of the king who reigns there today. Saich, hearing of the danger, immediately deployed soldiers to the defense of Tezà and, gathering a huge army, went to attack Maomet. And although Maomet was taken by surprise, nonetheless, he bravely sustained the siege and assault of the king's soldiers. As I have already said, Dubdù, which is situated on a mountain, is very strong through its position; therefore the king's men were thrown back once or twice by those of the city, with death to many of those outside. But the king reinforced his camp with many catapults and guns, and did much damage to the city, resolving not to depart from that siege until he had captured the city and taken Maomet prisoner. There were frequent skirmishes, and usually those within the city had the worst of it.

Seeing this, and better considering his case, Maomet realized that he had committed a very great error in wanting to wage war on Saich King of Fez, to whom he could in no way be equalled. And in the end, having thought over and over a thousand thousand ways by which he might relieve himself of the present war and remain good friends with the said king, not finding any means which might be helpful to his case, he remained very unhappy. Finally, after infinite discussion, one method by which he hoped to find his way back to safety came to his mind: and this was for him to put himself in Saich's hands and to try his courtesy and mercy.

Having reached this decision within himself, he wrote a letter to King Saich with his own hand and, dressing himself in the outfit of a messenger, went himself as an envoy of the ruler of Dubdù, knowing that the king would not recognize him. And passing through the army of the enemy, he presented himself at the royal pavilion and was introduced into the presence of the king. There, making the proper bow to the king, he presented his letter, which was his credential. The king, taking the letter, handed it to a secretary, bidding him read it. When it had been read in the presence of those who were there, the king, turning to Maomet, thinking he was a messenger, said to him, "Tell me, what do you think of our lord, who has become so arrogant that he has dared to wage war on me?"

To this replied Maomet, "Truly, o king, I think that my lord has been a great fool to seek to offend you, having ought always to have kept you as a friend. But the devil has the power to deceive the great as well as the small, and has turned the brain of my lord, forcing him to act insanely."

"By God," added the king, "if I can get him in my hands, as without doubt I will because he cannot escape me, I will give him such a punishment that he will be an example to all not to take arms against one's neighbor without a just cause. I promise you that I will tear the flesh from his body little by little and keep him alive as long as I can to his greater torment."

"Oh!" replied Maomet, "if he came humbly to your feet and, prostrating himself on the ground, begged your pardon for his insanities and supplicated to you to have mercy on him, how would you treat him?"

To this the king said, "I swear by this head of mine, that if he in this manner demonstrated the recognition of his mad error, I would not only pardon him for the injuries he has done me, but besides the pardon I would make a blood alliance with him, giving him two of my daughters as wives for the two sons which I hear he has, and I would confirm him in his state, also giving him the dowry which befits my rank. But I cannot believe that he will ever bear to humiliate himself, he is so arrogant and crazy."

Maomet did not wait to reply, and said, "He will do it all, if you assure him in the presence of the chiefs of your court that you will keep your promise."

"I think," continued the king, "that these four who are here among the others, that is my chief secretary, that other man the captain general of the cavalry, the third my father-in-law, and the fourth the chief magistrate and priest of Fez, may suffice for him."

Hearing this, Maomet threw himself at the king's feet and with tears in his voice said, "King, behold I am the sinner who has recourse to your mercy."

The king then raised him and lovingly, with suitable words, embraced and kissed him. Then, summoning his two daughters and Maomet his sons, they made the weddings with greatest ceremony. From then on

Saich always had Maomet as a kinsman and friend, and today Saich's son does the same, who has succeeded his father in the kingdom of Fez.

III, 62
From Bandello to the very kind gentleman Domenico Cavazza.

Heaven when it is at its brightest and clearest does not look at earth with as many eyes as the number of varied events of fortune that happen in this mortal life. And if ever there was an age when one saw marvelous and different things, I think that this age of ours is one of those in which, much more than in any other, things are happening which are worthy of astonishment, compassion, and blame. For example, in matters pertaining to the worship of God, the saints and the Catholic faith, since Martin Luther raised his horns against the Church, any number of sects have been seen to spring up; and any number of cities and provinces now live variously, scorning their fathers' way of life, which had been approved by so many ancient, learned and holy men and generally observed by the public consensus of good folk since the birth of Christ; and thus today among those people who have separated themselves from the Church in order to live, not in the freedom of their good conscience but in the freedom of their appetites, there are as many sects as there are opinions, each man trying by himself to discover some new error, and everyone trying to be different. This seems to me a very clear indication and strong argument that our Redeemer Jesus Christ is not with them: for if he were with them, there also would be the Holy Spirit, whose virtue and property is to unite the disunited, and not to divide and separate those who ought to be one and the same and to walk on the same path.

Again in worldly matters this age of ours has seen the Turks take all of Syria, and the Sultan defeated with his mercenary crew, Belgrade conquered, Rhodes at war, most of Hungary subjugated, and Vienna in Austria besieged, and great damages done in those countries, with the expectation of worse, to the unspeakable shame of all Christendom, which has by now been reduced to a corner of Europe thanks to the discords which grow greater every day among the Christian princes. Those who ought to stand up against the Turkish might and cruelty have spilled so much Christian blood that it would have been sufficient to recapture the Empire of Constantinople and the Kingdom of Jerusalem. Between the house of Anjou and the house of Aragon, how many fights have there been for the kingdom of Naples, so that Naples has frequently changed *three or four rulers within a short time? Milan has seen itself commanded now by the Sforzas, now by the French and now by the Spanish. In Spain the people have taken arms against their rulers; part of Navarre has passed from the house of Lebretto into the hands of the Aragonese, and all of Spain has become subjected to the Germans. The very blood of the royal house has been rebellious to the King of France, and the Duke of Bourbon, fleeing from the king, has gone to join the Emperor. We have seen the Great Shepherd of Rome, a prisoner of the Germans and Spanish, buy his freedom from the Emperor Charles, and Rome cruelly sacked, the churches pillaged, the nuns raped, and all the cruelties one can imagine perpetrated, so that the Goths of former times were more merciful. Germany, divided within itself, is destroying itself with its Diets.[9] The Emperor and the King of France are now at war and now at truce, and yet one sees no peace agreement. The Venetians have been forced to buy peace from the Turks and to give them part of their land which they had acquired in the Levant. The King of England, a tributary to the Church who wrote such a learned and Catholic piece against the errors which had sprung up in our day, overcome by his own passions and disordinate appetites, has rebelled from the Church and made himself the head of a new heresy, arousing on the island a new sect and a new way of living never before seen or heard of. And certainly we can say that very few ages have seen as sudden changes as we see daily, nor do I know where all these things will end, because it seems to me that we are going from bad to worse and that among Christians there is more discord than ever.*

Speaking, then, about the nature of our age and the many wives which the King of England has taken, Lord Liberio Almadiano of Viterbo, who had long done business in England, narrated the whole thing briefly. Having written it down and added it to the number of my tales, I wanted to publish it under your name, as witness to the friendship which recently in Linguadoca began between us. Stay well.

Giambattista Basile
(1575–1632)

B orn in Naples, Giambattista Basile lived there most of his life at the court of the prince; he also served as governor in various places within the kingdom. His three sisters were singers, one of whom became immensely popular. Basile wrote odes and madrigals for his sisters to sing, occasional poems for members of the court, and court entertainments, such as the musical five-act tragedy *Venere addolorata* or *Sorrowing Venus*. He belonged to various academies at which members read their latest works to each other and set each other literary projects. One result of such projects was a series of poetic "Portraits" of seventy-one ladies of Naples and thirty-five other persons, all based on anagrams of their names. The search for exotic enterprises led Basile to follow the steps of his friend Giulio Cesare Cortese by writing literature in the Neapolitan dialect, perhaps partly to show the Tuscans that Naples too was a cultural center. Basile's *Muse Neapolitane* or *Neapolitan Muses* are nine verse dialogues in dialect, named for the nine muses and depicting scenes of popular life in Naples.

Lo Cunto de li Cunti, overo lo Trattenemiento de Peccerille (The Tale of Tales, or Entertainment for the Little Ones) was similarly written in Neapolitan dialect; indeed, Basile sometimes sought out or even made up Neapolitan versions of common Italian words. The book, published in 1634–1636 after Basile's death, was later called the *Pentameron* because it divides the days and treats the differences between appearance and reality, the use of wording to make good seem bad and vice versa, the tedium which ends all ambitions and pleasures, and universal cupidity. The framing tale is much like the stories it includes, and unlike previous frames it makes no attempt at historical veracity but revels in the creative play of the fabulous. The frame theme of making a melancholy girl laugh may derive partly from the *Decameron* with its aim, expressed in the conclusion, "to chase away the melancholy of women."

The tales are nearly all of folk origin and include such well-known favorites as "Cinderella" and "Puss in Boots." Several were taken over by

Charles Perrault for his French *Tales of Mother Goose (1697)*. Carlo Gozzi in the eighteenth century dramatized some of the stories, one of which, *The Love of Three Oranges* (V, 9), was made into an opera by Sergei Prokofiev. The brothers Grimm became fascinated by Basile's work and listed analogies between his tales and the German folktales which they were collecting. Basile's style, however, is much more sophisticated than his material. His musical sensitivity and verbal playfulness make his language particularly difficult to translate; for the rhythms, alliterations, rhymes, and puns which make his writing sparkle—sometimes even without our being aware of them—are often impossible to transfer into another language.

I have selected tales to represent both the diversity of themes and also their interplay from tale to tale, using the Neapolitan text edited by Mario Petrini, Scrittori d'Italia 260 (Bari: Laterza, 1976), which includes a bibliography of editions but no notes. Further bibliography can be found in Porcelli's *Novellieri Italiani*. Benedetto Croce's translation into modern Italian is inaccurate but well annotated. N. M. Penzer unfortunately translated the *Pentameron* from Croce's version, but included Croce's introduction and notes and added notes and appendices of his own (New York: E. P. Dutton, 1932). Sir Richard Burton's *Pentameron, or the Tale of Tales* (London, 1893) is another inaccurate translation. The Pentameron has been translated partially and inaccurately by J. E. Taylor with illustrations by George Cruikshank (London, 1848). *Stories from the Pentameron*, ed. E. F. Strange (London: Macmillan, 1911) makes use of Taylor's translation. Thomas Keightly, with the help of Dante Gabriele Rossetti, translated a few stories in his *Tales and Popular Fictions*, where they are grouped with analogous stories from other sources. Eight tales have also been translated by Anne Macdonell in *The Italian Fairy Book* (London: T. F. Unwin, 1911). A few can be found in the anthologies of Pasinetti and Valency. Lacy Collison-Morley, *Italy after the Renaissance Decadence and Display in the Seventeenth Century* (London: G. Routledge & Sons, 1930) offers a general introduction to Basile's context.

Introduction

It is an established proverb, one of ancient coinage, that he who seeks what he shouldn't, finds what he doesn't want; and it is known that the monkey, by shoeing himself with boots, remained caught by the feet,[1] as happened to a ragged slave who, never having worn shoes on her feet, wanted to put a crown on her head. But because the grindstone takes off all the rough spots, and there comes a day when everything is paid for, in the end she who by evil ways had usurped what was meant for

*others, was caught in the wheel of kicks[2] and the higher she had risen to
the top, the greater was her precipitous fall, in the manner that follows.*

*I say that there was once a king of Vallepelosa, who had a daughter
named Zoza, who, as if she were a new Zoroaster or a new Heraclitus,[3]
was never seen to laugh. For which reason, the unhappy father, who had
no other joy than this only daughter, omitted nothing which might dispel
her melancholy; and to provoke her laughter he summoned now men
who walk on stilts, now others who jump through hoops, now acrobats,
now master Ruggiero,[4] now sleight of hand, now the strength of Hercules,[5]
now the dog that dances, now the trained monkey that leaps, now the ass
that drinks from a glass, now "Lucia canazza,"[6] and now one thing and
now another; but it was all time lost, for not even the remedy of master
Grillo,[7] not even the Sardinian herb,[8] not even a poke in the ribs would*

Franca Trippa.   Fritellino.

*have creased her mouth into the slightest smile. So the poor father, not
knowing what else to try, as a last attempt gave orders that a great fountain of oil should be opened before the gate of the palace, with the idea
that as it sprayed people who passed through the street coming and going
like ants, they would, so as not to spot their clothes, leap like crickets,*

jump like goats, and run like rabbits, slipping and knocking this fellow and that, and in this manner something might happen to excite his daughter to a burst of laughter. When the fountain, then, was turned on, and Zoza was standing by the window, so sour that she seemed like a pickle, there came by chance an old woman who, sopping up the oil with a sponge, was squeezing it out into a jug of hers. And while, with a great bustling, she was performing this operation, a little devil of a page from the court threw a pebble so right on the mark that, hitting the jug, he reduced it to fragments. Whereupon the old woman, who had no hair on her tongue,[9] nor was used to letting anyone ride her, turning around to the page, began to say to him, "Ah, you snivelling, idle, shitty, bedpissing, leaping goat, diaper-assed, hangedman's knot, bastard mule! Lo even fleas have a cough![10] Go and may paralysis seize you! May your mother receive bad

Cap: Babeo.   *Cucuba.*

news of you! May you not see the first of May! May you be thrust by a Catalan lance, or may you be strangled by a rope, so that no blood is spilled! May a thousand curses come to you with haste and speed and wind in their sails! May your seed be lost, rascal, beggar, son of a taxed woman,[11] rogue!"

The boy, who had little hair on his cheeks and less discretion, hearing this delicious tirade, repaid her with the same coin, saying: "Don't you want to cork up that sewer, grandmother of Parasacco,[12] bloodsucking witch, baby-smotherer, shitdressed, fartface?"

The old woman, hearing this news of home, flew into such a rage that losing the compass bearings of phlegm[13] and escaping from the stall of patience raising the curtain from the stage, she revealed a bushy scene in which Silvio could have said, "Go open their eyes with your horne,"[14] at which spectacle Zoza was seized with such laughter that she nearly fainted. The old woman,

Cap. Cardoni.   Maramao.

hearing herself laughed at, was so enraged that, turning towards Zoza a snout to make anyone terrified, she said to her, "Go, may you not find the shadow of a husband, unless you take the Prince of Camporotondo!"

The princess, hearing these words, had the old woman called in and wanted to know at all cost whether she had insulted or cursed her; and the old woman replied, "Know now that the prince whom I mentioned is a lovely person and is named Tadeo, who because of the wicked spell of a fairy has put the last touch on the painting of his life and has been placed in a tomb outside the walls of the city; where there is an epitaph written

on the stone that any woman who fills a pitcher which is hanging there
on a hook with her tears in three days, will bring him back to life and
have him for a husband. But because it is impossible that two human eyes
can pour so many drops as to fill to the brim a pitcher so large that it contains half a bushel, unless it were, as I have heard tell, that Egeria who
was turned into a fountain of tears at Rome,[15] I, seeing myself derided
and mocked by you, gave you this curse, which I pray Heaven may come
to you in full, in revenge for the insult which has been given me." This
said, she slipped away and down the steps, afraid of a beating.

But as Zoza, at the same moment, was ruminating and chewing over
the words of the old woman, the tempter spirit entered into her head,
spinning a wheel of thoughts and a mill of doubts around this information; and in the end, carried away in the cart of that passion which blinds
the judgment and enchants the rationality of man, after having taken a
handful of money from her father's coffer, she slipped away out of the
royal palace and walked until she arrived at the castle of a fairy. When
Zoza had unburdened her heart to her, the fairy, in compassion for such
a pretty young girl, who had her young age and the overpowering love of
the unknown as two spurs to prick her forward over a precipice, gave her
a letter of recommendation for one of her sisters, also a fairy. This sister
welcomed her with many courtesies, and in the morning, when Night
sends out an announcement by the birds promising a good tip to whoever
will bring her notice of a flock of lost black shadows, she handed her a pretty
walnut, saying to her, "Take it, my child, and hold it dear, and never
open it except in a moment of great need." And with another letter she
recommended her to another sister. Having arrived at this second sister's
house after a long journey, Zoza was welcomed with the same loving
manners and in the morning received another letter for another sister,
along with a chestnut and the same warning that had been given her
about the walnut. After more walking she reached the castle of that fairy,
who, making a big fuss over her, at her departure in the morning consigned
to her a hazelnut, with the same admonition: never to open it unless
necessity had her by the throat. Having taken these things, Zoza set her
legs in motion and wandered through so many countries, passed so many
woods and rivers, that after seven years, just at the moment when the
Sun has saddled his horses to run the usual stages, wakened by the
roosters' bugles, she arrived almost exhausted at Camporotondo. Here,
before entering the city, she saw the marble sepulchre by the foot of a
fountain which, at seeing itself shut in a porphyry prison, was weeping
crystal tears. Taking from it the pitcher which was hanging there and

setting it between her legs, Zoza began to perform the play of the Two
Lookalikes[16] with the fountain, never raising her head from the mouth of
the pitcher; so that in less than two days, she had filled it two fingers up
the neck, which needed not quite another two and the pitcher would be
full; but worn out from so much weeping, she was despite herself deceived
by sleep and constrained to withdraw for a couple of hours behind the
curtain of her eyelids.

Meanwhile a certain cricket-legged slave-girl who often came to the
fountain to dip in a cask, and who knew the business about the epitaph,
for it was talked about everywhere, having seen Zoza weep so much that
she made two streams of tears, stayed to spy until the pitcher should be at
a good point, in order to take the work out of her hands and leave her
there with a fistful of flies.[17] And now that she saw her fallen asleep, taking advantage of the opportunity, she dextrously pulled the pitcher from
under her and, bending her eyes over it, in four winks filled it to the
brim. It was no sooner full than the prince, as if he were waking from a
deep sleep, rose up from that chest of white marble and grabbed hold of
that mass of black flesh, and immediately taking her to his palace, he
made her his wife, with parties and wonderful public illuminations.

But when Zoza woke up and found the pitcher on the ground, and
with the pitcher her hopes, and saw the tomb open, her heart closed up
so that she was on the point of unbaling the bundle of her soul at the cus-
tomhouse of Death. Finally, seeing that there was no remedy for her evil
plight, and that she could complain only against her eyes that had ill
guarded the heifer of her hopes,[18] she made her way with slow steps into
the city; where, hearing about the prince's parties and about the fine sort
of wife he had taken, she imagined clearly how the business had happened and said, sighing, that two black things had stranded her on bare
ground, sleep and a slave. Nonetheless, in order to try everything possible against death, from which every animal defends itself as much as it
can, she rented a pretty house facing the prince's palace, from which, if
she did not succeed in seeing the idol of her heart, she could at least con-
template the walls of the temple in which was enclosed the good that she
desired. But one day, when Tadeo had noticed her, he who had been like
a bat always flying around that black night of a slave became an eagle
looking always fixedly at the person of Zoza, who was the apex of the
privileges of nature and the "Gin rummy" of the bounds of beauty.
Aware of this, the slave raised hell and, being already pregnant by
Tadeo, threatened her husband by saying, "If from window you no go,
me give belly blow, and beat baby Giorgio!"[19]

Tadeo, tender for his offspring, trembling like a reed for fear of causing it any shock, tore himself away, like a soul from the body, from the sight of Zoza; who losing even this small comfort to the weakness of her hopes, not knowing at first what course to take in this extreme necessity, *remembered the gifts of the fairies. And when she opened the walnut, out came a little dwarf as big as a dolly, the most delicious little creature ever seen in the world, which, setting itself at the window, sang with so many trills, gurgles, and cadenzas as to seem equal with Biondo, to surpass Pezzillo and to leave far behind him the Blindman of Potenza and the king of the birds.[20] The slave, seeing and hearing it by chance, became so enchanted that, calling Tadeo, she said to him, "If no have her that's singing so, me give belly blow, and beat baby Giorgio!" The prince, who had donned moorish horse-trappings,[21] sent at once to ask Zoza whether she would sell it; she replied that she was no merchant, but that, if he would accept it as a gift, he might take it, for she gladly made him a present of it. Tadeo, who was making every effort to keep his wife happy so that she might carry the birth to term, accepted the offer. But four days later, Zoza opened the chestnut and out came a hen with twelve golden chickens which, being placed at the same window, were seen by the slave, who desired them from her very heels; and calling Tadeo and pointing out to him that lovely object, she said to him, "If you no get that hen-o, me give belly blow and beat baby Giorgio!" And Tadeo, who was letting himself be intimidated and wagged like the tail of that she-dog, sent anew to Zoza to offer her whatever she wished to ask as the price for such a pretty hen; and from whom he got the same answer as before, that he should rather take it a gift, because to speak of terms for selling it would be a waste of time. And he, who could not do without it, let need chase out discretion; and carrying away this pretty mouthful, remained astonished at the generosity of the woman, as that sex is by nature so greedy that it would not be satisfied with all the gold bars that come from the Indies. But when as many days had passed again, Zoza opened the hazelnut, from which out came a doll that was spinning gold, a thing truly to be wondered at, which had barely been placed in the same window when the slave, sniffing it out, called Tadeo, saying to him, "If buy dolly you no go, me give belly blow and beat baby Giorgio." And Tadeo, who let himself be spun like a skein-winder and led by the nose by the pride of this wife by whom he had let himself be saddled, not having the courage to send to Zoza for the doll, decided to go there in person, recalling the proverbs: "There's no messenger better than yourself"; "He who wants*

*goes, and he who doesn't want sends someone else"; and "He who wants
to eat fish must get his tail wet." And as he begged her heartily to pardon
the impertinent wishes of a pregnant woman, Zoza, who was in raptures
at the presence of the cause of her labours, fought against herself and let
herself be begged again and again in order to keep the boat sailing and to
enjoy for a longer time the sight of her lord, stolen from her by an ugly
slave; in the end, she gave him the doll as she had done the other things,
but before she handed it to him, she whispered to the figurine that it
should instill in the slave's breast the wish to hear tales told. Tadeo, who
saw himself with the doll in hand without disbursing so much as a penny,
thunderstruck by such liberality, offered her his state and life in exchange
for that favor. And returning to the palace, he gave the doll to his wife,
who had no sooner taken it into her lap to play with when it resembled
Cupid in the form of Ascanius in the lap of Dido, who kindled a fire in
her breast;*[22] *for such a burning desire seized the slave to hear tales that,
unable to resist and fearing to touch her mouth and make a child that
would outpester a whole shipful of beggars,*[23] *she called her husband and
said to him: "If people no come and tell tales-o, me give belly blow and
beat baby Giorgio!" Tadeo, to rid himself of this March worry,*[24] *ordered
an announcement published that all the ladies of the country should
come to him on a given day; and on that day, at the first peeping of
Diana's star,*[25] *which rouses Dawn to deck the streets through which the
Sun must pass, all the women assembled in the appointed place.*

*But, as Tadeo did not want to keep that whole rabble from their busi-
ness on account of a particular fancy of his wife, besides his suffocating
at the mere sight of such a crowd, he selected from them only ten, the
best of the city, who seemed to him the most lively and chattering; and
they were lame Zeza, twisted Cecca, goitered Meneca, big-nosed Tolla,
hunchback Popa, drooling Antonella, snout-faced Ciulla, rheumy Paola,
mangy Ciommetella, and diarrhetic Iacova. Having written these names
on a piece of paper and dismissed the others, he and the slave arose from
under their canopy and made their way with measured step to a garden
of the same palace, where the leafy branches were so tangled that the Sun
with the poles of his rays was unable to part them; and when they had sat
down under a pavilion covered with a pergola of grapes, in the middle of
which ran a large fountain which daily instructed courtiers in the art of
murmuring, Tadeo spoke thus:*

*"There is nothing in the world that more whets the appetite, my good
women, than to hear about the doings of others, nor without obvious*

reason did that great Philosopher set the supreme felicity of man in hearing pleasant tales; because, as you listen to things to your taste, cares evaporate, irksome thoughts are dispelled, and life is prolonged. On account of this desire, you see artisans leave their shops, merchants their trade, lawyers their cases, shopkeepers their business, to go with open mouth to the barbershops and the circles of gossipers to hear false news, invented notices, and fabricated newssheets.[26] Therefore I must excuse my wife if she has gotten into her head this melancholy humor to listen to tales. And so, if it please you to fill the pitcher of my princess's desire and to strike the bullseye of my wishes, each of you will agree, for the four or five days until her belly is unburdened, to narrate one tale every day of the sort that old women are wont to tell to amuse the children, meeting always in this same place where, after having eaten, we will begin the chattering, ending the day with some eclogue which will be recited by our own servants, in order that we may pass joyfully through life, and sad be he who dies!" At these words all accepted with a nod of the head Tadeo's command; meanwhile, as the tables had been set and the food brought, they began to eat, and when they had finished gulping it down, the prince gave a nod to lame Zeza that she should put fire to the gun. Zeza, making a great bow to the prince and his wife, thus began to speak.

I, 4
Vardiello

VARDIELLO, WHO IS A REAL DUNCE, AFTER HAVING DONE HIS MAMA A HUNDRED BAD SERVICES, LOSES A PIECE OF HER CLOTH; AND WANTING IN A FOOLISH MANNER TO GET IT BACK FROM A STATUE, BECOMES RICH.

When Meneca had finished the tale, which was considered no less pretty than the others for being stuffed full of curious events which held the listeners' minds in suspense until the end, Tolla followed her at the prince's command; and without losing time spoke in this manner.

If nature had given animals the need to clothe themselves and to spend money on victuals, the quadruped race would undoubtedly have died out; therefore they find food ready without the gardener gathering it, the cook preparing it, the waiter trimming it; and their own fur defends them from rain and snow without the merchant furnishing cloth, the tailor sewing a suit, and the delivery boy asking for a tip. But to man, who has intelligence, nature has not bothered to give similar conveniences, because man knows by himself how to get what he needs; and this is the reason why one sees ordinarily that wise men are beggars and stupid folk rich, as you will be able to gather from the tale which I am about to tell you.

Grannonia of Aprano[27] was a woman of good judgment, but she had a son named Vardiello, the most unlucky simpleton of that region; nonetheless, because a mama's eyes are bewitched and see distortedly, she loved him devotedly, and was always bending over him and stroking him as if he were the prettiest creature in the world. This Grannonia had a hen that was laying eggs from which she was hoping to get a pretty brood of chickens and make a good profit; and having to go out for some necessary matter, she said to her son, "Handsome son of your mama, come here, listen: keep your eye on this hen, and if she gets up to peck around, see that you quickly make her return to her nest; otherwise, the eggs will get cold and you won't have either eggs or chickies."

"Leave it to this guy," replied Vardiello, "for you haven't spoken to the deaf."

"Another thing," added the mama [indicating a jar of pickled walnuts], "see, blessed son, that inside that cupboard there is a glazed vessel with something poisonous in it; watch out lest you be tempted by the ugly sin of touching it, because you would stretch out your feet stiff."

"Far be it!" replied Vardiello; "poison won't get me! And you are a wise woman with a crazy head to warn me of it; because truly, I could have chanced upon it, and there was neither thorn nor cross-bones on it."

And so when his mama had gone out, Vardiello, who was left at home, not to lose time, went out into the garden to dig little holes covered with straw and earth to make children fall in; when, in the thick of his work, he noticed that the hen was strolling around outside the room, wherefore he immediately began to say, "Shoo, shoo, this way, go over there!" But the hen did not move back one step and Vardiello, seeing that the hen was a bit of an ass, after saying "shoo, shoo," began to stamp his feet; after stamping his feet, to throw his cap at it; and after the cap, he hurled a rolling-pin at it, which, hitting it right on, made it fall in agony and stretch out its claws. Seeing this sad mishap, Vardiello thought to repair the damage; and making a virtue of necessity, so that the eggs would not get cold, he immediately pulled down his pants and sat down on the nest; but, pressing them with his weight, he reduced them to an omelette. Seeing that he had rolled a double, he was on the point of hitting his head against the wall; but in the end, since every sorrow becomes a treat, feeling a pang in his stomach, he decided to swallow down the hen; and therefore, plucking it and sticking it on a fine spit, he lit a big fire and began to roast it; and when it was almost cooked, so that everything would be ready on time, he spread out a pretty and freshly-washed cloth over an old chest and taking a pitcher, went down to the wine-cellar to uncork a small barrel of wine. But in the middle of pouring the wine, he heard a noise, a crash, a confusion in the house, which sounded like armed horses; whereupon all alarmed, turning to look, he caught sight of a big cat who had snatched the hen along with the whole spit, and another cat was behind him, crying to have its share. Vardiello, to repair this damage, threw himself on the cat like an un-chained lion, and in his haste left the barrel uncorked; after having played tag through all the corners of the house, he recovered the hen, but meanwhile, the wine had all run out of the barrel. Returning to the barrel and seeing that he had let it all stream out, Vardiello also spilled the vat of his soul through the spouts of his eyes. But because judgment aided him, to repair the damage so that his mother would not notice so much ruin, he took a sack full full, heaped heaped, loaded loaded, stuffed stuffed, brimming brimming with flour and strewed it on the wet spots. With all this, counting on his fingers the disasters that had occurred, and thinking that because of having committed an excess of stupidities he was losing the game along with Grannonia's favor, he made a firm resolution not to let his mother find him alive; therefore opening the vessel with the pickled walnuts, which his mama had told him was poison, he did not take his hand from it until he had uncovered the whole shiny surface within; and having filled his belly well, he thrust himself into an oven.

In the meantime his mama came home; and after having knocked for a long while, perceiving that nobody heard her, she gave a kick to the door and came in; and calling her son in a loud voice and seeing that no one was answering, she cried out more loudly: "O Vardiello, O Vardiello, are you deaf that you don't hear me? Do you have spavins that you don't come running? Do you have hen's pip that you don't answer? Where are you, gallows-face? Where have you slipped off to, bad seed? Would that I had smothered you at the source when I made you!"

Vardiello, who heard all this shouting, finally, with a small piteous voice said, "Here I am, I'm inside the oven, and you will not see me again, mama mine!"

"Why?" responded the doleful mother.

"Because I have poisoned myself," replied the son.

"Alas!" said Grannonia, "and how have you done it? What motive did you have to commit this suicide, and who gave you the poison?" And Vardiello told her, one by one, all his fine accomplishments for which he wanted to die and remain no longer in the world as a reject. Hearing these things, his mama was mournful, was unhappy, and had much to do and to say in order to get that melancholy humor out of Vardiello's head; and since she bore him a devoted affection, by giving him some other syrupy thing, she took from his brain the fear of the pickled walnuts, which were not poison but made for the stomach. Having thus calmed him with kind words and made him a thousand sweet caresses, she pulled him out of the oven, and giving him a fine piece of cloth, told him to help her sell it, warning him not to do business with people of too many words.

"Fine!" said Vardiello, "I will serve you elegantly, don't doubt it."

And taking the cloth under his arm, he went walking with his merchandise through the city of Naples, uttering his cry: "Cloth, cloth!" But to all who asked him, "What sort of cloth is it?" he replied immediately, "You won't do for my business, for you have too many words." And if another asked him, "For how much are you selling it?" he called him a chatterbox who had broken his eardrums and given him a headache. In the end, discovering a plaster statue in the courtyard of a house, uninhabited because it was haunted by a spirit, the poor boy, footsore and weary from so much wandering around, sat down on a low wall; and not seeing anyone come or go from that house, which seemed like a sacked village, he said wonderingly to the statue, "Say there, comrade, doesn't anyone live in this house?" And seeing that it did not reply, he judged it a person of few words, and said, "Do you want to buy this cloth? I will give you a good price." And seeing the statue remain silent, he said, "In faith, I have found what I was looking for! Take it and examine it, and pay me whatever you think is right; tomorrow I will return for the money." This said, he left the cloth where he had been sitting; and the first mother's son who entered that courtyard to do something necessary, finding luck with him, carried it away.

When Vardiello came home to his mother without the cloth and reported to her what had happened, the poor woman felt her heart break, saying to him: "When will you put your brain in order? See how many troubles you have caused me! Remember them! But the fault is mine because, being too tender of heart, I did not at the first moment straighten you out with a good beating; and now I see that a tender-hearted doctor lets the wound become incurable! But you give me so much trouble that in the end you will fall into it yourself; and then the reckoning will be a long one!"

Vardiello for his part kept saying, "Quiet, mama mine, for it won't be as you say. Do you want something other than new-minted pennies? What do you think, that I come from Ioio[29] and don't know my own reckoning? Tomorrow is yet to come! From here to Belvedere is not far, and you will see whether I know how to put the handle on a shovel!"

In the morning, when the shadows of Night, pursued by the policemen of the Sun, quit the country, Vardiello took himself to the courtyard where the statue was and said to it, "Good day, Sir! Is it convenient for you now to give me those four little coins? Come now, pay me for the cloth!" But seeing that the statue remained mute, he picked up a stone and hurled it with all his might right in the middle of its chest, so hard that he broke a vein in it; and this was the salvation of his house for, having smashed four chunks of plaster, he uncovered a pot full of gold crowns, and grabbing it up with both hands, he ran at breakneck speed towards home, shouting, "Mama, mama, see how many red lupins! How many, how many!"

Mama, seeing the crowns and knowing that her son would go publicizing the event, told him to set himself in front of the door to see when the ricotta seller would pass by, because she needed to buy a pennysworth of milk. Vardiello, who was a glutton, at once sat down by the door; and his mother, from the upstairs window, rained down on him for over half an hour more than six packages of raisins and dried figs; which Vardiello picked up shouting, "Mama, o mama, bring basins, get tubs, put out vats, for if this shower lasts, we will be rich!" And when he had filled his belly full with them, he climbed up stairs to sleep.

It happened that one day while two laborers, rogues well-acquainted with the courts, were quarreling over the claim to one gold crown that they had found on the ground, Vardiello came by and said, "What arch-asses you are to quarrel over one red lupin of this sort, which I don't consider of any worth since I found a pot brim full of them." The members of the court, hearing this and opening wide their eyes, interrogated him and asked how, when, and with whom he had found the crowns. To which Vardiello replied, "I found them in a palace, inside a mute man, when there was a shower of raisins and dried figs." The judge, who heard him throw out this diminished fifth,[30] smelled out the business and decreed that he should be sent to an asylum as the competent place of judgment for him. So the ignorance of the son made his mama rich, and the good judgment of the mother made up for the asininity of her son, by which we see clearly that

> A ship steered by a good pilot
> rarely breaks on a rock.

II, 4
Cagliuso

CAGLIUSO, THROUGH THE INDUSTRY OF A CAT LEFT TO HIM BY HIS
FATHER, BECOMES A LORD; BUT SHOWING HIMSELF UNGRATEFUL, HE
HAS HIS INGRATITUDE THROWN IN HIS FACE.

The great enjoyment cannot be expressed that everyone got from the good fortune of Viola, who with her cleverness knew how to work things out well for herself despite her sisters, who, enemies of their own blood, had tried so many times to trip her up and make her break her neck. But it was Tolla's turn to pay the tax she owed; disbursing from her mouth the golden coins of pretty words, she satisfied her debt.

Ingratitude, ladies, is a rusty nail which, hammered into the tree of courtesy, makes it dry up; it is a broken drain which wets and weakens the foundations of affection; it is soot which, falling into the cooking-pot of friendship, takes away its fragrance and flavor; as is apparent and plainly proven, and you will see its design sketched in the tale that I am about to tell you.

There was once in my city of Naples an old beggar, who was so poor, penniless, homeless, hopeless, bare, and without the scent of a cent in his satchel,[31] that he went as naked as a louse. Having reached the point of shaking out the sacks of life, he called his two sons, Oratiello and Pippo, saying to them: "Now I have been summoned according to the terms of the contract for the debt which I owe to nature; and believe me (if you are Christians) that I would take great pleasure in leaving this stew of troubles, this sty of travails, if it weren't that I leave you destitute, as poor as the nuns of Santa Chiara,[32] at the five roads of Melito[33] and without a stitch, clean as a barber's basin, quick as cops, dry as a prune pit; for you have not so much as a fly carries on one foot, and if you run a hundred miles, not a farthing falls your way, since Fortune has led me down to where the three dogs shit; for I have nothing but my life, and as I see myself so I describe myself; for as you know, I have always made yawns and crosses,[34] and gone to bed without a candle. With all that, I want nonetheless to leave you some token of my love at my death; therefore do you, Oratiello, who are my first-born, take that sieve which hangs on the wall, with which you can earn your bread; and you, who are the fledgling, take the cat, and remember your daddy." So saying, he burst into tears, and shortly thereafter said, "Good-bye, for it is night!"

Oratiello, having his father buried by charity, took the sieve and went sifting here and there to earn his living; so that the more he sifted, the more he earned. But Pippo, taking the cat, said, "Now see what a mournful inheritance my father has left me, who have no means to live for myself and now I must shop for two! What's to be made of this sorry bequest? I'd have been better off without it!"

But the cat, who heard this lament, said to him, "You are complaining too much and have more luck than sense; but you don't recognize your own luck, for I can make you rich if I put myself to it."

Pippo, hearing this, thanked His Catship, and stroking its back three or four times, warmly recommended himself to it until the cat, feeling sorry for the bereaved Cagliuso,[35] betook itself every morning, when the Sun with a bait of light on a golden hook fishes for the shadows of the Night, to the seashore at Chiara or to the Fishstone,[36] and eyeing some fat mullets or some good giltheads, it would snatch them and carry them to the king, saying, "The Lord Cagliuso, humble slave of Your Above-the-roof Highness, sends you this fish with reverence and says, 'For a great lord, a small gift.'"

The king, with a merry face such as one is wont to wear who receives presents, replied to the cat, "Tell this lord, whom I don't know, that I thank him very much."

At other times, the cat would run to places where there was a hunt, at the Marshes or at Astrune,[37] and when the hunters had made some oriole or titmouse or blackcap fall, he would gather it up and carry it to the king with the same message. And so many times he used this artifice that the king said to him one morning, "I feel so obliged to that Lord Cagliuso of yours that I desire to make his acquaintance in order to offer him a return for the affection he has shown me."

To whom the cat replied, "The desire of Lord Cagliuso is to offer his life and blood for your crown; and tomorrow morning without fail, when the Sun has set fire to the stubble of the fields of the air, he will come to pay you his respects."

When morning came, the cat appeared again before the king, saying to him, "My lord, Lord Cagliuso sends his apologies for not coming, because this night certain of his servants robbed him and fled, leaving him without even a shirt."

The king, hearing this, at once had some clothing and linens fetched from his wardrobe and sent them to Cagliuso; and not more than two hours later he came, guided by the cat, to the palace, where the king paid him a thousand compliments and, bidding him sit beside him, gave him a magnificent banquet. But while he was eating, Cagliuso would from time to time turn to the cat saying, "My kitty, I put my four rags under your protection that they may not come to harm!"

And the cat would reply, "Be quiet, shut up, and don't say such beggarly things!" And when the king wanted to know what Cagliuso needed, the cat replied for him that he would like to have a little tiny lemon; and the king sent at once to the garden for a whole basketful. And Cagliuso repeated the same song about his tatters and rags; and the cat told him again to close his mouth; and the king asked once more what he required; and the cat was ready with another excuse to cover up Cagliuso's baseness. Finally, after they had eaten and chatted a while about this and that, Cagliuso took his leave, and the foxy cat stayed on with the king, describing the valor, wit, judgment, and above all, the great wealth that Cagliuso happened to possess in the countryside of Rome and of Lombardy, for which he deserved to ally himself in marriage to a crowned king. And when the king asked how much this wealth might amount to, the cat answered that it was not possible to count all the furnishings, the real estate, and the movable goods of this very rich man, for he himself did not know what he owned; and that if the king wanted to inform himself about it, he should send some of his men out of the kingdom, and they would let him know by experience that there was no wealth in the world equal to it.

The king, summoning certain persons whom he trusted, commanded them to gather detailed information on the matter; they followed the steps of the cat, who with the pretext of going to find refreshments for them along the way from place to place when they had passed the boundaries of the kingdom, kept running ahead, and whenever he met flocks of sheep, herds of cows, or troops of horses, he would say to the shepherds and keepers, "Hola, be on guard, for a band of brigands want to plunder whatever they find in this countryside. However, if you want to save yourself from their fury and want them to respect your property, tell them that it's all the stuff of the Lord Cagliuso, for then they won't touch a hair of it." And he said the same at the large farms that he found by the road; so that wherever the king's men arrived, they found the flute tuned, for everything they saw was said to belong to Lord Cagliuso, until weary of asking further, they returned to the king, speaking oceans and mountains of Lord Cagliuso's wealth. At this report the king promised a handsome tip to the cat if he could arrange the marriage; and the cat, having played the shuttle back and forth, at last concluded the match.

When Cagliuso had arrived, the king gave him a large dowry and his daughter; and after a month of celebrations, Cagliuso said that he wanted to take his bride to his own lands, and accompanied by the king as far as the border, he left for Lombardy, where, at the cat's advice, he bought territory and lands and made himself a baron. Now Cagliuso, seeing himself fabulously rich, thanked the cat as much as possible, saying that he owed his life and grandeur to the cat's good services, and that the designs of a cat had brought him greater profit than the wits of his father; and therefore the cat could deal and dispose at its wish and will with all his goods and with his life, promising that when the cat died—and he prayed it would be a hundred years off!—he would have it embalmed and placed in a golden casket in his very own bedroom in order to keep its memory always before his eyes.

Not three days after the cat had heard this swaggering, feigning to be dead, it let itself be found stretched out long, long, in the garden; which when Cagliuso's wife saw, she cried, "O my husband, what a great calamity! The cat is dead!"

"May every evil go with him!" answered Cagliuso. "Better him than us."

"What shall we do?" replied his wife.

And he said, "Take him by the paw and throw him out the window!"

The cat, hearing this pretty reward when he would least have imagined it, began to say, "This is the 'great thanks' for the lice which I took off your back, this is the 'thousand thanks' for the rags which I made you throw away, rags from which one could barely hang spindles? This is the exchange for having set you up like a spider, and for having fed you when you were hungry, you beggar, ragamuffin, who yesterday were tattered, torn, threadbare, frowsy, and lousy? That's how it is when you wash an ass's head!³⁸ Go, cursed be all that I have done for you, who don't deserve that I spit in your throat! A fine golden casket you lined for me! A fine burial you gave me! Be a servant yourself, struggle, labor, sweat, to obtain this fine reward! Oh wretched is he who sets his cooking-pot on his hope in others! Well spoke the philosopher: he who goes to bed an ass wakes up an ass! In sum, he who does most can expect to get least. But good words and sorry deeds deceive both wise men and fools!" So saying and shaking its head, it slipped out the exit; and for all that Cagliuso, with the lung of humility,³⁹ sought to appease it, there was no remedy to bring it back; but as it kept running without ever turning its head, it said:

> God keep you from a rich man grown poor
> and from a beggar grown rich and cocksure.

IV, 9
The Crow
IENNARRIELLO, IN ORDER TO PLEASE HIS BROTHER, MILLUCCIO, THE KING OF FRATTA OMBROSA, MAKES A LONG VOYAGE AND BRINGS HIM

WHAT HE WANTED, AND FOR FREEING HIM FROM DEATH, IS CONDEMNED
TO DEATH HIMSELF; BUT BECOMING A STATUE OF MARBLE STONE IN
ORDER TO DEMONSTRATE HIS INNOCENCE, BY A STRANGE OCCURRENCE
HE RETURNS TO HIS FORMER STATE AND HAPPILY REJOICES.

I f I had a hundred pipes in my throat, a lung of bronze, and a thousand tongues of steel,[40] I could not explain how much Paola's tale
pleased them, hearing how not one of the good deeds she had done
was left without reward; so much did the tale please them that they had
to heap a good dose of begging on Ciommettella to have her tell hers, as
she wanted to get out of having to pull, like everyone else, the carriage of
the prince's command. However, unable to avoid obeying, in order not
to spoil the fun, she spoke thus:

It is truly a great proverb this one: we see crooked and judge straight;
but it is so difficult to apply it that few human judgments hit the nail on the
head; rather in the sea of human affairs most people are freshwater
fishermen, who catch crabs, and he who thinks he is taking the measure of
his intentions more closely, is all the sooner mistaken; from which it arises
that everyone is thinking distortedly, everyone is acting idiotically, everyone is judging randomly, and most of the time, with a sorry tumbling for
a foolish resolve they buy themselves a sensible repentance, as did the
King of Fratta Ombrosa, whose story you will hear if you will call me into
the circle of modesty with the bell of courtesy and give me a brief audience.

Now I say that there was once a king of Fratta Ombrosa named Milluccio,
who was so addicted to hunting that he mortgaged the things most necessary to his state and household in order to follow the tracks of a rabbit or
the flight of a thrush; and he continued on this path until one day fortune
brought him to a forest which had made a tight-packed phalanx of earth
and trees not to be broken through by the cavalry of the Sun, where on a
beautiful marble stone he found a freshly killed crow. The king, seeing
that bright bright blood splashed on that white white stone, heaved a
great sigh, and said: "Oh heaven, if only I could have a wife as white and
red as that stone, and with hair and brows as black as the feathers of this
crow!" And he fell to pondering this thought in such a way that for a
while he played the Two Lookalikes with that stone, so that he looked
like a marble statue making love with that other marble; and locking this
sorry caprice inside his head and feeding it all the while with the pap of
desire, he turned it in four winks from a toothpick into a pole, from a
pippin into an Indian melon, from a barber's brazier into a glassblower's
furnace,[41] and from a dwarf into a giant, such that he thought of nothing

but the image of that object inlaid in his heart like a stone in a stone. Wherever he turned his eyes, he always found that image before him which he carried within his breast, and forgetting all his other affairs, he had nothing but that marble in his head, until he wore himself so thin over that stone that he dwindled hair by hair, this stone being a millstone which ground away his life, a porphyry which pulverized the paints of his days, a flint which set fire to the sulphur of his soul,[42] a magnet which drew him, and finally a gall-stone which would not let him rest.

At last Iennariello, his brother, seeing him so deathly pale and wan, said to him, "My brother, what's the matter with you that you carry dolor quartered in your eyes and despair enlisted under the pale flag of your face? Speak, open your heart to a brother! Fumes of coal enclosed in a chamber make a person sick, powder compressed in a mountain makes fragments fly through the air, infection shut into the veins corrupts the blood, gas retained in the body generates flatulence and colic; therefore open your mouth and tell me what you are feeling; in the end you can assure yourself that if there is anything I can do, I will lay down a thousand lives to help you."

Milluccio, mumbling words and sighs, thanked him for his kind love, saying that he had no doubt of his brother's affection, but that his ill had no remedy, because it sprang from a stone on which he had sown his desires without hope of fruit, a stone from which he did not hope for even a mushroom of gladness, a stone of Sisyphus which he was carrying up the mountain of his intentions, and whenever he got to the top it rolled bumpety-bump to the bottom; finally, after being begged a thousand times, he told him all about his love. Iennariello, having heard the matter, comforting him as well as he could, told him to be of good spirit and not to let himself be dragged on the ground by this melancholy humor, for he himself, to give his brother some satisfaction, was resolved to travel all the way around the world in order to find a woman who was the original of that stone; and immediately furnishing himself with a large ship full of merchandise, dressing himself as a merchant, he headed for Venice, the mirror of Italy, welcomer of the virtuous, the greatest book of marvels of both art and nature, where, being granted safeconduct to pass to Levant, he set sail for Cairo; and entering the city, seeing someone who was carrying a most beautiful falcon, he bought it at once to bring to his brother, who was such a hunter; and shortly thereafter, encountering another man with a wonderful horse, he acquired that too; and entering a tavern, he refreshed himself from his past toils on the sea.

But the following morning, when the army of the stars at the command of the general of light takes down its tents from the palisade of heaven, and abandons the post, Iennariello began to walk through the city, eyeing it all over as a wolf does a stag, looking at this woman and that, to see if by chance he might find a face of flesh similar to a stone; and while he went wandering here and there, always turning around like a thief afraid of the cops, he encountered a beggar who wore a whole hospital of bandages and a Giudecca[43] of rags, who said to him, "My gallant man, what's the matter with you that I see you so bewildered?"

"Do I have to tell you my business?" answered Iennariello; "as soon as I've made my bread, I'll report my case to the police!"

"Gently, my handsome young man," replied the beggar, "for the flesh of men is not sold by the weight! If Darius had not recounted his troubles to a groom in the stables, he would not have become the ruler of Persia![44] Therefore it would not be strange if you told your business to a poor beggar, for there is no twig so thin that it can't serve you to pick your teeth."

Iennariello, hearing this poor man speak to the point and with good sense, told him the cause that had brought him to his country and what he was seeking with such diligence; hearing this the beggar responded, "Now see, my son, how necessary it is to take account of everyone! For although I am dung, yet I will be good to manure the garden of your hopes. Now listen: under the pretext of seeking charity I will knock on the door of a beautiful girl, the daughter of a necromancer; keep your eyes open, look at her, consider her, check her out, think her over, measure her, for you will find her the image of what your brother desires."

And so saying, he knocked on the door of a house not far away, where Liviella came to answer, and as she threw him a morsel of bread Iennariello as soon as he saw her thought her built according to the model given him by Milluccio, and handing the beggar a good sum, he sent him away. And going to a tavern, he changed his dress to that of a ribbons-and-pins vendor, carrying in two boxes all the goods of the world, and he walked back and forth in front of Liviella's house until she called to him, and taking a look at those pretty little nets, veils, ribbons, kerchiefs, laces, linens, and lotions, brooches, pins, rouges, and bonnets, which he was carrying, and looking over all the merchandise several times, finally she told him to show her something else pretty, and he replied, "My lady, in this box I carry things trifling and cheap; but if you would deign to come to my ship, I could show you things out of this world, because I have treasures of beauty fit for a great lord."

Liviella, who was not lacking in curiosity lest she harm the reputation of women's nature, said to him, "In faith, if my father weren't away, I would love to give it a glance!"

"You can come all the better," replied Iennariello, "for perhaps he would not concede you this pleasure; and I promise to show you luxuries that you'll be crazy about. What necklaces and earrings! what belts and corsets! what enamels! what laceworks! In sum, I want to amaze you."

Liviella, hearing of this great collection of things, calling over a neighbor of hers to accompany her, went to the ship; once she was on board, while Iennariello held her enchanted by showing her so many pretty things that he had brought, he skillfully had the anchor raised and the sails spread, so that by the time Liviella lifted her eyes from the merchandise and saw herself far from land, they had gone several miles; realizing the trick too late, she began to do like Olimpia in reverse, because whereas that lady lamented being left on a rock, this lady lamented leaving the rocks.[45] But Iennariello, telling her who he was, where he was taking her, and the fortune which awaited her, and moreover depicting to her the beauty, valor, and virtue of Milluccio and finally the love with which he would receive her, did and said enough to calm her down; indeed she was praying the wind to take her immediately to see the full-color version of the sketch which Iennariello had made for her.

And so as they were sailing merrily, lo they heard the water whispering under the ship, which although it spoke in an undertone, the captain of the ship understood and shouted, "Every man on the alert, for now a storm is coming, and may God help us!" To which words were added the testimonial of a whistle of wind, and lo the sky became covered with clouds and the sea full of whitecaps; and because the waves, curious to know other people's business, without having been invited to the wedding jumped up into the ship, some men were scooping them with a ladle into a basin, some were driving them out with a pump; and while every sailor, because his own cause was at stake, attended some to the tiller, some to the sail, some to the sheet, Iennariello climbed up to the crow's-nest to see with a telescope whether he could discover any land where they might cast anchor. And lo, while he was measuring a hundred miles of distance with two palm-lengths of tube, he saw a male and female dove fly by and alight on top of the lateen yard; the male said, "Rukke rukke."

And the female answered, "What is it, my husband, that you are complaining about?"

And the male said, "This doleful prince has acquired a falcon which as soon as it is in the hands of his brother will peck out his brother's eyes; but if he doesn't bring it there, or if he warns him to beware, he'll turn to stone of marble rare!" And having said this, he went back to crying "Rukke rukke."

And the female dove said to him again, "And still you're complaining! Is there anything more?"

And the male said, "There's another little problem, for he has also bought a horse, and the first time his brother rides it he will break his neck; but if he doesn't bring it there, or if he warns him to beware, he'll turn to stone of marble rare; and rukke rukke!"

"Oh dear, so many rukke rukkes!" continued the female dove; "What else is there to be dished out?"

And the male said, "This man is bringing a pretty wife to his brother, but the first night that they go to bed they will both be eaten by a hideous dragon; but if he doesn't bring her there, or if he warns him to beware, he'll turn to stone of marble rare!"

And when he had said this, the storm ceased, and the fury passed from the sea and the rage from the wind, but there stirred a much greater tempest in the breast of Iennariello on account of what he had heard, and more than four times he wanted to throw all these things into the sea in order not to bring the cause of his brother's destruction; but on the other hand he thought about his own welfare, and the first cause began with himself;[46] worrying that if he did not bring these things to his brother or if he warned him about them, he would turn to marble, he resolved to look more closely at the proper noun than at the generic,[47] because the shirt pinched him more than the coat. And arriving at the port of Fratta Ombrosa, he found his brother at the shore, who, seeing the ship return, was awaiting it with great relish; and having seen that it was bringing her whom he held in his heart, comparing one appearance to the other and seeing that there wasn't a hair's difference between them, he was so happy that his overloaded joy was about to break under the burden, and embracing his brother with great pleasure he said, "What falcon is this which you carry on your wrist?"

And Iennariello said, "I bought it to give to you."

And Milluccio replied, "It well appears that you love me, because you go about seeking to give me things to my liking; and certainly if you had brought me a treasure you couldn't have given me greater pleasure than by this falcon!" And as he tried to take it onto his hand, Iennariello quickly with a big knife that he was wearing at his side made its head fly off, at which action the king remained stunned and considered his brother crazy for having done such an inappropriate deed; but in order not to trouble the joy of his arrival he said nothing about it. But seeing the horse and asking whose it was, he heard that it was for him; whereupon he wanted to ride it, and while he was having the stirrup held for him, Iennariello suddenly with a knife cut its legs; which sorely offended the king, and he thought he was doing it to spite him, and his innards began to seethe, but it did not seem to him the proper time for expressing his resentment, in order not to poison at first sight the maiden, whom he could not get enough of gazing at and squeezing by the hand.

And when they had arrived at the royal palace, he invited all the lords of the city to a fine feast, where they looked just like a school of riders in the hall making curvets and serpentines, and a herd of fillies in the form of women; but when the dance was finished and they had gotten the better of a huge banquet, they went to bed. Iennariello, who had no other thought in his head than to save his brother's life, hid himself behind the bed of the newlyweds, standing ready to see when the dragon would come, and lo at midnight a hideous dragon entered the chamber, who threw flames from his eyes and smoke from his mouth, which would have been good for making the grocer sell all his wormseed to cure the terror it brought to the beholder.[48] When Iennariello saw this, with a damascene sword which he had placed under his cloak, he began to set about him perilously, striking forehand and backhand, and among his other blows he struck one so powerful that it cut in two a poster of the king's bed; at which uproar the brother awoke, and the dragon vanished. But Milluccio, seeing the sword in Iennariello's hand and the poster cut in two, began to shout, "Ho there, four of my men, ho there people, hola, help, help, help, for this traitor brother of mine has come to kill me!"

At which cry a band of servants who were sleeping in the antechamber rushed in, and the king, having him bound, sent him that very hour to prison, and as soon as the Sun in the morning opened his bank to pay back the deposit of light to the creditor of the day, the king called a council and when he had reported the deed, which matched the evil intent demonstrated in killing the falcon and in wounding the horse, they sentenced Iennariello to die, and the prayers of Liviella had no power to soften the heart of the king, who said, "You do not love me, my wife, while you think more of your brother-in-law than of my life! You saw him with your own eyes, this assassin dog, with a sword which could slice a hair in the air, come to cut me in pieces so that if that poster of the bed (poster of my life!) had not protected me, at this hour you would be shorn!"[49] So saying he gave orders for justice to be carried out. Iennariello, who heard notice of this decree and saw himself brought to such evil for doing good, did not know what to think of his case; because if he did not speak, it was bad; if he spoke, worse; a sorry itch and a worse scratch; and whatever he might do was to fall from the tree into the wolf's mouth; if he stayed silent he would lose his head under a blade, if he spoke he would end his days inside a stone. In the end, after many turbulent changes of mind, he decided to reveal the business to his brother, and as long as he had to die anyway, he deemed it a better resolution to inform his brother of the truth and end his days with the title of innocence than to keep the truth to himself and be expelled from the world as a traitor. And therefore, sending word to the king that he wanted to speak with him on an important matter of state, he was summoned into the king's presence, where he made a long preamble about the love which he had always borne him; then he entered into the trick played on Liviella in order to give him satisfaction; what he had heard the doves say about the falcon, and how in order not to turn into a marble stone he had brought it to him and, without revealing the secret, had killed it so as not to see his brother eyeless; as he said this, he felt his legs grow hard and turn to marble, and continuing with the matter of the horse in the same way he became visibly stone up to his waist, wretchedly hardening, a thing for which at another time he would have paid ready cash and now he wept for it in his heart;[50] finally coming to the matter of the dragon he remained completely stone like a statue in the middle of the hall. When the king saw this, blaming his own error and the rash judgment he had made of a brother, so good and so loving, he wore mourning for more than a year, and whenever he thought of it he made a river of tears.

In the meantime the young Liviella produced two sons who were two of the most beautiful things in the world; and after a few months, while the queen was out for amusement in the countryside and the father was staying with his children in the middle of the hall, gazing with streaming eyes at that statue, remembering his folly which had taken away the flower of men, lo there entered a very old man, whose long hair covered his shoulders and whose beard hung down over his chest, who bowing to the king said, "How much would your majesty pay to see this fine brother return to what he used to be?"

And the king answered him, "I would pay my kingdom!"

"This is not a thing," replied the old man, "which exacts a price of wealth, but being a matter of life it must be paid for with another life."

The king, partly for the love which he bore Iennariello and partly because he felt himself guilty of the damage, replied, "Believe me, my good sir, I would pay my life for his, and if only he could come out from that stone, I would gladly be turned into a stone myself."

Hearing this the old man said, "Without putting your own life in this danger,[51] because it is so difficult to bring a man to adulthood, it will suffice that the blood of these children of yours be smeared on this marble to make him immediately come back to life."

The king at these words answered, "Children one can make! There is still the mold for these dolls, and others can be made, but I have only one brother and no hope ever to have another!"

So saying he made before the idol of stone a miserable sacrifice of two innocent little kids,[52] and the statue, smeared with their blood, immediately came to life and was embraced by the king, rejoicing with him more than one can tell; and as the poor children were being put in a casket to give them the honorable burial which was due them, at that same moment the queen returned from outside, and the king, bidding his brother hide, said to his wife, "What would you pay, my heart, to bring my brother back to life?"

"I would pay," answered Liviella, "this whole kingdom."

And the king replied, "Would you give the blood of your sons?"

"That no," answered the queen, "for I would not be so cruel as to tear out with my own hands the pupils of my eyes!"

"Alas," continued the king, "to see a brother alive I have cut the throats of the children! For this alone was the price of Iennariello's life!"

So saying he showed her the children in a casket; seeing this bitter spectacle, shrieking like a madwoman, she said, "O my children! O props of my life! O delights of my heart! O fountains of my blood! Who has cast this pitch upon the windows of the sun? Who has let blood without a doctor's license from the principal vein of my life? Alas, my children, children, my broken hopes, darkened light, poisoned sweetness, lost support! You are pierced by a blade, I am punctured by grief, you are drenched in your blood, I am drowned in my tears! Alas, to give life to an uncle you have killed a mama, for I can no longer weave the cloth of my days without you, pretty counterweights of the loom of this mournful life! The organ of my life must be silenced now that its bellows have been taken away! O children, o children, why don't you answer your mummykins, who already gave you blood within her body and now gives it to you through her eyes? But since my fortune makes me see the fountain of my joys dried up, I want no longer to live as a burden to this world; now I will follow in your steps to rejoin you!"

So saying she ran to a window to throw herself out; but at the same moment through the same window there entered her father the necromancer in a cloud, who said to her, "Stop, Liviella, for after having made a journey and performed three tasks, I have taken vengeance on Iennariello, who came to my house to steal away my daughter, by making him stay so many months like a clam in the sea inside that stone; I have paid myself back for your wicked behavior when you went off on a ship without regard to me, by making you see your two children, rather two jewels, slaughtered by their own father; and I have mortified the king for his caprice, like a pregnant woman's, which he had brought on himself, by making him first the criminal judge of his brother, then the executioner of his sons. But because I wanted to shave and not to flay you, I want all your poison to turn to a royal pasty; and therefore go take your children and my grandchildren, for they are prettier than ever; and you Milluccio embrace me, for I accept you as son-in-law and as son, and I pardon Iennariello his offense, since he did what he did in service to a brother so worthy." When he had spoken, here came the children, whom the grandfather could not get enough of hugging and kissing, into which joys Iennariello entered as a third, who having passed through the noodle press now went into the macaroni soup,[53] although with all the pleasures which he felt in his life he never forgot the past perils, thinking of his brother's error and how alert a man must be not to fall into a pit, as

Every human judgment is false and distorted.

V, 1
The Goose
AT THE MARKET LILLA AND LOLLA BUY A GOOSE THAT SHITS COINS; IT IS BORROWED FROM THEM BY A NEIGHBOR WHO, FINDING NO COINS IN ITS EXCREMENT, KILLS IT AND THROWS IT OUT THE WINDOW. IT ATTACHES ITSELF TO THE REAR OF THE PRINCE WHILE HE IS UNBURDENING HIMSELF, AND NO ONE CAN DETACH IT EXCEPT LOLLA, FOR WHICH REASON THE PRINCE MARRIES HER.

It was a great saying of that great honest fellow that artisan envies artisan, cesspool cleaner envies cesspool cleaner, musician musician, neighbor neighbor, and the poor man the beggar;[54] because there is no space in the edifice of the World where the cursed spider of envy does not weave his web, who feeds on nothing but the next man's ruin, as you will hear specifically in the tale I will tell you.

There were once two sisters so reduced to bare nothing that they only managed to live on as much as they could get by spitting on their fingers from morning to evening to make a bit of thread to sell. Yet, notwithstanding this wretched life, it was impossible for the billiard ball of necessity to hit that of honor and knock it out. For this reason Heaven, which is as generous in rewarding good as it is stingy in chastising evil, put it into the head of these poor girls to go to the market to sell certain skeins of thread and, with the little money that they got from it, to buy themselves a goose; having done this and brought the goose home, they set such affection on it that they took care of it as if it were their sister, letting it sleep in their own bed. But dawn peeps out and makes a good day; the good goose began to shit Spanish crowns, so that, dropping by dropping, they filled a large coffer; and such was that excretion that they began to lift up their heads, and one could see their coats shine again, so that certain neighbors of theirs who observed this, finding themselves together one day to gossip, said to each other, "O Vasta, my neighbor, have you seen Lilla and Lolla, who the day before yesterday didn't even have a place to fall dead in and now they are so much better off that they look like high-class ladies? Have you seen their windows always hung with chickens and pieces of meat, which strike your eye? How can this be? Either they have tapped the key of honor or they have found treasure!"

"I am struck dumb like a mummy," answered neighbor Perna, "because where before they were dying of hunger, I now see them fat and up again, so that it seems like a dream to me."

Saying these and other things, pricked on by envy, they made a small hole which went through from their house to that of the two girls, in order to spy and see if they could give some food to their curiosity; and they kept on spying until one evening, when the Sun beats with his rays on the ships of the Indian Ocean to give a rest to the Hours of the day, they saw Lilla and Lolla spread a sheet on the ground and set the goose on it, who began to spurt out a discharge of crowns, at which simultaneously the neighbors' eyeballs bulged out from their eyes and the throats from their necks. And in the morning, when Apollo with his golden wand conjures the shade to retreat, a third neighbor, Pasca, went to pay a visit to those girls and, after a thousand preambles and windings, shillying and shallying, came to the "wherefore" and begged them to lend her the goose for two hours, in order for it to help certain goslings which she had bought get used to the house. And she knew how to talk and beg so well that the two ingenuous sisters, partly because they were kindly and did not know how to refuse and partly because they did not want to make the neighbor suspicious, lent it to her, with a promise that she would bring it back as quickly as possible. The neighbor went to find the other women, and together they immediately spread a sheet on the ground, setting the goose on it, which, instead of showing in its bottom a mint that coined crowns, uncorked a sewer pipe and decorated the white linen of these unfortunate women with yellow dirt such that the smell filled the whole lodging, as it does from the good wives' cooking pots on Sundays. Seeing this, they thought that by feeding it well they could give substance to the philosophers' stone[55] to satisfy their wishes; and so they stuffed it until food was coming out of its throat, but when they placed it on another clean sheet, if before the goose had shown itself lubricous, now it revealed itself downright dysenteric, for digestion played its part. Whereupon, the neighbor women, feeling scorned, became so angry that they twisted its neck and threw it out the window into a blind alley where garbage was dumped.

But as fortune had it, which when you least expect it makes the bean grow, there passed by that area one of the King's sons, who was going to hunt; and there at the instigation of his body, he gave his sword and horse to a servant to hold and entered into that alley to unburden his belly; and having finished this business, not finding in his pocket any paper to clean himself with and seeing that goose freshly killed, he used it for a rag. But the goose, which was not dead, gripped so strongly with its beak onto the buttocks of the sorry prince that he began to cry out; at which all the servants came running to him, but though they tried to pull it off from his flesh, it was not possible, for it had attached itself there like a Salmacis of feathers and a Hermaphrodite of skin;[56] therefore the prince, unable to bear the pain and seeing the efforts of his servants come to nothing, had himself carried in their arms to the royal palace, whither all the doctors of the city were summoned; and consulting with each other on the spot, they tried everything they could to remedy this accident, applying ointments, using pincers, strewing powders. But seeing that the goose was a tick that would not be detached with quicksilver, a leech that would not come off with vinegar, the prince then ordered an announcement to be published that whoever succeeded in removing this annoyance from his rear, if a man, would be given half the kingdom, and if a woman, would be taken as his wife. Here you saw people running in a crowd to poke in their noses; but, the more they applied remedies, the more the goose tightened its grip and tortured the poor prince, until it seemed truly that there had allied themselves all the recipes of Galen and the Aphorisms of Hippocrates and the remedies of Mesoè[57] against the

Posteriors of Aristotle[58] to the torment of that unfortunate man. But as chance had it, among the many many who came to make a try, there arrived Lolla, the younger of the two sisters, who, when she saw the goose, recognized it and cried, "My plumpikin, plumpikin!" The goose, hearing the voice of one who loved it, at once released its grip and ran into Lolla's lap, stroking against her and giving her kisses, not minding to exchange the rear end of a prince for the mouth of a poor girl. The prince, who saw this wonder, wanted to know how it had come about; and hearing of the neighbor woman's deceit, he had her beaten all across the town and sent into exile; and marrying Lolla with the goose as her dowry, which kept excreting a hundred treasures, he gave another rich husband to Lilla; and they remained the happiest people in the world, despite the neighbors who, wanting to close off one road to riches that Heaven had sent, opened for Lolla another road to become queen, recognizing in the end that

Hindrance is often help.

<h1 align="center">V, 9</h1>
<h2 align="center">The Three Citrons</h2>

CENZULLO DOESN'T WANT A WIFE, BUT HAVING CUT HIS FINGER ABOVE A RICOTTA CHEESE, HE DESIRES ONE WITH A COMPLEXION AS WHITE AND RED AS THAT RICOTTA AND BLOOD, AND FOR THIS HE WANDERS THROUGH THE WORLD, AND ON THE ISLAND OF THREE FAIRIES HE OBTAINS THREE CITRONS. UPON CUTTING ONE OF THEM HE ACQUIRES A BEAUTIFUL FAIRY TO MATCH HIS HEART'S DESIRE; WHEN SHE IS KILLED BY A SLAVE, HE TAKES THE BLACK WOMAN INSTEAD OF THE WHITE ONE, BUT DISCOVERING THE DECEIT, HE HAS THE SLAVE KILLED, AND THE FAIRY, RETURNING TO LIFE, BECOMES QUEEN.

One cannot describe how much the tale of Carmosina pleased all her companions; but as it was Ciommetella's turn to speak, and she had been given the sign, she said thus:

That wise man truly said it well: "Don't say as much as you know, nor do as much as you can," for both one and the other bring unknown danger and unexpected ruin, as you will hear about a certain slave, speaking with respect of my lady the princess, a slave who in doing as much harm as possible to a poor girl caused so much evil in the matter that she became the judge of her own crime and gave herself the sentence of punishment which she deserved.

The king of Torre Longa had one son, the apple of his eye, on whom he had placed the foundation of every hope, and he could not wait to find him a good match and be called grandpa; but this prince was so far from love and so unsociable that when one spoke to him of a wife, he shook his head and was a hundred miles away. So that the poor father, who saw his son reluctant and obstinate, and the family line in danger of ceasing, was more irked, angry, knotted in the throat, and frustrated than a prostitute who has lost a payment, than a merchant whose agent has failed him, than a peasant whose ass had died; for his papa's tears did not move the prince, his vassals' prayers did not soften him, the counsels of good men did not persuade him, though they set before his eyes his sire's pleasure, his people's need, his own best interest, as he was the period at the end of a line of royal blood; for with the stubbornness of Carella, with the obstinacy of an old mule, with a skin four fingers at its thinnest, he had so planted his feet, stopped his ears, and blocked his heart, that they could sound the alarm. But because often more happens in one hour than in a hundred a years, and one cannot say "I won't go this way," it befell while they were all together at the table one day, that as the prince was trying to cut a ricotta in two while paying attention to some crows that were flying by, he accidentally cut his finger, so that two drops of blood fell on the ricotta, making such a pretty and lovely mixture of colors that, either by the chastisement of Cupid who was lying in wait for him at the pass, or by the will of heaven to console that good man his father, who was not so pained by his own hernia as he was tormented by that unsociable colt, he got the capricious idea of finding a wife as white and red exactly as the ricotta colored with his blood, and he said to his father, "My lord, if I don't get something of that complexion I am ruined! Never did a woman stir my blood, and now I want a woman like my blood. Therefore resolve, if you want me alive and well, to give me the means to go through the world seeking a beauty that precisely matches this ricotta; otherwise I will end my course and die accursed."

And the king, hearing this bestial resolution, felt the house fall down around him, and as he sat stock still, one color left him and another came over him; and when he came to himself and could speak, he said, "My son, vital organ of this life, delight of this heart, prop of my old age, what delirium has seized you? Have you left your senses? Have you lost your wits? You roll either a one or a six![59] Before you did not want a wife in order to deprive me of heirs, and now do you have such a hunger for one as to drive me from this world? Where, where do you want to go roaming, consuming your life and abandoning your home? Your home, your hearth, your place of rest? Don't you know to how many toils, to how many dangers he submits himself who travels? Let this caprice pass, o son, pay heed! Don't wish to see your life ruined, your house fallen, your state come to an end!" But these and other words entered at one ear and exited at the other, and all were thrown into the sea; finally the doleful king, seeing that his son was like a deaf crow in the bell tower, giving him a good handful of coins and two or three servants, granted him leave, feeling as if his souls were parting from his body; and leaning out on a balcony, weeping as if his life were at an end, he followed him with his eyes until he lost him from sight.

The prince then, having departed and left his father mournful and sorrowful, began to trot through fields and forests, across mountains and valleys, over plains and hills, visiting various countries, dealing with diverse peoples, and always with his eyes open to see whether he could find the object of his desire; until at the end of four months he arrived at the coast of France where, leaving the servants at a hospital with a migraine in their feet, he embarked on board a Genoese boat, and heading towards the Strait of Gibraltar, he took there a larger ship and continued towards the Indies, always seeking from kingdom to kingdom, from province to province, from city to city, from street to street, from house to house and from room to room to see whether he might encounter the exact original of the pretty image painted in his heart. And he moved his legs and turned his feet until he arrived at the Island of the Orcs,[60] where casting anchor and disembarking onto land, he found an old old woman, who was dry dry and had an ugly ugly face; when he had told her the cause which had dragged him to that country, the old woman was beside herself hearing the fine caprice and capricious fantasy of this prince, and the toils and risks undergone in order to satisfy his whim, and she said, "My boy, beat it, for if my three sons, who are butchers of human flesh, catch sight of you, I wouldn't set your worth at three farthings, for half alive and half roasted you will be coffined in a baking pan and buried in a belly! But be quick as a rabbit, for you won't go too far before you find your fortune."

Hearing this the prince all frightened, chilled, aghast, and dismayed, took to his legs and without even saying "good-bye" began to wear out his shoes, until he arrived at another village where he found another old woman worse than the former, who being told his business from A to Z said to him, "Get out of here fast if you don't want to serve as a snack for the little orcs, my daughters, but be quick, for night is upon you; a little farther on you will find your fortune."

Hearing this the melancholy prince began to take to his heels as if he had blisters on his tail, and he went until he found another old woman, who was sitting on a wheel with a woven basket on her arm, full of little cakes and confections which she was feeding to a group of asses, which afterwards began to leap on the banks of a river, kicking up their heels at certain poor swans. The prince, having come into the presence of this old woman and made her a hundred salaams, told her the story of his wanderings; and the old woman, comforting him with kind words, gave him a meal so good that he licked his fingers, and when he had arisen from the table, she handed him three citrons which seemed to have been just freshly plucked from the tree, and gave him also a fine knife, saying at the same time, "You can return to Italy, for you have filled your spindle and have found what you are looking for! Get along, then, and when you are not far from your kingdom, at the first fountain which you find cut a citron, and a fairy will emerge saying to you, 'Give me something to drink!' and do you be quick with the water, otherwise she will vanish like quicksilver; and if you miss your chance with the second fairy, look sharp and be careful with the third, lest she get away from you, and by giving her immediately something to drink, you will have a wife after your own heart."

The prince all gladdened kissed a hundred times that hairy hand, which looked like the back of a porcupine, and taking his leave, he left that village and, arriving at the shore, sailed towards the Pillars of Hercules. Having crossed into our seas, after a thousand storms and dangers, he entered a port only one day away from his kingdom; and reaching a beautiful forest, where the shadows made a palace for the fields so that they might not be seen by the Sun, he dismounted by a fountain which with a crystal tongue called to people in a murmur to refresh their mouths, where sitting on a Syrian carpet made by the grass and flowers, taking the knife out from its sheath, he began to cut the first citron. And lo, out came like lightning a beautiful girl as white as milk and cream, and red as a clump of strawberries, saying, "Give me something to drink."

The prince was so stunned, open-mouthed, and astonished by the beauty of the fairy that he was not quick to give her water, so that her appearance and disappearance were both in an instant. Whether this was a blow to the prince's noddle, let him judge who, desiring a great thing and having it right in his paws, loses it; but when he cut the second citron, the same thing happened, and it was a second cudgel to his pate, so that making two streams of his eyes, he spouted tears head to head, face to face, eye to eye, and tête-à-tête with the fountain, not yielding to it a bit; and lamenting all the while he said, "What a wretch I am, cursed be this year! Twice I have let her escape as if I had arthritis in my hands, may paralysis seize me! I'm moving like a rock when I ought to be running like a greyhound! In faith, I've made a fine job of it! Wake up, poor man! There's one to be, and at three, the king's home free! Either this cut gets the damsel or I'll do something dismal!"

So saying he cut the third citron, out came the third fairy, who said as the others, "Give me something to drink," and the prince immediately offered her water, and lo he had in hand a girl as tender and white as a junket, with an intermingling of red that looked like a prosciutto from the Abruzzi or a salami from Nola, a thing never seen in the world, beauty without measure, whiteness beyond the beyond, grace more than the most; on her hair Jupiter had rained down in gold, with which Cupid was making arrows to pierce the heart;[61] on that face Cupid had set a stain[62] so that some innocent soul might be hanged on the gallows of desire; at those eyes the Sun had lit two lamps of light so that in the breast of whoever saw her, fire was set to the gunpowder, and they heaved rockets and fireworks of sighs; at those lips Venus had passed with her temple, giving color to the rose in order to prick with the thorn a thousand enamoured souls; at that bosom Juno had pressed her breasts to nurse human wishes. In sum, she was so beautiful from head to foot that nothing could be seen more lovely, so that the prince did not know what had happened to him and marveled beside himself at such a beautiful offspring of a citron, at such a beautiful cut of woman spawned from cutting a fruit, and he said to himself, "Are you asleep or awake, o Ciommetiello? Is your vision enchanted or have you put your eyes on backwards? What a white object has come forth from a yellow peel! What a sweet confection from the acid of a citron! What a pretty scion from this seed!"

In the end, realizing that it was no dream and that they were playing for real, he embraced the fairy, giving her a hundred and another hundred French kisses and afterwards they said to each other a thousand amorous words about this and that, words which like a *cantus firmus* were set with a counterpoint of sugary kisses,[63] and the prince said, "My soul, I do not want to bring you into my father's country without the pomp worthy of your beautiful person and without the escort proper for a queen; therefore climb up in this oak tree, where nature seems to have provided for our need a little hollow like a small chamber, and wait for me until I return, for certainly I will put on wings, and before this spittle is dry, I will come to fetch you, dressed and accompanied as you deserve, into my kingdom." And so with the proper ceremony they parted.

Meanwhile a black slave had been sent by her mistress with a pitcher to fetch water at that fountain, and seeing the reflection of the fairy by chance in the water and believing it was her own, she began to say in astonishment, "See, poor Lucia pretty daughter, but boss-lady make you fetch water; and you take this lying down, o Lucia poor clown?"

So saying she broke the pitcher and returned to the house. Asked by her mistress why she had performed this misdeed, she replied, "At fountain bad luck, broke pitcher on rock." The mistress, swallowing this fib, gave her a pretty jug to fill with water the next day; returning to the fountain and seeing that beauty appear again in the water, she said with a great sigh, "Me no thick-lipped slave, me no Moor, no flabby-ass, me so pretty, and carry jug to fountain!"

And so saying, she banged and smashed the jug once again making a thousand fragments of it, and returning to the house all grumbling said to her mistress, "Donkey walked, jug knocked, to ground crashed, all smashed."

The annoyed mistress, hearing this, had no more patience, and setting her hand to a broom handle, gave her such a flogging that the slave felt it for several days; and taking a wineskin, the mistress said, "Run, make haste, you beggar slave, cricket-leg, asshole, run, don't shilly-shally or dance around, and bring me this skin full of water or else I'll beat you to a pulp and give you such a whipping that you will remember it!"

The slave ran lickety-split, for she had seen the lightning and was afraid of the thunder, and filling the skin she turned again to admire the beautiful reflection and said "Me an ass to fetch water! Better to marry my George! This no beauty to be killed with rage and serve a boss who always cross!"

So saying she took a pin which she wore in her hair and began to pierce the wineskin until it looked like a garden fountain with water sprinkling out, making a hundred little spouts, seeing which the fairy began to laugh as if she would burst. The slave, hearing this and looking about, became aware of the hidden observer and speaking to herself said, "You cause me beating, but you no care!" And afterwards she said to the fairy, "What you doing up there, pretty girl?"

And the fairy, who was the mother of courtesy, set forth to her all that she had within, not leaving out one jot of what had happened with the prince, whom she was expecting from hour to hour and from minute to minute with gowns and an escort to go to his father's kingdom and enjoy herself with him. Hearing this, the slave, elated, thought to win this prize for herself, and replied to the fairy, "Because you wait for husband, let me come up, and me comb your hair and make you more pretty!"

And the fairy said, "You are as welcome as the first of May!"

And as the slave was climbing up, the fairy held out to her a white little hand which, grasped by those black twigs, looked like a crystal mirror in an ebony frame; up climbed the slave and, beginning to examine the fairy's hair, jabbed a long pin into her head; but the fairy, feeling herself stabbed, cried, "Dove, dove!" and turning into a dove, spread her wings and flew away. The slave, stripping herself naked and making a bundle of the rags and tatters which she was wearing, threw them a mile away and remained as her mama had made her, up in that tree like a statue of jet in an emerald house.

Meanwhile the prince, returning with a large cavalcade and finding a jar of caviar where he had left a pan of milk was for a while struck senseless; finally he said, "Who has made this ink blot on the fine white paper where I was intending to write my happiest days? Who has draped in mourning the freshly whitewashed house where I was planning to have all my fun? Who has made me find this dark touchstone where I had left a silver mine to make me rich and happy?"

But the shrewd slave seeing the prince's astonishment said, "Don't be astonished, my prince, me Moor by enchantment, one year white face, one year black ass."

The prince, poor man, since the evil had no remedy, resigning himself like an ox, swallowed this pill, bidding the moor come down, he dressed her from head to foot, decking her out with a brand new gown and adorning her all over; and irritated, frustrated, sulky, and surly, he took the road to his country, where he was received by the king and queen, who had come out six miles from town to meet him, with the same pleasure with which a prisoner receives notice of the sentence that he is to be hanged, seeing the fine results of their crazy son who had gone all over to find a white dove and had brought home a black crow; nonetheless, as they couldn't help it, renouncing the crown in favor of the children, they set the circlet of gold on that head of coal. Now while splendid feasts and stunning banquets were being prepared, and the cooks were plucking geese, slaughtering pigs, skinning goats, basting roasts, stirring pots, beating pulps, stuffing capons, making a thousand other delicious morsels, there came to a window of the kitchen a pretty dove, singing,

> Cook in the kitchen, what is stewing?
> What are the king and the Saracen doing?

To which the cook paid little attention; but as the dove returned a second and a third time to repeat the same song, he ran to tell it at the table as a thing of wonder; and the bride, hearing this music, gave orders for the dove to be caught at once and immediately chopped up and cooked. Therefore the cook tried until he caught it, obeying the commandment of the black-amoor and having scalded it to pluck it, he threw the water and feathers off the terrace into a large flowerpot, where not three days later there came forth a pretty citron shoot, which grew in four winks; it happened that the king, coming to a window which overlooked that area, saw this tree which he had not seen before, and calling the cook asked him when and by whom it had been planted. And hearing the whole story from Master Ladler, he became suspicious about the business, and thus he gave orders under pain of death that no one should touch the tree, but that it should be tended with thorough diligence. And after a few days there began to grow three beautiful citrons similar to those which the Orc had given him, and when they were full-grown, he had them picked, and closing himself in a chamber with a large cup of water and with the same knife which he always wore hanging at his side, he began to cut; and after it had befallen him just as before with the first and second fairies, finally he cut the third citron, and giving drink to the fairy who came forth the way he had hoped, he remained with the same young lady whom he had left up in the tree, from whom he heard all about the wicked deed of the slave.

Now who can tell the smallest part of the joy which the king felt at this good fortune? Who can tell the rejoicing, reveling, prancing, and dancing[61] that he made? It figures that he was swimming in sweetness, bursting out of his skin, going into ecstasy and into seventh heaven; and pressing her in his arms, he had her dressed to the nines, and taking her by the hand, led her into the middle of the hall where all the court ladies and men of the town were assembled to honor the feast, and calling upon them one by one he asked them, "Tell me: whoever did harm to this beautiful lady, what punishment would such a one deserve?" To which some replied that she would deserve a necklace of rope, some a dinner of stones, some a blow with a sledgehammer on the hide of her stomach, some a soup of scammony, some a bracelet of a millstone, and some one thing and some another.

In the end, when he called upon the black queen and posed her the same question, she replied, "Her deserve to burn for malice, and ashes thrown from roof of palace."

Hearing this the king said, "You have written your doom with your own pen! You have swung the hatchet at your own foot! You have erected the block, whet the knife, mixed the poison, for no one has done more evil than you, you dog, you bitch, you ugly snout! Do you know that this is the pretty girl that you stabbed with a pin? Do you know that this is that pretty dove which you had slaughtered and cooked in a pot? What do you think, Cecca, of this jade! Shake, for it's all come down! You've made a fine mess! He who does evil can expect evil done to him; he who cooks green branches ladles out smoke." So saying he had her seized and put, all alive, on a big heap of wood, and when she had turned to ashes, they strewed her from the palace roof into the wind, making true the saying:

> He who sows brambles shouldn't go barefoot.

Conclusion to the introduction of the entertainments, which takes the place of the tenth tale of the fifth day.[65]

ZOZA NARRATES THE STORY OF HER TROUBLES; THE SLAVE, FEELING HER KEYS TOUCHED, MAKES SCISSORS SCISSORS[66] IN ORDER TO INTERRUPT THE TALE, BUT, DESPITE HER, THE PRINCE WANTS TO HEAR IT AND, DISCOVERING THE TREACHERY OF HIS WIFE, HAS HER KILLED, PREGNANT AND ALL, AND MARRIES ZOZA.

All ears were pricked to hear the tale of Ciommetella, and some praised the skill with which she had told it, others murmured about it, taxing her with lack of judgment as she should not in the presence of a slave-princess publish the shamefulness of another similar person, and they said that she had run a great risk of spoiling the game. But Lucia acted truly like Lucia, fidgeting all over[67] *while this tale was being told, for to the jitters of her body were matched the turbulence which she had in her heart, having seen in the tale of another slave the identical portrait of her own deceits, and she at once put an end to the discussion; but partly because she could not do without tales, the doll had put such a fire in her body, just as the victim of St. Vitus's Dance cannot do without music, and partly in order not to give Tadeo reason to suspect her, she swallowed this egg yolk with the idea of making a big fuss about it at another time and place. But Tadeo, who had taken a liking to this pastime, nodded to Zoza to tell her tale; who, making her curtsy, spoke.*

"Truth, lord prince, was always the mother of hatred, and therefore I would not like my obedience to your commands to offend anyone who is here, because not being used to making up lies and weaving fables, I am constrained both by nature and by accident to tell the truth. And although the proverb says 'Piss clearly and make a fig at the doctor,' nonetheless, knowing that the truth is not always welcomed in the presence of princes, I tremble to say something which may perhaps make you angry."

"Say what you wish," replied Tadeo, "for from that pretty mouth of yours nothing can come out which is not sugared and sweet."

These words were a dagger blow in the heart of the slave, and she would have shown sign of it if black faces like white ones were the book of the soul, and she would have given a finger of her hand to be free of these tales because her heart had become blacker than her face; and worrying lest the previous tale had been a first warning of ensuing disaster, from the morning she foresaw a bad day.[68] But Zoza meanwhile began to enchant those around her with the sweetness of her words recounting from the beginning to the end all her troubles, beginning right from her natural melancholy, the unhappy omen of what was to come, carrying with her from the cradle the bitter root of all her evil fortunes, which with the wrench of an impulsive laugh impelled her to so many tears; then she continued with the old woman's curse, her own wandering with so many hardships, her arrival at the fountain, her weeping with open floodgates, and the traitor sleep, cause of her ruin. The slave, hearing her hesitate[69] and seeing the boat on a bad course, shouted, "Be quiet, hush up! if no, me give belly blow, and beat baby Giorgio!"

Tadeo, who had discovered a new land, had no more patience, but taking off his mask and throwing his harness to the ground said,[70] "Let her tell it to the end, and stop making these threats about little George and big George, for in the end you haven't caught me alone, and if the mustard rises to my nose, it would be better for you to have been run over by a carriage wheel!"[71]

And as he commanded Zoza to go on despite his wife, she, who wanted nothing but the sign, continued with her finding the pitcher broken, and the deceit of the slave who took this good fortune from her hand; and so saying she burst into such tears that there was no person present who stood firm under the blows. Tadeo, by Zoza's tears and the silence of the dumbfounded slave, understood and fished out the truth of the matter; and giving Lucia such a head-washing as would not be given to an ass,[72] making her confess with her own mouth this treachery, he immediately gave orders that she be buried alive with her head barely out so that her death would be slower; and embracing Zoza, he had her honored as a princess and his wife, notifying the king of Vallepelosa to come to the celebration; and with this new wedding he put an end to the

*grandeur of the slave and to the entertainment of the tales, and much
good may it do us, and bring us health, for I came away step by step with
a spoonful of honey.*

The end

Notes

Introduction

1. For a list of other Italian tale collections in English, see the bibliography. Many of them have gone out of print, but can sometimes be found in libraries. Valency's anthology, one of the more readily available, has both French and Italian stories; it includes a greater number of authors than mine, but usually only one or two tales from each. Painter's translation was made during the English Renaissance, often using French intermediary translations as a basis and in any case freely elaborating on the tales. Almost all of the listed volumes are without any annotations and without any of the original framing narratives.

2. *Delle novelle italiane in prosa bibliografia* (Venice: Tip. di Alvisopoli, 1833). See also Marcus Landau, *Beitrage zur Geschichte der italienischen Novelle* (Vienna: Von L. Rosner, 1875), p.16.

3. Therefore I have left out the rather tedious tales of Gentile Sermini and Sabadino degli Arienti from the fifteenth century, and Anton Francesco Grazzini and Girolamo Parabosco from the sixteenth, even though a thorough history of the Italian novella might warrant their inclusion.

4. Peter Burke, *Culture and Society in Renaissance Italy* 1420–1540 (London: B. T. Batsford, 1972), pp.242–43.

5. Gene Brucker, *Renaissance Florence* (New York: John Wiley, 1969), p.85.

6. On the reflection of real-life marriage practices in medieval literature, see Georges Duby, *Medieval Marriage: Two Models from Twelfth-Century France,* trans. Elborg Forster (Baltimore: Johns Hopkins University Press, 1978), pp.11–15.

7. Lauro Martines, *The Social World of the Florentine Humanists,* 1390–1460 (Princeton: Princeton University Press, 1963), pp.60–61, 69. This was in the mid-fifteenth century.

8. David Herlihy, "The Natural History of Medieval Women," *Natural History* (March, 1978), p.67.

9. E.g., Brunetto Latini, *Li Livres Dou Tresor,* ed. Francis Carmody (Berkeley: University of California Press, 1948), III, 41, p.353. Cicero defines the three types of narration in *De Inventione* I, 19, 27 and in the *Rhetorica ad Herennium* I, 8, 3. See E. R. Curtius, *European Literature and the Latin Middle Ages,* trans. W. Trask (New York: Harper Torchbooks, 1963), pp.452–55 on the repetition of these definitions by Isidore.

10. On the meanings of *novella* see Walter Pabst, *Novellentheorie und Novellendichtung* (Hamburg: Cram, De Gruyter and Co., 1953), pp.27 ff.; Robert Clements and Joseph Gibaldi, *Anatomy of the Novella* (New York: New York University Press, 1977), pp.4–5.

11. "Sopra il comporre delle novelle," in *Raccolta di Prose Fiorentine* Part II, (Florence: Tartini e Franchi, 1727), I, p.169.

12. Ibid., pp.176–79, see especially p.172.

13. "Donne e Muse," in *Italica* 15 (1938), pp.132–41, and "The Structure and Real Significance of *The Decameron*," in *Essays in Honor of Albert Feuillerat*, ed. Henri Peyre, Yale Romantic Sudies 22 (New Haven: Yale University Press, 1943), p.69.

14. On the origins of the European novella, see Alessandro D'Ancona, "Del *Novellino* e delle sue fonti," *Studi di critica e storia letteraria* (Bologna, 1912), II, 3–163; Rudolf Besthorn, *Ursprung und Eigenart der alteren italienischen Novelle* (Halle: M. Niemeyer, 1935); Clements and Gibaldi, *Anatomy*, pp.37–40; Letterio di Francia, *Novellistica* (Milan: F. Vallardi, 1924), I, pp.1–97; John C. Dunlop, *History of Prose Fiction* (London, 1896), II, pp.2–47; and Salvatore Battaglia, *Contributi alla storia della novellistica* (Naples: Raffaele Pironti, 1947).

15. Di Francia, *Novellistica*, I, p.10.

16. Trans. John Sinclair (Oxford: Oxford University Press, 1961).

17. Di Francia, *Novellistica*, II, pp.21, 24, 37–40.

18. For the sources of *The Hundred Old Tales*, sometimes called the *Novellino*, see D'Ancona, "Del *Novellino*"; I. Pizzi, "Riscontri orientali," in *GSLI* 22 (1893), pp.225–26; and L. Di Francia's notes to his edition of the *Novellino ossia le cento novelle antiche* (Turin, 1930).

19. Bonciani, "Sopra il comporre. . . ," p.210. In contrast, the author of *The Hundred Old Tales* presents them as examples of fine speech, or *bel parlare*. See Di Francia, *Novellistica*, I, pp.31–32.

20. Both Salutati and Filippo Villani in their praises of Boccaccio list his Latin works while referring in a deprecating manner to the Italian ones; see Villani's life of Boccaccio in Angelo Solerti, ed., *Le Vite di Dante, Petrarca e Boccaccio scritte fino al secolo decimosesto* (Milan: Dottor Francesco Vallardi, n.d.) and also Vittore Branca, *Boccaccio Medievale* (Florence: Sansoni, 1956), p.8.

21. Clements and Gibaldi, *Anatomy*, pp.6–7.

22. Cesare Segre, ed., *Decameron* (Milan: Mursia, 1970), p.254, n.2, refers in this regard to Dante's *Epistole* XIII, 10, which connects the humble style and use of vernacular with the speech of women.

23. Bonciani, "Sopra il comporre . . . ," p.183.

24. Glending Olson, *Literature as Recreation in the Later Middle Ages* (Ithaca: Cornell University Press, 1982), ch.2, MS. pp.9–10.

25. Ibid., ch.5, MS. pp.10–11. This whole chapter discusses *The Decameron* in relation to medical advice on protecting oneself from the plague.

26. *Novellentheorie*, pp.35–40.

27. In the introduction to the third topic.

28. Dunlop, p.43.

29. For a few international examples of the "disaster cornice" and the "carnival cornice" see Clements and Gibaldi, pp.43–45, 47–48.

30. Mikhail Bakhtin discusses some of the implications of carnival in *Rabelais and His World*, trans. Helen Iswolsky (Cambridge, Mass.: M. I. T. Press, 1968), pp.4–9. Carlo Muscetta, *Giovanni Boccaccio* (Bari: Laterza, 1972), pp.300–303, suggests Macrobius's *Saturnalia* as a model for the sociable gathering of speakers during carnival.

31. William Bascom, "The Four Functions of Folklore," in Alan Dundes, ed., *The Study of Folklore* (Englewood Cliffs: Prentice-Hall, 1965), pp.285–90.

32. Carl Gustav Jung, "On the Psychology of the Trickster-Figure," in *Four Archetypes,* trans. R. F. C. Hull, Bollingen Series (Princeton: Princeton University Press, 1973), pp.140–41.

33. Kenneth Burke, *The Rhetoric of Religion* (Boston: Beacon Press, 1961), pp.186–87, discusses this point in regard to the story of Adam and Eve in *Genesis.*

34. Johan Huizinga, *Homo Ludens* (Boston: Beacon Press, 1970), p.2.

35. Ibid., pp.6 and 10.

36. Millicent Marcus, "Wit and the Public in the Early Italian Novella" Ph.D. diss., Yale University, 1973), pp.93–94.

37. The fifteenth century too produced a few *novelle sciolte* or loose tales such as "Fatso the Carpenter," included in this book, and Aeneas Silvius Piccolomini's *History of Two Lovers* in Latin.

38. Originally the council was intended to restore the unity of the church; but meeting under papal control and without the participation of Protestants, it managed only to widen the split by ending much of the pre-Reformation debate and flexibility of belief within Catholicism.

39. Ultimately the censure against criticism of the clergy outweighed the censure against lustful tales, and a "corrected" *Decameron* in which all monks, nuns, friars, and priests were replaced by townspeople was allowed publication. See G. Rosadi, "Il Boccaccio e la Censura," *Miscellanea Storica della Valdelsa,* 21 (1913).

40. Bruno Maier, *Novelle italiane del cinquecento*, Collana dei classici 8 (Milan: Edizioni per il Club del libro, 1962), p.xxxv.

41. Giuseppe Rua, introduction to his edition of Straparola, *Le Piacevoli Notti,* Scrittori d'Italia 100 (Bari: Laterza, 1927), pp.55 and 93.

42. Giambattista Basile, *Pentameron*, trans. N. M. Penzer with notes (New York: E. P. Dutton, 1932), p.ix, with reference to Ferdinando Galiani, *Del dialetto napoletano* (Naples: G. M. Porcelli, 1789).

43. On variety as a principle explicit in the composition of novella collections, see Clements and Gibaldi, pp.15–16.

44. William Painter, *The Palace of Pleasure* (New York: Dover Publications, 1966), I, 6 and 14.

45. *Elizabethan Critical Essays*, ed. G. G. Smith (Oxford: Oxford University Press, 1971), I, 2.

The Hundred Old Tales

1. Matthew 12:34 and Luke 6:45.

2. Frederick II (1194–1250), king of Sicily and Roman emperor; famous for his learning, he founded the University of Naples, sponsored translations of scientific and philosophic works from Greek and Arabic, and had at his court the first center of Italian poetry.

3. *Schiavine:* the attire suggests they have come from far away; later the word was used for certain wool robes worn by pilgrims.

4. Ezzelino da Romano (1194–1259), a leader of the Ghibellines, known as a cruel tyrant. Dante mentions him in *Inferno* XII, 110.

5. A kind of coin.

6. Dante mentions him in *Purgatorio* XVI, 46.

7. Although the writer says "not long after his death" there were in fact five centuries between the Roman emperor Trajan and Saint Gregory, who became pope around 600 A.D. Dante tells this story in *Purgatorio* X, 73–93.

8. The twelfth-century sultan of Egypt and Syria, famous in the west through the crusades.

9. The devil.

Sacchetti

1. Suspension points indicate gaps in the manuscript.

2. A well-known Dominican preacher of Florence (d.1359).

3. The arm was brought into Florence in 1352 and discovered to be a fraud in 1356.

4. Armor for the throat and arm.

5. An obscene gesture made by placing the thumb between two fingers of the closed fist.

6. A freshwater fish.

7. Sacchetti tells several tales about this character, who seems to have liked playing tricks. Alastair Smart, *The Dawn of Italian Painting* 1250–1400, p.118 (Ithaca: Cornell University Press, 1978), suggests that the early fourteenth-century painter Buonamico Buffalmacco is the jolly trickster of both Sacchetti's and Boccaccio's tales.

8. The patron saint of Perugia.

9. Literally, cast from a mold.

10. A friend of Sacchetti's who wrote verses on current events and on the sights of Florence. His most famous poem describes the market square.

11. The mule could be a reference to illegitimate birth.

12. A nonsense threat.

13. Gonnella, a trickster figure from popular tradition, appears in several stories by Sacchetti and also in the work of other writers, including Bandello. A fifteenth-century collection of Gonella stories and oral anecdotes appeared in book form, the *Buffonerie del Gonella*.

14. Salerno was a famous center of medical studies.

15. Possibly Taurus or Tunisia.

16. The loser at dice paid not only his bets but also the expenses of the evening.

Ser Giovanni Fiorentino

1. Boccaccio's preface to the *Decameron* is similar.

2. Near Forlì.

3. Urban is called the "true" pope and "an Italian of ours" as opposed to the unmentioned Clement VII, elected pope in the same year by the French.

4. *Cortesia* implies generosity and thus, like Aristotle's magnanimity, is a virtue which requires money.

5. This phrase is from the speech of the famous lover Francesca in Dante's *Inferno* V, 100.

6. A kiss given as part of the church service.

7. There is a proverbial phrase: to make one's reckoning without the innkeeper.

8. Bologna was famous for its law school.

9. Venisi or Venaissin, a region in southern France.

10. The leek, with its white root or "beard" and green shoots, was a common image for an old man who still possessed sexual vitality. Cf. Boccaccio's *Decameron* I, 10."

Sercambi

1. **G** ià trovo che si diè pace Pompeo
   I mmaginando il grave tradimento,
   O micidio crudele e violento,
   V olendo ciò Cesare e Tolomeo.
   A n' Ecuba quel (. . . . . .) reo
   N ativo d'Antinor (il cui nom sia spento)
   N ascose in su l'altare, e con gran pasione
   I l convertì ringraziando Deo.

   S otto color di pace ancora Giuda
   E l nostro salvator Cristo tradìo
   R endendo sé di vita in morte cruda.
   C onsiderando ciò dommi pace io:
   A vendo sempre l'anima mia cruda
   M ossa a vendetta, cancello il pensier mio.
   B en dico che la lingua colla mente
   I nsieme non disforma in leal gente.

2. *Bonzora*, close to the priest's name.
3. *Roncare*, again a play on the priest's name, cf. *bonzora*.
4. The main square of Lucca.
5. Vergil was reputed to have performed various magical works for the city of Naples, near which he was buried.
6. Sercambi seems to have confused Medea with Ariadne, left on an island by Theseus.
7. Zuccarina means "little sugar."
8. Suspension points represent a gap in the manuscript.
9. This pair of lines rhymes in Italian.

Masuccio

1. The ending *-ino* is diminutive.
2. Latin: although unworthy.
3. Margarita was crowned in 1381, ruled until 1387, and died in 1412.
4. Textile Street.
5. 1452–1516.
6. Masuccio labels the parts of his tales according to Cicero's account of the parts of an oration.
7. Conventual: a less strict branch of the Franciscan order, as opposed to the stricter "spiritual" Franciscans.
8. Duns Scotus was a Franciscan, St. Thomas a Dominican; the two theologians held opposing views.

9. His fear of the dead pursuer was greater than his fear of being accused of the murder.

10. A form of torture.

11. The marriage occurred in 1415.

12. Dominicans and Franciscans were famous as rival organizations. Santa Croce was run by the Franciscans.

13. A port town in Calabria.

14. There are several pictures of Mary attributed to Luke and now in Rome, including a drawing in the Lateran and, in Santa Maria Maggiore, a famous icon which is carried to St. Peter's on the feast of the Immaculate Conception.

15. The use of these expressions imitates Boccaccio's *Decameron* III, 10, where the sexual act is called putting the devil in hell.

16. Joan of Arc (1412–1431).

17. *Salute* means both physical health and spiritual salvation.

Fatso the Carpenter

1. Ammannatini (d.1450), a maker of wooden inlays.

2. The famous Florentine architect (1377–1446) who built the cupola of Santa Maria del Fiore and other churches in Florence.

3. Knew him thoroughly.

4. Another famous Renaissance artist (1383–1466).

5. A character from the *Decameron*, the stupid and gullible butt of several jokes.

6. Member of one of the famous noble families of Florence.

7. References to classical literature and mythology: Apuleius' *Golden Ass* tells the story of a man turned into an ass by a magical potion; for the story of Actaeon, see Ovid's *Metamorphoses* III, 138–253.

8. A hospital which took in lost children.

9. Quiet and happy.

10. This would permit Matteo to avoid arrest for a specified amount of time.

11. Could notice tiny imperfections.

12. Antonio di Matteo, Michelozzo, and Andreino were sculptors; Feo Belcari wrote *The Life of the blessed Colombini*, which can be found in the same volume of *Prosatori volaari del quattrocento* from which this story is taken; Luca della Robbia is famous for his painted ceramic sculptures and reliefs; Antonio di Migliore Guidotti was an architect and woodworker; Michelino was a painter and a student of Fra Angelico. All these artists lived in the fifteenth century, the last of them dying in 1491.

Luigi da Porto

1. Lucina Savorgnana was a cousin of the author.

2. Bartolomeo della Scala ruled Verona from 1301 to 1304, and was host to the exiled Dante.

3. A branch of the Franciscans.

4. Members of the clergy were under jurisdiction of the ecclesiastical court and not the secular court.

Straparola

1. There is an inconsistency in the story here as we are never told in what way Biancabella transgresses the serpent's commandments.
2. Now Dubrovnik.

Bandello

1. Because of her suicide.
2. Corneto is the name of a real town but is used here only for the pun on *corna,* the horns of a cuckold.
3. Amalfi, within the Kingdom of Naples.
4. A family famous for their ugliness; cf. Boccaccio's *Decameron* VI, 6.
5. Antonio Bologna was murdered in 1513.
6. Filippo Visconti. His brother Gian Maria died in 1412.
7. Various kinds of coins.
8. A lively popular dance, here used as a euphemism.
9. "Diet" is a congress of representatives from the confederate states of Germany.

Basile

1. As monkeys imitate human behavior, it was popularly thought that the way to catch a monkey was to put on and take off a pair of boots several times, and then to put lime in the boots and leave them outside so that the monkey would get stuck when he put them on.
2. Reference to a children's game in which one child tries to break into a circle defended by the other children's feet.
3. The ancient philosophers Heraclitus and Democritus were commonly held to represent the tragic and the comic view of life. In re Zoraster, Augustine wrote in the *City of God* XXI, 14, p.991: "Infancy, indeed, starts this life not with smiles but with tears; and this is, in a way, an unconscious prophecy of the troubles on which it is entering. It is said that Zoroaster was the only human being who smiled when he was born, and yet that portent of a smile boded no good for him." (Tr. Henry Bettenson, New York: Penguin Books, 1977).
4. A popular singer.
5. Gymnastic games.
6. The dance of Lucia or Sfessania was very popular in Naples in the sixteenth and seventeenth centuries; it was said to come from Malta and used Moorish costumes. *Lucia canazza* is part of the sung refrain. Basile refers to this dance many times throughout the book.
7. There was a very popular book, published in Venice in 1521 and many times thereafter, called *A new merry and amusing work about a peasant worker named Grillo who wanted to become a doctor,* in which Grillo cures a princess by making her laugh.
8. The Sardinian herb is famous for its bitterness. Hence our word "sardonic," meaning with bitter laughter. Possibly Basile is suggesting that the herb might make her grimace.
9. Proverbial phrase meaning she was not shy to speak.
10. Proverb implying impudence or presumption; the cough refers to clearing one's throat when wanting to speak up and be heard.

11.   Prostitutes paid a monthly tax in return for being allowed to ply their trade.

12.   A wicked spirit or boogey-man used to frighten children.

13.   A bodily fluid; according to medieval science it is one of the four humors, and supposedly causes apathy or coolness. In this mixed metaphor, Basile says that the old woman lost all calm.

14.   Quotation from Guarini's *Pastor Fido* I, 1, a pastoral play. The "bushy scene," appropriate to pastoral drama, is of course also obscenely meant here; and in this context "horn" also becomes obscenely suggestive.

15.   Egeria wept so much for the death of her husband King Numa of Rome that Diana turned her into a fountain; see Ovid's *Metamorphoses* XV, 482–92 and 547–51.

16.   The *Twin Menaechmi* by Plautus or one of its many imitations.

17.   Proverbial for empty-handed.

18.   Reference to the myth of Io who was turned into a heifer by Juno and guarded by the hundred-eyed Argus lest Jupiter continue his affair with her; see Ovid's *Metamorphoses* I, 568–750.

quently makes her speeches rhyme.

20.   Biondo and Pezzillo were famous popular singers during Basile's time; the Blindman of Potenza was perhaps another popular singer unknown to us.

21.   Another reference to the dance of Lucia; it also suggests that the prince has let his wife saddle and ride him, i.e., take control.

22.   Cupid, disguised as Aeneas' son, made Dido fall in love with Aeneas; see *Aeneid* I, 657–722.

23.   Reference to a popular belief that a pregnant woman, when unable to satisfy her whims, would, if she touched any part of her body, impress some sign of her desire upon that part of the body of her baby. Thus the slave is afraid that by touching her mouth she will give her baby the disposition to make persistent demands.

24.   March is described by Basile in V, 2, as an "impertinent" month which "with such ice and rain, snow and hail, winds, whirlwinds, fogs, and storms, and other worthless things make life tedious for us."

25.   The moon-rise.

26.   Printed newspapers were beginning to appear at this time. Basile mentions also *avvisi* or handwritten notices.

27.   Village near Naples.

28.   Spavins are hard growths on the joints of a horse's legs; cf. the following sentence with pip, a hen's disease of the throat.

29.   To "come from Ioio" seems to be a proverbial phrase. It has been suggested that Ioio refers to a particularly low-class neighborhood; thus *not* coming from Ioio is an assertion of one's own value and respectability.

30.   An especially discordant interval in music. Basile, whose sisters were singers, uses many metaphors from musical terminology.

31.   *Senza 'na crespa 'n crispo a lo crespano.*

32.   An order of nuns sworn to poverty.

33.   A gathering-place of beggars between Naples and Aversa.

34.   The sign of the cross was supposed to keep the devil from entering one's mouth when one yawned. The yawns may be intended here as a sign of hunger.

35.   Basile uses Pippo a few times and then switches to Cagliuso for no visible reason.

36.   Place of the wholesale fish market.

37.   Hunting areas near Naples.

38. "Washing an ass's head" is proverbial for wasting one's efforts.

39. Lung was considered a delicacy for cats.

40. Cf. *Aeneid VI,* 625–7: "Non, mihi si linguae centum sint oraque centum,/ferrea vox, . . ."

41. *Focono da varviero fornace de vritraro.*

42. *Arma,* a pun on soul and gun.

43. A ghetto area.

44. See Herodotus, III, 85–87.

45. Reference to Ariosto's *Orlando Furioso* X, 1–34.

46. A pun between the First Cause and the prime consideration.

47. *Proprio,* a pun meaning both proper noun and own good.

48. Wormseed was sold as a remedy for fright.

49. It was a custom in Naples that a widow's hair would be cut off, and she could not remarry until it had grown back out.

50. The remark that he would have paid cash to become hard is another of the author's obscene jokes.

51. *Cemiente,* a pun meaning both danger and cement.

52. This is a pun on the tradition of sacrificing young goats.

53. He passed from a painful situation to a good one.

54. From Hesiod, *Works and Days,* II, p.25–26, with variations.

55. The fabled philosopher's stone turns other materials into gold.

56. Salmacis hung on to Hermaphrodite until the gods fused their bodies together; see Ovid's *Metamorphoses* IV, 285–388.

57. Galen and Hippocrates were famous doctors of antiquity. Mesoè was the Arab doctor of Harun el Raschild in the ninth century; his writings were translated into Latin and Italian.

58. Aristotle's *Analytica Posteriora,* with a pun.

59. The lowest and highest possible score in rolling dice.

60. Orcs are man-eating giants or ogres.

61. Jupiter descended to Danae as a shower of gold; see Ovid's *Metamorphoses* IV, 610–11.

62. A blush, but also the crime of making marks on the wall of someone else's house.

63. Another musical mataphor: *cantus firmus* is a pre-existing melody; *counterpoint* refers to one or more independent melodies added as accompaniment to the primary melody.

64. These four verbs all rhyme, as do the four adjectives *irritated, frustrated, sulky* and *surly* on p.266. The two sets of words form a contrasting pair.

65. One of the narrators is sick on the last day, and the prince invites Zoza to speak in her place. Her tale is last.

66. This refers to an old folktale about an insistent woman who, when forbidden to speak any more, kept on making a sign with her hands. The scissors sign in Basile's context suggests the slave's desire to cut short Zoza's tale.

67. *Cernennose,* a pun on *Cierne Lucia,* the popular dance to which Basile keeps referring. It was a dance of lively movements. See the illustrations at the beginning of the Basile section.

68. *Malanno,* a pun meaning disaster but also, literally, a bad year, thus paired with *male iuorno,* a bad day.

69. *Larga,* a pun meaning both to hesitate and to push a boat off from shore or set sail.

70. Cf. the initial frame story, p.6, where Tadeo is said to wear moorish horsetrappings; and see n.21.

71.   The usual Basilean mix of images and allusions. "You haven't found me alone," i.e. you haven't caught me at a disadvantage "if the mustard rises to my nose," i.e. if I get mad (uncontrollable seizure from peppery stuff).

72.   See note 38.

Bibliography

I. English Anthologies Containing Renaissance Novellas

Bishop, Morris. *A Medieval Storybook*. Ithaca: Cornell University Press, 1970.
_____. *A Renaissance Storybook*. Ithaca: Cornell University Press, 1971.
Calvino, Italo. *Italian Folktales*, trans. George Martin. New York: Harcourt Brace Jovanovich, 1980.
Crane, Thomas. *Italian Popular Tales*. Boston: Houghton Mifflin, 1885.
Hall, Jr., Robert. *Italian Stories*. New York: Bantam Books, 1961. With facing Italian.
Painter, William. *The Palace of Pleasure*. New York: Dover Publications, 1966.
Pasinetti, P. M. *Great Italian Short Stories*. New York: Dell, 1959.
Pettoello, Decio. *Great Italian Short Stories*. London: Ernest Benn, 1930.
Roscoe, Thomas. *The Italian Novelists*. London, 1836.
_____. *Tales of Humour, Gallantry and Romance*. London: Charles Baldwin, 1824.
Speroni, Charles. *Wit and Wisdom of the Italian Renaissance*. Berkeley: University of California Press, 1964.
Taylor, Una. *Early Italian Love Stories*. London and New York, 1899.
Trevelyan, Raleigh. *Italian Short Stories*. New York: Penguin, 1965. With facing Italian.
Valency, Maurice, and Levtow, Harry. *The Palace of Pleasure*. New York: Capricorn Books, 1960.

II. Basic Critical Studies of the Novella

*Most scholarly and critical work in this field has been done in Italian. A few of the basic studies on the novella are:

Battaglia, Salvatore. *Contributi alla storia della novelistica*. Naples: R. Pironti, 1947.
_____. *La coscienza letteraria del Medioevo*. Naples: Liguori, 1965.
_____. *Le epoche della letteratura italiana: Medioevo-Umanesimo-Rinascimento*. Naples: Liguori, 1965.
Bonciani, Francesco. "Sopra il comporre delle novelle," in *Raccolta di Prose Fiorentine* Part II, vol. I. Florence: Tartini e Franchi, 1717, pp.161–212.
Borlenghi, Aldo. *La struttura e il carattere della novella italiana dei primi secoli*. Milan: La Gogliardica, 1958.
Chiari, A. "La fortuna del Boccaccio," in *Questioni e correnti di storia letteraria*. Milan: Marzorati, 1949, pp.275–348.
Di Francia, Letterio. *Novellistica*. Milan: F. Vallardi, 1924.
Graedel, Leonie, *La cornice nelle raccolte novellistiche del Rinascimento e i rapporti con la cornice del Decameron*. Florence: Stamperia il Cenacolo, 1959.

Maier, Bruno, Introduction to *Novelle italiane del cinquecento*. Collana dei classici 8. Milan, 1962.

Porcelli, Bruno. *Novellieri italiani dal Sacchetti al Basile*. Ravenna: Longo, 1969.

M. Righetti. *Per la storia della novella italiana al tempo della Reazione Cattolica*. Teramo: Fabbri, 1921.

P. D. Stewart. "Boccaccio e la tradizione retorica: la definizione della novella come genere letterario," *Stanford Italian Review* I (1979), 67–74.

*There are also a number of general studies in German:

Auerbach, Erich. *Zur Technik der Frührenaissancenovelle in Italien und Frankreich*. Heidelberg: Carl Winter's Universitätesbuchhandlung, 1921.

Besthorn, Rudolf. *Ursprung und Eigenart der älteren italienischen Novelle*. Halle: M. Niemeyer, 1935.

Kunz, Josef, ed. *Novelle*. Darmstadt: Wissenschaftliche Buchgesellschaft, 1968.

Landau, Marcus. *Beiträge zur Geschichte der Italienischen Novelle*. Vienna: Von L. Rosner, 1875.

Neuschäfer, Hans-Jorg. *Boccaccio und der Beginn der Novelle*. Munich, Wilhelm Fink Verlag, 1969.

Pabst, Walter. *Novellentheorie und Novellendichtung*. Hamburg: Cram, De Gruyter & Co., 1953.

*Some general studies in English which may be useful are:

Bascom, William. "The Four Functions of Folklore," in *The Study of Folklore*, ed. Alan Dundes. Englewood Cliffs: Prentice-Hall, Inc., 1965, pp.279–98.

Clements, Robert and Gibaldi, Joseph. *Anatomy of the Novella*. New York: New York University Press, 1977.

Dunlop, John C. *History of Prose Fiction,* vol. II. London, 1896.

Ehrmann, Jacques, ed. *Game, Play, Literature*. Boston: Beacon Press, 1971.

Freud, Siegmund and Oppenheimer, D. E. *Dreams in Folklore,* trans. A. M. D. Richards, ed. J. Strachey. New York: International University Press, Inc., 1958.

Jung, Carl Gustav. "The Phenomenology of the Spirit in Fairytales" and "On the Psychology of the Trickster-Figure," in *Four Archetypes*, trans. R. F. C. Hull. Bollingen Series. Princeton: Princeton University Press, 1973.

Keightly, Thomas. *Tales and Popular Fictions: Their Resemblance and Transmission from Country to Country*. London, 1834.

Marcus, Millicent. "Wit and the Public in the Early Italian Novella," diss. Yale University, 1973.

Nelson, William. *Fact or Fiction: The Dilemma of the Renaissance Storyteller*. Cambridge: Harvard University Press, 1973.

Olson, Glending. *Literature as Recreation in the Later Middle Ages*. Ithaca: Cornell University Press, 1982.

_____. "The Medieval Theory of Literature for Refreshment and its Use in the Fabliau Tradition," *Studies in Philology* 71 (1974), pp.291–313.

Propp, Vladimir. *Morphology of the Folktale*. trans. Laurence Scott. Austin: University of Texas Press, 1968.

Rodax, Yvonne. *The Real and the Ideal in the Novella of Italy, France and England*. Chapel Hill: University of North Carolina Press, 1968.

Rotunda, Dominic Peter. *Motif Index of the Italian Novella in Prose.* Bloomington: Indiana University Press, 1942.

_____. *A Tabulation of Early Italian Tales.* Berkeley: University of California Press, 1930.

Symonds, John Addington. "The Novellieri," *Renaissance in Italy,* vol. II. New York: Modern Library, 1935, pp. 199–229.

Thompson, Stith. *The Folktale.* New York: Dryden Press, 1946.

*Studies in English on specific authors and further sources of bibliography can be found at the end of the preface to each author.

III. Critical Studies on Boccaccio & the Novella

Although Boccaccio's *Decameron* is not included in this anthology, so much study has been focused on the work that some brief, selected bibliography may be helpful in illustrating an array of possible approaches to the novella. The English version is listed whenever one exists. There are two collections of essays in English on the *Decameron: Critical Perspectives on the Decameron,* ed. Robert Dombroski (Toronto: Hodder and Stoughton, 1976) and *The Decameron: 21 Novelle, Contemporary Reactions, Modern Criticism,* trans. and ed. Mark Musa and Peter Bondanella (New York: W. W. Norton & Company, 1977). They will be referred to hereafter as "Dombroski" and "Musa."

For historical criticism see V. Branca, *Boccaccio: The Man and His Works,* trans. R. Monges (New York: New York University Press, 1976), also an excerpt in Dombroski; Giorgio Padoan, "Mondo aristocratico e mondo communale nell'ideologia e nell'arte di Giovanni Boccaccio," *Studi sul Boccaccio* II (1964), pp.81–216; Giuseppe Petronio, "The Place of the *Decameron,*" in Dombroski; Raffaelo Ramat, "Indicazioni per una lettura del *Decameron,*" in *Scritti su Giovanni Boccaccio* (Florence, 1964), pp.7–19. For an opposite view, the separation between history and fiction, see Giuseppe Mazzotta, "The *Decameron.* The Marginality of Literature," *University of Toronto Quarterly* 42 (Fall 1972), pp.64–81; Guido Almansi, *The Writer as Liar: Narrative Technique in the Decameron* (Boston: Routledge & Kegan Paul, 1975). Glending Olson, *Literature as Recreation in the later Middle Ages* (Ithaca: Cornell University Press, 1982) partly bridges this gap by relating the book to contemporary medical theories about the health value of recreation and amusement, especially with regard to the plague.

For stylistic analysis, see Erich Auerbach, "Frate Alberto," in *Mimesis,* trans. W. Trask (New York: Doubleday Anchor Books, 1957), pp.177–203, also in Dombroski; Alfredo Schiaffini, *Tradizione e poesia nella prosa d'arte italiana dalla latinità medievale al Boccaccio* (Rome: Edizioni di Storia e Letteratura, 1969); Marga Cottino-Jones, *An Anatomy of Boccaccio's Style* (Naples: Cymba, 1968); Wayne Booth, *The Rhetoric of Fiction* (Chicago: University of Chicago Press, 1967), pp.9–20, also in Musa. For its relation to previous genres, see Enrico de' Negri, "The Legendary Style of the *Decameron,*" *Romanic Review* 43 (1952), 166–89, and reprinted in Dombroski; Hans-Jörg Neuschäfer, *Boccaccio und der Beginn der Novelle* (Munich: Wilhelm Fink Verlag, 1969); Victor Shklovskij, "Some Reflections on the *Decameron,*" in Dombroski.

On possible schemes for the structure of the whole work, see Ferdinando Neri, "Il disegno ideale del *Decameron,*" *Storia e Poesia* (Turin: Giuseppe Gambino, 1936), pp.51–60; Branca, *Boccaccio;* Edith Kern, "The Gardens of the *Decameron* Cornice," *PMLA* 66, no.4 (June 1957), pp. 505–23; Joan Ferrante, "The Frame Characters of the *Decameron:* A Progression of Virtues," *Romance Philology* 19 (1965), pp.212–26; Tzvetan Todorov, "Structural Analysis of Narrative," in *Novel: A Forum for Fiction* 3 (1969), pp.70–76 and in Musa; Pamela Stewart, "La novella di madonna Oretta e le due parti del *Decameron*," *Yearbook of Italian Studies* 1973/75, pp.27–39; Lars Peter Rømhild, "Osservazioni sul concetto e sul significato della cornice del *Decameron*," *Analecta Romana Instituti Danici* 7 (1974), pp.157–204. Janet Smarr, "Symmetry and Balance in the *Decameron*," *Medievalia* 2(1976),pp.159–186; for structures and patterns within single days, see Cesare Segre, "Funzioni, opposizioni e simmetrie nella giornata VII del *Decameron*," *Le strutture e il tempo* (Turin: Einaudi, 1974), pp.117–44; G. Bosetti, "Analyse 'structurale' de la sixième journée du *Decameron* de Boccace," *Studi sul Boccaccio* 7 (1973), pp.141–58; Victoria Kirkham, "Love's Labors Rewarded and Paradise Lost," *The Romanic Review*, 72 (January 1981), pp.79–83.

For intertextual readings, see Millicent Marcus, "The Sweet New Style Reconsidered: A Gloss on the Tale of Cimone (*Decameron* V,1)," *Italian Quarterly* 81 (Summer 1980), pp.5–16; Robert Durling, "Boccaccio on Interpretation: Guido's Escape (*Decameron* VI,9)," in *Dante, Petrarch, and Others: Studies in the Italian Trecento*. See also *Essays in Honor of Charles Singleton*, ed. Aldo Bernardo and Anthony Pellegrini, Medieval and Renaissance Texts and Studies (Binghamton: State University of New York Press, in press).

For semiotic analysis, see Franco Fido, "Retorica e semantica nel *Decameron*: tropi e segni in funzione narrativa," *Le metamorfosi del centauro* (Rome: Bulzoni, 1977), 63–76; Giovanni Sinicropi, "La struttura del segno linguistico nel *Decameron*," *Studi sul Boccaccio* 9 (1975–6), pp.169–224.

For thematic interpretations see Branca and other works already mentioned; see also Guido Di Pino, *La Polemica del Boccaccio* (Florence: Vallecchi Editore, 1953); Giovanni Getto, *Vita di Forme e Forme di Vita nel Decameron* (Turin: G.B. Petrini, 1958); Thomas Greene, "Forms of Accommodation in the *Decameron*," *Italica* 45 (September 1968); Marga Cottino-Jones, "Fabula vs. Figura: Another Interpretation of the Griselda Story," *Italica* 50 (1973), pp.38–52; Mario Baratto, *Realtà e stile nel Decameron* (Vicenza: Neri Pozza, 1974); Guido Almansi, *L'estetica dell' osceno* (Turin: Giulio Einaudi Editore, 1974), pp.131–182; Cesare Segre, "Comicità strutturale nella novella di Alatiel," *Le strutture e il tempo*, pp.145–160; Millicent Marcus, *An Allegory of Form: Literary Self-Consciousness in the Decameron*, Stanford French and Italian Studies 18 (Saratoga, California: Anma, 1979).

IV. Social Histories

For a fuller understanding of life in Renaissance Italy, one can turn to many good recent studies. The old and now qualified, but still classic work is Jacob Burckhardt, *The Civilization of the Renaissance in Italy* (New York: Harper Torchbooks, 1958), in two volumes with many illustrations. A more recent study covering not just Italy but all of Europe, treating many fascinating topics, such as how long people lived, what they ate, what they did with their garbage, how people travelled and how long it took them to get from place to place, is J. R. Hale's *Renaissance Europe: Individual and Society, 1480–1520* (Los Angeles: University of California Press, 1977). Gene Brucker's *Renaissance Florence* (New York: John Wiley & Sons, 1969) and Brian Pullan, *A History of Early Renaissance Italy From the Mid-Thirteenth to the Mid-Fourteenth Century* (New York: St. Martin's Press, 1972) consider economic changes and their social effects; Brucker's book also surveys the physical appearance of

Florence and its buildings in the Renaissance and includes an annotated bibliography on specific topics. Chapter two of Lauro Martines' *The Social World of the Florentine Humanists* 1390–1460 (Princeton: Princeton University Press, 1963) offers a portrait of the ruling class, its desires and its means for trying to accomplish them; the importance of the family is discussed at some length.

Several books relate social and economic history to the arts: Peter Burke, *Culture and Society in Renaissance Italy* 1420–1540 (London: B. T. Batsford, 1972) provides a wealth of information on society and life as well as on art; J. Larner, *Culture and society in Italy, 1290–1420* (New York: Charles Scribner's Sons, 1971) has an excellent chapter on booksellers, libraries, and the educational system as well as chapters on the market for art works; Dennis Hay, *The Italian Renaissance in its Historical Background* (Cambridge, 1961); Arnold Hauser, *The Social History of Art,* vol. II (New York: Vintage Books, 1951); Millard Meiss, *Painting in Florence and Siena after the Black Death* (New York: Harper Torchbooks, 1964) documents changing attitudes as expressed in art.

Some diaries of Renaissance Florentines have been translated into English: *Two Memoirs of Renaissance Florence: The Diaries of Buonacorso Pitti and Gregorio Dati,* ed. G. Brucker, trans. Julia Martines (New York: Harper & Row, 1967); Luca Landucci, *A Florentine Diary from 1450–1516,* trans. Alice de Rosen Jervis (New York: E. P. Dutton & Co., 1927).

"A must for the student of European narrative, Elizabetha
drama, and folklore."

Aldo Scaglio
The University of North Carolina at Chapel H

"These *novelle* will be of particular interest to studen
of Dante, Boccaccio, Chaucer, and Shakespeare, but a
worth knowing in their own right. The translations are cle
and lively."

Robert Hollander, Princeton Universi

"Janet Smarr's intelligent selection of story materials co
tributes to a better knowledge of a trend in literature whic
stresses the importance of narrative from Boccaccio o
Italian Renaissance Tales will be useful not only
the classroom, but to anyone seriously interested in the a
of storytelling."

Dante Della-Terza, Harvard Universi

Solaris Press, Inc.
Rochester, MI 48063

ISBN: 0–933760–03–
$13.9